THE RECRUITER

A RICK CARTER NOVEL

GREGG PODOLSKI

THE RECRUITER

BLACK STONE PUBLISHING

Published in 2024 by Blackstone Publishing
Cover and book design by Alenka Vdovič Linaschke

Printed in the United States of America

First edition: 2024
ISBN 979-8-212-02640-6
Fiction / Thrillers / General

Version 1

Blackstone Publishing
31 Mistletoe Rd.
Ashland, OR 97520

www.BlackstonePublishing.com

*For Kristina, Kayla, and Evan. Everything I do, I do it for you.
And now you have that Bryan Adams song stuck in your head.
You're welcome.*

CHAPTER ONE

The story made the front page of the City section. Below the fold, no picture, but that's only because Ian was so good at what he did. In the hands of a lesser professional, it would have been the top headline, paired with a full-color photo of a grisly crime scene. Police would already be searching for suspects and there would be whispers of the first move in an underground turf war.

I smiled. There was none of that. Thanks to Ian and his impeccable attention to detail, it was being treated as a crime of passion. Both bodies had been found naked in the man's apartment. There was mention of his suspected ties to organized crime, but he wasn't a major player and the reporter clearly didn't feel that was a thread worth tugging on.

The woman had bruises around her neck. One hand cuffed to a bedpost, the other lying limp in a pool of blood. This came from a hole in the man's jugular, which was only partially plugged by the stem of a broken champagne flute. The rest of the pieces were on the floor next to the nightstand. Her prints were all over the stem. There were heavy amounts of amphetamines in both their systems. No sign of forced entry. No other prints found at the scene. A wild night of rough sex gone horribly wrong.

Ian was an artist. I should have charged Leon double. He'd balked at my fee during our first meeting, but that wasn't unusual for new clients. People who have never worked with a recruiter—or have only worked with bad recruiters—don't always appreciate our value when it comes to finding top talent. That was as true when I worked in corporate America as it was with mid-tier crime bosses like Leon White. Then they'd see the quality of candidates I bring to the table, and suddenly money wasn't an issue.

I finished reading the article and closed the paper, confident it would be treated as an open-and-shut case. My "No Cops Guarantee" track record remained unblemished. A part of me—buried deep inside—took a small measure of pride in that. The rest of me was just cold.

The early spring temperatures a few days ago proved no more than a tease. Winter had returned to Brussels with a vengeance, well-rested from its brief vacation. I was the only person sitting outside my favorite café on that sunny but blustery morning, trying to freeze out another hangover with a bowl of melon and a thirteen-degree windchill. Unorthodox, but it worked. Better than any of the other home remedies I'd tried over the years. By the time I popped the last piece of not-quite-ripe cantaloupe into my mouth, I felt almost human again.

I left the paper on the table, weighed down by my empty coffee mug so it wouldn't blow away, tucked my gloved hands into the pockets of my wool overcoat, and pulled it tighter. Halfway through the walk back to my apartment, my phone rang. I didn't recognize the number.

"Hello?" I said, slightly out of breath from the cold.

"I wanted to wait until you finished reading," Leon said. The thick Serbian accent was unmistakable. "Did you see the story?"

I stopped and looked around. There were a few people sharing the sidewalk with me, and a few more across the street. One guy rode past on a bike. The two cars that drove by never slowed. No obvious signs I was being followed.

"I did," I said. "Can you believe Wu-Tang Clan's gonna play Forest National this summer? I had no idea they were so popular over here. Wanna go halfsies on a club box?" I scanned the windows. None were open, and the sun glare was too bright to see anything through the rest of them. Certainly no sign of a lens, a scope, or any other type of surveillance device.

"Your candidate does good work, Mr. Carter," he said, ignoring my attempt at ignorance. "I am very impressed."

"And I am very busy. You paid your fee, so unless you have another search for me, I'm going to hang up."

"You should learn how to take a compliment."

"I prefer them over text. In a secure chat room. The way we've always communicated."

"And how about referrals?" Leon asked. "Do you only take those over text as well?"

"Ideally, yes," I said impatiently. This call, which never should have happened in the first place, was already taking far too long and was far too public. Still not sure where his eyes were but convinced I wouldn't be able to find them, I started walking again. My apartment was a straight shot from the café, but two blocks away I turned right, just to be safe.

"Are you not going home?" he asked.

I stopped again. The melon and coffee suddenly felt very unwelcome in my stomach. Leon White owned a strip club on the outskirts of the red-light district and made most of his money running drugs and whores from the back room. He was a medium fish in a big pond who hired me to find someone to take out one of his rivals. We'd met in person exactly twice, neither time giving the impression that he had the ability to track me the way he was, and he damn sure shouldn't know where I lived.

"I play bridge every Tuesday morning," I said. "We drink tea and discuss Oprah's latest book club selection. Why do you care?"

"I have someone I want you to meet."

"Great, give me their name and number and I'll be happy to reach out."

"No, no," he said, amused. "They do not do business over the phone."

"And I don't do business on my living room couch."

"They will be at your apartment in one hour," he said, the humor gone. "It would be a shame if you're not there to greet them."

Go ahead and run, Rick.

That's what he was really saying.

Try to figure out which of those sun-stained windows has a sniper rifle behind it. Think you can get it right before the bullet enters your brain?

"I guess I can skip my game today," I said. "I wasn't a fan of Oprah's pick this month anyway."

"Good," he said. "I gave you a glowing recommendation, Mr. Carter. Don't make me regret it."

Before I could reply, the line went dead. I stared at my phone for a few seconds, then redialed the number. I hung up while a recorded voice explained that it was no longer in service.

CHAPTER TWO

The knock came at 10:57 a.m. Eight minutes early. I stood up from my worn leather couch, buttoned my black suit jacket, took a deep breath, and let it out slowly. Then I walked to my door and looked through the peephole.

There were two of them, a little younger than me. Midthirties, maybe. Each with close-cropped dark hair and matching dark suits. One looked like a banker, the other a lawyer. A slick one, the kind that handles divorce cases because he enjoys it, not just for the money. Both wore sidearms on their belt, and neither tried to hide it.

Obviously not a banker or a lawyer. Cursing Leon under my breath, I opened the door.

"Rick Carter?" said the one closest to me, the banker. I couldn't place the accent. Not another imported American, like me, but he definitely wasn't Belgian.

I nodded.

"Our car's waiting outside." He held out his arm, beckoning me into the hallway. The overhead light two doors down flickered and buzzed, bathing the fresh piss stains on the green, threadbare carpet in an irregular fluorescent glow. I didn't move.

"Great," I said. "Where are we going?"

"Brussels Airport. There's a private jet waiting."

"The airport?" More alarm bells went off in my head. Too many. "Where exactly is this meeting taking place?"

"No idea," said the first guy again. Other than checking his watch, the second guy standing behind him might as well have been a cardboard cutout. His presence was far from insignificant, however. Two guys made backing out more challenging. Two guys made it less of an invitation and more of an order.

"Our instructions were to pick you up here and drop you at the plane," the first guy said. "Whatever happens after that . . ." he shrugged to indicate his guess was as good as mine. There really wasn't a choice. The second guy made sure of that.

I opted to play this out, at least as far as the airport, without making a fuss. Diplomacy was always my default tactic. I could handle myself if things got physical—it was a prerequisite when dealing with my clientele—but I am not James Bond. I had no urge to escalate the situation.

Until I stepped into the hallway.

Guy #1 put his hand on my chest before I had my other foot out the door.

"Sorry," he said, "we need to take your piece." He reached under my coat, toward the Glock holstered beneath my left armpit, but I slapped him away and stepped back.

Guy #2 drew his gun, but Guy #1 held his hand toward him and told him to be cool. He had his other hand, the one that had reached under my jacket, stretched out to me, trying to keep things civil.

"No need to get worked up, Mr. Carter," he said. "Just precautionary. Take it out and leave it here, if you'd rather not have us hang on to it."

"Thanks, but I prefer to leave it right where it is," I said, patting the grip. Guy #2 flinched. Guy #1 never broke eye contact. "Just precautionary."

"Sorry," he said again. "Can't let that happen."

"Well then you can tell your boss that I respectfully decline his meeting request."

"Can't let that happen either." He dropped his hand and rested it on the butt of his own weapon. That made it official. Rejection was not an option.

"I don't know how your employer does business," I said, "but I only agree to a pat-down when I know what I'm walking into. This right here," I motioned in a circle encompassing the three of us and our little standoff, "is not the way you make a potential partner feel comfortable. So either my peace of mind comes with me," I tapped it again and this time both men flinched, "or you can go fuck yourselves."

Guy #1 dropped his eyes and bent his mouth into a half smile. I saw the move coming a half second before he made it. He pulled his gun and I grabbed his arm in the same motion, yanking it hard into the edge of the doorframe. His hand popped open and the gun went skidding across my apartment floor toward the kitchen. Still holding his arm, I ducked as he swung at me with his other fist, then stood up straight, driving the crown of my skull into his chin. His legs went wobbly, making it easy to grab two handfuls of his shirt and toss him into my TV stand. The set crashed to the floor with a flash of sparks, a pop of smoke, and the sweet smell of burnt electrical components.

Nice job, genius, I thought. *I guess pushing him* out *of the apartment made too much sense.*

With his partner on the ground, Guy #2 had a clear shot at me. I flung the door shut and stepped to the side as two bullets splintered the wood where my chest had been. I clicked the dead bolt just as he tried to ram through, shaking the entire frame. A second later it shook again as his partner, back on his feet, lowered his shoulder into my spine and drove me into the wall. The air rushed out of my lungs, and I dropped to my knees after he landed two point-blank kidney shots. I turned just as he was raising his knee to deliver the knock-out blow and was able to block it with my forearms. Before he could reload to try again, I shot my hand out, grabbed his testicles, squeezed, and twisted.

The cry that came out of him was part animal, part wounded child. He collapsed without even trying to brace the impact. His head smacked on the hardwood floor but I don't think he noticed. Both hands clutched his ruptured genitals and didn't move to defend his face as I stomped it with the bottom of my foot. There was a single, sharp snap, like a pencil breaking in half. Nose, orbital bone, jaw—something was now in worse shape than it had been when he woke up that morning.

The door shook as his partner collided with it again.

"Mike, you okay?" he shouted.

I heard wood crack and saw the frame around the dead bolt curve outward. One or two more good hits and he'd be inside. It was a miracle it had held up this long. Putting two in his chest as he entered the room would have ended things quickly, but I still didn't know who they worked for and didn't want to step into an even bigger pile of shit by capping one of their people or holding him at gunpoint until I figured out what to do next. There was also the serious question as to whether or not I'd even be able to pull the trigger when it mattered. I talk a good game, but the next person I shot would be my first. All I wanted at that moment was to get somewhere safe, call Leon, and demand to know who the fuck he sent to my apartment and why.

The window.

I ran to it and pulled it up as Guy #2 slammed into the door again. My apartment was on the third floor and there was no fire escape. Jumping meant a broken leg at best, so that was out. I looked around, my head outside in the frigid winter air, hoping to find anything resembling a viable option. That's when I saw the drain spout.

It was about four feet to my left, secured to the side of the building by metal clamps bolted into the brick. No idea if it would hold my weight, but I was out of time. Not thinking, just moving, I stepped onto the windowsill, pushed off, and caught the pipe with both hands. Tore the skin off all my knuckles as they scraped between the brick and the spout, but I got a grip. The bracket closest to where I grabbed bent outward and the bolts pulled free, but the ones above and below it maintained their hold. I half rappelled, half fell down the pipe, and landed on the sidewalk hard enough to lose my balance and tumble onto my back. When I looked up, I saw Guy #2 leaning out my window. I scrambled to my feet and ran, waiting for the sound of gunshots.

Would the bullets ricochet off the concrete around my feet, sending up little puffs of debris like in the movies? Or would this bad guy actually have decent aim and put one in the back of my head on the first try?

As it turned out, neither of those things happened. I had just enough time to wonder why before I rounded the corner and the large man blocking my path jammed an electric stun gun into the side of my neck.

It was an interesting sensation. First there was the pain, sudden and blinding and unexpected. It felt like two white-hot needles had punctured my skin and began burning my flesh from the inside.

After the initial jolt, the electricity worked its way through my muscles, seizing every one of them. My body went limp and I crumpled into the behemoth who I assumed was the third member of my collection party. He caught me under the arms and put the stun gun back in his pocket. Then he removed my Glock from its shoulder holster and tucked it into his belt.

All that and they still took my frigging gun.

Feeling started to come back—quicker than I expected—but everything was pins and needles, like when you've been sleeping on your arm and roll over, allowing the blood to rush back in. Though I could stand on my own, doing much else was out of the question. Guy #3 made it a moot point when he pinned my arms behind my back and secured my wrists with a length of white plastic zip tie.

He grabbed my elbow and led me to a black, four-door sedan idling at the curb by the entrance to my building. Guy #2 came through the front doors as we approached, his arm beneath his partner's shoulders, dragging him along.

"What the fuck happened?" my guy asked.

"Asshole freaked out," Guy #2 said. "Broke Mike's nose."

Among other things.

Mike attempted to lunge at me, but it was half-hearted. More for show and to salvage what was left of his pride than anything. Guy #2 restrained him, but it didn't take much effort.

"So what do you want me to do?" Guy #3 asked.

An elderly couple shambled toward us on the sidewalk, bundled tight beneath coats that looked as old as they were, their arms around each other as much for warmth as affection. Otherwise, the street was empty. In my neighborhood, anyone not at work by 11:00 in the morning was either drunk, high, or dead from doing too much of both.

Guy #3 squeezed my arm hard enough to bruise and shot me a sideways glance. *Don't try anything*, it said. He flashed a thin smile to Ma and Pa Kettle, who nodded politely and crossed the street, wanting no part of our little congregation.

"I'll arrange for a pickup, get him to a doctor," Guy #2 said, nodding toward Mike. "Can you handle the drop-off by yourself?"

"No problem. He's restrained, and if he gives me any shit, I'll just hit him again with my little friend."

"Don't be so hard on yourself," I said. "I'm sure it's perfectly average-sized." It was a lame joke, I know, but cut me some slack; I'd just started getting feeling back in my tongue. Guy #3 didn't find it funny. He opened the rear driver's side door and tossed me in like a bag of takeout food. My head clipped the roof of the car and then thudded against the passenger door for good measure. All my nerve endings were still tingling but I managed to work myself into a sitting position as he got in and drove away.

"Do you think Mike's gonna be okay?" I asked. I was feeling better and wanted to make up for the lazy dick joke. "You guys didn't have a date planned tonight, I hope."

I saw his eyes steal a look at me in the rearview mirror. Then he took the stun gun out of his pocket, held it up, and pushed a button on the side of its smooth black handle. A tiny blue arc crackled between the twin silver pins at the top.

"Keep talking, asshole, and I'll give you a shot in the mouth."

"Come on, man, that's just setting me up for a blowjob joke. Do you not hear how that sounds when you say it?"

I make jokes when I'm nervous, okay? Sometimes it works and breaks the tension, other times it gets me beaten and tasered. I would have kept it up, but those two little pins jammed into my leg and everything went all tingly again. Seems this was one of the latter situations. I rode the rest of the way in silence, my head leaning against the cool glass of the window.

CHAPTER THREE

We drove straight onto a tiny runway at the far end of Brussels Airport, reserved for private charter jets. At the guard booth, my chauffeur flashed a badge and was waved through. From the backseat I couldn't make out the full ID, but it definitely wasn't local police.

Interpol maybe?

That would be interesting. Despite what the movies and TV shows tell us, Interpol doesn't have "agents," at least not in the gun-toting, busting-bad-guys-on-the-street sense. It's not even an actual law enforcement agency, but rather a means for agencies across the globe to work together when the situation calls for it. Their "agents" are really just analysts, plucking away at keyboards in a cubicle in their headquarters in France. Which means if the badge my driver flashed was real, he was either packing heat against company policy, or he was on loan from some other agency and carrying Interpol credentials temporarily.

I also didn't get a good enough look to tell if the badge was a fake. If he and his two buddies were indeed actual agents on the take, coupled with the G550 idling on the runway, it all pointed to some serious bankroll behind Leon's referral. Not to mention the potential they had via Interpol to access corrupt agents anywhere in the world.

My driver parked the car a few feet away from the $42 million luxury suite with wings and pulled me out of the backseat. Over his shoulder, I saw another dark-suited agent-type approaching from the lowered steps of the aircraft.

"He's all yours," my driver said, shoving me toward my next handler. "He's got a mouth on him."

"Don't act like you didn't love it," I said.

"It's okay," the new guy said, "I have a ball gag on board that looks to be just his size." My eyes grew wide and I made an excited gasping noise, while my driver cringed at his colleague's choice of words.

"Seriously," I said to both of them, "did you guys rehearse this? Because you're making these jokes WAY too easy."

New Guy grabbed me by the arm, then stopped. "Is he supposed to be cuffed?" he asked, holding up my bound wrists.

"He got a little rebellious back at his place," my driver explained. "Figured better safe than sorry."

"Is he armed?"

"Not anymore."

"Then what's there to worry about?"

"I'll have you know," I said, "I have a black belt in Jeet Kune Do. Okay, that's a lie. I do watch a lot of Bruce Lee movies, though. And sometimes, late at night, I practice along with the fight scenes. In my underwear. It's not pretty. I have a lot of moles on my back."

New Guy had the same sense of humor as my driver. "Cut him loose," he said. Reluctantly, my driver took a folding knife from his pocket and sliced the zip tie in half. The plastic strip fell to the ground.

"Let's go," the new guy said, shoving me toward the jet.

"Aren't you going to pick that up?" I asked my driver. "Nobody likes a litterbug." He spit on the severed zip tie and turned back to the car.

My new handler ushered me up the cabin steps and not-so-gently into an otherwise very comfortable leather seat. Way nicer than the cracked, bargain store leather of my couch. Then he went back and sealed the outer door before disappearing into the cockpit. Fifteen minutes later we were airborne, on the way to who-the-fuck-knew.

At least we'd get there in style. The table in front of me was small and round, freshly polished. Cherry, or something equally expensive. A TV hung from the ceiling, but no remote that I could find. The phone next to my chair was dead when I picked it up. They'd let me keep my cell, but there was no one to call at thirty thousand feet anyway. To my left was a long panel door, about knee high. I lifted the handle and it slid up to reveal a drink compartment. Inside was a bottle of Macallan 18. I removed the bottle, found a glass in the cabinet over the sink behind me, and filled it a little more than halfway.

"Here's to a long flight," I said, then cheered my glass to no one.

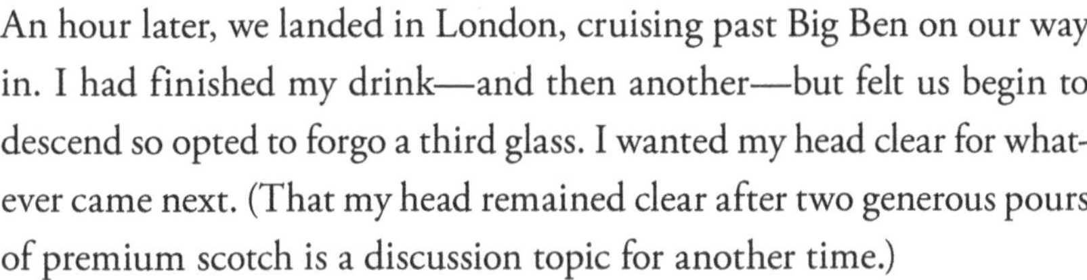

An hour later, we landed in London, cruising past Big Ben on our way in. I had finished my drink—and then another—but felt us begin to descend so opted to forgo a third glass. I wanted my head clear for whatever came next. (That my head remained clear after two generous pours of premium scotch is a discussion topic for another time.)

We taxied into an empty hangar where another car waited. Two more agent-types stood next to it. The guy who escorted me onto the plane—we'll call him Guy #4—emerged from the cockpit and opened the door. There was a Guy #5 in the copilot's seat, but he never turned around to acknowledge me.

"Let's go," #4 said, motioning toward the door.

"I enjoy our little talks," I said as I walked past him. As soon as both my feet were on the tarmac, he folded the steps up and slammed the door shut behind me.

The two agents—because who was I kidding, that's what they were—approached. One was a Black male, late twenties. The other was a female, Caucasian, around the same age. At least we finally had some diversity in the group. Corruption opportunities in law enforcement should be open to anyone who qualifies, I always say, not just boring white dudes.

"Are you guys Interpol too?" I asked. Neither one answered or reacted to the question in any way. The woman opened the back door—same make and model as the car that picked me up in Brussels—and beckoned me over.

I got in, looked up at her, and said, "Don't suppose you can tell me where we're going?"

She shut the door in my face.

Albert Street is a tree-lined collection of middle-class row homes just outside the main business district in London's Camden Town. The London Zoo and Regent's Park are minutes away. It's the kind of neighborhood that London urbanites settle in to raise their kids without fully committing to suburban life.

We pulled up to a house that had been painted an unappealing blend of white and tan. A pink tricycle with plastic tassels sprouting from each handlebar sat just inside the black, wrought-iron fence guarding the tiny, well-manicured lawn.

The female agent opened my door and led me up the short flight of concrete steps. There were no other cars parked at the curb. A stack of coupon circulars and other assorted junk mail protruded from the mailbox next to the door. It had all the trappings of a safe house, further cementing my Interpol theory.

The male agent stepped around me with a key and unlocked the door. Inside, the house was silent. The living room was furnished in turn-of-the-century IKEA and everything was covered with a thin layer of dust. The female agent took the lead while I followed behind. Her partner shut and locked the door and brought up the rear. We walked single file down a short hallway, hung a right, and went down a flight of stairs to the basement.

The steps were old and rickety. They creaked beneath our weight. At the bottom was an equally old door, its white paint faded, cracked, and peppered with black mold. The female agent opened it and stepped into a dank washroom, illuminated by a single exposed, hanging bulb with a pull chain. There was a washer and dryer against one bare, cinder block wall. Next to them stood a water heater wrapped in a sheet of yellow fiberglass insulation to shield it from the cold. The wrap was secured in the front with three strips of frayed duct tape that were slowly losing their battle against time and the elements. The space was tight, so much so that the male agent had to hang back on the steps.

"Cozy," I said. "Is your boss going to pop out of the washing machine, or did we make a wrong turn back at the half bathroom?"

The female agent crouched in front of the water heater and pulled apart the bottom edges of the insulation, exposing a metal plate covering the temperature controls. She loosened the top and bottom screws with her fingers and pulled the plate off, revealing not little dials regulating the heat of the water in the tank, but a telephonic keypad. She punched in a nine-digit code (I made out an eight and a two, but missed the others) and a hydraulic hiss escaped from behind the wall to my right. The outline of a door formed in the mortar between the cinder blocks as an entire section pulled backward, revealing the entrance to a corridor, brightly lit with fluorescent overhead lighting. I took an involuntary step backward and knocked into the male agent, who shoved me back toward the door.

The female agent replaced the plate over the keypad and ushered me through the hidden passageway, which was a first for me. I'd attended client meetings in plenty of sketchy locations over the past decade, but none of them were accessed through the washroom of an empty row home.

Keep your shit together, Rick. These guys aren't playing around.

I wiped my palms on my pant legs, hoping my escorts didn't notice how badly I'd started sweating.

Everything about this . . . bunker, I guess? . . . was the exact opposite of the house that camouflaged it. The walls were white and the floor was shiny gray linoleum. Nothing cracked or faded. Everything sleek and new. We formed a single line again and walked down the corridor, past two sets of standard office doors, one on each side. There was a final pair of doors before the corridor ended in a T junction, and we turned into the one on the left.

It was an interrogation room. Clearly soundproofed, with foam walls and the low, persistent hum of noise-canceling speakers filling the air. There was a metal table with two chairs, one on each side. A steel bar was welded to the table by the chair on the left. If I'd been wearing handcuffs, that's where they'd have secured them.

"Please, sit," the female agent said. Her accent was rich, smooth. Upper-crust British all the way.

"It speaks," I replied, sitting in the chair without the handcuff bar in front of it. She smiled.

"Would you like anything?" she asked. "Coffee? Water?"

"I'm good, thanks."

"Then I'll let our host know that you're here. Won't be more than a few minutes."

"And what is our host's name?" I asked, but she only smiled, as if the question amused her, and left the room, her brown ponytail bouncing behind her. Her partner hung behind, standing guard by the door.

I took a quick survey of my surroundings. No glass, so no two-way mirror. No visible cameras, but there was no doubt they were there. Tucked into the lighting, most likely. Or embedded in the walls.

Curbside, the place screamed safe house. The inside too. But down here, this was different. Safe houses are just that: houses. They may have a crawlspace or a false floor somewhere to hide in case of emergency, but nothing like this. This was something else.

There was no clock on the wall, but I still heard one ticking. For a brief moment I thought it was my heart, pounding in my ears, but then realized it was the male agent's watch. He stood motionless by the door, his arms straight down in front of him, crossed at the wrists.

"Nice timepiece," I said. "Mine has Spider-Man on it, but I only wear it on special occasions."

The door opened, ending my attempt at witty banter. Ponytail entered, followed by a woman wearing a white suit with sharp edges. She had a blue blouse beneath the jacket, and her blonde hair—though styled short—was accented by darker roots. She could have been forty just as easily as she could have been sixty. I stood as she approached and shook her hand. There was a thin gold band on her right ring finger. No other visible jewelry. Not even a tiny pair of earrings.

"Mr. Carter?" she said, still holding my hand. "My name is Patricia Baum. It's a pleasure to meet you."

"Likewise," I said. She had the same sophisticated air to her accent as Ponytail, but it was disingenuous. It came off as something practiced. Polished and fine-tuned over many years.

"Please sit," she said. I did, and she took the other chair. The two agents bracketed the door. "How was your flight? Did you enjoy the Macallan? I do hope we got that right."

"The scotch was delicious and the plane was immaculate," I said. "Can't say I cared for the pickup service, though."

She lowered her head and tried to look disappointed. It rang as empty as her accent. "Yes, I apologize for that. I hope you understand why we need to take precautions in regard to allowing outside parties to carry weapons into a meeting, but it could have been handled more delicately."

"In all honesty, Trish—can I call you Trish?" Her lips smiled but her eyes didn't. "I don't understand any of this. Don't get me wrong, I'm grateful for the opportunity and value all the referral business that comes my way, but there are some unspoken rules that weren't followed here."

"Indeed there were," she said. "Regrettable, but necessary."

"And why is that, exactly?"

She sat back in her chair. Crossed her slender legs and folded her hands across her knee. "You come to us very highly recommended, Mr. Carter. May I call you Rick?"

"Please, call me Trish." Behind me, one of the agents stifled a laugh.

"Not just by Leon," she said, unfazed, "although his glowing review of your work was what finally convinced us to reach out. In particular, we were impressed with your ability to find professionals who are adept at, shall we say, sleight of hand."

I raised an eyebrow.

"We are dealing with a very delicate situation. It needs to be resolved quickly and efficiently but can never be traced back to us or our business partners. From what we've been told, you're the best there is at finding people capable of pulling that off."

"Who is 'we'?" I asked.

"My superiors."

"And they are?"

"Let's call them the Board of Directors."

"Fine," I said, waving my hand at the cloak-and-dagger nonsense. "When do I get to meet them?"

"The same day you get to meet God, Mr. Carter." There was so much ice in her voice, I almost expected to see her breath. "In the meantime," she continued, "you go through me."

"Go through you for what? This is the part where we talk about exactly what it is you need my people to do."

Trish motioned for the male agent to come over. He punched up something on his phone and placed it in front of me. On the screen was a file photo of an agent in the FBI. Her freckles folded into the wrinkles just starting to deepen on her face. The text next to her head shot showed her to be a twenty-year veteran of the Bureau. Her name was Nadia Spencer.

He swiped left and a new photo appeared. Another FBI agent, this one named Frank Portis. His bio revealed him to be Nadia's partner, although he looked at least a decade younger. Both were on assignment in Saudi Arabia.

He swiped left again. Another agent, David Lofton, but this one was MI5. Blonde hair, blue eyes. More Daniel Craig than Sean Connery.

Swipe. David's partner, Lewis Reed. Both men stationed here in London.

Swipe. Yosef Abram. Mossad operative. No file photo this time, just a grainy black-and-white snapped from a distance.

Swipe. Yosef's partner, Leah Abram. A rare husband-and-wife duo. Risky, but effective for deep cover work if the marriage was strong enough to handle it.

The agent withdrew his phone, and I looked up at Trish. I already knew I wouldn't be taking the job, but I wanted to at least hear her out. Professional courtesy still mattered to me, even if it didn't to them.

"Together," Trish said, "these six agents represent an international task force that has become more problematic than we originally anticipated. We need them removed. The sooner the better."

I plucked a speck of fuzz off my sleeve and dropped it on the floor, then rubbed my fingers and thumb together several times. I was stalling. I needed to choose my words carefully. In my old firm, when I found white collar executives for white collar companies, passing on a search opportunity was a sign of strength. It proved you didn't need to chase work outside your niche; that your services were so in demand, you had the luxury of choosing which projects to take on and which to turn down.

As I found out early on, however, clients in my new industry didn't view rejection the same way and tended to react . . . poorly.

"Can't you just buy them off?" I said at last. "If you've got Interpol in your pocket, bribing a half dozen other agents should be well within your means."

"We tried. Several times. It seems possessing an impenetrable set of moral standards was a prerequisite for joining this particular task force."

"What about your own people? If you have a Board of Directors, don't you also have a . . . project management team, let's say . . . that can handle this?"

"Oh yes," she said. "One of the best in the world. But as I said, we need to be as far removed from this as possible. That's where you come in."

I sighed and looked for more lint to pick off my suit, but there was none. "Unfortunately, Trish, it's not."

"Excuse me?" For the first time since she sat down, her accent broke. Just a little. Enough for a whiff of her cockney upbringing to seep through.

"Frankly," I said, "I'm surprised I'm even sitting here. If you went to all the trouble to find out my favorite brand of scotch, then you must have also learned that I don't get involved with hits on law enforcement. Never have."

"We did," she said. The cracks in the accent were gone, sealed up by the return of her icy tone. "We hoped we could convince you to make an exception."

"I don't see how—"

"Three million dollars."

I blinked.

"That's our budget for all six hits, plus your fee of course. You can divvy that up among your candidates however you see fit. At your going rate of 30 percent, that will net you a nine-hundred-thousand-dollar payday."

My mouth was dry. Nine hundred thousand dollars was almost double what I had stashed in all my accounts combined. But Trish wasn't done.

"Nine hundred isn't a very psychologically satisfying number though, is it? It's so close to the edge of being something more, something much grander. It's a tease, really. Which is why we took the liberty of depositing a hundred thousand into your Swiss account this morning. Call it an engagement fee. Or better yet, call it our way of apologizing for breaking those unspoken rules you care so much about."

My hand reflexively reached for my phone but I pulled it back. Trish saw and laughed.

"Go ahead and check with your bank," she said. "I won't be offended."

I hesitated just a second before I did. Sure enough, the money was there. *How the hell did they get my account information?*

"That's a million dollars total, Mr. Carter. Unless our facts are wrong, that's more than you've earned at one time in your entire career."

Her facts were not wrong. And if I were in this for the money, we'd already have been shaking hands. But the money stopped being important to me the minute I stopped needing it. By that time, of course, I'd lost everything else of value in my life, and no number of zeroes would bring them back.

I was in it now because getting out wasn't an option. Sleeping at night was never easy, but one of the ways that still made it possible was telling myself that the people involved in every deal I closed were all on the wrong side of the law. When no one hurt by my actions was innocent, it made it far easier to suppress my own guilt. That went out the window the minute I started accepting jobs where the targets were good guys.

"While I'm flattered," I said to Trish, "and you're not wrong about the fee, I'm still going to have to decline. I've built my career doing what I do best, and it isn't jobs like this."

"Jobs like what," Trish said, "finding people to kill other people? Forgive me, but I thought that's exactly what you built your career on."

"You're forgetting my work in smuggling, money laundering, and online hacking," I replied.

"We operate in those areas, too," Trish said. "And it would be wonderful to have someone as talented as you on hand to help us recruit for those projects, when the need arises. But for now, *this* is our need. And it trumps everything else."

"I'm sorry, but you're going to have to find another recruiter." I tried to strike a firmer tone without coming off too aggressive. The male agent moved away from the door and stood next to me.

Careful, Rick.

"If you like," I said, wishing very much that the holster under my jacket wasn't empty, "I'd be happy to recommend a few names that are just as good in this niche as I am in my own."

"If we wanted a different recruiter, Mr. Carter, they'd be the one sitting in that chair right now."

How many lives have been ended by your actions, Rick? How many innocents, even if they were involved with the wrong people? Did that make them guilty, too? Did the woman Ian strangled deserve to die just because she was sleeping with Leon's rival? How many others like her? Don't kid yourself about who you are or what you do, just because the bodies in your wake don't get buried with badges.

This wasn't the first time I'd been offered a job like this, notwithstanding the enormous fee. Do what I do long enough, and eventually the bad guys want you to find people to take out the good guys. Each time, I'd turned down the offer without burning a bridge. Each time, I'd gone home and scrolled through the memories of who I used to be, deluding myself into thinking a part of that man still remained. That I hadn't buried him along with all those other bodies.

So why does this time feel different?

"It's not gonna happen," I said, derailing my train of thought before it led me somewhere I didn't want to go.

"That's too bad," Trish said. Her eyes flicked over my shoulder and before I could react the male agent's arm wrapped tightly around my neck, compressing my trachea at the Adam's apple. His gun pressed into the side of my head. My hands shot up like pistons to loosen his grip, with little effect. Panic hit hard and fast, erasing any lingering questions about who held the power in this negotiation.

"If you kill me," I choked out, pulling at his arm to gain an extra breath, "then you'll just have to find someone else anyway."

"Killing you is certainly on the table, Mr. Carter," Trish said patiently, "but there are several steps to go before we get there. We've only begun trying to talk you into it, after all."

"Please," I said. The tremble in my voice was bad, but I couldn't help it. "I won't say anything to anybody. You know that about me."

"Oh, we're not concerned about you going to the authorities, Rick. Your reputation in that regard is spotless. But we didn't fly you all the way out here and pay you a hundred thousand dollars just to buy your silence."

"You can take the money back. I don't want it."

"That has become abundantly clear, but we still need you to do what you do best. The good thing is, I'm fairly certain you can do your job even without the tip of your finger."

"NO!" I screamed, or at least intended to. What came out was little more than a squeak. The agent's arm constricted even tighter, cutting off all but the faintest trickle of air. I tried to resist when Ponytail grabbed my left wrist and pulled it onto the table, but the gun dug deeper into my temple and the world started to go gray as my oxygen supply dwindled. With one quick motion, she pulled a knife from her pocket—a Smith & Wesson foldout, the same model my driver used to remove the zip tie from my wrists in Brussels—and used it to remove the tip of my left pinkie finger from the rest of the digit. Just below the top knuckle. The grip on my throat eased enough for me to scream, which was likely the intent.

Trish wanted to hear it, and I didn't disappoint.

When the spots cleared from my vision, I saw my hand resting in a pool of blood. Someone had wrapped the severed tip of my finger in a cloth napkin, balled it up, and set it on the corner of the table.

If they get that on ice fast enough, someone might be able to reattach it, I thought naïvely.

"Rick?" Trish said, almost cooing my name. "Do I have your attention?"

I nodded and tried to answer but all that came out was a hacking series of coughs. The male agent's arm, though loosened, still had a snug embrace on my neck and was ready to reengage on her command. He'd put away his gun, but it was overkill by that point anyway.

"Good, because I'm going to extend our offer again. You may have lost a tiny bit of yourself, but you haven't lost any money. Turn us down a second time, however, and you will lose an eye."

My head snapped up as the agent's arm went back to work once more. Ponytail took the tip of her blade, now flecked red, and pressed it ever so slightly into the corner of my left eye. A bead of blood formed on my lower eyelid and dripped down my cheek. Through that thin layer of skin, I felt a tiny ball of pressure. Not enough to do any damage; just enough to let me know it was there. Almost like a stye.

I concentrated on two things: sucking in what little air my bruised windpipe would allow, and not shitting or pissing my pants. I was succeeding at both, but just barely.

"Okay," I said, managing no more than a whisper. I would have nodded as well, but all I could picture was the knife plunging into my eye as a result, a warm trail of bloody goop sliding down my cheek.

Trish motioned to the male agent, who removed his arm from my throat, and to Ponytail, who pulled her knife away. I gulped at the air, but it was like trying to chug water through a straw. Every fresh breath brought a new seizure of coughs. After a few minutes, I got myself under control and pulled my aching, mutilated hand to my chest. I didn't even have a tissue to stem the bleeding, so I made a fist and squeezed it tight, hoping that would at least slow it down until it clotted. Blood dripped down my arm in warm rivulets, staining my sleeve and the front of my shirt.

"I'm glad you came around," Trish said, smiling. "Things go so much smoother when we're all on the same page."

I stared at her and said nothing. My throat and finger screamed in rhythm with my pulse.

"How long before we can expect to see our first candidates?"

"Two weeks," I croaked. Then I cleared my throat, which felt like gargling with broken glass, and repeated myself, stronger this time.

"We'll give you half that," Trish replied.

"You don't understand. This is a multipronged job requiring three candidates, minimum, and a high level of precision planning. I want to make sure the vetting process is done the right way."

"I can appreciate that, but we are under somewhat of a time crunch. Your candidate pool is legendary, Mr. Carter. We're confident that you'll be able to source quality people within a week's time."

I didn't protest. Any control I had over these proceedings was now balled up in a bloodstained napkin on the corner of the table. Instead, I just nodded.

"Good, it's settled then. I believe you require half your fee up front and half when you deliver the candidates, yes?"

I nodded again.

"The money will be in your account tomorrow morning. Same one we used for the first hundred, unless you wanted it spread out amongst the other banks you use?"

I shook my head. "The one will be fine." It was a Swiss bank, and $450,000 would barely register as water-cooler talk around their offices. "When I have candidates ready to present, how do you want it done?"

"We'll send a link to our secure chat. Let us know when you have a sufficient list put together and we'll arrange a meeting."

"Do you need me to give you my cell number?"

"Oh darling," Trish said, amused, "we already have it."

Of course they did.

I nodded again and squeezed my fist tighter, wincing at the pain.

"Let's get you cleaned up before your flight home, shall we? Edward, fetch some bandages from the first aid kit, please."

The male agent—Edward, apparently—clapped me hard on the back and left the room.

"I'll be going as well," Trish said, standing up. She extended her hand across the table. I glared at it for a moment before standing and taking it. "It was a bumpy start, Mr. Carter, but I look forward to our partnership. I think it will prove extremely beneficial for both sides."

I released her hand but said nothing. She started to leave then stopped, turned, and grabbed the balled-up napkin containing my fingertip off the corner of the table. She clenched it in her fist as she walked out the door. I heard her heels clicking on the linoleum but they soon faded away, leading me to wonder how far this underground facility actually stretched.

So much for having that reattached. Pinkie tips are overrated anyway.

Edward returned with a wad of white gauze and medical tape. He dropped them on the table in front of me, and I wrapped my still bleeding finger as tightly as I could.

"Little help?" I asked, as I tried awkwardly to hold the gauze wrap in place while also securing it with the tape, all one-handed. He grimaced, as if I'd just asked him to put in an extra hour of overtime on a Friday, but took the tape and looped it around several times while I held the wrap. A red bloom formed quickly at the tip of the gauze, but it stopped spreading not long after it started. The pain eased a bit, too, but that was likely more mental than anything. Like when you're a kid and a Band-Aid is a cure-all. I opened and closed my fist a few times to make sure the tape would hold, satisfied with the job Edward had done.

"Thanks," I said to him. "Now take me the fuck home."

CHAPTER FOUR

Guy #3 dropped me off at the curb in front of my building, waving goodbye with just his pinkie finger, laughing as if he'd just reinvented comedy. He never did give me my gun back, but I'd taken the Macallan 18 when I left the plane, so call it even. The bottle, now half-empty, sloshed as I trudged up the stairs, past Sem, the homeless fixture in the corner of the lobby. He was slumped in his usual spot against the potted tree that hadn't been watered since I moved in three years ago, snoring away contentedly. Lucas, the night manager, would usher him out around eight o'clock. Sometime before morning he would reappear, like a speck of dust that gets swept away only to land in another room.

It drove Lucas nuts, but Sem was the reason I chose this place out of all the other shitholes I looked at when I moved to Brussels. When you have money but live in the gutter, people who might want to find you for the wrong reasons will often step right over you as they search the kind of places where they assume you'll be. (Hating yourself makes living that way a lot easier, too.) A homeless guy by the stairs who often has flies buzzing around his mouth was the final piece of security that sealed the deal.

I was mildly surprised to see that nothing appeared to have been disturbed inside my apartment, especially with the demolished door hanging impotently open on its hinges. There was a dried bloodstain on the floor where Mike's face had met my foot, and the TV remained shattered a few feet away, but other than that, the place looked just as shitty as when I left it. Owning nothing of value remains the most effective anti-theft system I've ever discovered. I wasn't worried about noise complaints from the neighbors, either. Meth tends to block out a lot of the nuisances that trouble reputable members of society.

I took off my suit coat and tossed it on the couch, the only piece of furniture in the room other than the dinner tray I called an end table, and the TV stand that was currently missing a TV. I grabbed a rocks glass off the kitchen counter, one that still had a pool of melted ice sitting in the bottom, and filled it with the Macallan that hadn't splashed out of the bottle on the way up the stairs. Then I went back into the living room, collapsed onto the couch, and drained half the glass in a single swallow. Somehow, it felt more dignified than swigging straight from the bottle.

My mind swirled with possible next steps, failing to settle on one.

Go see Leon and demand to know how he's connected to Trish and her people?

Withdraw all the money from my accounts and disappear, hope for the best?

Start recruiting right away just to get it over with?

Drink more scotch?

Checking Facebook was not one of the choices on the merry-go-round of bad decisions in my mind, and yet I found myself with phone in hand, doing just that. I needed a shot of something positive. To smile, even if it was only at memories.

Denise had her profile set as private, but that wasn't a problem. One of the perks of knowing bad people who do bad things is learning how to hack your ex-wife's social media accounts in less than two minutes. At first, I'd needed the written steps in front of me, but now I could walk somebody else through it without trouble.

Her profile picture had changed since the last time I'd checked in. A selfie at a beach somewhere. Her brown curls had adopted the lighter, almost dirty-blonde color they got after baking in the summer sun, so

I assumed it was taken about six or seven months ago. It couldn't have been much older than that because the wisps of gray, though less noticeable, were still prevalent around her ears.

Her background picture was the same one as before: her and the kids sitting on the front steps of the house, before going out for her birthday. It still amazed me to see Maggie as a teenager. Take away her dimples and she could be Denise when we first met. Then there was Ethan. At twelve years old, he looked ready for high school. A far cry from the towheaded toddler who used to follow me around everywhere I went, giggling the way only a two-year-old can when you blow raspberries on their belly.

Ordinarily, my next move would've been to scroll through her photos, looking for the one of her in the black dress and matching heels. The one taken at the wedding of a coworker we attended a year before everything turned to shit. The one she wore in anticipation of a night alone in a hotel room without the kids but wound up being torn off in an elevator instead, the emergency bell ringing in our ears, an act of passion that never would have happened without hours' worth of free drinks leading up to it. In ten years, she hadn't deleted the picture. Probably because I wasn't in it.

But tonight, I never made it past the newest entry on her timeline. It was a photo, but not of her. She'd only been tagged in it. Her sister, Carol, was smiling that big, broad smile of hers. The kind that endeared her to all the kids in the daycare she ran out of her home. The same one that lights up the pages of our wedding album (assuming Denise hadn't thrown it out), where she appears as the Maid of Honor.

Shorter than Denise and frumpy, she could easily have grown up to be a bitter, middle-aged woman. The kind who argued with the checkout person in a grocery store over an expired coupon she insists should still be deducted from her total. Especially after her husband, Bill, left her childless, her prime motherhood years all but gone, while he started a family with his tall, decidedly not-frumpy office manager.

Carol was the exact opposite of bitter, though. We always got along well. It was impossible not to get along with Carol.

Tonight, I hated her. Not for who she was, but more by association.

In the photo that Carol had posted, she was holding a single sheet of paper. Heavy cardstock with eloquent script and silver embroidering around the edges. I could make out the words "You are cordially invited to the wedding of" but had to zoom in to read the rest. It was Denise's name, a date (August 4), and a second name: *Robert Baglioni.*

"So excited to be my big sister's Maid of Honor for a second time!" the caption read. It had racked up 124 likes and over 60 comments. Friends, family, coworkers. All wishing Denise well, telling her how happy they were for the two of them, and that they couldn't wait to be there on the big day.

Denise had been dating him for about a year. He wasn't in any pictures, but that didn't mean anything. Cops can be notoriously shy when it comes to social media. After their first date, she'd written a post that included his full name. He must have said something to her, because the post was gone the next time I hacked in, and she referred to him only as Robert from then on. I'd just gotten lucky.

A simple Google search yielded only the skimpiest of biographies. The first hit was a 2015 article in *The Philadelphia Inquirer* about a drug bust in Kensington. The arresting officer was one Robert Baglioni. No photo. I scrolled some more. Found an article about another drug bust from 2016, an obituary for what appeared to be his grandmother, and an old link to his graduating class for the police academy. No photos anywhere. No social media presence at all that I could find.

If I wanted to dig deeper, I could have. I still had connections back in the States that would tell me everything I wanted to know about Detective Baglioni. But what was the point? By all accounts, he made her happy. And he must be good with the kids. Denise wouldn't tolerate any man who wasn't. So I opted to do the grown-up thing and accept it. She had moved on, and so would I.

At least, that's what I told myself. Truth was, I didn't want to know what he looked like, or what kind of man he was, or how many friends he had. I didn't want to start tallying up our side-by-side stats and find that I came up way short. Easier to pretend to be the bigger man and just let the two of them live their lives.

But I never expected her to marry the son of a bitch.

"To Denise and Robert," I said, holding my drink up to the empty room. I finished it in a single swallow and hurled the empty glass at the wall. It exploded, the broken shards joining the remnants of my TV screen on the floor.

I had every intention of side-arming the phone against the same spot, eyeballing the fresh gash in the blue paint as my target, but the last few brain cells that weren't swimming in scotch stopped me before I went through with it.

There are more productive uses for the device in your hand, they suggested.

I stared at the screen, as if realizing for the first time that it could perform functions other than flagellation by way of social media.

"This is Rick," I said into it after dialing a number I swore I'd never call again. "Carter."

On the other end of the line, a female voice spoke. Quietly. Knowingly. "Thirty minutes," she said.

I considered sweeping up, brushing my teeth, maybe showering while I waited. In the end I just sat and watched the minutes silently tick by on the same phone until the knock came against my useless door. I got to my feet, wobbling a little, and went to her.

She wore a black dress with matching heels. Her brown hair hung to her shoulders in curls. In one hand, she clutched a small purse. With the other she reached up and stroked the side of my face, her skin soft against the rough stubble.

"Poor baby," she purred in passable English. "You look awful." Her hands slid down my sides and stopped at my bandaged finger. "Oh my God, what happened to your—"

I grabbed her around the waist and pulled her into me. Our mouths met, and her tongue quickly began searching for mine. I swung the door shut and pressed her against it. Her hands fumbled at the front of my pants while I hiked her dress up above her hips and pulled her panties to the side.

A few quick thrusts. Some muffled moans. The earth didn't move. It didn't have time.

I stood there for a moment, panting into her shoulder. When I felt her shift uncomfortably against the door, I took a step back and pulled my pants up while she flattened out her dress. She started toward the kitchen but I held up a folded wad of cash to block her way.

"You don't need to pay me now, sweetie. You've got me for the whole hour."

"Just take it," I said.

She considered the cash, then turned her eyes toward mine. "Honey, what's wrong?"

"Just take it and go, please," I said again.

"Are you sure? I can fix you something to eat, or we can just—"

"I said take the fucking money!" It was louder than I intended, and my throbbing throat hated me for it, but I didn't care. I crushed the bills into a ball, took her by the wrist, and shoved it into her palm. "Get out!"

Her features—full of sharp angles yet somehow still soft in a way that reminded me of Denise even more than the black dress I insisted she wear for all our encounters—twisted into a sneer. She was no longer every man's fantasy, a woman who could become whatever you desired, but a contract worker who just realized the guy who hired her is a piece of shit. To put an exclamation point on the transformation, she spit in my face and stormed into the hallway.

I slammed the door shut behind her, which was pointless with the lock and doorknob both broken. She kicked it once, swinging it back toward me, and shouted, "Asshole!" before stomping off. I gave the door a hard kick myself, decided that wasn't enough, and punched it too. Then I turned and collapsed against it. My legs gave out and I slid to the floor where I hugged my knees and started to sob.

CHAPTER FIVE

The next morning, I showered, dressed, vomited, and made breakfast, though not in that order. Everything hurt, and I wanted nothing more than to lie in bed for a week, but that wasn't an option. The extra $450,000 in my bank account ($550,000 if you count the "engagement fee") staring back at me from my phone screen was a reminder that I had a pressing obligation to some very serious people. As if the one they sent me home with yesterday wasn't enough.

I'd cleaned the nub of my finger as best I could in the shower—that'll wake you up—and wrapped it in fresh gauze afterward, but it needed real medical attention. The bleeding had mostly stopped, save for a little seepage here and there, but the skin around the wound had turned an ugly, purplish black. The bone was still exposed, and the entire finger had yet to regain feeling beyond the second knuckle. Going to the hospital meant paperwork, so that was a nonstarter.

Didn't matter. I knew a guy. Finding a medical professional who accepted cash and asked no questions was priority number one whenever I set up shop in a new location. He and I were set to meet later that day. Before that, though, I had a call to make.

I'd only met Leon White two weeks ago and knew very little about him. Since he hadn't shared anything useful about his relationship with

Trish's group at the time, and what I knew about him only made his ties to them more puzzling, I decided to back up one degree of separation and talk to the person who connected me with Leon in the first place. He picked up on the second ring.

"Hey Rick, good to hear from—"

"Who tipped you off about Leon White?" I interrupted.

"What?"

"Your lead about the White contract, Freddie, where did it come from?"

"I don't know, some guy. Why are you pissed? Did Leon not pay? I read the paper yesterday. Contract looks like it went smoothly."

"Oh it did," I said, "right up to the point when Leon hooked me up with a very well-funded referral who cut off part of my finger when I turned down their search opportunity. So, if you want me to continue paying off your gambling debts, you better come up with a better answer than 'some guy,' Freddie. I need to know who told you about White, because whoever he was neglected to mention that Leon knew people that high up on the food chain."

"Look, he was new, what do you want me to say? I'd never worked with him before, but he dropped all the right names and I knew the contract would interest you. It's not the first time I've sent you a lead from a source like that. Did they really cut off your finger?"

"Focus, Freddie. What did he look like?"

I could almost hear him shrug over the phone. "Average height, average build. Short brown hair, like a crew cut."

"Great, you just described half the guys in Belgium. Anything else, anything I can use? A name, maybe?"

"No name, but the ones they give me are almost always fake anyway." He snapped his fingers. "Oh, he had a neck tattoo! Some kind of Chinese symbol."

"Okay, that's at least mildly interesting. Nothing else, though? Nothing that seemed suspicious?"

"Not that I recall," he said. "Sorry, man, I've got a lot on my mind." His voice became more annoying than usual when he wanted pity. Sounded like someone slowly letting the air out of a balloon.

"Why?" I asked, rubbing my eyes. "Who's going to break your legs this time?"

"Nobody, as long as I get them the thousand I owe. Fucking sure thing trips up in the final lap. Just my luck."

"You got no luck Freddie, never have. Which is why I keep telling you to stay away from those dog races."

"Yeah, but Rick, this was a ten-to-one *sure thing*."

I sighed. "They're all sure things, Freddie, until they trip and fall."

"Rick . . ."

"The contract went off without a hitch, just like you said, and your referral fee will be in your account tonight. Don't get all squeaky."

"Thanks, Rick. And hey, I'll make it up to you next—"

I hung up.

Chinese neck tattoo. I don't know what else I was expecting. Freddie was a middleman, nothing more. A weaselly little guy who had his ear to the ground and passed on whatever he thought might be valuable to me, which in turn was valuable to him. He wasn't going to launch an investigation into every new contact he made, nor had I ever expected him to.

It didn't matter anyway. Identifying the person who fed Freddie intel on Leon White's station in the criminal underworld wouldn't change the fact that the people he referred me to were expecting candidates for their job, and the quicker I produced some, the quicker I could be done with the whole thing. Then it would be time for damage control.

If my candidates successfully completed Trish's contracts—and they would, I had no doubt—then word would soon spread that Rick Carter had started taking on searches he'd previously turned down. It would be harder to back out of those conversations with clients. Those bridges I'd managed to keep intact would begin to smolder.

Candidates would start asking questions, too. Both new and ones already on my roster. Wanting to know if it was true that I'd started handling those types of jobs, which often paid better than the ones I'd become known for. If I told them that no, it was a one-time thing, that might not sit well with all of them. Especially if the steady stream of work I promise, the thing I stake my reputation on, starts to dwindle because clients start to utilize my competitors as retaliation for doing a job for Trish that I refused to do for them. Wouldn't happen with all my clients, but I'd be a fool to think it wouldn't happen with any. Dominos would fall. That much was inevitable. The only questions would be how many and for how long.

Or, alternatively, Trish's job becomes but the first step over a line I soon leave far in my rearview. I prove as successful finding candidates for similar contracts as I'd been in the others so far. More clients come my way. More jobs. More candidates. More money. And more notoriety—more visibility—at the agencies that employ people whose job it was to put guys like me away for a long, long time.

Both options sucked. And in either scenario, the agents on Trish's list—six people who put their lives on the line every day to uphold justice—would be dead. Because of me.

Happy fucking Wednesday.

CHAPTER SIX

The tail was on me the minute I stepped out the front door of my building. It was Guy #2, the smarmy lawyer look-alike, keeping pace about twenty feet behind. He had on a similar suit to the one he'd worn yesterday, except he'd added an earpiece to the ensemble. The small white cord curled down noticeably from his right ear to the tiny microphone clipped to his shirt collar. I couldn't be sure if he wanted me to know he was there or he just sucked at his job, but either way, even on a sidewalk swollen with weekday foot traffic, he stood out.

After a few blocks, it was apparent his task was merely to observe, rather than intimidate. There really was no need for the latter. Trish had delivered that message loud and clear during our meeting.

When I ducked into the emergency clinic—a nondescript sliver of building tucked between a butcher and a hookah shop—he crossed the street and parked himself on a bench. He didn't bother pretending to read a newspaper or check his phone. Just lit up a cigarette and watched me through the clinic's front window. It wasn't much of a show. I was the last scheduled patient, and the physician on duty had sent the office staff home thirty minutes ago. He ushered me into a back room before I could enjoy the three-month-old magazines and stale coffee in the meager waiting area.

"What the fuck did you do?" the doctor asked as he removed the bandage from my pinkie. The space heater in the corner of the exam room was set to high, pumping out tropical waves of hot air. Sweat glistened from the thick black hair on his arms, but he never washed up before snapping on his surgical gloves. I bet the butcher next door had better sterilization practices.

"I slipped and fell," I said.

"Uh huh, we get a lot of those." He rinsed the wound with alcohol and called me a pussy when I winced. Or to be more accurate, he called me a *kut* as he didn't speak a word of English. I'd moved to Brussels from Germany a little over three years ago and my Dutch was still choppy, but getting better. I knew all the curse words, though.

"I'm assuming you didn't save the tip?" he asked.

"Sold it for beer money," I replied.

He grunted and pulled several medical tools out of a drawer, each a little less shiny than I would have preferred. One of them was a needle full of novocaine that he jabbed directly into the exposed tissue without so much as a heads-up. Despite the nerve damage, it still gave me a jolt.

"*Kut*," he muttered again.

Twenty minutes later, he was finished. He cut away the loose, dead skin around the edges and filed down the protruding bone until it was short enough to stitch the remaining flesh closed around it. Finally, he slathered the entire tip with antibiotic ointment and re-bandaged it. I paid him five hundred euros in cash, and he let me leave through the back door. When I emerged from the alley, Guy #2 was nowhere to be found.

I made it all the way to O'Reilly's without seeing him reappear. It was my last stop of the day, so I'd soon find out if he called it quits or was waiting for me back at my apartment. In the meantime, I had one more meeting on my schedule.

I was at the bar, halfway through my first beer when Joey sat down next to me. He was carrying a cigar box, wrapped in brown paper.

"What's a nice gal like you doing in a place like this?" he asked.

"Waiting for you, handsome," I said. "Buy you a beer?"

"Heineken."

I signaled the bartender and told her to put it on my tab. When she put the glass down in front of Joey, her name and phone number were written on the napkin underneath. He gave it a cursory glance and stuffed it in the back pocket of his jeans, where there were probably three more just like it. His ass hadn't had time to warm the barstool yet and already that chiseled jaw and those baby blue eyes had worked their magic. Some girls just liked that ripped, 3 percent body fat look I guess.

"I'm going to start meeting you in places where the employees are all old and ugly," I said, shaking my head. "Try to salvage what's left of my self-esteem."

"Could always hit up Delirium," he said, "mingle with the tourists. Place is so thick with them, I'd get lost in the crowd."

"Ten bucks says the hottest girl in the place finds you anyway."

Joey chuckled and sipped his beer. "Twenty says we're back here next time, so it doesn't matter."

He wasn't wrong. O'Reilly's was the only place in town where I actually had a tab. A traditional sports bar, the walls were lined with TVs and the waitresses poured into tight-fitting uniforms. It was filled with guys who didn't give a shit about what I did for a living. Somewhere I could have a beer without worrying whether the couple at the next table were eavesdropping on my conversation. Which was good because Joey and I had a lot to discuss. Unfortunately, it wasn't as fruitful a dialogue as I'd hoped.

"So you have no idea who they are?" I said, after giving him the CliffsNotes version of my past twenty-four hours. "Patricia Baum. Crooked Interpol agents. Safe house on Albert Street in London. None of this means anything to you?"

"Nada," Joey said. "I wish I could help you out."

I'd met Joseph Walls a little over a year ago, and I could count on one hand the number of times he'd disappointed me when it came to providing reliable information. Wouldn't need more than two fingers, either. After getting dishonorably discharged from the Army for dealing hash on base, instead of going back home to Michigan, Joey decided to remain in Brussels and picked up right where he left off. Only now, unencumbered by the security protocols inherent to an active member of the armed forces, his client list was much bigger. He expanded his services, too, adding gunrunning to his thriving drug business. That made him a very well-connected individual. Way more so than Freddie. He was a golden goose to a man in my position.

"It doesn't make sense," he said. "Why fly you all the way to London and show off their operation instead of meeting at a neutral site?"

"Power play. Prove how big and resourceful they are, how far their reach extends, in case I have any thoughts about backing out or going to the authorities."

"And you're sure their guys were carrying Interpol creds?" he asked.

I sipped my beer, a delicious amber local brew, and nodded. "Yup. I thought at first they might be bogus, but I've been around enough corrupt cops to tell the real ones from the phonies. They knew all the moves, and sported matching hardware."

"Looks like they weren't afraid to use it either."

I wiggled my pinkie. The novocaine was starting to wear off, but the beer was picking up the slack. "They could have done a lot worse." I thought of the knife point pressed against my eyelid, that unwelcome, unpleasant little bump pushing through the skin.

"You at least get a few shots in, use any of the moves I taught you?" he teased, punching me in the arm. It hurt more than I bet he intended, but with the size of his biceps, there probably wasn't much he could do about it.

"I held my own," I said. "Broke a nose, popped a couple testicles."

"My man," he said, raising his glass. We toasted my dirty fighting tactics and laughed.

"I can't believe Leon knows people that high up," Joey said, shaking his head. "He's a drug-running pimp, not a criminal mastermind."

"I have a feeling Leon doesn't know the first thing about who they are or what they do. He serves some useful purpose for them, but he's a tool and nothing more."

"You gonna go talk to him about it, see what he does know?"

I shook my head. "Thought about it, but I can't trust that fat bastard not to blab to his buddies that I'm asking around about them. I just want to wrap this up without causing more problems than I already have."

"Fuck it," Joey said, raising his glass again. "At least you're getting paid, right?"

I spun my pint glass between my hands and didn't answer.

"I mean, it's not like you had much of a—"

"They're federal agents, Joe." I looked up, wiping my hand over my lips, as if the words left behind a stain. "Six of them."

Joey waited, his mouth hung partially open, before he exhaled and played with his own pint glass. After a minute he said, "What were you supposed to do, Rick? Refuse? They'd have slit your throat, found somebody else, and those agents would still wind up dead. Might as well do the job, take the money, and live to regret it."

"Yeah," I said, because there really was nothing else to say. This was happening. I'd just have to find a way to live with it. Christ, what a shitty fucking thing to say. I finished my beer in one long swallow, set the empty glass down on the bar harder than I intended, and cleared my throat. "Anyway, after this is done, I'll be going away for a while."

"Where?"

"I don't know. Someplace with a beach. Europe's been good to me, but I need a healthy dose of sand and bikinis, if you know what I mean." I laughed to show I was taking it all in stride, but it was a feeble attempt. Joey's expression didn't change.

"You take care of yourself, okay?" he said.

"You too."

"Here, this will help," he said, sliding the cigar box over to me. "Maybe now you'll take my advice and keep a spare around."

I reached into my inside coat pocket, pulled out an envelope wrapped in a rubber band, and set it on the bar in front of him. He didn't disrespect me by counting its contents.

"You got time to help me break this in?" I asked, holding up the box. "Friday night at ten?"

"Works for me." I stood to leave but he grabbed my arm.

"There's something else in there, too. A lead."

"Somebody good?"

"Somebody new. Never met him. He's supposed to be young and raw, but brimming with talent. Just your type, right?"

I slapped him on the back. "You know me so well, buddy."

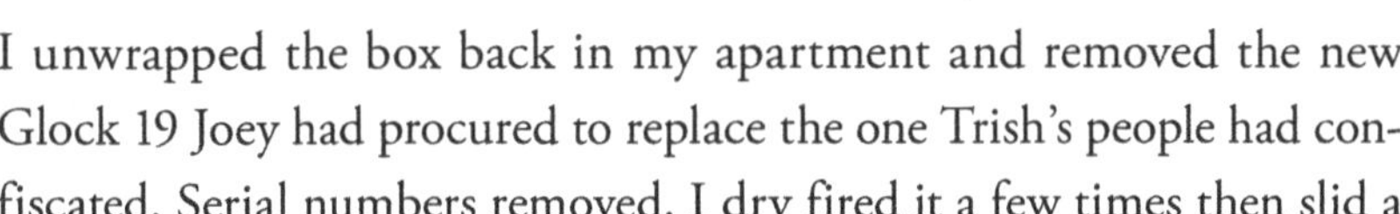

I unwrapped the box back in my apartment and removed the new Glock 19 Joey had procured to replace the one Trish's people had confiscated. Serial numbers removed. I dry fired it a few times then slid a fresh magazine in.

I had one more bit of housekeeping to attend to before I started contacting candidates, but so far I was stuck on hold, waiting for my guy to get back to me. Not that I was surprised. Techies can be notoriously fidgety, and this one was new to me. I'd been impressed with a hack he pulled last month on a dark web bidding site for stolen military goods and had been keeping him on the bench, waiting for the right job to come along.

Never thought the right job would involve him working for me, but my life was all about adapting to the unexpected.

It was a search for a similar type of candidate, a guy with computer skills who used them to do illegal online shit, that got me into this life. I didn't go looking for the search. Rather, the client found me through an innocuous mutual connection, an accountant who did the books for the side of this person's business that was legal and above board. When his boss said he was looking for someone with an IT background, he recommended he contact me. I'd done some IT recruiting for my firm, even though we didn't specialize in that area, and my friend was always happy to toss me a bone.

What his boss told me was that he wanted someone to hack into his company's servers to test their security measures. What I learned later was that he'd paid the candidate a helluva lot more to then hack into a bunch of smaller businesses in the area and steal their customers' stored credit card information. What neither of them knew was that I was at a time in my life when financial circumstances left me prone to making bad decisions. The kind of bad decisions I would not normally have made otherwise. Like saying yes when the same client referred me to someone else looking for a similar candidate, even though by then I'd figured out what was really going on.

If I'd known then what I know now, about where that first bad decision would lead, would I have still done it? I'd like to say no, but that's a lie. Or an optimistic assumption, at best. People who aren't prone to making bad decisions often fail to foresee just how life-altering a truly bad one can be. How trying to do the right thing for your family can put them in more danger than you'd ever imagined. The kind of danger that makes your stomach clench and your bowels loosen. The kind of danger that robs you of any of the joy you used to have just by being with them, because all you could think of, every minute of every day, was what the people you now worked for would do to them if you ever tried to correct that initial bad decision. The kind of danger that leaves a man no choice but to disappear in the middle of the night, move half a world away, and set up an entirely new life, simply to protect the one he'd left behind.

Before closing my blinds and turning in for the night, I waved to the car parked across the street, the physical representation of my latest bad decision. It had been waiting for me when I returned from O'Reilly's. In the dim light it looked empty, until a tiny orange circle appeared, just barely visible on the driver's side. The cigarette was one of many that would be in a pile by the curb the next morning.

CHAPTER SEVEN

That cigarette pile was precisely why I needed to connect with my tech candidate. If Trish was going to the trouble of tailing me around town and staking out my place, then it stood to reason she was also listening in whenever possible. They might have bugged my apartment, but I didn't care; they could listen to me drink and jerk off all they wanted. But if they somehow tapped my phone—or at the very least were tracking numbers and reading texts—then that was a problem.

All recruiters are protective of their database, so there was that initial, knee-jerk territoriality. But there was a bigger risk involved. If they were able to contact my candidates directly and bypass the middleman, then that not only saved them a hefty chunk of change, it also made me very expendable. I had no idea if tapping a cell phone to that extent was within their realm of capability, but I wasn't rolling the dice to find out. I needed a new device.

Fortunately, when I got out of the shower that morning, I had a new chat message waiting for me. My tech guy had responded.

I'm interested, his text said.

Good, I wrote back. *Where do you want to meet?*

Park bench by the fountain. Noon.

I'll be there.

Time to make a trip to the bank.

Guy #2 followed me the entire way. I tried to make it interesting. Darting across intersections right when the light changed. Weaving in and out of throngs of pedestrians on their way to work. I even circled one block three times just to fuck with him, but credit where it's due: for a guy who'd just spent the night in his car and smoked like he was angry at his own lungs, he kept pace without much effort. When we finally made it to the bank, he waited across the street, casually leaning against a light pole, smoking a cigarette while I went inside. On the one hand, it was comforting. Trish clearly wanted me to know she was watching, which meant the purpose of the shadow was not to garner any new intelligence on me (like say, my candidate list) but rather just to make sure I was doing my job and not talking to the authorities. On the other hand, I didn't like being followed.

The meeting with the tech guy by itself wouldn't arouse any suspicions—could just be a candidate interview as far as they knew—but any type of handoff would undoubtedly garner their attention. The good news was they seemed content to give me privacy indoors, which opened up my playbook a bit. I couldn't risk another meeting at O'Reilly's, though. That would be pushing my luck. But I already had something else in mind, assuming the initial meeting went well.

I accepted my cash in large bills, thanked the teller, and left. Outside, I waved to Guy #2. He puffed his cigarette and waved back.

Tech guys tend to show up for meetings early. I sat down on the bench at 11:30, and he joined me less than ten minutes later. Guy #2 was taking a slow stroll around the fountain behind us. A mom and her two little ones were the only other people in the area. The kids took turns tossing loose change into the fountain while their mother ignored them and talked on her phone.

My candidate was young. Dark hair, gray eyes. His heavy, green parka was zipped to his chin with the collar popped, obscuring the lower half of his face. What remained visible was all sharp angles and pale skin, covered in a fine sheen of windblown mist from the fountain.

"Mr. Carter?" he asked, without looking at me. Thick accent. Croatian, maybe.

"That's me," I said. "Nice to meet you Mr. . . . ?"

"Call me Sergei."

A hacker named Sergei. He must have found that one in the discount bin at Aliases "R" Us.

"Pleasure to meet you, Sergei. Nice job with the Atlanticorp breach," I said, referring to the dummy corporation that served as a front for the military black market he'd hacked. "I was impressed. How did you get around their firewall?"

"You have job for me?" he asked.

Maybe one day I'll meet a hacker who doesn't mind small talk, but apparently not today.

"Kind of," I said. He finally stopped staring straight ahead and looked at me. I glanced quickly over my shoulder and saw Guy #2 working his way around the kids, who had gone from taking turns throwing change to arguing over who got to toss in the last euro coin. Their mother was still on the phone, still oblivious to anything they were doing, but had no problem giving Guy #2 a nasty look when he blew out a cloud of smoke as he walked past. "I need a phone."

Sergei raised an eyebrow.

"Ideally, one that bounces its signal across a dozen or so countries and has top-of-the-line text encryption."

"That is very special phone," Sergei said slowly.

"I'm self-conscious about my *Pokémon Go* habit," I said. "Don't want anyone to find out."

"How soon do you need it?"

"Tonight. Tomorrow at the latest."

Sergei laughed. It was not a pleasant sound. Like a hyena choking on a rabbit. "I took this meeting for job, not jokes."

"So you're telling me you can't do it?"

"In twenty-four hours? No, I cannot do that."

"I'll pay you ten thousand, cash."

"I can do it, sure, yes."

I smiled and clapped him on the shoulder. He flinched and drew back. "That's what attracted me to you, Sergei," I said. "Your can-do attitude."

He smiled awkwardly, at least I thought he did. It was hard to tell with the collar up around his face. Guy #2 passed in front of us about twelve feet away. He didn't slow and Sergei didn't seem to notice him. "I will text you when phone is ready," he said.

"Nope, sorry, that won't work. My current phone is slow and glitchy. It's all gunked up with Pikachus and porn."

Sergei raised an eyebrow again, this time in visible disgust.

"Here's what we're gonna do instead," I said, leaning in.

I had my hand on the front door to my apartment building when Guy #2 called out to me.

"Who was the guy on the bench?" he asked as he walked up, an ever-present Winston clasped between two fingers.

"Just a connection," I said. "Don't you know secondhand smoke kills?"

He took a deep drag, exhaled in my face, and stubbed the cancer stick out on the brick wall of my building. "How's your finger?" he asked.

"How're Mike's balls?"

His face stiffened. "The guy on the bench, asshole, who was he?"

"I told you; he was just a connection. Why don't you take that thing out of your ear so you can hear better?" I reached for the curly cord dangling beside his neck, but he grabbed my hand and twisted.

"Ouch," I said, pulling it free. "So aggressive."

"He was a kid who looked like he was about to piss his pants when you touched his shoulder. If that's the type of candidate you plan on presenting, I might as well just kill you now and save us a week's worth of wasted time."

"I said he was a *connection*, not a candidate."

"What's the difference?"

"A *connection* is someone who can put me in touch with an in-demand *candidate*," I explained, rubbing my wrist. "This isn't an afternoon drive-by your boss wants done. She's paying me for quality talent, and quality is hard to find. I need to work several channels to uncover the best people. That's what today's meeting was about."

This, of course, was total bullshit. I already knew who I planned to present for the job and had three backups in mind in case any of my preferred options were already under contract, unresponsive, or just plain uninterested. You don't pay a top recruiter to start looking for fresh candidates—you pay them for the years spent building their database so those candidates are already in their pipeline. But he didn't need to know that.

"Okay, fine," he said. "Just remember that I'm watching you."

"And you should know that *I'm* also watching *you*. Mostly through the window of your car, as you sleep." I leaned in close and whispered, "While I touch myself."

He jerked back, trying to cobble together any kind of rejoinder before he gave up and bumped me with his shoulder as he walked away.

"There's a spark between us, admit it," I called after him. "Don't try to fight this feeling!"

He hurried across the street and got into his car without ever turning around. I smiled and went inside.

And later that night, while he dozed behind the wheel, did I go up and tap on his window? Press my phone against it while it played "Can't Fight This Feeling" at top volume? Draw a heart in the frost on the glass, then plant a kiss right in the middle as he looked on, bleary eyed, confused, and, yes, more than a little disgusted?

Of course, I did.

REO Speedwagon 4ever.

CHAPTER EIGHT

The $10,000 was in an envelope, tucked into the inside pocket of my coat. It was half of what I withdrew yesterday, after making a transfer from one of my other accounts. The Swiss bank where Trish deposited my first payment was one of many. I learned early on that it was best to spread my funds around in not only multiple banks but multiple countries. Most of the banks were located near a charity to which I'd make regular anonymous donations. Homeless shelters, libraries, various medical research facilities and clinics. The proximity kept people from wondering too much about where the money was coming from, and the donations themselves were another way I helped myself sleep at night.

I had some concern that after our chat last night, Guy #2 would up the intensity of his surveillance, maybe start each day with a pat-down on the sidewalk that would reveal my envelope full of cash. Those fears turned out to be unfounded.

He was waiting across the street, the pile of discarded cigarette butts next to his car window larger than the day before. When he saw me, he stepped out onto the curb, added a butt to the pile, and maintained his usual distance. That was good. I was betting on business as usual if this exchange was going to go off undetected. I blew him a kiss and feigned disappointment when he didn't catch it or blow one back.

They knew my habits, so I assumed that ducking into the café down the street for a cup of coffee and a Danish wouldn't raise any red flags, and it didn't. He lit a fresh cigarette and watched me through the window. I ordered, grabbed my food and drink, and took a seat at a table near the front, providing him an unobstructed view.

I gave it ten minutes. Finished my Danish and read two articles in the paper, or at least pretended to. Then I stood and walked back to the men's room. I left the paper on my chair and the coffee cup half-full, so as to indicate to any passersby that I would return. I tried to walk casually, but the harder I concentrated on looking natural, the more unnatural and suspicious I felt. I kept waiting for the bells above the door to jingle and to hear the gasps of the other patrons as Guy #2 rushed in from behind and tackled me to the ground.

I fought the urge to look over my shoulder and entered the restroom. Other than the far stall door being closed, it was clear. One of life's little favors.

I entered the middle stall, locked the door, sat on the toilet seat and said quietly, "Sergei?"

"*Da*," came his reply from next door.

"Slide it under."

A yellow envelope, the kind with the bubble lining for shipping fragile packages, emerged on the floor from the stall next to me. I scooped it up and checked the contents: One black Android smartphone.

"This has all the specs we talked about, right?"

"*Da*," he said again. "Your *Pokémon* secret is safe."

I smiled. I was starting to like this kid. When this was over, I'd have to find a real contract for him. I slid the envelope filled with cash back under in return.

"Pleasure doing business with you," I said. "You wear a hat and a different jacket than yesterday, like we talked about?"

"*Da*."

"Good. Wait five minutes after I leave, then zip up the coat and pull the hat low, but not too low. Walk outside and hang a right at the first corner. Don't look around."

"Okay."

I stood, tucked the phone into my outer coat pocket, flushed, and opened the stall door just as Guy #2 walked in.

My breath caught in my throat and my eyes grew wide. It required a conscious effort to reduce them and breathe normally.

"Hey," I said, walking to the sink. He didn't reply. His eyes were focused on the stall where Sergei was hiding. I smoothed the flap over my coat pocket holding the phone, to make sure no bits of yellow envelope protruded. In my mind, the bulge stood out like a bowling pin against my hip.

"You shit that quickly," he asked, "or do you always piss in the stalls?"

I turned the water on and pumped some soap from the dispenser, more aggressively than I probably needed to, then started washing and said, "Are these the kind of questions that keep you up at night?"

He ignored me and kept looking at Sergei's stall door, which I prayed would remain closed until we left the restroom. I finished washing and grabbed a handful of paper towels from the stack beneath the mirror. "Coffee goes right through me. I love it, but my stomach doesn't. Feel bad for the poor guy next to me. But by all means, let's keep talking about it and make him even more uncomfortable."

Guy #2 took his eyes off the stall, looked at me, and frowned. Then he went over to the row of urinals and unzipped his fly. Watching him to make sure he didn't kick open Sergei's door would be weird, so I went back to my table and took a sip of lukewarm coffee that I didn't taste. Less than a minute later, Guy #2 walked past me and out the front door, but he set up shop against the mailbox just outside rather than across the street. If Sergei's disguise was off at all, or if Guy #2 decided to stop every patron who exited before I did, then we were fucked.

And when Sergei came out of the restroom, I *knew* we were fucked. His ball cap was too low. His jacket was zipped up as requested, but way too high. Everything about him was conspicuous. I knew his cover was blown before he stepped foot out the door.

But just as soon as the thought entered my head, Sergei walked out, past my unwelcome babysitter, and hung a right at the corner, as instructed. I waited for Guy #2 to follow, but he didn't. Three more people left before I finished my coffee, and he paid no special attention to any of them either. I was so relieved, I bought Guy #2 a blueberry scone and tossed it to him as he started following me back to my apartment. It bounced off his chest and landed on the ground. He made no move to stop and pick it up.

"I want to see you start doing some actual work, Carter," he said, wiping crumbs off his shirt, "or we might need to dip into our bag of motivational tricks."

"Been working this whole time," I said, walking backward. Then I flipped him off and spun around before he could respond.

Lucky for me, that work was about to pay off.

CHAPTER NINE

Of course I'm interested, read the text from Ian.

This is the big one, kid, I wrote back. *You're ready for it.*

He was. The MI5 agents were most ideal. They were within his operating range, geographically, and my preference was to stay as local as possible. As a rule in recruiting, corporate or otherwise, it's always better to find a local candidate rather than one that requires relocation. Transplanting a CEO from one state to another means extra money, extra time, and extra hassle for both sides—all of which hold the potential of torpedoing the deal.

For this job, less travel meant less of a trail for anyone to follow. And once this went down, there would be *plenty* of people looking for any kind of trail to follow.

Ian was still in Brussels, fresh off the masterful double hit he did for Leon, but London was drivable, especially for the fee he would receive. More important than the money, though—and for a kid who grew up robbing homeless people for enough spare change to purchase a school lunch, $1 million was *very* important—was what this contract would do for his career. Pull it off, and he'd be elevated into the upper echelon of hitters for hire, which is where I knew he belonged. Helping candidates achieve that kind of success was why I started recruiting in the first place. For just a second, I was able to forget what "success" meant for a man in Ian's field, and enjoy the moment.

I put my old phone down on the couch cushion next to me and picked up the one I'd bought from Sergei for the equivalent of nearly one year's rent. There were two chat rooms open on the new one, each in a different encrypted site so far down the dark web, it was illegal just to know they existed. Both chat rooms contained a single text, encased in a blue box that indicated it was written by me:

Got a job.

Ian had responded to my initial text within five minutes. I hoped my other two candidates responded within the five days I had left before Trish's submission deadline expired. If they did, this would be the easiest million I ever made. If they didn't, well, that's what backup plans were for.

Candidates D through F had already confirmed that they were in the area and were available if needed. I never told them what the job was or that they were contingency plans, of course, but I didn't have to. None of them had any work lined up in the next few days and were willing to wait to see if my contract "came to fruition," which was the standard euphemism I used when I wanted to keep a candidate engaged without letting them know they weren't my first choice.

Problem was that my babysitter wanted to see me do "actual work," and everything was already wrapped up. That's when I remembered the slip of paper Joey had given me, tucked into the box with my new Glock. On it was written a phone number and a name: Eric Krieg.

No way would I submit a new candidate on a job this big, but an interview, someplace public, would get Guy #2 off my back. I texted the number on the paper and Eric responded almost instantly.

Where do you want to meet? he asked.

Coffee shop on Adolphe Max by the bank, I wrote back. *2:00.*

I'll be there.

Look for the guy in blue jeans, black blazer, and a bandage wrapped around his left pinkie finger.

I like to arrive early whenever interviewing a new candidate. Let them come to me instead of the other way around. Allows me to get a lay of the land, make sure nothing looks suspicious. We'll typically only meet in person once or twice during our time working together, so it's critical I make a commanding first impression. I need them to trust me from the beginning and know just how well-connected I am. Which is why I do my homework on everyone before we ever set eyes on each other.

Joey had never met this guy, but from what he'd heard, Eric Krieg was tall and blonde. Former German Special Forces (KSK). (Joey sent me a lot of ex-military.) Dishonorably discharged after assaulting his commanding officer. Operated in and around Belgium the last two years doing low-level contracts for low-level thugs. Debts that were never paid. Snitches that needed silencing. Revenge hits. The kind of emerging talent for which I was always on the lookout. Again, not ready for the prime time of Trish and her people, but worth checking out to stash on the bench for something more his speed down the road. A full pipeline of quality candidates is a recruiter's lifeblood.

The café, a different one than where I'd met Sergei earlier, was busy but not packed. I'd secured a round, two-person table by the side window that afforded me a full view of both the front door and anyone approaching from the side street. Guy #2 was at a table in the back, alone, his earpiece hidden in his pocket.

"I'm fine if you want to play peeping Tom," I'd told him as he followed me to the interview, "but if you make yourself as obvious as you are now, our man will turn around and walk away."

Guy #2 wasn't happy, but he lost the earpiece and agreed to stay on the sidelines.

"Try anything funny," he warned, "and all bets are off. I've been easy going so far, letting you do whatever it is you do, but I'm not a man you want to fuck with."

"Okay, John Wick."

"It's Colin, actually."

"I don't care."

At precisely 2:00 the café door opened, ringing the quaint little bell suspended above it. A few seconds later a tall blonde sat in front of me, which I expected. What I didn't expect was that the tall blonde also had boobs. And not man-boobs, like the kind I try to stave off by doing push-ups on the mornings when I'm not busy vomiting, but real ones. The kind that men without any class stare at for too long.

"Eric?" I asked, trying not to be classless. I failed.

"Erica," she said, emphasizing the *a*. Her accent was thick, but decidedly un-German. Swedish? Maybe Dutch? I couldn't be sure. And I was still staring.

She smiled. White teeth. Straight. Expensive. "Were you expecting someone else?"

"Yes and no," I said, looking her in the eyes for the first time. Brown, like the tight leather jacket she wore. Pretty. "So who's your plastic surgeon? He does *great* work."

She smiled again. No teeth this time. "I heard you were a wiseass."

"And I heard you had a penis."

"Who told you that?" she teased.

"Somebody who's normally more reliable."

"Well, don't be too upset with him," she said. "A lot of hard work went into cultivating that lie."

"Seems like a lot of effort for nothing. Unless you usually attend client meetings wearing a bald cap and a fake mustache, people will realize that not only are you a woman, you're also full of shit. Not a great first impression."

"You're right, it's not," she said. "I thought if I could just get in front of clients who would never consider a woman for a job, that I could convince them to give me a chance. It worked a few times, but I've burned more bridges than I built. Being a woman in this field isn't the easiest way to earn a living."

"Not true," I said. "One of the top hitters in the world is a woman."

"The Persian, I know. She's a legend. And you represent her."

That was when the sound drained out of the room and all I could hear was my heart beating in my ears. Nobody knew about my connection to The Persian except the handful of clients that were able to afford her, and they would never talk. Just being associated with her, with the things she'd done, would earn you a life sentence. Likely more than one.

A thought occurred to me. I shifted in my seat, looked around the room, and said, "Are you a cop?"

"You mean like your friend back there, trying to blend in?"

"No," I said without missing a beat. "He's dirty. Are you the kind that's actually good at your job?"

Of the six or seven people in the tiny coffee house, none of them looked out of place. No suspicious vans or random strangers standing around, killing time outside the windows. If she was a cop, I couldn't spot her backup.

"Do you want to frisk me here in public?" she said, spreading her arms slightly.

"Don't tempt me."

Frowning, she leaned over and opened the collar of her blouse, letting me peer down. She'd hooked her thumbs under the straps of her bra so the cups pulled away, defiantly showing me everything.

No wire.

"Who told you I worked with The Persian?" I asked, easing back in my seat.

"Sorry," Erica said, doing up the top button on her blouse, "I can't tell you that."

"If we're going to play games, then this interview is over."

"No," she said, grabbing my arm. Tight at first, then quickly letting up. "No games. But come on, would you tell me who provided the information you have on me?"

I shook my head. "My interview, my questions."

She sighed. "I can't—"

"We're done," I said, pushing my chair back.

Her grip tightened again and she said, "Wait." I waited.

"When I was with the KSK, my unit came under scrutiny for fostering extremist right-wing ideology. Nazi propaganda, disgusting shit like that." She let go of my arm and I pulled my seat back to the table. "Nothing ever came of it. Beckett, my CO, was a lifer, with pull in all the right places. He just told us to be more discreet and pretty soon all the attention went away."

"Is he the one you decked to earn your dishonorable discharge?" I asked.

"Best right hook I ever landed." She smirked. "Still worth it."

I didn't trust her, but I was starting to like her.

"Anyway," she went on, "a few months after they kicked me out I got word that he'd been killed. Official report labeled it an accident during a training exercise. His Barrett M82 jammed and the round exploded in the chamber. Those rifles are designed to take out tanks, so it wasn't just a little pop. Shrapnel took off half his head."

"Ouch."

"Served him right. During the investigation into the 'accident,'" she put air quotes around the word, "they discovered details for an attack he was planning on a mosque. The whole unit was in on it, but he was the one calling the shots. When he died, the plan fell apart. Everyone was court-martialed, and countless lives were saved."

"You don't think his death was an accident, do you? You think it was The Persian."

"I *know* it was The Persian."

So did I, as a matter of fact. I earned $100,000 in commission for putting her on that job. Turns out her CO's fucked-up belief system also justified rape, at least when his victim was a different color than him. If he'd had half a brain, he wouldn't have picked the daughter of an imam whose followers included at least one person with deep pockets and no compunction about revenge killings. He didn't, however, so now he *literally* had half a brain.

One less rapist in the world is always a win in my book, regardless of who he chooses to victimize. When I took the job, I had no idea he'd been planning a domestic terror attack. Thwarting that was a nice little bonus on top of one of those rare jobs that already made me feel good about myself.

"We'd all heard about her," she said, "The Persian, but she was a myth. A ghost story told around campfires in Afghanistan the night before a raid. After Beckett died, though, the rumors started that it was her. So I started digging. I found nothing that proved she had anything to do with his death, but I did find out more about who she was, the things she'd supposedly done. And the more I learned, the more I wanted to be like her."

"Someone who kills people for a living."

"I've always been someone who kills people for a living," she said flatly. "At least this way it would be on my own terms—and for much better pay."

"I'm still waiting for the part that explains how you got to me."

She shrugged. "Just connecting the dots. You were a name that came up more than once the deeper I looked into her history. I wasn't sure if there was a real relationship between you two or not, but when you texted me, I knew it was my chance to find out." Her eyes pleaded with mine. "It is true, though, isn't it? You do represent her?"

I took a sip of coffee. "And what if it is?"

Her eyes went from pleading to hopeful. "Then you can help me. I'm not just in this for a quick cash grab. I want a career. But I can't do that on my own. I've tried. Open the doors for me that you opened for her. You won't regret it."

When I first recruited her, The Persian was well on her way to elite status with no help from me. I didn't know much about her, but what I did know painted the picture of a born killer. She had no documented connection to any military or intelligence outlet but had seemingly done work for all of them. Her first suspected kill came when she was only nine years old, poisoning a top Shiite militia leader in Iran. Some say it was revenge for a bombing that killed her parents. Others swear it was just because she wanted to see what it felt like, not only to kill a man, but to get away with it. Either way, it was the first of many. By the time she was twenty years old, she had a body count rivaling some dictators. Everyone from top government officials to terrorist groups offered bounties for her head. The Persian was beholden to no particular flag or ideology. Her only loyalty was to her next contract.

Our partnership was one of convenience: She existed outside of the spotlight and waited for me to bring jobs directly to her, while I collected handsome fees and doubled my referral business in the process. I didn't open a single door she couldn't have opened on her own. The only reason she had me do it for her was because, if there was a gun or a cop standing behind that door, she'd rather have me take the bullet or do the time.

Erica had a long way to go to get to that level. Didn't mean she couldn't, though. And if The Persian was the standard by which I measured all prospective candidates, then my pipeline would soon run drier than a sawdust martini.

"Okay," I said, "Let's start over. How long you been in the game?"

"Four years."

"I heard two."

"You also heard I had a pair of balls and a hairy chest."

"Touché." That was strike two for Joey. We were going to have an interesting conversation when I saw him at the shooting range later that night.

"What's your number?" I asked. She raised an eyebrow. "Of jobs completed. I'm not a creep."

"Six," she said without hesitation. That matched what Joey told me. Maybe I wouldn't rip him all the way apart when I saw him.

"All singles or any multiples in there?" I asked.

"Just did my first double last job."

"How did that go?"

A young couple walking from the counter to a table behind us accidentally bumped into Erica's seat.

"*Pardon*," the woman said, looking every bit the French touristy type.

"*C'est bon*," Erica replied. Her eyes darted around the room. It was starting to get crowded.

"Don't worry," I said, "I've done interviews here before. It's filled with some of the most pretentious people in Brussels. They're too busy talking about themselves to hear anything we say."

She laughed. It was a deeper sound than I would have expected, but full. Smooth. I took another sip of my coffee.

"So," I said, speaking a little louder to be heard over the growing din. "Your last job?"

"It went fine. Client was very pleased."

"Business or personal?"

"Does it matter?"

I smiled. That was the right answer.

"You have any other offers at the moment?"

"No. I just got back in town. Still getting settled."

"Good. If you draw interest from other parties during that time, I want you to let me know."

"I can do that," she said. She brightened. "Does that mean you have a job for me?"

I considered for a moment then said, "Not right now. But I know a few clients who'd be interested in your services, whenever the need arises."

The disappointment on her face was evident, although she did her best to hide it. Now that her confidence was shaken a bit, the time was right for a little skills assessment. Without preamble, I leaned in and said, "Far right corner by the restroom, table for two, what kind of watch is the man wearing?"

"Bulova," she said, no hesitation. The disappointment was gone. She was all business. "Black."

"Woman standing by the front door, what's she drinking?"

"Espresso, double shot."

"My right, your left, what's the cover story on the magazine somebody left behind on the table?"

"'New diet promises to give you the bathing suit body you crave.'"

"How many scones are there in the display counter right now?"

"None. This place doesn't sell scones."

I nodded approvingly.

"Did I pass?" she asked.

"Part One, yes."

"What is Part Two?"

"Part Two is I need to see you complete a job."

"Is that part of your typical interview process?"

"Depends. You talk a good game, but I need proof you can back it up. Call it a working interview."

"And will I be compensated for this working interview?"

"Not by me. Next time you score a contract on your own, let me know. Use the same chat room to text me a time and place. Give me enough notice to get there early and make sure I can slip away undetected. I get pinched for anything you do, then your career is over before it even gets started. I'll make damn sure of that."

"Understood."

"If the job makes it difficult for me to observe in person, I'll need proof you pulled the trigger. Nothing that can be faked."

She nodded. "So what now?"

"I'll wait to hear from you," I said, and this time I did stand up. Before leaving, I decided to give her one last test.

"*War mir eine Freude*," I said, offering my hand. "*Bis wir uns wiedersehen.*"

She gripped my fingers, gently, and pulled herself up. "*Danke*," she said. "*Ich freue mich auf die Zusammenarbeit mit Ihnen.*"

At least she really did speak German. Joey's intel wasn't a total bust, anyway.

I watched her walk out the door. I put my hand on Colin's chest as he came up beside me.

"She totally made you," I said, my eyes still on Erica as she passed by the front window.

"She did not," Colin said, insulted.

"Don't beat yourself up," I said, turning to him. "It's just because you're terrible at your job."

"Me?" he scoffed. "You said she was a guy. How do you fuck that up?"

"We all have our off days," I said. Except this didn't feel like an off day. No, this felt like one of those days where I stumbled onto something special.

CHAPTER TEN

"Like, a *woman* woman? Tits and all?"

"No, Joey," I replied. "She was one of those women you see all the time with no breasts. They're everywhere."

"Don't be a dick. Maybe she was one of them gender neutral types. You really need to be more progressive in your thinking, Rick. Like me."

"Yeah, you're the poster boy for the LGBTQ community."

"Damn straight," Joey said. "No pun intended." Then he fired off three quick shots. Each one found its mark. Head. Heart. Gut.

Joey was a lot of things, but a bad shot wasn't one of them. Well, except when he was trying to cap a guy in the back of the head as he got into his car. Then, Mr. Steady Hand turned into Shakes the Clown and blew off the mark's ear instead. Shooting skulls is different than shooting targets, you see. Even for a former Army Ranger with seven confirmed kills in Afghanistan under his belt. It's harder when the life you're taking is up close and personal instead of just a dot in a sniper's scope.

Lucky for Joey, I was watching the whole thing go down from a rooftop across the street. He was a candidate on my radar at the time. I'd heard he was trying to make a move from drugs and guns to wet work. Though the attempted hit was a total Turkish clusterfuck, I *was* impressed with how he scored such a lucrative contract without any representation. Takes someone very well-connected to land a five-figure hit in a turf war. I bailed him out of jail and paid off the cops to drop the attempted murder charge in exchange for Joey doing a little networking on my behalf.

His client was so appreciative that I'd gotten the heat off of them for the botched hit, they agreed to use me to recruit for their next job. And Joey was more than happy to let me tap into his network for whatever I needed. The personal training and marksmanship lessons he provided were just added bonuses. His real value was the wealth of insider information his vast number of contacts provided, which was normally impeccable.

"And your sources definitely told you she was a man?" I asked again.

"Rick, come on, you know me," he said. "I hear something, I tell you. I don't embellish, I don't interpret, and I damn sure don't confuse 'she' with 'he.' Girl's good at building a cover. That has to count for something, right?"

I turned back to my paper target hanging thirty yards away and emptied the rest of my clip. I hit the black torso outline with each shot, just not exactly where I intended. "Close enough," I muttered, popping the empty magazine out and slapping in a new one.

"You're still flinching," Joey said. He'd pressed the red button on the side of his stall and moved his target back another ten meters. "We've worked on that."

"Yeah, well, it's been a while."

"And whose fault is that?"

"Don't start with me, Joey."

"Look, you want my help, you gotta put in the work. I ain't gonna waste my time—"

I drowned out the rest of his sentence by squeezing off fifteen rounds in rapid succession. They all missed wildly. I didn't care.

"Real mature," he said.

"It's been a long couple of days." I took the empty magazine out and started filling it with new shells. Three stalls over, Colin fired off steady, three-round bursts from some type of semiautomatic rifle he'd brought with him. The sound was almost hypnotic. I didn't even realize Joey had come up behind me until he spoke.

"Is it okay for us to be talking with him around?" He said it quietly, but I still jumped about a foot in the air.

"Jesus Christ!" I took my yellow safety glasses off and tossed them on the counter next to the Glock and the box of ammo. I pinched the bridge of my nose, took a deep breath, and let it out slowly. "Yeah, he's cool," I said at last. "Colin's harmless."

"Colin?"

"Badass name, right?"

"Sure," Joey said, "if you're the lead in a romantic comedy."

We both laughed. Then Joey turned serious and said, "Everything okay? You seem a little on edge."

"I'm fine," I said, putting the safety glasses back on. "Just getting real, you know? I have to present my people in a few days, and then . . ." I fired a single shot that missed the target completely.

"We don't have to do this tonight."

I fired again, hitting the top-right corner. Perfect, if my goal was to kill the white space next to the guy's head. "I need the practice," I said.

Joey stared at me a minute, debating whether to push the issue. In the end, he settled for one of his patented shrugs. "Okay bud, whatever you want." He slapped me on my shoulder and walked back to his stall. From the other side of the wall between us he said, "So did you tap it?"

"Tap what?"

"That blonde ass from this morning. Or can you only get it up when you pay for it?"

"You know what," I said, "my target's swinging just a little bit. Would you mind going down there to hold it steady?"

He laughed. "Shit, I'll stand in front of it. With your aim, that's the safest place to be."

The Glock sat on the cushion, taunting me. Daring me to pick it up. I stared at my phone, the glow from its screen the only light in my dark living room, and thought about tasting the bitter, oily barrel again.

Maybe this time would end differently. I hadn't attempted that particular escape route since I first moved to Europe. Maybe this time I'd have the guts to finish the job.

My last two candidates had responded. The Persian yesterday, and now Ghost. They were both interested in Trish's job. One day to spare before her deadline, too.

Ghost was my other ace. Unlike The Persian, I actually *had* made him what he was. Carefully crafted his career as one of the world's most notorious—and expensive—contract killers. He's what Ian was close to becoming, and a much more apt comparison for what Erica wanted me to do for her.

Rick Carter, creator of monsters.

I'd spent the last two days putting together a list of backup candidates that was now rendered moot. Trish would take my top three without a second thought. Ghost and The Persian were slam dunks, and Ian had cred coming off the double hit for Leon that had impressed her mysterious Board of Directors so much. As I suspected, it would be the easiest million I'd ever made.

Ironic that my lowest moments often came during the high points of my career.

I eyed the Glock again, knowing I wouldn't pick it up. It wasn't a way out, at least not one I was willing to take. Same as turning myself in. Prison would not be kind to me, and I knew it. If I lacked the courage to end things permanently, I sure as hell lacked the fortitude to survive a lengthy stretch behind bars. And with my rap sheet, "lengthy" is the only kind of stretch I'd do.

Sure, I could rat out my clients. Shave some years off my sentence, maybe even earn a new life in a witness protection program. I'd be John the Insurance Salesman. Quiet guy who keeps to himself in the tiny rancher at the end of the street in some backwater town. For a while. Until just one of those clients figured out where I was. Then we were back to the same problem I had with the Glock sitting next to me. Much as I hated my life, I was more terrified by the prospect of not living at all. Great way to spend your days.

So just stop, you might say. *If you hate your job so much, get a new one. Plenty of ways to earn a living that don't end up with anyone dead in the morning.*

True enough, in theory. Problem was that once I stopped providing my particular service, I no longer held any value to my clients. Instead, I became a liability. And liabilities have a very short shelf life in this business.

Candidates are ready, I texted in the chat room Trish had set up. Before she could respond, I turned off the phone and buried my face in my hands. After a minute, I pulled them away and examined the stitches on the tip of my pinkie. Then my eyes shifted to the next finger over.

It was invisible, but still there. A ring of skin around the base of the fourth finger on my left hand. For eight years, that skin had been covered by a wedding band. Until I broke my knuckle, and it didn't fit anymore.

I was the only one home on a Friday afternoon. Denise was at work. Maggie was in kindergarten. She had recently gotten into watching the NBA with me on TV, so we decided to surprise her with an adjustable basketball hoop as a birthday present. I'd taken the day off to complete the project before Denise, very pregnant with Ethan, picked her up from the school's aftercare program.

It was windy that day, and no sooner had I stood it up than a strong gust sent the entire thing on a collision course with my car's windshield. I caught it before it even touched the hood, but my left hand took the brunt of the fall, cracking the knuckle on my ring finger.

If Denise had been home, she would have immediately run outside to see why I was filling our quiet little corner of the neighborhood with words that would make Quentin Tarantino blush. Then she would have taken one look at my swollen finger and demanded I go to the emergency room, or at least the urgent care center. After I refused, she would have nagged me into the passenger seat of her SUV and driven me herself.

Fortunately, I was alone, so it was easier to be stupid.

I reset the hoop and stacked bags of sand on the base before it could topple over again. The pain in my finger went away as soon as I saw my daughter's face through the window of Denise's Ford Escape as it pulled into the driveway.

"Daddy, I love it!" She squealed, running into my arms. "Is that for me?"

"You bet it is, Peanut," I said, scooping her up. Didn't feel any pain then, either. "You like it?"

"Yes I do, thank you! Can we play?"

"Well, you might need a ball for that," Denise said. She held a gift bag that had been hidden in my trunk for the past week. It was purple and had a gaggle of Disney princesses on the front. The basketball inside was legit, though. No pink and flowery ball for my little superstar. No way. Her wide eyes only grew bigger as she tossed the tissue paper to the side and pulled it out.

"It's a real one, just like the men use on the TV!" she exclaimed.

"And the women," Denise said.

"Happy birthday, sweetie," I said.

"Thank you, Daddy! Thank you, Mommy!" She gave us both the same hug, tight around the neck. The special kind only five-year-olds know how to give.

The ball looked gigantic in her tiny hands. Even with the rim lowered to its minimum height of six-and-a-half feet, it would've been a miracle if she made one shot out of ten. Denise had argued that we should get her a smaller ball, but Mags wanted a real one like the Sixers played with, so that's what she got. The hoop I had growing up didn't lower at all. I had to practice free throws every day in my driveway for an entire summer before I'd built up the arm strength to do more than just brick it off the bottom of the ten-foot rim. But my dad was right there with me every day, which was really all that mattered. Making a shot was a bonus.

We spent the next hour shooting hoops. By the end, her free throw percentage was about where I expected, but she was an absolute beast at dunking the ball from Daddy's shoulders. That night, we took her to her favorite restaurant for a proper birthday dinner of pancakes and ice cream with chocolate milk. She beat me in two out of three games of placemat tic-tac-toe, and I only let her win one of them. At bedtime, we tucked her in with not only her ragged teddy bear, but her brand-new basketball as well.

After we shut her door, Denise helped me slather my finger with dish soap to slide my wedding ring over my badly swollen knuckle. For a minute I thought I might have to go to the ER just so they could cut it off, but finally it came free. Denise scolded me for being a stupid man, and I suggested she was even stupider for marrying me. She didn't put up much of an argument.

Before I went to bed, I set the ring in the top compartment of her jewelry box. A month later, when the swelling had subsided, I discovered the ring no longer fit. Likely the result of my knuckle healing haphazardly, without the proper medical treatment. I promised Denise I'd get it resized at the jeweler near my office during my lunch break one day that week.

As far as I knew, the ring was still sitting in the same spot in her jewelry box, although I doubted it. More likely it was displayed in a glass case at a pawn shop somewhere, or perhaps buried in mud at the bottom of the Delaware River. One place it wasn't for sure was on my finger.

But that didn't mean I couldn't still feel it there. Especially when I closed a deal. On those occasions, it felt like a vise, trying to crush my finger all over again.

CHAPTER ELEVEN

"Really, we have to do this again?" I asked.

Colin sneered and unbuttoned my suit jacket. He reached inside and pulled the gun out of its shoulder holster. Unlike my preferred Glock, the shaft of this one was bright orange, and the word Nerf was printed in yellow block letters on a sticker glued to the butt.

"Careful," I said, "it's loaded."

Colin tossed the dart gun on the floor, but behind him his partner laughed. Like before, they allowed me to keep my keys, wallet, and phone. (The original one. Sergei's phone was beneath the floorboards in my closet, secured inside a small electronic safe along with my collection of passports and $10,000 in various currencies.)

"Let's go," Colin said, and started walking down the hall.

"Where to this time?" I asked, shutting and locking my newly repaired apartment door.

"You'll see."

"Did you buy me more scotch? Last time I got scotch."

"Don't you ever stop talking?" he asked.

"That's what the scotch is for." I jerked my head over my right shoulder and said, "Who's the new guy?"

"That's Nigel."

"Nigel," I said, turning and offering my hand, which he shook cautiously. "I'm Rick. Do you know if they bought me scotch?"

It was the same place as before. Same house on Albert Street. Same hidden corridor. Same room. So as not to break precedent, I even sat in the same chair.

It made sense. By limiting what I knew about their operation, they also limited what I would be able to tell anyone should I ever decide to talk to the wrong people. I didn't care where we met, honestly. The plane *did* have scotch. Macallan 18 again. And this time, I helped myself to four glasses.

"Well done, Mr. Carter," Trish said as she gathered the three candidate profile sheets into a neat stack. "We'd heard rumors of your ties to Ghost and The Persian but couldn't be sure they were true. The Board will be very pleased. *This*," she said, tapping the pages in front of her, "is the reason we wanted to work with you so badly."

"I thought it was my ability to find people who are good at covering their tracks," I said. The last few words slid a little bit against the alcohol that coated my tongue, but I didn't care about that either.

"Well I should say you succeeded," she said with a laugh. "Even this one." She held up Ian's profile.

"He doesn't have the résumé of the other two, but he does have the talent," I said, getting defensive for no reason. "And he's the best option within driving distance of the London targets."

"Oh, I don't doubt it," Trish said. "Leon raved about his work, as you know." She tucked his profile back with the others. "As per our agreement, we will deposit the second half of your fee within twenty-four hours."

"Once I confirm it's there, I'll connect you with each candidate in three separate, encrypted chat rooms." She knew this already, but it felt good to reiterate the rote mechanics of my process. My attempt at convincing myself this was just another job, rather than a potential turning point for my entire career. My entire life. "You talk details and timelines with them. I don't need to know anything and I don't want to know anything. I step back. When each job is completed, you text me and disable the chat room. Should something go wrong, let me know so I can work on replacing the candidate. Cops get involved, then and only then do you tell me what went down so I can deal with the fallout."

"Yes, your 'No Cops Guarantee.' Leon was particularly impressed with that part of your service agreement. How exactly do you back it up?"

"I've never had to, but when it happens, I'll let you know."

"For your sake, Mr. Carter, let's hope the first time isn't *this* time. If these three pan out," she said, sliding their pages into a large yellow envelope, "we have plenty of other work to keep you occupied. I hope you don't intend to take your money and run."

That was exactly what I intended to do, as soon as I received confirmation that all three jobs had been completed successfully, but I wanted this meeting to end so I merely said, "You know how to reach me."

Trish grinned, then stood and left. And just like that, six agents—six of the good guys—were living on borrowed time. They had what, two weeks? Maybe less?

I needed a shower. I needed a drink.

I needed to get the fuck away. From everything.

CHAPTER TWELVE

There was a 3:45 afternoon flight to Mexico City, and a 6:00 to Cozumel. I had told myself I would book the first flight out to anywhere in Mexico, but Cozumel was on the coast. I decided the beach was worth the extra couple hours' wait. After all, that's why airport bars were invented.

I had promised Trish that I would be available until the contracts were completed, which was what kept me from hopping the first flight last night to a Mexican beach, somewhere to lie low while I figured out my next move or until I died from alcohol poisoning, whichever came first. But that promise applied to my typical jobs with typical scum-of-the-earth targets. After a night of sleep that came in fits and starts, when every pop or crack from the walls as my apartment settled sounded like a gunshot, I knew I couldn't wait that long. It wasn't that I was scared—Colin's car was no longer at my curb, the pile of cigarette butts the only monument to our time together—but I couldn't escape the feeling that everything had changed, and not for the better. I needed to sort out what that meant someplace where no one knew who I was.

In the morning, I took the $10,000 I had left over from the amount I'd withdrawn to pay Sergei, combined it with the $10,000 I had in my safe, gathered up all my passports, packed a small bag, paid my landlord the next three months' rent in advance (which still was less than a single mortgage payment on my old house), did the same for the parking garage where I kept the Audi I never used, and took an Uber to the airport before noon.

I didn't care if Trish ever deposited the other half of my fee. I didn't care if my candidates pulled off their jobs or not. I didn't care if they got busted and I had to live up to my guarantee for the first time ever. I didn't care if Trish had Colin and Nigel, the *Downton Abbey* twins, follow me all the way to Mexico and sip margaritas ten feet from my beach chair.

I didn't care about anything anymore. Except what I was going to drink while I waited for my flight. It was the closest I'd ever come to doing more than taste the barrel of my Glock. I still couldn't pull the trigger myself, but for the first time, I didn't care if the gun went off by itself.

"What can I get you?" the bartender asked. He was about my age, wearing one of those standard issue T-Shirts that bar and grills have turned into the unofficial industry uniform. This one was a god-awful shade of yellow with his name, Frank, stitched in blue above the name of the bar, Beers & Cheers.

"Cheeseburger and fries," I said, handing him the laminated menu.

"Anything to drink with that?"

"1800 and lime on the rocks, please."

Frank flicked his eyes at the clock above the door leading to the airport concourse, the one that said it was just a few minutes past 11:30 in the morning, but left without saying anything. I'm sure I wasn't the first traveler to booze up before brunch was over, and I sure as hell wouldn't be the last.

There was a guy in a sweater and khakis three stools down from me, taking his time with a plate of nachos while he scrolled through something on his phone. At one of the four tables behind me, a young couple sipping fruity drinks laughed and talked almost as loudly as the Hawaiian shirts they were wearing.

Otherwise, the place was empty. If Colin, Nigel, or any of their colleagues were still assigned to follow me, then their orders must have been to pull back significantly, because they were nowhere to be seen. Or maybe I just wasn't looking hard enough. Maybe Gilligan and Mary Ann with the loud shirts were just waiting to see what flight I boarded so they could notify another team who would keep an eye on me in Cozumel. I didn't care. Are you sensing a theme here?

My food arrived. I ate and watched a muted midday game show on the TV hanging in the corner. It was dull as hell, yet oddly mesmerizing. When my phone rang in my pocket, I didn't react until it was about to kick over to voicemail. It was my old phone. Sergei's was tucked into my carry-on. I'd use that for all outgoing calls moving forward, but I wanted to make sure Trish could reach me in case anything *did* go wrong. Old habits die hard, I guess. Or maybe I was more afraid of that gun in my mouth going off than I wanted to believe.

"Hello?" I said.

"Rick?"

The voice, deep and American, broke my trance the rest of the way.

"Ian?" I said, alert. "What's wrong?"

"You always said to give you a call if I had a question about a job that I didn't feel comfortable asking the client." This was true, but it rarely happened. In most cases, it was because my client changed the terms of the deal or the specs of the job that I had presented. I had placed Ian on a dozen jobs before this, and he had never called me after accepting a contract. I didn't like it.

"Christ, that was quick," I said, checking the time above the door. It was 12:04. "Did they already contact you?"

"Yeah, like five minutes after you sent us the chat invite last night."

"Well, these are serious players," I said, trying to persuade myself as much as Ian that everything was copacetic. "People like that don't dick around."

"Yeah, no, that part was fine," Ian said. "The call was over quick, like they usually are. We set up a time to meet at their location tomorrow, but in the meantime they gave me the names of the principals to go over. They wanted me to do some research, see how good I was at the preliminary stuff I guess."

"So what's wrong with that?"

"Nothing, I'm used to it. The weird thing though is she gave me three names, not two. You said it was supposed to be two, right?"

I had been swirling the ice in my glass, waiting to say something else placative, but that last line got my full attention. I sat straight up on the stool and forgot about the rest of my fries.

"What are you talking about?" I asked. Somewhere deep in my brain I was aware that we were having this conversation on my old phone, the one that may or may not have been compromised, the one that Trish may or may not have been eavesdropping into. But any concern I had about talking on a tapped phone was buried under my growing unease about the extra name.

Did everyone get three names? And did their contract rates go up accordingly?

Could be Trish was just trying to save money on my fee, but I never liked it when a client altered terms behind my back. It spoke to a lack of trust. And bad things tended to happen to people that criminals didn't trust.

"There were the two you told me about," Ian said, "and a third guy. Not even in London; he's over in the fucking States."

This wasn't good. My tongue felt very heavy. And dry. "What's his name?"

Ian paused. "You sure? Over the ph—"

"What's his goddamn name, Ian?"

"Some cop in Philly," he said, suddenly sounding a little concerned himself. "Robert Baglioni."

You are cordially invited to the wedding of Denise and Robert on August 4 . . .

Fuck fuck fuck fuck fuck

I squeezed the phone so tight I thought I might shatter the screen. I shut my eyes and let my head fall until it landed in a puddle of condensation where my glass had been resting. I took a deep breath and exhaled. It came out very shaky. My legs were tingling and the muscle controlling my sphincter all at once felt suspect. There were still the same four people in the bar, but my ears filled with a loud rumbling as my blood pressure skyrocketed.

"Rick?" Ian said. "You there?"

I tried to answer but nothing came out, so I took another breath instead. This one was a little steadier.

"Rick?"

"I'm here," I said. It came out the way it sounds when someone gets off a roller coaster and is trying to convince you they're fine while also not throwing up.

"It's not a big deal," he went on, "and they're paying me extra for it. You just always said to call you if anybody ever changes the deal, so I wanted to—"

"How much?" I asked.

"How much what?"

I sat up straight and opened my eyes. Blue and black dots swam in my vision for a few seconds until they cleared. The bartender gave me a glance, then went back to watching the boring TV game show.

"How much more are they paying you?" I asked.

"One point two for all three. Are you sure we should really be talking about this—"

"I'll give you an extra fifty."

"What?"

"One point two-five, but I want you to back out."

There was another pause, longer this time. "Rick, what the hell are you—"

I stood up, grabbed my carry-on bag, and started walking. Fast. Almost running.

"Hey," Frank the bartender called after me, "you didn't pay!"

I pulled out my wallet, cursing and jerking my arm as it got stuck in the folds of my jeans pocket, and tossed a pair of twenties over my shoulder.

"I need you to bail on this one, Ian."

"Why? Who is this guy?" Ian sounded as frantic as me. A routine call had gone sideways and he wanted an explanation.

"He's nobody," I lied.

My eyes were everywhere as I moved. Scanning every kiosk, every coffee stand, every bench for one of Trish's agents. Knowing she wouldn't send anyone I had seen before. Becoming more paranoid as a result. Everyone looked suspicious. Every mother pushing a stroller, every elderly couple on a bench holding hands, every businessman chattering away on his Bluetooth was tailing me. And I suddenly cared *a lot.* My earlier apathy had been replaced by abject fear. I felt my pulse quicken again and concentrated hard to get it under control.

"Please, Ian, I just need you to do this as a favor. You'll be helping me out and you'll pocket an extra fifty grand."

"Do you even have that kind of money?" he asked, not liking any of this.

"I do as of this morning." Another lie. I still hadn't checked to see if Trish's second payment had gone through.

"Rick, none of this makes sense. I just wanted to keep you in the loop and now you want me to bail on the biggest job of my career? This could set me up for life."

"You're going to make more money from me NOT to do it. And I'll get you other jobs, Ian. You know I will."

He sighed. "Yeah, but ones like this? If I back out, my rep will be shot. No one's going to want to—"

"IAN, FOR GOD'S SAKE JUST TRUST ME!"

They all stopped. All the spies, corrupt agents, and deep cover families of four within a hundred feet of me froze and gawked at the crazy man shouting into his phone. The one with the beady, shifty eyes who had started sweating right through his cotton shirt.

I raised my hand and patted the air in a feeble attempt to convince them that this was just a normal, everyday public meltdown, rather than a precursor to something that would land everyone on the nightly news.

It worked. Kind of. They stopped gawking, but they also gave me a wide berth as they resumed whatever they'd been doing. A few of them had a sudden urge to use the restroom. At least I knew they weren't following me.

"I'm sorry," I said quietly as I started walking again. Not quite so fast this time, but still with some urgency. "I just need you to do this for me. I can't say you owe me one because you've lined my pockets as much as I've lined yours, so I'm just asking. As a personal favor. Don't do this job. Let me pay you a shit ton of money NOT to do this job, Ian."

The silence lasted a long time. No more than thirty seconds in actuality, but it felt eternal. "A hundred," he said at last.

"What?"

"I want an extra hundred, not an extra fifty. And I want it in cash. Tonight."

I stopped walking and put my hands on my knees. My breath came easier and my muscles got their strength back. I heard Ian call my name two, then three times, and put the phone back to my ear.

"Thank you," I said. "Meet me at the place we first interviewed. Ten o'clock." Getting my hands on that kind of cash in less than ten hours wasn't going to be easy, but I could make it work. Knowing a bunch of unscrupulous people comes in handy sometimes.

"Who is this Baglioni guy, Rick?" Ian asked. "No bullshit." He sounded calmer too, but still more than a little worried. About me or him I couldn't be sure. Probably both.

I started to tell him. Wanted to tell him.

"I'll see you tonight," I said instead and hung up. Then I shifted the strap for my travel bag higher up my shoulder and continued toward the pickup zone outside where a line of Ubers waited, not seeing or not caring about the dirty looks they received from the taxi drivers further up the curb.

Inside my bag, Sergei's phone bounced against a pair of socks. I barely felt it.

CHAPTER THIRTEEN

Robert Baglioni, the man who would soon become my children's stepfather, being targeted for murder by an organization that was clearly involved in some global-level illegal shit, raised a lot of questions.

Was he somehow involved with the task force that Trish referenced during our meeting, the one comprised of agents from multiple intelligence agencies? If so, what the fuck did a cop from Philly have to contribute to whatever they were investigating?

Or did he pose a different kind of threat to Trish and her Board of Directors? Something more direct? Something more personal?

All deserved an answer, but they were secondary in my mind. At that moment, all I cared about was:

Why didn't Trish tell me he was on the list? Why hide that name in particular?

There were a few possible answers to that simple question, and I didn't like any of them. The most benign reason was that Trish really *was* just trying to save some money.

It had happened before. It's why I tell all my candidates to call me if anything changes after they accept the offer. I get paid 30 percent of whatever the contract pays. If a client offers my candidate more money for extra work after I've already delivered them, then they don't have to pay me as much for my services. Doesn't take an evil genius to hatch that scheme. Maybe Ghost and The Persian got extra names as well, and just didn't bother to let me know.

But I'd already determined that Trish wasn't the penny-pinching type, so I forced myself to disregard it as the least likely motivation, comforting though it was.

The second possibility scared me because it meant that Trish knew about Robert's connection to my family. Which meant she knew about my *family*. It was bound to happen sooner or later. I'd changed my name, bought new IDs, deleted all my social media accounts, only used cash whenever possible, and obtained a new social security number. Done everything I could to vacuum up whatever breadcrumbs connected me to my old life and the people in it. But no matter how hard I tried, with some of those crumbs out there and online, there was only so much vacuuming I could do.

Denise still had years' worth of photos on social media in which I was featured prominently. There were articles where I was quoted and blog posts I'd written for my old recruitment firm that still came up in Google searches. All under my actual name, of course, not Rick Carter, but anyone who was willing to dig would find out enough about my past to do some damage. My hope was that by setting up a new life with a new identity, several thousand miles and one large ocean away from who I used to be, I could protect those who might get hurt.

The plan worked for ten years. In retrospect, that was longer than it should have.

Trish had to have known that Robert being on the hit list would be a nonstarter for me. Sure, she could have still used her charm to convince me to take the job—

I touched my eye, remembering the way the knife point felt against it.

—but the risk of me breaking my rule about not going to the authorities went way up. Maybe, deep down, I really was a monster who secretly relished the idea of helping knock off the guy who would replace me in all future family photos, but she couldn't take that chance. (Nor should she have. I'm an asshole, an alcoholic, and an accessory to many murders, but I'm not a monster. Even if the previous truths don't make for the most compelling argument.)

In this scenario, she didn't tell me about Robert because she honestly believed I represented her best chance to find the kind of professionals she needed for the job. So she neglected to include the one name that could derail the whole thing to ensure I would fulfill my responsibility without distraction.

I hoped it was one of the first two reasons. Trish being cheap or Trish being strategically deceitful. Because the third option terrified me.

In that scenario, she knew about my family. Knew about Robert's connection to them. And rather than that relationship being a threat to our partnership, one that needed to be avoided, it was instead integral to it. They cut off my fingertip and refused to take no for an answer not because I was the best in the business, but because when it was all over, I was going to take the fall. And not just as part of my "No Cops Guarantee" if one of my candidates got caught.

The more I thought about it, the more obvious it became. This was an organization with immense reach and resources. If they wanted to, I had no doubt there were people within their ranks skilled enough to execute all six members of the task force as efficiently as the three professionals I provided. But then there would be a direct link between them and the hits. Their people were good, so it wouldn't be glaring, but it would be there for anyone who looked hard enough.

And when six agents across three different intelligence communities go down at the same time, there are plenty of people afterward who are looking at *everything*. Maybe they connected the dots back to Trish and her Board of Directors, maybe not.

Why take the chance, though, if you can just hire yourself a patsy? Robert gave me motive. Flimsy, sure, but Trish would take care of that. (Asking Ian to take out Robert was likely laying the groundwork. He was easier to connect to me than the more clandestine Ghost or The Persian.) Evidence would be planted, witnesses would be bought, and overnight I would go from ancillary player to underworld kingpin. The buck would stop with me. All for the low, low price of one million dollars. A bargain, really.

I'd deny it all, of course. When they brought me in—whatever agency that might be—I would tell them everything. Every last detail. I'd recite every word of my conversation with Trish verbatim and draw them a frigging oil painting of the house on Albert Street with its fancy water heater, my "No Cops Guarantee" be damned.

Trish had to know this was true as well. Which meant after the jobs were finished, my time on this earth would be measured in hours. Things go much smoother when your patsy is too busy being dead to defend himself.

This raised a fourth possibility, that Robert was on the list simply to frame me, tie me into everything on a personal level. But that meant she would also have to plant false evidence on Robert after his death that connected him in some way to the task force's investigation, which seemed like a lot of extra trouble to go through when she could just frame me in some other way. Much as I wanted to believe Robert was just a pawn in all this, I couldn't get there without making some leaps in logic. No, he was involved. I just didn't yet know how.

Pulling Ian from the equation wouldn't prevent any of those scenarios from playing out, it would merely delay them. That was the only move I had, though, so I was going to make it.

Tomorrow, Ian would no-show for his meeting with Trish. He wouldn't tell her he was backing out and provide some bullshit explanation; he would just ghost her. It would buy me extra time. Not a lot, but every little bit helped. Depending on her mood, Trish would either try to reach him on her own or reach out to me to see if I could track him down. Either way, I would hear from her. She would poke around to see if Ian had told me about Robert without showing her hand, so I'd have to watch what I said, but that was fine. I'd gotten good at tap dancing with criminals. I'd apologize for Ian flaking out—

The kid's rep really would be shot; he was right about that. Collateral damage that I would spend a long time cleaning up, but necessary. It wouldn't happen overnight, but I'd find him more jobs. His career wouldn't be derailed as much as it would be delayed.

—and tell her I'd spend a day trying to track him down, then would start searching for a new candidate right away. She'd want to know why I didn't have a backup option in place from the start and I'd explain that I did but that person had just accepted another contract, so I needed to dive back into my database and pull out someone else. Given the nature of the job, it couldn't be just anyone, but give me two, three days at the most and I'd have a new candidate for her.

When I failed to produce anyone within that timeframe, give or take, she'd tell me my services were no longer required and that she'd find someone on her own. At that point she'd offer the hits on the two MI5 agents and Robert to either Ghost or The Persian, rather than bringing in a third operative and risk expanding the pool of people who knew about what was going on. She'd be hard-pressed to find anyone better anyway, at least on short notice. Whichever one she chose would be in the US within a day, assuming Robert became a higher priority than the MI5 agents, given my newfound knowledge of his involvement.

If all of that played out like it did in my head, that gave me four days on the low end, six on the high end. Split the difference and I had five days to get to New Jersey, locate Robert Baglioni, and somehow convince him that his fiancée's estranged ex-husband popped up after ten years to save him from one of the world's top assassins who, by the way, was only there because of me.

Piece of cake. But first I needed to pay off Ian.

Loan sharks don't need my services. Along with death and taxes, one of the universal truths is that there will always be desperate people who need money fast but for whom banks and other legitimate lending institutions are not viable options. And people like Matteo Claes will always be there to fill the void. They don't need an intermediary to find them work; business comes to them and it never slows down.

The relationship between Matteo and I was similar to the one I had with Joey Walls, but much more symbiotic. In short, our clientele overlapped. The people to whom he lent money often owed it to the same people that could use my services. When he came across a new name or caught wind of a potential job, he kicked it my way. I, in turn, referred him to my clients when they were in need of any of his offerings, such as illegal gambling or money laundering. It worked out great. We're both professionals who respected and valued what the other brought to the table. The look he gave me that afternoon, however, was not one of respect. And any value I held in his eyes was not apparent as he asked me to repeat my question.

"One point three million in cash, Matteo," I said. "Do you have it or not?"

We were sitting in his office, a room off the back of the check cashing place that was his hide-in-plain-sight corporate front. He even had business cards printed up. I was standing on the other side of his desk, the generic gray metal kind that furnishes the cramped offices of warehouse managers and accounting supervisors everywhere. The only difference was the glass hookah sitting on its corner. The silver pipe at the end of the hose dangled from Matteo's long, dainty fingers as he exhaled a plume of sweet-smelling smoke into the already clouded air.

"What kind of operation do you think I have here, Rick?" he asked.

"A successful one," I said. "Come on Matteo, just for the bookmaking alone you're liable to have that much on hand. Don't fuck with me on this, okay? It's important."

He took another hit from the pipe. The water gurgled in the bowl, like a kid slurping the last of his soda from a paper cup. The sound made me think of Ethan, of all the sodas I'd bought him and Maggie over the years.

"Please," I said.

Matteo sighed and clipped the pipe to the side of the hookah. "Three percent fee. That's my friends and family discount, so don't even try to negotiate."

"Done," I said. There really was no need for a vig of any kind since I was about to pay off the loan before I walked out the door, but a million in cash isn't easy to withdraw from any legitimate bank without raising eyebrows and he was going to just hand it over. Three percent seemed more than fair. He opened the laptop sitting next to the hookah and pulled up his account info, then spun it to face me. I bent over and logged into my own accounts. Trish had made the second deposit of $450,000 that morning. I'd checked from the backseat of the Uber on the way in from the airport.

Within ten minutes, $1,300,000 (plus his $36,000 fee) was in his account and my total net worth had gone from nearly seven figures to a little over $300,000 in less than twenty-four hours. Five minutes later, one of his employees brought in a square brick made up of hundred-dollar bills. The bills were strapped together in packs of a hundred, all held together with Saran Wrap. The entire brick weighed about twenty pounds and fit into my carry-on bag with room to spare. Being a millionaire never felt so insignificant.

"That's a lot of money for a man who buys his suits off the rack," Matteo said as I zipped up my bag. A loose edge of plastic wrap got caught in the teeth, so I had to undo it and try again without breaking the zipper. My fingers were shaking. Matteo glanced at the bandage around my pinkie and said, "You in some kind of trouble, Rick?"

"Nope," I replied, getting the bag all the way closed this time. I hefted the strap over my shoulder and across my chest. "Just going away for a little while. Need some walking around money."

Matteo whistled. "That's a lot of walking."

"God willing, brother."

Nobody followed me. At least, nobody that I saw. They either weren't there or they were very good. The complete opposite of Colin and his remain-visible-in-plain-sight style of surveillance.

Or maybe that had all been an act to make me drop my guard and Colin had never stopped following me, he'd just started doing it the right way.

Either way, I made it to my apartment and found it unmolested. Nothing ransacked, nothing out of place. I retrieved my Glock from the safe and stuck two extra magazines into the clip holders on my shoulder strap. I tucked the gun in its holster and locked the door behind me for what felt like the last time. I hoped I was wrong.

CHAPTER FOURTEEN

At 9:57 p.m., I pulled into the empty parking lot and killed my engine. Thirty feet away, Ian sat on his motorcycle. The neon green paint job of the Kawasaki crotch rocket matched the stripes on the sleeves of his jacket. He had it idling when I pulled up—the exhaust was visible beneath the light where he was parked—but when I got out of the car, he shut it off and flicked open the kickstand.

I'd used this parking lot a handful of times earlier in my career before moving on to more secure locations. It was secluded, nestled in between four long-abandoned packaging and distribution facilities, at the end of a road that served as the sole artery for the industrial complex where it was located.

Ten feet past the entrance to the lot, the road dead-ended with a chain-link fence guarding what probably began as a pile of leftover construction dirt but was now a thriving ecosystem of weeds, broken glass, and used condoms. The fence had rusted to the point where the dead end sign, a browned, decayed version of its former bright-yellow self, hung by a thread, its final fall from grace imminent.

People long ago stopped giving a shit about the empty complex at the end of that road, which was what made it so attractive as a meeting site. The more experience I gained, however, and the more interviews

I logged, the more I realized that while it might be ignored by most people, it wasn't invisible to any of them. In fact, with its wide-open lot and still-functioning light poles, it was a voyeur's dream.

The more candidates I met there, the more exposed I began to feel. Ian was the last interview I ever held in that spot. Nobody else I'd interacted with in the last two years knew about it. I was banking on that to keep us both safe.

Ian's footfalls echoed in the empty night air, his feet heavy in his leather boots. I scanned our surroundings as I moved to meet him, but there wasn't much to see. No cars had followed me. We were alone.

I searched the roofs of the buildings and the holes in the dirty windows, looking for a gleam of moonlight off a sniper's scope, but nothing flashed. That should have calmed my nerves but it didn't. I pulled the canvas duffel bag off my shoulder and ran my fingers through my hair, convinced there were more grays mixed in with the brown than when I rolled out of bed that morning. The temperature was close to freezing, but my palms were sweaty.

"Hey Rick," Ian said when we met, halfway between our vehicles.

"Ian."

"This definitely brings back memories," he said, taking in the scenery.

"Sure does."

He'd been wearing a Detroit Lions baseball cap the last time. Ten pounds lighter, lost in a heavy winter coat. Two nights earlier, he'd taken that coat off the customer in front of me in line at a liquor store. This was after he'd shot the store owner in the head and then put another between the eyes of the tough guy by the wine rack who'd seen one too many movies and thought he could be a hero using only a bottle of cheap merlot. Ian never hesitated with either shot. Hand was steady, eyes were cool. He had natural talent but no one to manage it. It didn't take me long to track him down.

"You look like shit, man," he said, snapping me back into the present.

"Got a lot on my mind."

"I'd say."

Was that concern in his eyes? Pity? Maybe a little disgust? Hard to tell.

“That my money?” he asked, pointing to the bag.

“Yup.” I slipped the strap off my shoulder and unzipped it. I’d taken out my clothes and other travel stuff back at the apartment. All that was inside now was one hundred and thirty stacks of hundred-dollar bills. I pulled the flaps open and held it out so he could see inside. He nodded. I zipped the bag back up and handed it over to him. “Did you call and tell them yet?”

“No,” he said. “I wanted to meet with you first, make sure you hadn’t changed your mind.”

“Not likely,” I said.

“First you break your own rule about avoiding jobs with law enforcement targets, now you’re paying me to back out. You ready to tell me what’s going on, or have I not earned that level of respect from you yet?” He set his eyes on mine, and I held his gaze.

“It has nothing to do with respect, Ian.”

“How many other candidates on your roster would have agreed to what you asked me to do?” he asked, slinging the bag over his shoulder. “Can you name even one?”

“No,” I said honestly.

“You helped me back when I had nothing. I always swore that if there was ever any way I could repay you for that, I’d do it. This is me making good on that promise. But this is a big fucking favor, man.”

“You still got paid, Ian.”

“Fuck the money!” he shouted, stabbing his finger at my face. “You know damn well it’s not about that. Word of this gets around—and it will—a lot more than just my career could be over. Don’t nobody wanna work with a guy who backs out of the big jobs. You’re good, Rick, but are you good enough to still book me quality gigs with that hanging around my neck?” He shook his head. “There’s better than a fifty-fifty chance I just reset my entire life by helping you out. Least you can do is tell me why.”

“Ian—” I started.

Then stopped.

Then held my hands up in frustration.

Then looked around, down at the ground, and back into his eyes again.

Then I took a deep breath. If we were going to continue working together—and I had every intention of making damage control for his career my top priority as soon as all of this was over—it was only fair that he knew the truth.

Then a bullet opened a hole just above his right eyebrow and blew out the back of his head.

I heard his brains hit the asphalt before I heard the gunshot. A wet, unsettling sound. Oatmeal being dropped on the kitchen floor. A thin line of blood snaked down the side of his nose from the hole above his eye, which was wide open, staring at nothing. He swayed on his feet for a moment before his knees gave out and he crumpled backward, like a puppet whose strings had been cut. It wasn't until he landed in the pile of his own gray matter that I started to scream.

My legs felt unsteady so I began dancing on my feet to keep them active, spinning in half circles where I stood, looking for the shooter. After a few seconds, whoever was at the controls in my head flipped the logic switch to the "On" position and I realized twirling in the middle of an open parking lot next to a dead man wasn't the best way to avoid getting shot. I fumbled in my pocket and pulled out my car keys.

Get the money, that same logical voice suggested.

"Good idea," I said, in a high-pitched half-whisper. Ian had landed on top of the bag, so I bent to roll him over when something ricocheted off the ground by his shoulder. A second later, I heard the crack of another gunshot.

Shooter's a couple hundred yards away, give or take, the voice said.

I tugged on the strap, hoping to yank it off his body by sheer force, when a third bullet bounced off the ground next to my foot. I felt tiny daggers of splintered asphalt pepper my ankle through the thin black sock I had on.

Forget the money. Run.

I didn't need to be told twice and broke into a full sprint for my car. That's when the bullets started coming in bunches. They were bouncing all around me. I heard one zip past my head so close I reached up and expected to feel blood in my hair, or a ragged mess of dangling flesh where my earlobe used to be, but everything appeared to be intact.

The voice tried to assure me that if the shooter really wanted to hit me, I'd be in the same position as Ian right now, but I was no longer paying attention. I had tunnel vision for the driver's side door of my 2016 Audi A3, terrified that its silver finish would erupt in an explosion as the shooter hit the gas tank. The voice calmly explained how that kind of thing only happened in the movies, but my all-encompassing panic was having none of that logical nonsense.

I hit the door without slowing down, so hard my hip actually pinned it shut for a brief instant as I tried to pull the handle open. Once I got inside I stared at the six keys on my keychain as if they were relics from a lost civilization, their purpose a mystery to me.

Then the back, left window exploded and everything snapped into place. I jammed the key into the ignition, started the engine and floored the gas pedal so hard I almost jumped the curb across the street pulling out of the lot. I swerved at the last second to stay on the road and watched the speedometer needle climb past sixty. The wind coming in through my shattered window swirled the mess of broken glass around my backseat and floor. I reflexively pressed the button on my armrest that would roll the back window up, then made a sound that was supposed to be a laugh but came out more like a nervous bark when I realized there was nothing left to roll up.

Tires squealing, I pulled onto the main road without applying the brakes. I fully expected one of the handful of cars parked in the shoulder to come to life, its headlights piercing the night, and begin to give chase.

None did.

At the first traffic light, I turned left on red. The car approaching from the other way honked, but we weren't close to colliding. He was just pissed.

There was no plan, no destination. I was zigzagging, trying to make myself more difficult to follow, even though I had yet to spot a single suspicious vehicle or individual tracking me since I fled the airport. To my anxiety-riddled mind, Trish's people were everywhere. The hole in Ian's head didn't do much to assuage my paranoia.

It wasn't until the third or fourth random turn that I passed a street I recognized and got my bearings. That grounded me and stopped all of the synapses in my brain from firing at once, allowing rationality and intelligence to take over. My next two turns were more deliberate.

By the time I passed the Gare du Nord train station, I knew exactly where I was going. But I couldn't go alone. I pulled out my phone and started to dial, then stopped and stared at the screen. Reflected in the glass, behind the white numbers and the digital keypad, Trish stared back at me. Waiting for me to make a call or send a text, so she could take a peek at my next move. I blinked and she was replaced by Ian's lifeless face, dark red blood oozing from the wreckage the hollow point left behind, his brown skin already turning ashen. I let go of the wheel, took the phone in both hands, snapped it in two and tossed the pieces out the window.

I opened the center console and pulled out Sergei's phone from the top compartment, praying Joey would pick up despite not recognizing the number.

"Who's this?" he said when he answered.

"Joey, it's me," I said. Although shouted is probably more accurate.

"Rick? Why'd you switch up your number? Shit, you got five-oh problems? How long they been listening in?"

"No five-oh, but I've got problems. I'll explain later. Right now, I need you to do something for me."

Joey never hesitated, never gave it a second thought. When I was done going over everything, he simply said, "You're going to need one more."

CHAPTER FIFTEEN

Leon's was a small club on the outer edge of Brussels's red-light district. Two blocks past where prostitutes stopped patrolling the streets and the beat cops working the overnight shift started.

Situated between a cigar shop and a pawn shop, the only way anyone knew that the entertainment inside was of the adult variety was by word of mouth. Fortunately for Leon White, that word was strong and the club was packed most nights, even on a Wednesday. I parked in the only open spot on the street by the entrance, right in front of a fire hydrant. There was no line, but just inside the front door a bouncer with a goatee and a chest the size of my refrigerator stepped in front of me as I walked past the ticket booth toward the doorway into the club's main room. He had to shout to be heard over the thumping bass of the '90s dance pop the DJ was spinning. A remix of Madonna's "Justify My Love," which came standard on every strip club playlist.

"Ten euro cover," he said, putting his hand on my chest. I thought about grabbing his pinkie and snapping it but decided to avoid making a scene. For now, anyway.

"I'm not here for the show," I said. "I just need to see your boss. Tell him it's Rick Carter."

"Is he expecting you?"

I took out my wallet and removed two hundred-dollar bills. "No," I said, holding them up. He thought about it for maybe half a beat, then the hand came off my chest and snatched the money.

"Wait here," he said, and disappeared into the club. From behind the glass of the ticket booth, a twenty-year-old human tattoo with a dozen facial piercings watched me with an almost insulting lack of interest.

"Long day?" I asked. She continued observing me the way a kid on Christmas regards a new pair of socks. Her expression didn't change when a gray-haired man in a cheap three-piece suit came up and paid his admission, so at least I knew it wasn't just me that she found boring. As the old guy pushed through the curtain into the club, the bouncer with the goatee sidled past him.

"Arms out, palms up," he told me. I obliged. He removed my Glock and tucked it into the waistband of his pants against his lower back. The two spare clips he pocketed. Finding nothing else he said, "Follow me."

The curtain opened onto a small, narrow set of three steps that led to the club floor. Multicolored stage lights flashed above the DJ booth in the far corner, where a young Korean man was focused on queuing up the next track while protected from the riffraff below by three high, plexiglass walls. Not that the crowd looked like it was filled with much riff or raff. For the most part, it was middle-aged white guys hiding from their families. They fed dollar bills to the G-stringed dancer on the main stage or the ones patrolling the floor the way parents feed dollar bills into change machines for their kids at arcades on the Jersey Shore boardwalk. A few pods of younger men getting an early start to the weekend dotted the scene.

It wasn't a total sausage fest, though. There was a blonde sitting right by the main stage, getting what amounted to her own show from a dancer wearing six-inch heels and nothing else, and one table that featured a pair of twenty-something girls deep in conversation. They might have been a couple, or they might have just been best friends who thought hitting a strip club would make for a great story the next time they got together with the rest of the gals.

Either way, I didn't care. I had my eye on the table just past them.

More specifically, the empty beer bottle on top of it. I snatched it as we walked by and held it against the back of my leg. If the bouncer turned around I'd have been screwed, but he never did. Not until we got to the door just beyond the main stage, anyway. He opened it and held his arm out for me to go in ahead of him. I took a quick mental snapshot of the scene on the other side—

Leon seated behind a desk against the far wall, typing on a computer. White suit, red shirt, what little hair he had slick and glistening with Brill cream. Marcus, his bodyguard, standing just inside the doorway to my left, waiting for us. Sunglasses on, because of course they were. I'd never seen him without them, even though we'd never met anytime other than the dead of night. He had a cigarette in his mouth and was reaching for it with his right hand.

—then I gripped the beer bottle by the neck and smashed it against the doorframe. The bottom half of the bottle shattered, leaving a jagged, broken rim still connected to the neck, which did an excellent job of slicing open the goateed bouncer's cheek in three places. He screamed and slapped his hand against the flaps of flesh, which quickly sent rivulets of blood pouring through his fingers.

Under normal circumstances, I never would have been able to move a man of his size. But he was shocked and disoriented, so when I shoved him toward Marcus he went with no resistance whatsoever. As he fell, I pulled my gun from the back of his pants. Marcus was able to dodge the full weight of his body as he barreled into him, but it bought me enough time to fire a shot into the bodyguard's shoulder. Fortunately, I was only a few feet away, so aiming was more of a formality.

Marcus screamed—a little higher-pitched than the bouncer—and reached under his jacket for his own weapon as blood soaked one side of his shirt. Before he could draw it, I swung the Glock in a wide, arcing uppercut that caught him under the chin and sent him sprawling onto the couch behind him, next to where Mr. Goatee had landed. I put a bullet in each of their knees before either could get up. When I took Marcus's gun from him and tucked it into my waistband, he was too busy bleeding and crying to offer any resistance.

All this happened in the space of maybe five seconds. Not long, but plenty of time for Leon to reach into his desk drawer. Inside was either a gun or a button that would summon more security. I didn't care to find out which, so I put two bullets through the front of the desk, into the drawer just below the one he was fishing around in. He gave a small yelp, like a dog after its tail is stepped on, and withdrew his empty hand.

I covered the distance between us in three steps, grabbed the back of his head and drove his face into the computer keyboard before he could reach back in. The impact sent little plastic letter keys flying in all directions. When he came up, there was half a "K" stuck to his forehead. I slapped it away and put the barrel of my gun in its place.

"Hands up," I said, struggling to keep my voice even. He obliged. Behind me I could hear the moans and cries of Marcus and the bouncer. There didn't appear to be any panic or commotion coming from the club, but that wouldn't last. Even with the bass thumping and the general din of a bar at night, *someone* had to have heard the shots and the screams. They might not have recognized them for what they were, but if they had just a tiny bit of curiosity in them, then I'd have to make my exit far sooner than anticipated. "Stay," I said to Leon. His eyes told me that wouldn't be a problem.

Keeping the gun aimed at his head, I backed toward the door and kicked it closed with my foot. Reaching behind me, I found the dead bolt and locked it. Neither Marcus nor the bouncer made any move toward me while I was standing next to them. They were too busy bleeding out onto the hideous orange carpet and matching couch. Having bought myself a few extra minutes, I marched back across the room, grabbed a hold of Leon's shirt with one hand and yanked him out of his chair, which kicked backward and toppled over. I pinned him against the wall and drove the gun barrel into the side of his head. His own pudgy hands stayed where they were the entire time. Next to his ears, palms out, shaking.

"Wha—what the f—fuck is wrong with you?" he stammered.

"No no," I said through gritted teeth. "I ask the questions, not you. The people you set me up with, your referral. Who are they?"

"What?" he asked, eyes wide.

I pressed the barrel harder against his temple. He recoiled from the pressure, so I pulled him back and slammed him against the wall. A framed picture of he and several players from the Anderlecht soccer team fell off and shattered on the ground. One of the stitches popped beneath the crisscrossed Band-Aids on my damaged finger. I didn't feel it.

"Who are they?" It was getting harder not to shout, but I didn't want to lose my cool. The two men writhing on the ground ten feet behind me were the first I'd ever shot in my life, and it had been far easier than I'd anticipated. Far easier than I was comfortable admitting. I had a feeling that the third would be even easier if I wasn't careful. And tempting though it was, Leon did nothing for me dead.

"I—I don't know," he said. Sweat leaked from every pore, mixing with whatever cheap cologne he bathed in that morning. The resulting smell was a repugnant blend of musky sweetness.

I took the gun away from his head, pointed it toward the wall three inches from his left ear and fired a shot. He screamed louder than either of his employees who actually took a bullet earlier and covered his ear with his hand. The other remained in its quivering, upright position. His screams quickly turned to cries, and tears began to seep from behind his closed eyelids.

Good, I thought. *This is what happens when you fuck with my family, you greasy little bitch.*

Except it wasn't Leon who had put my family in danger. But I couldn't get my hands on Trish at the moment, and beating up myself never felt this good.

It feels a little too good, though, doesn't it? You're slipping, Rick.

I was. But there would be time for moral quandaries later. First, I needed answers.

His left ear was ringing and useless, so I replaced the gun against his temple and leaned close to his right. "Don't fuck with me right now, Leon," I said. "Who are they?"

"I don't know, I swear! I only started working with them six months ago. They wanted girls, lots of them, so they came to me. It's what I do. It's what I'm known for. What, was I going to say no?"

"Who was your contact?"

"He never gave me his name. Brown hair, maybe thirty. Shorter than you. He had a tattoo on his neck."

I thought of my conversation with Freddie.

"What did it look like?" I demanded.

"I don't know, some kind of Chinese symbol or something."

Son of a bitch.

"Was he Chinese?" I asked.

"No, he was normal."

I rolled my eyes at the casual racism and smacked him in his bad ear with the gun.

"Ow, Jesus Christ, Rick!" he shouted.

"How did he pay you?"

"Cash. Every time, cash. A lot of it. I couldn't say no."

"How many times?"

"Five, maybe six. About once a month."

"How many girls?"

"Ten, sometimes twelve."

"All at once? Do you even have that many girls on your payroll?"

"No, it wasn't like that. He didn't want dancers, he wanted *girls*."

It didn't register at first, but when it did the last levee against my boiling anger broke. An image of Denise, dirty and abused, being sold at auction to some wealthy sexual predator, flashed across my mind's eye.

An image of Maggie.

I pulled Leon away from the wall and slammed him flat against the desk. The edge caught him in his lower back and he bent awkwardly at the waist. His legs went limp and I pressed the gun so hard against his head that it flattened his cheek against the busted keyboard.

"You fucking sick piece of shit," I spat. Literally. Flecks of saliva splattered on his flushed face. "How old were they? Did you even care?"

"NO!" he cried. "No, Rick it wasn't like that, I swear!"

"Oh really? What was it like, huh? When you said you got them 'girls,' what exactly did you mean?"

"I mean I got them girls, but not girls like that. Women, not strippers.

The kind rich guys buy for themselves. But they were all of age, Rick, I swear. Every single one of them." His eyes were hopeful, begging me to understand that it wasn't a big deal.

So that's what my world had come to in a few short hours. A place where sex trafficking instead of outright pedophilia was considered a silver lining.

"You're a monster," I whispered.

Leon looked at me with the one eye that wasn't buried in a bed of chipped plastic computer keys. "You're one to talk," he said. I raised the gun and slammed the butt hard into the middle of his chest. His lungs voided all the air they had in them at once and he slid to a sitting position on the floor, coughing and wheezing, propped up by the desk. As I bent down and pressed the gun against his eye, I heard the first knock on the door. It was soon followed by another, then three in rapid succession along with a male voice calling Leon's name.

"Party's just about over, Leon," I said, "so talk quick. Did your contact ever mention a woman named Patricia Baum?" Words were still beyond his capabilities at the moment, but he shook his head. "What about the Board of Directors? Did he ever mention them?" This time he stopped coughing and looked at me with the one eye that wasn't staring down the barrel of a Glock.

"No," he choked. "What the fuck are you talking about?"

The knocking against the door turned urgent, and the male voice had gone from calling out Leon's name to talking to someone else about opening the door. Which meant one of the other bouncers had joined the action and would soon lead a charge into the office. The bouncer with the mutilated face and the blown out kneecap called to them to hurry up.

"The guy with the tattoo," I said, "where can I find him?"

"I don't know. He always came to me, here."

I grabbed his ear and twisted it, hard. There was so much adrenaline pumping through me, I could have ripped it clean off. As it happened, a streamer of blood ran down from where his lobe connected to his head. Turns out that part tears pretty easy.

"Not good enough," I half-whispered, half-snarled into his ear while he screamed.

"Okay!" he cried. "He races bikes. Motorcycles."

"Where?"

"The Atomium. I staked him a few times. He's good. Really good. We both made some extra money." He added that last part almost boastfully. I twisted his ear again and the sudden flash of pride disappeared.

"How do I find him?"

"He wears a bright-yellow helmet. It matches his motorcycle. Looks like a god damn bumble bee buzzing down the strip."

"Maybe you really are good for something after all, Leon," I said, letting his ear go. "Who knew?" Then I stood and pointed the gun at the middle of his forehead. Killing him would change nothing. He was merely a middleman, whose death would have no impact on anything Trish had set in motion.

Didn't matter. In that moment, I just wanted to see him die. God help me.

Looking back on it, maybe He did.

The door swung open and two men in suits came through with guns raised. Behind them was a third man, also dressed in a suit, but with a garish pink shirt and no tie. He dropped to his knees and tended to the men on the floor while the first two trained their sights on me and told me to drop my weapon. I did as I was told. Marcus's gun was still concealed in the back of my waistband.

"Hands up!" they ordered. I again obliged.

"Two federal agents for a shooting at a strip club?" I asked. "Do all the local cops have the night off, or were you both just here for a lap dance?"

"We got a tip that old Leon was doing more than running some drugs out the back of his club," said Agent #1. He and his partner were new faces to me. Older. Veterans. Instead of rushing me like a couple of adrenaline-fueled rookies, they were calm. Casual, almost. #1 was bearded, #2 was not. Both had their guns aimed at my chest. Most likely Belgian Federal Police, which meant Trish could have easily put some extra cash in their pockets through her connections in Interpol. Just because I hadn't seen them before didn't mean they weren't dirty. But it did mean I couldn't be sure. Still, if they wanted me dead, it would have happened by now.

"Human trafficking, sex slaves," Agent #2 chimed in. "Nasty shit. You back there, Leon?" From behind the desk, Leon first raised both his hands, then struggled to his feet and stood next to me.

"That's better," the bearded agent said. He reminded me of a French actor I'd seen in a bunch of movies but could never remember his name. Always played the villain. "Good to see you again, buddy."

I tried to read Leon's face from the corner of my eye, see if it registered any recognition for the two agents other than the relationship between a petty criminal and the cops that harass him for inside information. It wouldn't surprise me at all to learn that Leon was a snitch. It was how pricks like him continued to operate, unimpeded.

"Oscar," Leon said, "you know me. Would I go into that kind of business?"

"I'd hoped not, Leon, but we got this from a very credible source."

"Who?" Leon asked. "Who is spreading these lies about me?" Even if I didn't know the truth, I wouldn't have believed him. His acting wouldn't cut it for the exposition scenes in a porno movie.

"Come on, Leon," Agent Oscar said, "you know I can't tell you that. Let's just say they're credible enough that we need to continue this conversation downtown. Come on over here, both of you." He waved his arm to us and lowered his gun.

"I'm sorry," I said, "what am I being arrested for?"

Agent #1 laughed and gave me a *are-you-shitting-me* grin. He pointed to Marcus and Mr. Goatee, who were making an awful racket while they waited for the paramedics to arrive. Bunch of babies.

"Oh," I said, shaking my head while Agent Oscar cuffed Leon's hands behind his back. "Guys, this is all one big misunderstanding. See, Leon and his goons here kidnapped my daughter."

Both men perked up at that.

"Excuse me?" said Agent #1.

"I did what?" Leon said, genuinely surprised.

"Yeah," I went on, "she was meeting her friends at the airport for this European vacation, and one of his guys followed her back to her hotel. She called me to check in and while we were on the phone a bunch of thugs broke into her room." Everyone was staring at me now, including the bouncer with the ugly pink shirt who was still kneeling over Marcus, pressing a bar rag against his shredded knee.

"Now, she's a smart girl," I said. "She hid under the bed, but I knew they would find her. So I told her, very calmly, 'Honey, you're about to be taken.'" The two agents shared a glance. Their expressions had gone from rapt attention to confusion, and were on their way to full disbelief.

"'I need you to pay attention,'" I continued. "'Look for any details. Identifying marks, tattoos, anything. Shout them out to me.' But she never got the chance. When she screamed, it was all I could do not to cry. One of the men picked up the phone. I took a deep breath and told him, 'If you are looking for ransom, I don't have money. What I do have is a very particular set of skills. Skills I have acquired over a long career. Skills that make me—'"

"Hold on," Agent #1 said, putting his hand up. "Isn't that a scene from *Taken*?"

"Yes! Best purchase I ever made from the $5.99 DVD bin at Walmart." I flicked my eyes over their shoulders. "But I don't remember what happens next, so you wanna hurry this up?"

"What?" said Agent Oscar as he turned to see what had caught my eye. He made it halfway around before Erica broke his jaw with a single swipe of her retractable steel baton. Blood and tooth fragments ejected from his mouth as he dropped to the floor. Agent #1 swung his gun up from his hip as he spun to face her, but she struck his wrist and he dropped it instantly. The blow also likely broke a few bones based on the sound it made and the way he screamed, but his cries were short lived. With her free hand she delivered a quick strike to his windpipe, silencing him like a valve cutting off water from a faucet. He dropped to his knees and tore at his throat, trying to pull his trachea open from the outside.

Leon started to call for help, so I came around the desk, covered his mouth with my hand and kneed him in the groin. He dropped as well. Agent Oscar staggered to his feet, the hinge of his jaw swollen and lumpy. Erica took the baton in both hands and pulled it tight across his neck from behind. Oscar started to cough and gurgle while he fought to push the baton away.

"Wait!" I said. "No killing. We don't know that they're dirty."

Erica rolled her eyes. In one swift move she replaced the baton with her left arm while she used her right to press against the back of his head. I'd never seen a sleeper hold administered in real life, other than when I was twelve and my dad took me to WrestleMania. Pretty sure the one Hulk Hogan put on Ravishing Rick Rude was a fake. This one, however, worked like a charm. And fast. Within thirty seconds, Oscar was out.

Agent #1 was starting to get his wind back, but another sleeper hold did the trick on him as well. Erica grabbed him by the arms while I did the same to Oscar, and we pulled their unconscious bodies toward Leon, who was still on his knees. I picked my gun up off the floor, held it to Leon's head for what seemed like the fiftieth time that night, and told him to hold his cuffed wrists out. He did, and we looped the agents' arms around his before cuffing them both. The three of them were now linked together like the interlocked rings in a magic trick. Except in their case, smoke and mirrors wouldn't be enough to get them apart. Erica and I took both sets of handcuff keys from the agents' pockets and put them in Leon's desk drawer along with their guns.

"What took you so long?" I asked her as we finished up.

"Did you see the ass on that girl with the heels?" she replied. "I wasn't leaving until her set was over."

"Jesus Christ," I said, shaking my head. "If I'd known that was going to be a problem I might as well have brought Joey in and left you outside to drive the car."

"Joey wouldn't have gotten her number."

"You're dead," Leon said. "Both of you. You know that, right?"

I crouched down, close enough to smell the garlic on his breath. "Leon," I said.

Then I headbutted him. It was a perfect shot. I heard his nose splinter at the bridge. His eyes rolled in the back of his head and he fell forward, landing on top of Agent Oscar.

"Let's get out of here," I said to Erica.

We walked past Marcus and the lead bouncer (Erica had taken care of Pink Shirt on her way in; he laid next to them on the floor, a baton-shaped welt rising on the side of his head) and closed the door behind us. Drops of blood from Leon's shattered nose were on my face and Erica still had the baton in her hand, but I'd holstered my gun. Nobody said anything to us, but we got more than a few stares as we made our way across the floor to the exit.

The DJ had segued from Madonna to something more modern and local from the Belgian artist Stromae.

We didn't see the cop right away. He was stationed on the other side of the curtain separating the main floor from the front ticket area. The two young women who were at the table by Leon's office stopped to talk with him on their way out. Erica and I were too far away to hear what they said above the pounding electro-beat of "Alors on danse," but we didn't need to. When one of them turned and pointed at us while the other nodded her head, the message was pretty clear.

Erica, the consummate pro, casually pivoted toward the bar but I froze. When the cop thanked the two women and stared at me, I stared right back. I'd paid off plenty of people in the Brussels-Capital Ixelles police force, but this guy's face was foreign to me. The drops of blood on my own face from Leon's busted nose felt like bright, glowing neon. Erica noticed I wasn't with her and came back to grab my arm, just as the cop pressed the button on the side of the walkie pinned to his shoulder.

"They may not be here for us," I said, knowing how foolish it sounded. Erica didn't dignify it with a response, other than to sigh as she pulled Marcus's pistol from the back of my pants. She raised it into the air and fired twice, the reports cutting through the French hip-hop and sending the two dozen or so patrons to their feet in unison. Instant panic and the few seconds of cover we needed.

"Run," she said, pulling me toward the back corner behind the

DJ booth. I had just enough time to register the cop's *oh shit* expression before my attention turned to dodging a sea of middle-aged men with suddenly shriveled hard-ons all scrambling for the front door at the same time. Erica weaved among them like a seasoned slalom skier while I elbowed and shouldered through the mass like a drunk hockey player. I almost dropped my phone twice as I dialed but managed to get it to my ear.

"Joey!" I shouted when he picked up. "Change of plans, we're coming out the back. Meet us around the block at the end of the alley."

"Good idea," he said. "There were two patrol cars waiting out front and I can hear a bunch more on their way to join them."

"Fuck," I said as I hung up.

"What's wrong?" Erica asked. We had made it to the swinging double doors leading to the small kitchen where Leon's staff reheated frozen bar food and microwaved bowls of soup for anyone pathetic and lonely enough to order a meal here.

"Our getaway isn't going to be easy," I said.

She scrunched her eyebrows at me and said, "You thought it would?"

We made our way through the kitchen—empty, the workers likely having fled after they heard the shots and the screams—and opened the door to the alley. I saw the first cop but didn't have time to warn Erica before his partner grabbed me from behind and slammed me against the wall, my right arm bent up and pinned against the small of my back. I tried to push off with my left but he kicked my feet out from under me while keeping the pressure on. The rough, sandpaper edges of the brick scraped the top layer of skin from my face as I slid down the wall.

I grunted through the pain and collected myself for one last push before he had a chance to secure my other arm and cuff my wrists together. In my head, I counted down.

Three . . . two . . . one

On *two*, the pressure against my back went away and my right arm fell free, but I was already committed. When I reached *one*, I pressed off as hard as I could against nothing but air, effectively launching myself into a puddle of oily alley water. Erica held out her hand and grabbed my forearm, pulling me to my feet. Both cops were unconscious, their foreheads bleeding.

"Two more seconds and I had him," I said, rotating my sore right arm.

"Your ass is wet," she replied.

"Your . . . Mom's . . . wet," I said, just in case she needed an example of a poor comeback for when we bantered in the future.

From the rear mouth of the alley came the sound of screeching tires, and Joey's voice shouting, "Move!"

He'd pulled up on the other side of the empty cop car that was blocking the exit from the alley, its blue lights still flashing. We ran to Joey's little hatchback—which he thought helped him remain inconspicuous, despite the fact that a man his size driving a car that small was the main attraction in most circuses—and slid over the roof of the cop car into his backseat. Before he pulled away, Erica shot out the front and rear passenger-side tires on the patrol car.

We could hear shouts of other officers running through the alley as we pulled away. Erica and I both lay as flat as we could across the narrow backseat. At the intersection Joey turned left, away from Leon's and the swirling blue lights collecting in front of it. It wasn't until two blocks later, when another patrol car—its own blue roof lights flashing—sped past us without stopping that I felt safe enough to sit up. The streets were otherwise deserted at this early morning hour.

"Joey," I said, "I owe you one."

"You owe me five thousand, to be exact," he said, "but you don't have to pay me right now." I laughed and slapped him on the shoulder.

"Where to?" he asked.

"We can go to my place," Erica said. "They won't be watching it."

"Rick?" Joey asked, his eyes in the rearview mirror waiting for my approval.

"We have to make a stop first," I said.

CHAPTER SIXTEEN

Located on the Heysel Plateau in the Laeken section of Brussels, The Atomium was originally constructed for the 1958 Brussels World's Fair. A massive work of modern art standing over three hundred feet tall, it consists of five silver spheres surrounding a larger, sixth sphere in the center, all connected by great silver spokes. The overall shape resembles an atom as it would appear in a Sharper Image catalog, hence the name Atomium.

Conceived as an example of futuristic—and fully livable—architecture, it's now a popular museum, and an iconic landmark for the city. Unfortunately for the quiet suburb in which it's located, the circular roads surrounding it are also ideal for illegal street racing.

The main concern is the cars, and they're the worst on the weekends. Residents regularly complain, not only about the noise generated by dozens of souped-up engines and modified mufflers at 3:00 in the morning, or the dangerous speeds at which they take hairpin turns, leading to more than one inevitable crash per Saturday night, but by the drivers themselves. Though the races don't typically begin until close to midnight, the party starts well before then as racers come from all over the city to compare rides, drink beer, and generally mistreat any pedestrian—especially those of the young, female persuasion—who venture too close to their territory. Apparently, illegal street racers *aren't* all charming rogues with hearts of gold. The *Fast and Furious* movies are full of shit.

Cops do what they can, often impounding several cars per weekend, but the races keep going despite a police presence that has only gotten more pronounced. That's why the motorcycle racers do their business during the week.

There're less of them, too, and while they aren't going to be helping old ladies cross the street any time soon, they aren't actively looking to piss off the locals either. Why attract more attention than necessary, especially with the cops focused entirely on shutting down the muscle-car aficionados?

When we pulled up, there were ten riders waiting their turn, each paired off, while the first pair in line revved their engines at the crosswalk that served as the starting line. A heavily tattooed bald man with a paper-thin mustache stood between the bikes with his arms raised. The high-pitched whines of the foreign crotch rockets pierced the night while the bystanders lining each side of the street cheered. There were maybe fifty people in all, mostly girlfriends of the racers and men like Leon who were there to make a quick buck. It wouldn't have surprised me at all if this was where Freddie first met up with Neck Tattoo. My little friend had never been able to walk away from anyplace capable of separating him from his money.

"Do you see him?" Erica asked as we approached the crowd. Joey was waiting in the car, parked behind us in a lot reserved for the museum. Buses transporting students on field trips and minivans driven by stay-at-home moms with small children would fill the spaces in the morning. He had the engine running, just in case Neck Tattoo decided he wasn't in the mood to talk to us, or if the cops showed up and *we* weren't in the mood to talk to *them*.

"There he is," I said, pointing two rows behind the riders who had just peeled off down the empty street after Baldy dropped his arms. The bright-yellow helmet was the only one in the pack, and his bike did indeed look like a bee with its yellow frame offset by the black tires and chrome piping. His opponent to the right of him was decked out in a more traditional red and black ensemble. Between the riders and spectators, the amount of leather on hand was enough to fully clothe a Freddie Mercury convention.

In addition to my jeans, button-down, and suit blazer, I might as well have been wearing a sign around my neck that said, "I don't belong here." Fortunately, Erica blended in better, so I just stuck close to her.

Scanning the crowd as we made our way to the riders, I could see why Freddie might come here for reasons other than losing whatever cash he had in his pocket. There were more than a few faces I knew from my networking efforts, although they probably didn't know me. This could be a prime business development spot.

But I wasn't there to network, and the guy in the yellow helmet was the only person I was interested in.

"What's his name?" Erica asked as we pushed through the crowd forming a horseshoe around the starting line.

"No idea," I said. The guy he was racing against was talking to a few other people, probably his buddies. Neck Tattoo had no one. He was lightly revving his engine with a subtle flick of his wrist, bouncing gently on the seat, waiting for the two riders in front of him to go so he could assume his place at the starting line. I tapped him on the shoulder. "Hey."

He stopped revving the engine and turned to look at me. The face shield on his helmet was raised, but all I could see was his eyes and the top of his nose. They didn't convey much, but it was clear he wasn't happy about being disturbed. The Chinese ink poked out from the top of his leather jacket collar, forming a bridge to where it disappeared beneath his helmet.

"Who the hell are you?" he asked, his young voice muffled by the helmet.

"We have a mutual business associate, Leon White."

The eyes narrowed, but he said nothing.

"You tipped off another friend of mine about a job Leon had," I continued, "looking for someone to take care of his competition across town."

Those eyes opened wide and I could tell his fight or flight was kicking in.

"Don't worry," I said quickly, "I'm not a cop. I just had some questions about the people you work for." Then, sensing that sounded *exactly* like something a cop would say, I added, "Leon tells me they pay well, and I'm always on the lookout for good work."

Erica remained silent next to me, but from the corner of my eye I could tell this wasn't the approach she would have taken. The two riders in front of us sped off as Baldy dropped his arms, and before I could react, Neck Tattoo slapped his face shield shut and peeled off right behind them.

"Shit!" I shouted.

"What the—that's a forfeit!" his opponent complained to Baldy, who looked equally perplexed.

Erica spun and turned her gun on the two riders behind us. "Off your bikes, now!"

They put their hands up, flicked open the kickstands, and stepped away from their expensive motorcycles, easily the most important things in their world. Not worth dying for though.

"Let's go," Erica said, straddling a bike with bright orange designs stitched across its sleek, compact frame. She nodded at the other one, implying it was for me.

"I don't know how to ride," I said.

"What?"

"I can't ride a motorcycle."

"Are you kidding?"

"Look at me! Does anything about this scream *Sons of Anarchy* to you?"

She rolled her eyes. "Get on."

I slid onto the back of the seat, one clearly not designed for two, and pressed my body as tightly against Erica as I could. My arms wrapped so far around her waist, I could have picked her back pockets.

"Breathing would be nice," she gasped.

"Sorry," I said, loosening my grip. But only a little. A half second later, we were doing 100 mph.

Or at least, that's how it felt. I'd only ever been on a motorcycle one other time in my life. My kid brother bought one after he graduated from high school, with money he'd saved waiting tables at the diner just outside our neighborhood. He tooled back and forth to the beach all summer before he wiped out driving home late one rainy night. The road was slick and he'd simply lost control on a turn. Had there been any other cars around, he likely would have wound up with a lot worse than some busted ribs and bad case of road rash.

He sold the bike soon after, but not before he took me for a ride. I'd been refusing his offer ever since he'd bought it, but he clearly wanted to show off his toy to his big bro. The accident had knocked some of the daredevil out of him, and he swore he wouldn't take it above 45 mph. Still, even at that pedestrian speed, I spent the entire twenty-minute ride feeling like I was about to slide off the back of his seat, no matter how tightly I held on to him. And his seat had way more real estate than the one I was on while Erica weaved through city streets like we were in a video game instead of real life. My jacket flapped behind me and the rush of the wind forced my eyes nearly shut. I had no idea how she was doing any of this.

Neck Tattoo had built a sizable lead by the time we finally got going, but Erica closed the distance fast. There wasn't much traffic on the roads at this time of night, but what little cars there were she swerved around—and between, in one particularly anus-clenching moment—without slowing down. An overhead street sign came into view when we were about twenty feet away from his buzzing bumblebee of a bike, advertising an on-ramp for the RO in one mile.

"We can't let him get on the highway!" Erica shouted above the wind and the whine of our bike's engine.

"What are you going to—"

Before I could finish, she kicked that whine up another octave. As Neck Tattoo drifted into the exit lane, we came up right beside him, close enough to touch hands, and blocked his way. The move surprised him and he nearly lost control, his tires making a sloppy, dangerous S pattern on the asphalt. Erica slowed her speed to match his, ensuring he wouldn't have time to recover and sneak onto the ramp at the last minute. He didn't, and pulled back onto the main road. She did the same, clipping the guardrail that lined the narrow strip of grass separating the ramp from the left lane with our exhaust pipe. Another fraction of a second sooner, and it would have been my foot that got pinched between the two hunks of metal.

Now aware of our presence, he became more brazen, making a sharp right turn against oncoming traffic down a residential street. I closed my eyes and held my breath as Erica followed, pretending not to hear the honking horns and screeching brakes of the little blue compact car and the massive taxi that were way too close to even consider making the move she had just executed. I never heard a crash, but I didn't turn around to look either once I opened my eyes.

"I'm going to pull up next to him," she said, turning her head slightly so I could hear, "then you jump off and tackle him."

I didn't say anything at first, as the only logical response to her suggestion was stunned silence.

"Rick, did you hear me?"

"Yes," I replied. "Did *you* hear you?"

"We're not going that fast right now. Just make sure you land on him and he'll take the brunt of the impact." She said this as if explaining to a toddler how it won't hurt if he falls off his bicycle as long as he lands in the grass.

"I don't think that's how physics works."

"Trust me."

"There has to be another way," I said. Except the last word elongated into "waaaaaaaayyyyyyy!" as Neck Tattoo turned left so suddenly we almost rolled the bike following him.

"There was another way," she said after we didn't die. "We could have pinned him between the two of us and forced him to slow down but you were never man enough to learn how to ride a motorcycle."

"Don't gender stereotype me."

"We're done talking," she said, then switched on the small audio system the owner of our bike had installed on his dash. Twin speakers mounted to the handlebars, each looking like they cost as much as the bike itself, started pumping out the first song on the pre-programmed playlist.

When Maggie was just a baby, we ran out of diapers in the middle of the afternoon. When I turned the car on to make a Target run, the opening guitar riff for "Bad to the Bone" by George Thorogood & The Destroyers was just starting on the radio. Not going to lie, I put my sunglasses on a little slower and backed out of the driveway like a badass that day. Super Dad, on the way to pick up some fresh Pampers. You don't want none of this, Society.

Never would I have guessed that, sixteen years later, I'd be involved in an actual high speed motorcycle chase, only instead of one of the most iconic blues-rock songs ever, my soundtrack would be "Nothing's Gonna Stop Us Now" by Starship. Because, apparently, the illegal street racer whose bike we commandeered had a thing for '80s power ballads.

Of course, that doesn't mean it's a *bad* song.

"You can turn this off if you want," I said into Erica's ear.

"Do *you* want me to turn it off?"

"Your call, you're the driver."

"I'm just gonna let it play."

"Sure, keep your hands at two and ten, I get it."

"It's a motorcycle, but point taken."

"Safety first. Speaking of which, is the plan still for me to—"

"Yes, you're still tackling him."

"Shit."

When we were about a foot to his left, the street temporarily free of parked cars as we'd entered more of a retail section with small shops replacing the houses, she shouted, "Now!"

As Mickey Thomas and Grace Slick were promising to build this dream together, I gathered what little footing I could and launched off the bike. It still amazes me that I had the nerve to do it. The younger, Target-run version of me would have been so impressed. Seeing my face locked in determination, outstretched arms reaching toward the object of our pursuit.

Then, slowly, that determined face evaporated into one of *oh shit* panic as instead of wrapping my outstretched arms around Neck Tattoo,

I sailed behind him. My hand brushed his coat, and strictly out of reflex I closed it and held on to the fistful of leather. It was enough to yank him off and we both smacked into the ground. I lost him as we tumbled, but he didn't go far, stopped by the tires of a delivery truck parked out front of a convenience store. I rolled a few more times before I clipped a parking meter, which killed the rest of my momentum.

So, pretty much the exact opposite of what Erica told me to do. But come on, it's not like I practiced this shit.

Blood dripped down my left hand from where another of the stitches at the tip of my finger had popped, and my shoulder was on fire. The whole left arm was limp and weak, in fact. I'd never dislocated a joint before, but I didn't need WebMD to tell me that's what had happened. My clothes, ripped and dirty, protected me from any serious road burn. My ribs were sore, but I could breathe and didn't think any were cracked. If I ever saw my brother again, I'd have bragging rights when comparing who took a better fall.

Yay.

The driver of the delivery truck had come out to see what happened, but Erica killed his curiosity by pointing her gun at him. When it became apparent he wasn't a threat, she turned her attention to Neck Tattoo, who was still struggling to get to his feet. His bike was lying in the middle of the street, a few random broken pieces scattered around it. His helmet had a dark black smudge where it must have hit the truck tire. Wear your headgear, kids.

My own head was bleeding—I couldn't tell from where, everything hurt—but I didn't think I had a concussion. There was no ringing in my ears and my vision was clear, but it was still a shock to see Joey's car idling behind Erica. Had he been keeping pace with us the entire time?

"Get up," Erica said, grabbing Neck Tattoo by his collar and ripping off his helmet. His legs were unsteady and he didn't put up a fight. She opened the back door of Joey's Fiat and forced him into the center, slid in next to him and told me to get in the other side, trapping him between us. I did and Joey sped off, the delivery truck driver watching us go, eyes and mouth agape, as Starship insisted that nothing would stop us now.

CHAPTER SEVENTEEN

"How much do you love this car?" Erica asked.

"I was actually thinking of trading it in, getting a nice Beamer," Joey said, his eyes on the road.

It was good enough for Erica, who grabbed Neck Tattoo's wrist, forced his hand open flat against the seat, and fired a bullet through the top of it.

"Fuck!" I shouted, clapping a hand against my ear. Joey cursed too and jerked the wheel, but our protestations were mild compared to the screams coming from Neck Tattoo. He clutched his mangled hand with the one that still worked and rocked his body side to side, then back and forth against the pain. The tendons in his neck bulged out like taut violin strings beneath his skin as he wailed, and it became readily apparent that he was not someone used to being tortured.

"Now," Erica said, her voice loud but controlled, refusing to feed into his hysterics, "let's try this again, because we don't have all night, but I do have plenty of bullets and you're full of soft targets." To emphasize her point, she pressed the barrel of her gun against his inner thigh, about two inches below the softest nonlethal target on his or any male body. "What's your name?"

"David," he said, the word coming out in little hitches, like a kid trying not to cry. A stark contrast to the attitude he'd taken as we pulled away from the crash scene, when he was full of the kind of bravado born not from an inherent disposition but from a sense of security that he couldn't be touched. That someone—in this case, Trish and her people—would protect him. Judging by the look on his face, that sense of security had leaked out along with a good amount of blood from the ragged hole in his hand. "David Wheeler."

"Okay David, my friend's going to ask you some of his questions again, only this time you're going to give him straight answers, right? None of that macho, cowboy bullshit like you tried before."

David shook his head vigorously from side to side, his eyes flicking toward the gun in his crotch.

"Rick," Erica said, inviting me to re-open the interrogation.

"Who do you work for?" I asked for the second time since we'd forced him into the back of Joey's car.

"Patricia Baum," he said, snapping his head toward me, and then quickly back to Erica. Probably to make sure she hadn't changed her mind about squeezing the trigger a second time.

"And what about the people above her, do you know who they are?"

"Only . . . only one of them," he stammered. My heart rate ticked up a notch. "Willem. Willem Van de Berg."

Well shit, that's interesting.

"The guy who got kicked out of Parliament?" I said.

David nodded.

"How do you know him?"

"I used to work for him, back when he was in the Senate. Made connections to people he couldn't be seen with in public. I know lots of people. Maybe I can help you out—"

"I know enough people already, Dave. Besides, you clearly aren't very good at your job. Otherwise, Van de Berg would still have a seat in the Palace, wouldn't he?"

"That wasn't my fault!" David said, forgetting about the location of Erica's gun for the first time. "He got greedy. I told him there were too many people I didn't know involved in that deal. If he'd have listened to me, he never would have gotten caught."

"Is that why he brought you along to his new venture with Trish, because he trusts you?"

"I don't know, maybe."

"What is it you do for him now?"

"Same thing. Make connections. Set up deals."

"What kind of deals?"

"Turn here," Erica said. Joey obliged and we disappeared down an unpaved road cutting through an open field. It was more dirt and rocks than flowers and grass. With every bump the pain in my left shoulder flared, sending a million daggers through every nerve ending in the area. It was definitely dislocated, but that was a problem for later. We were miles away from any hospital. The city lights faded behind us, but there was a dull glow coming from somewhere up ahead. Not man-made, though. Almost like the moon, nearly full, was reflecting off of something.

"Everything," David said. "They're into everything."

"Details, Dave," I said. "I need details." To help jog his memory, Erica pushed the gun harder against his thigh.

"I don't know! It's not just the two of them. There are others, but I don't know who they are. I've never met them and Willem never talks about them. Tells me not to ask. The only jobs he ever gives me involve girls."

"You mean like the ones Leon gets for you?"

He nodded. "But not just Leon. We deal with many other distributors."

Distributors. Jesus Christ.

I thought of Maggie and Denise again, of someone treating them like a product to be sold, of referring to the human dogshit that would profit off their abject slavery as a *distributor*, a word far too banal for that type of evil.

My fist broke his nose before I realized it was happening. A backhand, crisp but deliberate. The snap as the bone cracked just above the cartilage was so satisfying I hit it again.

Then again.

Then a fourth time.

I wanted to keep hitting him until he realized how poorly he'd chosen his words, but his face—painted red—and his demolished nose, a great, purple gob of blood-soaked snot hanging from one bulging nostril, stayed my hand.

It was too easy. Shooting Leon's guards, nearly killing Leon himself, beating David Wheeler into a pulpy mess—all too easy, even if I tried to justify it in the name of protecting my family. Ten years spent recruiting people who did this kind of thing for a living and in just under a few hours I'd discovered I had far more in common with them than I had ever believed. If the similarities ran any deeper, I didn't want to know.

"Was it your job to make sure Leon and I were connected?" I asked, my hand and voice both shaking.

"Yes," he said, although it came out muddy and thick. His head bobbed up and down, but it was hard to tell if he was nodding or just trying to keep from passing out.

"Why?"

"I don't know. They just said to make sure I got you two working together without making it obvious."

"Not good enough," I said, then I slapped him across the cheek. It wasn't hard, but with his damaged nose, it must have hurt like hell. "Why did they need us together?" I slapped him again, harder this time, barely giving him time to answer. "Why!"

"I don't know," he said again, only now he was sobbing. It was an ugly, congested sound. "I don't know, I don't know."

Jesus Christ, STOP.

But all I wanted to do was hit him again.

Erica removed her gun from his thigh (at that point, I'm not even sure he knew it was there) and shook her head subtly.

We're not getting anything else out of him, is what she meant.

"Hey guys," Joey said from the front seat, "am I driving through this gate or is there another way in?"

The glow I'd seen came from a limestone quarry. Blue limestone, to be exact, the exposed edges of which had been polished by the wind and rain to such a fine sheen, it glowed, ever so slightly, when the moon hit it right.

"Through," Erica said. "It's only secured by a chain, and only if someone has replaced it since the last time I was here."

Joey gave the little Fiat some extra gas and it split the ten-foot high, barbwire-topped gates with ease. The mouth of the quarry came up quicker than he expected, and we skidded to a stop on the loose dirt leading up to it.

"Get out," I said, dragging David Wheeler from the car. He collapsed onto the ground, sending up a little puff of dirt. I pulled him to his feet, walked him to the edge of the quarry, pulled my gun and pressed it to the back of his head. "Last chance." I cocked the hammer for effect. "Why did Trish want me and Leon working together?"

"I swear to God, I don't know," he blubbered. "They have so many people working for them. They don't tell us anything. Just what they need us to know. Please don't hurt me."

"Tell me!" I screamed. My voice echoed off the steep walls, which dropped over a hundred feet to the shallow pool of water below. I could have used a bullhorn if I'd wanted. The place was long abandoned.

"I don't . . ." he started, but the rest wasn't words as much as it was a nonsense jumble of sounds mixed with hysterical crying. There was nothing left to wring out of him. I lowered my gun.

"Rick," Erica said quietly, "if we let him go . . ."

She didn't need to finish the thought. We were on the same page. But I wasn't crossing that line. I'd already gotten far closer to it than I'd ever thought possible.

"I know," I said.

David's sobs quickly turned to full-fledged, panic-filled screams as Erica raised her boot and kicked him square in the back, launching him over the edge. I kept my back to the quarry, and didn't look when those screams came to an abrupt stop.

"Damn girl," Joey said, peering over the lip, "remind me never to ghost you after a date."

"Who's Willem Van de Berg?" Erica asked.

"He's a senator," I said, grateful for the chance to muffle the echo of David's screams in my head with some dialogue. I holstered my gun, my hand still shaking. "Or at least, he was. Young guy, rose up the ranks fast. Grew up on the streets of Brabant. Classic 'kid from the rough part of town makes good' story. Media ate it up. Except he never really left those streets behind."

"No he didn't," Joey said. "I was always trying to score a meeting with him. Guy rolled deep in the arms trade."

"Got busted a few years ago brokering a deal between one of his connections and the head of an Iraqi militia that Belgium voted not to support. Except his buyer was an undercover VSSE agent, not the militia leader. He was arrested and kicked out of Congress."

"And he's still walking around now?" Erica asked. "How did he get acquitted?"

"He never made it that far," I said. "Died in prison six months after his arrest, awaiting trial. At least, that was the story. Huge headlines here in Belgium. Got decent press in other parts of the world, too. Surprised you didn't hear about it."

"I don't follow the news." Erica took another look over the edge at the remains of David Wheeler. "So you're telling me they faked his death?"

"It certainly appears that way, assuming our buddy Dave was telling the truth about working for him. And if Trish's organization can fake the death of someone that high-profile without anyone catching on, then it means they're even more powerful and well-connected than I thought. Which means they'll be even more motivated to protect their interests and eliminate anyone who they see as a threat. Which means I've got to get to the States, although they'll be watching the airports, so I have no idea how I'm going to do that."

"What's in the States?"

"His family," Joey said before I could stop him.

"Are they in danger?"

"His ex-wife's fiancé has got a hit out on him from these people."

"Joey!" I said. I'd felt he deserved to know what was going on when I called to ask for his help, but was now regretting telling him as much as I did. Erica never asked for a reason when I called her. She just asked for a price.

"What, it's a fucking secret?" Joey shot back.

"It's my mess to clean up, nobody else's. Jesus Christ, you heard what that guy said, they have people everywhere. I already got Ian killed, I don't need anyone else getting hurt because of me."

"That wasn't your fault, Rick."

"Who's Ian?" Erica asked.

"A candidate of mine," I said. Then I corrected myself. "*Was* a candidate of mine."

"What happened?"

"I asked him to do me a favor, same as you two, except he took a bullet to the head for it."

"I'm sorry," Erica said, although there was no sympathy in the sentiment. It was spoken as more of a formality. "Were you close?"

"Not really. It's just . . . Ian was a good kid."

"There are no good people in this business, Rick."

"Whatever," I said, pulling an envelope from my jacket pocket, swollen with $20,000 in cash. It had been earmarked for cheap Mexican hotels and expensive tequila that I would never get to drink. In the same envelope was the plane ticket I bought what seemed like a lifetime ago. Useless now. I counted out $5,000 each for Joey and Erica. They'd earned it. "Thanks for helping me out tonight, but I don't need anything else from either of you."

I held a wad of cash in each hand, and winced as Erica took hers from my left. It was barely strong enough to grip the money.

"Looks to me like you could use one more favor," she said. Then, still holding my hand, she pulled my arm hard toward her. The pain was blinding and only got worse as she manipulated it up and then backward until the shoulder joint popped back into place. I dropped to one knee when she let me go, my right hand pressed against my shoulder, which still hurt like hell but not nearly as bad as before. I took a few breaths as the pain subsided, then got to my feet.

"Thanks," I said, slowly rotating my arm.

She nodded. "Your ex-wife's fiancé, is he a good man?"

"I don't know. Honestly, I don't really care about him. I mean, I do, but I care more about protecting my family. If he's in danger then they may be too. I can't just sit back and do nothing." Then, quieter, "My wife already lost one husband and my kids lost their father. They don't deserve to lose another."

Erica considered that for a moment and then said, "You need to get to the United States, yes?" I nodded. "I may be able to help you with that, too."

"How?"

"I still have some connections from my days with the KSK, could pull some strings," she said, shrugging her shoulders.

"Erica, that would be amazing. Thank you."

"One condition."

"Name it."

"I go with you. Your chivalry is admirable but fucking stupid. You can't possibly do this alone."

I was already shaking my head. "And I can't ask you to get involved. I've already got too many dead bodies on my conscience."

"You're not asking, you're buying."

"What?"

Erica smiled. "You wanted me to do a working interview. Now at least I'll get compensated for it."

It did make sense. I'd walked through every possible course of action in my head, and going to New Jersey to alert Robert personally was the only one that felt right. I couldn't just call him up and warn him. There was no way to guarantee that he'd believe me, and even if he did, the first thing he would do was tell the cops in his precinct. With what I now knew about Trish and her people, it was entirely possible she had somebody close to him, somebody who could walk him right into her crosshairs without raising any red flags. For all I knew, that could have been how she intended to tee him up for Ian.

Showing up in person was the only way to convey the gravity of the situation while also being on hand to make sure he and Denise took all the necessary precautions to stay safe, buying me enough time to figure out a way to call off the hit. Or, worst-case scenario, stop it before it went down.

On the latter point, Erica was right, much as I hated to admit it. I was a recruiter. My job was to find people who were good at pulling the trigger, not pull it myself. My recent foray into violence notwithstanding. This was going to be a lot more complicated than beating up some guy in the back of a car, or kneecapping a couple of cut-rate bodyguards.

"How much?" I asked.

She tilted her head side to side a few times, doing the calculations in her head. "A hundred thousand should do it."

"Shit," Joey said, "if that's the going rate, count me in too."

"Joey," I started.

"Joey what?" he replied. "Cops are already looking for my car anyway. If I'm gonna lie low, might as well do it overseas with a fresh hundred k in my pocket."

Two hired guns WERE better than one.

"They have my account information," I said at last. "If I move that kind of money, they might be watching and see whose accounts I move it into."

"There are ways around that," Erica said, pulling out her phone. In a few seconds, she'd pulled up a cryptocurrency app and held it out to me.

"What the hell is Bitcoin?" Joey said, looking over my shoulder.

"A way for us to get paid without getting caught," Erica said.

"How do you spend it?"

Erica regarded him like he'd just asked her how to program his VCR. "What kind of millennial are you?"

"Early generation."

"Well, don't worry Gramps, I'll show you how to spend your fancy Interwebs money," she said with dripping condescension.

"Kids these days," Joey said, but he was smiling.

I wasn't. I still didn't want them anywhere near this, but I didn't see any better options. My database was brimming with hired guns who would cost the same and had better credentials, but I couldn't trust any of them. If Trish *had* hacked my old phone, there was no way to know who she'd gotten to. And she could outbid me for every one of them.

So I bought two of the ones she didn't know about. A disgraced soldier turned drug dealer who'd fucked up his only attempted kill outside of the service and a former special forces operative who I'd just met and knew very little about. And all it cost me was half of my remaining net worth.

Team Carter, ready to roll.

Pretty sure we were all going to die.

CHAPTER EIGHTEEN

Erica was able to get a hold of her pilot contact, who agreed to fly us out the next day from an empty field an hour from the quarry. We opted to drive there and spend the night in Joey's car versus risking the drive back to her apartment and being spotted. The field was deserted, but to be safe, we took shifts standing watch for anyone who might approach, no matter how slim the odds. I volunteered for the first shift, watching the road we came in on while Erica and Joey slept. Once their breathing slowed to a deep REM rhythm, I pulled my phone from my pocket and stepped outside, opening and closing the door as if it were wired with C4.

All intelligence agencies have a twenty-four-hour tip line. It was automated, of course, but after punching in a few digits, I was transferred to a live person. She sounded bored.

If Sergei was as good as I thought (hoped) he was, then their trace would bounce around a few countries before zeroing in on my location. They wouldn't start it right away, but when they did, I estimated I had two, maybe three minutes, before their ping hit our field. Being outside the city would help, maybe buy me another thirty seconds or so.

"Thank you for calling the MI5 homeland security line. What is the nature of your call?"

"I'd like to report an assassination attempt on two of your agents, David Lofton and Lewis Reed."

That got her attention. "Hold please," she said. The trace was on.

A series of clicks and a new voice picked up. Older, more official. Not a station chief, but the highest ranking officer they could pull in at five a.m.

"Who am I speaking with?" he asked.

"Bugs Bunny," I said. "Your agents are part of a task force involving Yosef and Leah Abram with Mossad, and Nadia Spencer and Frank Portis of the FBI. Something to do with human trafficking, maybe more, I'm not sure. They've all been targeted for elimination." Talking fast but making sure my words were clear.

"How do you know this?"

"I'm the guy who was hired to find the hitters." I heard him snap his fingers at someone walking past his office, who was now on a mad dash to bring others, do whatever they could to pinpoint the origin of my call.

"Who did you put on the contracts?" he asked. "Give me names."

"The one assigned to your agents is dead."

"Who killed him? What was his name?"

"I don't know who killed him and his name doesn't matter. I'm sure the other two have names, but I don't know them. In my line of work, they're referred to as Ghost and The Persian."

Of course I knew their names, but this call was about saving their agents, not getting my people caught. I needed to preserve as much of my reputation as possible, or I'd have my entire roster gunning for me even if I somehow managed to survive my current situation.

There was silence on the other end of the line for a moment, and then he said, "Those two names are legendary in certain circles. Many have heard of them, but few actually know who they are, let alone have worked with them. How do I know you really—"

"Ghost is Asian. He has an L-shaped scar on his chin. The Persian is a female. Persian, obviously. She paints the nail on her trigger finger black, either because she has a flair for the dramatic or she's a big Avril Lavigne fan. Not sure which, but I've always hoped it was the Skater Girl."

I could hear him wet his lips through the phone, along with background rustling that grew louder by the second. There were at least a half dozen other people in the room with him by now, maybe more.

"You can stop stalling," I said. "If you have any kind of dossier on them at all, you know those details check out. You also know that the other four agents are likely already dead, but there's still a chance to save yours. If you move fast enough."

"Who hired you?" he said at last. "Give us some names and we can—"

I hung up and stopped the running stopwatch feature on my phone. It read 3:32. Three minutes, thirty-two seconds. Hopefully that was short enough to keep them guessing. It had to be. I did all I could for David and Lewis.

Next up was calls to the FBI and Mossad. The odds for their agents were not nearly as good, and with Trish's tentacles stretching who knew how far, it was a risk calling any of them at all.

I still had to try, though. Erica was right. There were no good people in this business.

But I wanted to be the first.

CHAPTER NINETEEN

Erica's old KSK buddy turned out to be a gunrunner named Madeline. Bright red hair and the personality to match. Driving in last night, I'd doubted the ability of anyone to land an aircraft larger than a drone in the limited amount of open space before the field ran into the surrounding trees, but Madeline pulled it off with room to spare. Her next run wasn't scheduled until Monday, but she agreed to move it up a few days as a favor to Erica. I tried to offer her the rest of the cash I had on me, but she wouldn't hear of it.

"I owe this one a lot more than an earlier flight," she said, nodding toward Erica, who was emptying a gas canister Madeline gave her all over Joey's car.

"What did she do?" I asked.

"Did you notice my two prosthetic legs?"

I looked down at the pair of brown boots sticking out from beneath the cuffs of her blue jeans. Hard to tell for sure, but based on the way she'd been moving, they certainly *looked* real. "No," I said.

Madeline smiled. "That's because of her," she said, nodding to Erica. "When the IED hit our convoy and the Taliban sniper opened fire on the wreckage where I was trapped inside, my legs pinched between the seat and a jagged, bent piece of smoldering Humvee, she laid down enough suppressing fire to keep the sniper from getting off a clean shot until a chopper could fly in and get us out. Fifteen minutes with no backup. The rest of our team was killed in the explosion. It was just me and her, and I was too busy bleeding out of both thighs to help her do much of anything. It was pitch-black. All she had to go off was his muzzle flash, yet she kept that son of a bitch so pinned down he never came close to hitting us. Used every last bullet we had on us. Ever since that day, if she needs help, I don't ask questions. And I sure as hell don't ask for payment. I still owe her for saving both my legs, not to mention my life."

I looked over my shoulder at Erica, but when I turned back to Madeline for more details, she had started toward the cockpit.

"That ass sure ain't prosthetic," Joey said behind me.

"Shut up, Joey," I said.

Erica struck a match and tossed it onto the car, slick and dripping with airplane fuel. It went up instantly, the windows shattering from the heat by the time she made it to the plane. I gave passing thought to the possibility of the grass and weeds around it going up, spreading to the woods a few hundred yards away, but the ground was damp with dew and remnants of a brief overnight shower. It would be okay. Probably. Besides, I had bigger things to worry about.

"You owe me a new car when we get back," Joey said. "And I want a damn BMW."

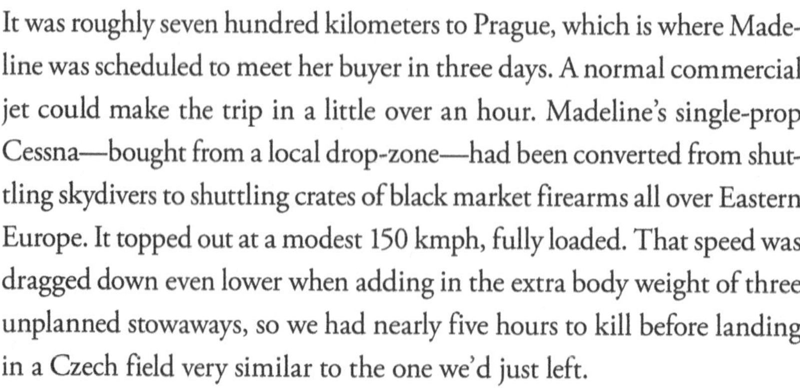

It was roughly seven hundred kilometers to Prague, which is where Madeline was scheduled to meet her buyer in three days. A normal commercial jet could make the trip in a little over an hour. Madeline's single-prop Cessna—bought from a local drop-zone—had been converted from shuttling skydivers to shuttling crates of black market firearms all over Eastern Europe. It topped out at a modest 150 kmph, fully loaded. That speed was dragged down even lower when adding in the extra body weight of three unplanned stowaways, so we had nearly five hours to kill before landing in a Czech field very similar to the one we'd just left.

Part of that time was spent by Erica repairing the two busted stitches in my finger and cleaning the minor cuts and scrapes on my face from my tumble off the motorcycle. If you were thinking that a night of fitful sleep crammed in the backseat of a compact car made my multitude of injuries feel any better the next morning, then I want to live in your world. Are there unicorns and fairies there, too?

Madeline had a standard military field kit on hand and insisted we keep it. Inside the zip-up nylon case was a shiny collection of scissors, needles, sterile wipes, bandages, and sutures. I worried that the motion of the plane would make fixing my finger tricky, but Erica was clearly used to patching up wounds under less-than-ideal circumstances. I was more concerned that some of Leon's blood from his busted nose had found its way into the cuts on my face, and now whatever unholy STD cocktail it contained was currently swirling around my system. Nothing I could do about that, unfortunately, except root hard for my immune system.

T cells don't fail me now.

I thanked Erica, but the rumble of the motor and the rattling of the crates against the metal interior of the cabin made lengthy conversation all but impossible, so I had the remainder of the trip to plot our moves once we reached US soil. Of all the things I'd fucked up in my life, it was crucial that this not be one of them.

Getting there would hopefully be the easy part. I had no doubt Trish had her people—both Interpol and internal—watching every airport, train station and bus terminal within a hundred miles of Brussels. Outside that radius, however, her resources would stretch thin, regardless of how vast they were. It was simply impossible for her to have eyes *everywhere.* (Or so I kept telling myself.) I hoped that buying three tickets to Scranton, Pennsylvania from an airport in the Czech Republic wouldn't attract any undue attention.

I considered flying directly into Philadelphia but opted against it out of an abundance of caution. It wasn't unreasonable to expect Trish to have eyes watching not only my potential points of departure but my destination as well. Scranton to Philadelphia was a two-hour drive, three at the most. Safer and it wouldn't take us too far out of our way. We'd bounce around a few different connecting flights, too. Bury our trail as much as possible without dragging out the flight time longer than necessary.

It was what to do once we arrived in Philadelphia that had me stumped. I knew I needed to find Robert and tell him what was going on. I knew I didn't want Denise and the kids to know I was in the country, no matter how badly the temptation to see them would seep in once I got there. And I knew it would be a matter of days—two, three if we were lucky—before either Ghost or The Persian arrived with their own agenda.

Preventing them from carrying out that agenda was where I was stuck.

Did we tell Robert, and then run? Let him tell the cops in his precinct and hope they could handle it?

Did we convince him that it was best to leave them out of it because A) Trish could have people within their ranks, and B) It was unlikely that even several squads of city cops would matter much whenever Ghost or The Persian made their move?

Would Robert believe me at all, or would he arrest me on the spot and blow everything up before it even got started?

Then there was the darker part of my mind, the one that wondered if Robert was only on Trish's hit list to frame me, or was there another reason. One that tied him more directly to Trish's business and the task force that was investigating it. One that made the threat to Denise and the kids even greater. I told myself that was just the jealous ex-husband coming out, that a homicide detective among a group of covert intelligence operatives would be the Thing That Didn't Belong in the classic *Sesame Street* quiz, but the thought nagged at me all the same.

When we landed fifteen miles outside of Prague, I was no further along in my strategizing than I'd been when we took off. Paralysis by analysis, as my old boss used to say.

We thanked Madeline and I again offered to pay her for the ride. Once more she refused, accepting a long hug and a lingering kiss from Erica instead. It was more than a parting peck between close friends. There was tenderness in it. Intimacy.

"Whoa, wait a minute," Joey said as Erica hiked her bag on her shoulder and walked past us. "Is she—"

I elbowed him in the ribs to prevent whatever juvenile remark that was about to leave his mouth, but he was persistent. I held back so Erica could get a few steps out of earshot and made him lower his voice.

"No wonder you never hit that," Joe said, snickering.

"What's that supposed to mean?"

"She's gay, right?"

"How should I know?"

"You interviewed her, didn't you?"

"Yes, but that's not one of my standard questions," I snapped, already tired of this conversation and almost certain Erica could hear us anyway.

"She pretended to be a man! How do you not ask a follow up question to that?" Joey shouted. I shushed him, then shook my head.

"I did ask a follow up, but—"

"But what," he said at a more respectable volume, "were you afraid the Professional Killers Union was going to sue you for discrimination?"

I started to respond but then decided to quit feeding the beast and began to follow Erica instead.

"Got a Human Resources manual you follow for all your interviews, do you?" Joey mocked as he fell into step behind.

"Please stop talking," I said without turning around. Behind me, Joey laughed, the deep kind, fueled by too much testosterone, that goes well with a beer and inappropriate jokes.

It was a short walk to the nearest town, and then we took an Uber to the airport. Though my head was on a swivel and my blood pressure nestled firmly in the red, we secured our tickets with no more trouble than the people ahead of us or behind us in line. We even had time to grab a late lunch of greasy fast-food burgers and fries in the food court before we boarded. All in all, it was as eventless and boring as a trip to the airport should be. Which, given the way my last trip to the airport ended, was an enormous relief.

We couldn't get three seats together, so I had time alone with my thoughts. The VP of Sales next to me, his paunch swollen large by many an in-flight meal and hotel room service, insulated himself with his laptop and earbuds before we were given the all clear to do so. He slipped his shoes off too, but that was fine. If it made him more comfortable and less inclined to strike up a conversation, I would put up with the smell.

Flight time was estimated at sixteen hours, forty-eight minutes, not including layover limbo. I was college educated and had built a successful career for myself in two drastically different realms of a highly competitive field. Surely I could come up with a logical, realistic plan to protect my family in that amount of time.

Granted, I had never done anything quite like this before, but all it required was some careful thought and consideration. Like chess. Think three moves ahead. I was good at chess.

CHAPTER TWENTY

This was nothing like chess. In chess, if you make a wrong move, you don't catch a bullet between the eyes. And I must have been absent in college the day they taught how to counteract the machinations of two highly trained covert assassins.

And yet, when we landed for our first layover in Paris, I still believed I had the capability to put everything together. I bought a notebook and a pen from one of the airport stores, along with a light gray Marc Anthony button-down and a new pair of blue jeans for $150. Airport markups are criminal. Joey and Erica picked up a change of clothes as well, and we each purchased a small bag to carry our old outfits after changing in the restroom.

Feeling refreshed, I opened the notebook and began jotting down ideas. By the time we landed in Barcelona for our second and final layover, I had a rough outline of a spy thriller that would feel quite comfortable nestled on a shelf at any airport *Hudson News*, but in terms of actionable, usable strategy, it was as unrealistic as the plots in those same thrillers.

We were somewhere over the Atlantic when I first texted Erica, airplane mode be damned. She sat three rows behind me, both of us in the middle section. Joey had the window seat that backed up against the lavatory wall. The barefoot VP from the first leg of our journey had been replaced by a college kid coming home from a semester abroad. At least, based on his age, backpack, and laptop covered with torn and faded stickers of bands I'd never heard of, that was the backstory I'd created for him. We never said more than "Hello" to each other before he covered his ears in a pair of headphones that looked like they cost more than my entire overpriced airport wardrobe.

Help me, I texted.

Oh come on, he's better than the last guy you sat next to, she texted back.

Not that. The plan. I have none.

That's encouraging.

I know.

You really do inspire confidence as a leader.

Hey, I never asked to be a leader, remember? You guys invited yourselves along and somehow got me to fork over $200k for the pleasure of your company.

We're worth every penny.

Start proving it. Help me figure out a way to stop this that only ends in us probably getting killed, instead of guaranteeing it.

Well, first we'll need guns.

That was stating the obvious. I'd gotten that far on my own before hitting a mental brick wall. There are ways to smuggle guns onto commercial flights, but none of them are easy and I wasn't in the mood to tempt fate so early in my suicide mission. None of us were carrying, our weapons all hitching a ride with Madeline, who promised to help them disappear.

I actually have that covered, I wrote.

Great! How?

One of my old candidates just outside Philly.

Is he still active?

I hoped so. It had been nine years since we last spoke, and his number was one of many I'd lost when I snapped my old phone in half. I didn't have it memorized and he wasn't in my cloud database, being of no use to me in Europe. He was strictly a local asset. One of those breadcrumbs I'd tried to sweep away. I knew where he operated, though, and planned to make that our first stop after leaving Scranton.

Yes, I wrote back.

Good. That's a start.

What do we do then? My job has always been to hire people to do this kind of work, not do it myself. Everything I come up with falls apart as soon as I start to pick at it.

Don't beat yourself up. There's no playbook for something like this. Most plans don't hold up entirely to scrutiny. Like everything else, it's all in the execution.

Poor choice of words. ☺

It took two seconds for my cheeks to flush red as I realized I'd just sent a smiley-face emoji to a former special forces operative, and another two seconds for the feeling to fade as I saw the middle finger emoji she sent back.

For the next six hours, we texted. Not constantly, and not always about our plan.

Enough that we each needed to plug our phone chargers into the USB port in the seatback in front of us.

Enough that when the flight attendant asked if I wanted anything to eat or drink, I didn't hear her at first and she had to tap me on the shoulder to get my attention.

Enough that if anyone hacked *this* phone—or Erica's, for that matter—our text thread would lead one to believe that we were old friends. Friends who were also planning what amounted to a double homicide, but whatever.

Bottom line, though: When we landed in Scranton, we had a plan. It was simple. It was direct. It was one of many I had come up with on my own and discarded, but with her seal of approval and critical adjustments, I felt more confident in our chances of success.

Okay, that part's a lie.

I was still pretty sure we were all going to die. But at least I felt assured it wouldn't be because of a shitty plan.

CHAPTER TWENTY-ONE

Like Brussels, the city of Scranton wears its age on its sleeve. Faded brick buildings. Rustic homes that feel lived-in, even if they're new. Nestled in the hills of northern Pennsylvania, in the fall when the leaves turn it takes on the aura of a Washington Irving story. Brussels is bigger by about one hundred thousand people, and more urban. But the two could easily be cousins, if cities shared such genealogy. Brussels the hip, trendy one that country bumpkin Scranton looks up to, but related nonetheless.

I'd visited the small city once before, to meet with a client back in the early days with my old corporate recruitment firm. I spent a night at the Marriott by the airport. Closed the deal, had dinner with my boss at a local bar, enjoyed the complimentary hotel breakfast of pancakes and runny eggs the next morning, and then drove home. Nothing special. One of a thousand memories that had been shoved into the recesses of my mental filing cabinet.

But now, setting foot on American soil for the first time in over ten years, it all came rushing back, in vivid sensory detail. The smell of the chlorine from the pool just off the lobby. The quiet of our footfalls on the carpeted hallways. The sweet, salty taste of the complimentary bacon as it mixed with syrup poured from a tiny plastic tub with a peel-off seal. Strange as it sounded, setting foot in Scranton, PA for only the second time in my life, it felt like coming home.

I wanted a Cinnabon. It was the most American airport food I could think of. Never mind that it was midnight and what few eateries the airport boasted were bound to be closed, I wanted a gooey clump of cinnamon-swirled dough, dripping with sticky icing. I wanted two thousand calories in a single dessert. I wanted a belly full of nostalgia and warm memories.

Alas, there wasn't a Cinnabon to be found, regardless of whether it would be open or not. The three of us were starving, however, so we settled on the one place that was still welcoming guests: an airport bar called the Tipsy Turtle, which just might be the most Scranton name ever.

I ordered a cheeseburger and fries—the second most American meal I could think of—while Joey chose the appetizer sampler featuring potato skins, mozzarella sticks, chicken fingers and onion rings. Not that those same dishes couldn't be had in Brussels, but they weren't the same. Like ordering a pizza anywhere but New York City.

Erica examined the menu the way a nun would read a list of dirty movies before she settled on a cheesesteak sandwich.

"No," I told her before the bartender could write down the order. "Wait until we get to Philly. You'll thank me later."

"Okay," she said, clearly annoyed at needing to scan the list of gastrointestinal nightmares a second time, "I'll have a bowl of French onion soup and a Reuben."

"Good choice," I said.

"I doubt that," she replied.

I ordered a round of beers to hold us over until the food arrived. We were the only three in the place, so it took longer than expected because they had to open the kitchen back up, but in the end it was worth it. If for no other reason than that the comfort food took my mind off the real reason for this homecoming. Ghost and The Persian weren't here—weren't even in America yet, no way—but their presence hung heavy as our footfalls reverberated throughout the near-empty airport on our way to the twenty-four-hour car rental agency.

We checked into the same Marriott as the one I'd bunked in on that unremarkable business trip all those years ago. Erica paid for her own room while Joey and I split one, although I barely saw him. When we passed by the tiny gym off the lobby on our way to the elevators, Joey spotted a twenty-something blonde wearing a pink sports bra and black yoga pants running on the treadmill.

"Can you take my bag up to the room, Rick?" he said. "Think I'm gonna get in a quick workout before bed."

"Oh yeah," I said, taking his backpack, "I hear that's great for jet lag. Just don't plan on working out in *our* room, okay? I'm exhausted."

Joey smiled. "If all goes well, we won't even have to leave the gym."

"You're such a classy guy, Joe."

When I woke up the next morning, Joey was crashed on top of his bed sheets, fully clothed. He grunted when I slapped his foot to wake him up, then wiped his eyes. I asked how he made out with Sports Bra, but he just said, "A gentleman never tells."

"Well since that term has never applied to you, why don't you fill me in?"

"Let's just say you should avoid the lat pulldown machine until the cleaning crew comes by."

"You're like a walking *Penthouse Forum* letter, you know that?"

"Nicest thing anyone's ever said to me, pal."

The complimentary breakfast featured the same pancakes as my first trip, but the eggs were better this time. By ten, we'd checked out and I was behind the wheel of our rented Ford Fusion.

"This guy works on a Saturday?" Joey asked from the backseat as I drove.

"He did nine years ago," I said. "I'm hoping his work-life balance hasn't changed since then."

"And this is our best option, some guy you haven't spoken with in a decade who may or may not still be in the game?"

"We could always stop at Walmart," I said sarcastically. "Fill out a few forms, wait a week or so. I'm sure Ghost and The Persian wouldn't mind taking a time-out until we're ready. They could see the sights. Maybe go visit Amish country or explore Crystal Cave."

"Don't be a dick," Joey said.

"I'm doing the best I can with what I've got, Joe," I said with less edge. "How long until we get there?"

"Couple hours, give or take."

Outside, the world was a dull palette of bare brown trees against a gray, overcast sky. The hills in the distance were still green with pine cover, but they were obscured by an early morning fog that hadn't yet lifted. Rolling farmland and patches of forest interrupted by the occasional housing development unfurled around us.

"It's so open," Erica said. "Not what I expected America to look like at all."

If Scranton is the kind of old town that makes you feel welcome, then Chester is the kind of old town that kicks you in the nuts and spits on you while stealing your wallet. Both are blue-collar—Scranton still has a working coal mine, for Christ's sake—but the blue-collars in Chester all get drunk after work and go looking for somebody to beat up.

While I was forging my new career overseas, they built a stadium for the Union—Philadelphia's MLS soccer team—with the hopes of developing the surrounding area into a thriving business district that people wouldn't be afraid to venture into after dark.

It didn't work. Based on what I saw as I drove past, the streets around the empty stadium were as littered with broken glass and torn garbage bags as every other avenue we'd traversed since entering the city limits.

"Okay, *this* is what I expected America to look like," Erica said as we rounded a corner and saw a homeless man urinating on the burned out husk of what used to be a slightly less-shitty car.

"Reminds me of home," Joey said, with a trace of genuine nostalgia in his voice.

"Where is home?" Erica asked.

"Benton Harbor, Michigan."

"Rick?" she said.

"Yes?"

"Do not ever take us to Benton Harbor, Michigan."

"Wonder if my dog's still alive," Joey said, almost to himself. Erica and I exchanged a glance in the rearview mirror.

"Your dog?" I asked.

He snapped his head around, as if surprised he'd spoken the words aloud. "Yeah," he said, sounding embarrassed. "She was seven when I left home, but still acted like a puppy, you know? I miss that dog. Probably long gone. She'd be damn near twenty now."

"Can't you ask your parents?" Erica said.

"We're not exactly on speaking terms."

We let that sit for a moment before I said, "What was her name, the dog?"

"Tinkerbell."

Erica tried to hold in her laugh, but it came snorting out from between her pressed lips.

"What?" Joey asked, defensive. "Big tough guy can't have a dog named Tinkerbell?"

"No, it's fine," Erica said, the giggles still just below the surface. "It's a very pretty name for a dog."

"And she was a very pretty dog. Beautiful collie mix. Best dog I ever owned."

"I'm sure she was," I said. "And hey, if she did pass away, maybe you can clap your hands together real hard and she'll come back to life."

That did it. Erica burst out laughing and I joined in right behind her.

"Fuck you and fuck you," Joey said, pointing to both of us in turn. "If she is alive, I'm going to have her bite your balls off, Rick."

We were still laughing when we pulled up to a scrap yard situated on the banks of the Delaware River. PPL Stadium loomed large just a few blocks away. Towering over it all was the Commodore Barry Bridge, a blue-gray relic from the '70s that was the perfect vessel to transition drivers from the bucolic farmland of South Jersey to the grit and grime of Chester, PA.

A lighted sign, the boxy kind that you can slide black plastic letters onto and off of, stood over the entrance to the parking lot. The top-right corner of the white background behind the letters was missing, the victim of a rock, bullet, or some other late-night projectile. The letters remained untouched, however, and spelled out *Enzo's Scrap*, just as it had the last time I was there. The guard booth a few feet into the lot was still there too, its white paint even more chipped and faded than the last time I'd driven up to it. Appropriate since "chipped and faded" could also describe the skin of the guard inside.

"We're here to see Frank. Is he working today?" I asked as we pulled up.

"Yeah, he's in the back of the warehouse somewhere," the old guy growled.

His voice sounded like rocks being jostled inside a paper bag. I remembered it well. He clearly didn't remember me.

"Just park anywhere?" I asked. He nodded and pressed a button that lifted the red-and-white striped wooden arm blocking our path. I thanked him and drove through.

"He didn't even ask to see ID," Joey mused.

"He didn't even ask your name," Erica elaborated. "What is his purpose, exactly?"

"To collect a paycheck and avoid his wife more than anything," I said as I pulled into a spot by the trailer that served as Enzo Moroni's office. "But, unless there's been a change in corporate policy, there's a shotgun in that guard booth strapped underneath a small counter and pointing roughly head level at the driver of any car that pulls up. The old guy—Cliff, or something like that—doesn't like what he sees, he has permission to pull the trigger and ask for forgiveness later."

"Who would want to rob a scrapyard?" Erica asked as we got out of the car. "Nobody," I answered. "But there's a lot more than scrap metal being processed here."

We entered through an open bay door where a forklift idled and immediately were hit with familiar warehouse smells. Oil, grease, and the faint musk of accumulated dirt. The weekend skeleton crew was in, so we passed unabated through aisles of metal shelving stacked high with everything from engine blocks to copper wiring to rusted backyard grills. At the opposite end was another open bay door that led to the yard where they took in larger items like cars, riding mowers, HVAC units, etc. Just before we passed through it a voice called to us from the end of the aisle to our right.

"Can I help you?"

The years had not been kind. His hair, thin and gray when last I saw him, had been reduced to a few strands clinging to a blotchy scalp through a sheer act of will. He wore glasses with simple frames, but the lenses looked thicker. Denim jacket over a flannel shirt. Blue jeans and steel-toed boots that had seen better days. I was pretty sure it was him, but just to be safe I said his name as a question, rather than a greeting.

"Frank Cochran?"

"That's me. If you have something to scrap you gotta bring it around front first so we can check it in, then we'll take it out back and weigh it."

I walked up to him so his thick lenses could do their work.

"Been a long time," I said. It took him a minute, but slowly his expression melted from confusion into recognition.

"Rick!" he said, and the smile wiped all nine years off his face. He took my hand and shook it like a long-lost uncle. "How the hell have you been? Where have you been? Are you home for good?"

I smiled right back—it was impossible not to—and clapped my other hand over his. "It's good to see you too, Frank."

"And who do we have back here, this your new lady friend?" He looked over my shoulder and winked as Erica and Joey approached.

"No, these are some business associates of mine." He shook hands with both of them, too, and said it was nice to meet them. "We've got some shopping to do."

The smile remained, but it thinned slightly and the eyes narrowed. It was the smile of a salesman smelling a fresh lead. Seventy-whatever years old and the guy still loved his work. Gotta admire that.

"What did you have in mind?" he asked.

The scrapyard was an open field of dirt and weeds with piles of junk metal sprouting from it like acne. There was no rhyme or reason to it, no discernible organization to the stacks. Some were nothing but heaps of jagged leftovers from a dozen different construction projects. Some had washing machines mixed with old piping mixed with kids' bicycles. It was an unalphabetized CD collection, a toddler's room with no parental supervision. It was a mess. And it was all intentional.

The washing machine with the scratch on the lid in the shape of a W? That one was filled with bricks of opium. The gas grill with blue spots of paint flecked on its red lid? Inside, beneath the cooking grates, a folder stuffed with stolen credit cards. And the 1984 Buick Regal sitting on cinder blocks with no wheels and a cracked windshield? Inside the trunk, under a false bottom, were half a dozen semiautomatic rifles. A Cadillac in another pile hid some handguns. The saddle bags of a beat-up Harley were loaded with C4. Frank showed us everything like a jeweler pulling out engagement rings from a glass case.

"You always had the best stuff, Frank," I said, dropping a brick of plastic explosive back into a leather saddle bag.

"Clean, too," he said with pride. "Practically like buying them off the rack."

"Except without all that messy paperwork."

He scrunched up his face. "Filling out forms gives me carpal tunnel, and besides, it's bad for the environment. Think of all the trees I'm saving."

"We all have to do our part," I agreed.

"So what'll it be?"

"I still qualify for the friends and family discount?"

"Oh I think we can work something out," he said with a wry grin.

"Great. We'll take one of the Berettas, the HK P30 and a Glock 19 for me. Two boxes of ammo for each."

"Going light, huh?"

"For now, at least."

On the plane, Erica and I had talked about the best way to arm ourselves. While strapping up with Uzis and rocket launchers might have given us a greater sense of security, in practical terms it wasn't necessary. Our primary objective was to protect Robert and my family while deterring Ghost and The Persian, not engaging in a full-blown firefight with them. If the latter was unavoidable, however, it was bound to happen quickly. And unless we planned to patrol the streets of my old neighborhood like extras from an Arnold Schwarzenegger movie, one pistol each was the easiest way to remain prepared yet inconspicuous.

"Well, you know where to find me if you change your mind," Frank said as he went back to the rusted out Caddy to fetch our orders.

If only changing my mind were an option, old friend.

We settled up in the trailer office. Enzo didn't work weekends, so Frank had full run of the place. He offered us coffee but we declined. In the end, I paid $2,500 for all three pieces, which was the equivalent of a Buy Two, Get One Free sale. Frank always knew how to treat the people who kept his bread buttered. Besides, I'd made him enough money over the years to pay for the free gun fifty times over.

Handing over the cash canceled out all the warm homecoming feelings I'd been having since we landed, though. It made things real. We weren't gearing up to go pop off at some paper targets or clay pigeons; these weapons were bought with the express purpose of killing people. Two of them, to be exact. Both of whom were far better at that particular skill than any of us.

Joey tucked the Beretta into his duffel bag with the same nonchalance as when he'd packed his socks before we left Brussels. Erica checked the sites on her HK in a manner that suggested it was but one step of a routine she had gone through many times before. I tucked the Glock in my waistband without checking anything. Placing the order was where my expertise ended. From here on out, I was a rookie climber on an Everest expedition. As I put the boxes of ammo in Joey's bag, I realized Frank was talking to me but I hadn't been paying attention.

"I'm sorry?" I said.

"I was just wondering if you had any work for me, now that you're back."

I smiled. "I'm not really back, Frank. Just a business trip. Besides, it looks like you're doing okay."

"Oh sure," he said, waving a hand. "Can't complain, especially at my age when you don't need much to be happy. But you always found me the best jobs, Rick. Paid good and were exciting, too."

"It's what I do."

"And you do it well." We shook hands. I tried not to convey how badly I wanted what he intended as a compliment to not be true. But deep down, just like after I'd read about the double hit Ian did for Leon, a part of me couldn't help swelling up a bit.

Everyone likes being recognized for a job well done, even if they hate the job itself. I thanked him again and the three of us started back toward our car. After a few steps, he called after me, so I stopped and turned.

"This business trip of yours," he said "You're just being overly cautious, right? Not like you to start mixing it up." He gestured toward the new, clean Glock beneath my coat.

"You know me, never can be too careful."

"I hope that's all it is."

I smiled. "See you around, Frank." He waved and I turned back, my stomach suddenly very unhappy with the Marriott's continental breakfast. In one final act of misguided hope, I pulled out my phone and opened the chat rooms where I communicated with Ghost and The Persian. After we landed in Scranton, as we taxied to the jetway, I tossed a Hail Mary, texting both of them individually, asking them to reach out. No context. No desperate plea. Nothing to indicate that I knew both I and my family had likely been added to their contracts. Just three simple words:

Can we talk?

Neither had responded. It had been foolish to even entertain the notion that they would. Still, those three unanswered words spoke volumes.

There would be no eleventh-hour reprieve. This was real now.

CHAPTER TWENTY-TWO

Step One of our master plan was complete. We were armed, but the playing field was far from level. Yes, we knew they were coming so technically had the element of surprise, but how useful was that when the people you're surprising were experts at not being seen? Despite the new gun pressed against the small of my back—my third in as many weeks—I wasn't exactly brimming with confidence. Making matters worse was that Step Two involved us splitting up, and that called for a massive leap of faith on my part.

We stopped at an Enterprise in a small town just over the Jersey side of the bridge from Chester. Joey rented a Honda minivan that would be practically invisible on my old suburban street. In the parking lot, I shook both their hands and thanked them.

"We got them covered, Rick. Don't you worry about it," Joey said as he slid behind the wheel. I'd given him my old address for the GPS. It was a short, ten-minute ride away. I'd passed by this Enterprise branch a thousand times before, in fact. There was an ice cream parlor down the road the kids used to love. Many a summer night was spent at a table in their small outdoor patio, licking the sprinkles off a cone filled with soft-serve, watching the cars roll by on Route 45, listening to the crickets chirp in the field behind the parking lot.

"I know," I said, but there must have been more of a tremor in my voice than I thought because he grabbed my arm before I could walk away.

"Hey," he said, "I mean it. First time in my life since I left the military, I'm getting paid to do something positive. It feels good. Nobody's gonna touch your family, Rick. Believe that. Just let those motherfuckers try."

I gripped his hand and nodded but didn't say anything. I wasn't sure I could. It was all hitting me in a big way.

I walked Erica around to the passenger side and pulled a picture from my wallet. Normally, it stayed in my hidden apartment safe next to my emergency cash and passports, but I'd taken it along with everything else for my trip to Mexico that wasn't to be. Folded into fours, its edges rumpled and worn white, it showed Denise and our kids sitting on the front step. She had her arms around them, Ethan at two years old on the left and Mags at seven on the right. All three were smiling the smiles of people without a care in the world.

We're content and we're happy, those smiles said. *We have all we need right here.*

It was Mother's Day. I had just surprised Denise with a gold necklace with her birthstone—a diamond—in the middle. The kids' stones, amethyst and pearl, hugged it. The diamond was not small, and the necklace was legit 14k gold, not the cheap spray-painted silver stuff that filled her jewelry box from past Mother's Days, birthdays, and Christmases. It was as much a gift for me as it was for her.

Not quite one year earlier, we had stayed up late into the night wondering how we would make our next mortgage payment. With the country mired in its worst recession in eighty years and nobody hiring at all, let alone paying someone to help them do it, my income had dwindled from a trickle to a slow, agonizing drip. Barely enough to keep the lights lit and food on the table.

But I'd fixed that. The necklace was my way of proving to her that I would keep the promise I'd made the day I proposed—when we were barely out of college and full of big dreams and bigger naïveté—to always take care of her. She'd questioned how we could afford such a gift. Our account was joint and, as far as she knew, had improved over the last few weeks but not enough to justify such luxuries. She didn't know about the other account I'd opened. It was the first of many lies.

I'd told her not to worry about it and clipped the chain closed around her neck while she held up her mass of curly brown hair with one hand. The kids were there and beaming. I'd taken them to the store and let them pick out the setting and their own individual birthstones, telling them all along how surprised Mommy would be, how she would love it so much she would cry. With them there, I knew she wouldn't press the issue any further, even though I'm sure she still had questions about where the money came from. Denise always worried about our finances. It was why I handled the bills and banking, which was how I was able to open additional bank accounts without her knowledge.

When she asked again that night as we lay in bed, both kids sound asleep, I gave her the same answer and silenced her follow up question with a long, deep kiss. The kiss turned into more and we never spoke of the necklace again. After so many lean months, it must have felt wonderful to wear tangible proof that things were finally turning around. I wanted a reminder of that feeling too, so I printed out the picture of her and the kids on the steps with the intention of putting it in a frame.

Ten days later I walked out my front door for the last time. I'd taken the picture and left behind my wedding ring. If I had my way, I wouldn't be walking back in. I hadn't earned that right.

"Keep them safe, okay?" I said to Erica, handing her the picture. I felt water fill my eyes and bit the edges of my tongue to keep it from spilling out.

"Nobody touches them," she said. My voice caught in my throat, so the best I could do in response was nod. She looked at the picture carefully, then put it back in my hand. "You keep this. I know what they look like."

Then she got in the van, shut the door, and they drove away.

Robert Baglioni was a homicide detective in the 3rd District. I tried calling him at the precinct on the off chance he was working on a Sunday, but wasn't surprised when I was told he wasn't. I politely informed the operator that I did not wish to leave him a voicemail.

The next call I made was to my old house line. I'd waited about forty-five minutes to give Erica and Joey a chance to drive there and get set up for their stakeout. If Denise or one of the kids answered, I would've hung up. My cell number was blocked, so they wouldn't be able to *69 me. This was assuming the house line was still in existence, or that anyone bothered to answer it anymore if it was. Ten years ago, land lines were already well on their way to extinction. The only reason we'd kept ours was so that we had a working phone in case of a power outage. Now, with most land lines running through a modem, even that one useful function had been removed.

On that cold, gray Sunday, though, I got lucky. Not only was the line still active—and still the same number as when I'd lived there—but Robert answered the phone on the third ring.

"Hello?" he said, and suddenly I was mute. I tried to respond but the words were like taffy in my mouth.

"Hello?" he said again, and I knew I had about two seconds before he hung up, thinking I was just one more person calling about extending his car's warranty, wondering why he even bothered to answer the damned thing in the first place.

"Detective Baglioni?" I said. It didn't come out sounding as strong and self-assured as I wanted, but just speaking was a victory at that point.

"Who is this?" The frustrated weariness of his previous tone was gone, replaced by straight up anger. "How did you get this number?"

"I got it from memory, Robert. It used to be mine."

There was silence on the other end, but I could hear him walking from one room to the other. I wondered if they were still using the old white cordless phone we hung in the kitchen by the laundry room. Then a door clicked shut on the other end of the line and he said, "Who is this?" Only this time, the anger was mixed with genuine curiosity.

"It's—"

I almost said Rick but caught myself. He had no idea who Rick Carter was. "—Ben. Ben Williams."

I'd played this scene in my head several times. In none of the run-throughs was his reaction pleasant. Nor was it indifferent, but to my surprise, that's exactly what I got.

"What do you want?" is what he said, almost like he'd been expecting my call. When my stunned silence drug on, he followed up with, "Do you want to talk with Denise? Because that's not going to happen."

"No," I managed. I had been gearing up for a fight and got a casual brush off instead. I didn't have a script ready for that.

"Who then, Mags? Sorry, champ, you missed her birthday by about a month."

Oh I didn't miss it, I thought. *I bought her a card. One with a horse, because they were always her favorite animal. Filled it out, signed it Love, Dad and everything. Then sealed it in an envelope and threw it in the trash. Just like I've done every year since she turned eight. And in four months, I'll do the same for Ethan. Champ.*

What I said instead was, "Actually, Robert, I wanted to talk to you."

"Oh really? What could you possibly have to say to me that I'd be interested in hearing?"

I took a shot. "Frank Portis and Nadia Spencer."

I could hear the names land, like two bombs from an empty sky.

"You've got my attention," he said. The bored tone was gone.

So you are *involved in this somehow. God damn it, I hate it when that dark part of my mind is right.*

"Not over the phone," I said. "Colonial Diner. One hour."

"How do you know those names?"

"Alone."

"Tell me how—"

I hung up.

And immediately called Erica.

"I gave him an hour," I said. "Let me know when he leaves and if he's with anyone."

"Want us to follow him?" she asked.

"No, stay with Denise and the kids." I doubted either Ghost or The Persian was in the country yet, but I couldn't be sure. If either was, I'd rather have my family protected than me and Robert.

"How's Joey been treating you?" I asked. "He can be a lot to take."

"I've dealt with worse."

"I bet you have," I said, thinking of her former Nazi-loving CO. "Where is Joey, by the way? It's awfully quiet."

"He stepped out of the car to talk to his girlfriend."

Sports Bra? Please tell me he didn't give some random one-night stand his phone number.

"Nice to know he's focused on the task at hand," I said.

"I told him it was fine. I could keep my eyes on them for a minute without his help."

I swallowed and heard a click in my throat. "Did you see her?"

"Your ex-wife? Yes, briefly."

"How did she look?" I asked, because I hate myself and enjoy being in pain, apparently.

I could feel Erica cycling through possible answers on the other end of the line. "She looked safe," she said at last, taking the cop-out route. I was grateful for it.

CHAPTER TWENTY-THREE

The Colonial Diner is quintessential New Jersey. In a state known for its all-night diners, this one hits every mark.

Stone façade with dark glass windows? Check.

Parking lot that's way too small for its total occupancy? Check.

Bar in the back serving watered down cocktails and light beer? Check.

Servers that all look like they either just extinguished or are about to light up a cigarette? Check.

Booths with fake leather cushions that are cracking and bite into your legs in the summer when you're wearing shorts? Check.

AMAZING food and coffee that could power a nuclear submarine? Of course.

Denise and I used to take the kids there once a week for dinner, although for me it was "dinner" in name only. A true Jersey diner aficionado knows you only ever order breakfast food when you're in such an establishment. I liked to mix it up—waffles one day, steak and eggs another—but my go-to was the scrapple omelet.

Scrapple is a brick of mushed up meat mixed with cornmeal. Originally concocted by German settlers outside Philadelphia in the eighteenth century but adapted by the Pennsylvania Dutch into the artery-clogging perfection it is today, the meat comes from the parts of a pig even the pig didn't want anymore. The kind of ingredients you don't list to someone who's never tried it when you actually want them to take a bite. It's seared to a crispy golden brown on the outside, but remains warm and gooey in the middle. I could eat it by the pound, assuming I didn't want to live to see fifty. Denise and the kids thought it was trash on a plate.

The Colonial mixed generous hunks of the stuff into a three-egg omelet with green peppers and onions. It might be the most perfect breakfast dish ever conceived. I hadn't had one in over a decade, and it called to me from the menu. It took more willpower than I anticipated to tell the waitress all I wanted was black coffee when she came to take my order. I was not looking forward to the conversation I was about to have, and if I was going to enjoy one of my favorite meals for the first time in a long time, I didn't want to worry about having to fight to keep it down right after I ate it.

I was on my second cup when Erica called from outside my house and told me Robert had left.

"Anyone with him?" I asked.

"Not right now, anyway. Sure you don't want us to follow?"

"No, thanks. I'll be fine."

I had a booth by the wall of windows overlooking the sidewalk leading from the always-full parking lot to the front door. I'd never seen Robert Baglioni before in my life—Denise had never posted a single picture, and I'd kept the promise I made to myself not to use my connections to dig up info on him—but when he walked past me on his way inside, I knew it was him right away. I assumed he knew what I looked like from old photos, the asshole husband who abandoned his wife and kids. He scanned the room from the small waiting area by the hostess podium before he found me.

He was shorter than me, but a lot of guys are. His hair was jet black and thick on his head. Longer than mine, but still professional. It hung just past the tops of his ears and almost to his shoulders in the back. He was clean shaven, but the first sprouts of five o'clock shadow were starting to show. He wore a black leather jacket over a plain gray thermal shirt and blue jeans. His badge hung from a beaded chain around his neck.

I was very aware of the gun holstered on his belt. Not that he would put me down in the middle of the diner like a sheriff in an old-timey western but . . . let's just say I was aware of it. Whatever bored annoyance existed when he first answered the phone—whether real or an act he put on to show how little he thought of his fiancée's ex-husband—was gone. He was in full cop mode now, and he wanted me to know it.

He slid into the booth seat across from me and set his arms on the table hard enough to ripple the coffee in my mug.

"Thanks for coming," I said. "I would have ordered you something, but I didn't know what you'd—"

"How the fuck do you know those names?"

Right to it, then.

"I know a few more names, too," I said. "David Lofton and Lewis Reed."

"Those mean nothing to me."

"What about Yosef and Leah Abrams?"

"No. Tell me about Frank and Nadia." He punctuated both of their names with a finger stab on the table. My coffee rippled some more. "How do you know them?"

"I don't. I only know *of* them. They're FBI agents working as part of a task force. The other four are agents from MI5 and Mossad. They're part of the task force, too." This was progressing a lot quicker than I anticipated. I expected more time spent on how I was a scumbag who ran out on my family and couldn't be trusted. Some measure of suspicion over my true motives for being here, or how I heard those names in the first place. Robert wasn't in the mood to dick around, though. I had to make sure the conversation didn't get away from me.

"How do you know all this?" he asked. "What, did you get caught up in some bad shit with the Feds? They got you in witness protection? Is that why you ran out on Denise?"

There was the shot I was expecting, tacked on at the end.

"Believe me, I'm the furthest thing from a snitch."

"Then what, an agent? Undercover?" He waved his hand. "Bull SHIT."

"How do you know Frank and Nadia?" I asked, trying to wrestle the wheel away from him.

He sat back. A spring creaked as he leaned against the booth. Chewed on his bottom lip. Let his hands fall to his lap. Then shook his head. "Nope." He put his hands on the edge of the table as if he was planning to stand up. "We're not having this conversation here. If you want to talk, we're doing it on the record, down at the station. Let's go."

He started to slide out of the seat but I said, "They're dead." And boy, if ever I felt like I was about to be the victim in an old-timey western shootout, that was it.

"What do you mean?" he said. His hands were still on the table, but it was a short trip to that gun.

"I don't know for sure, but the odds aren't in their favor. When was the last time you spoke with them?"

"Two days ago. We did our regular Friday debrief call. Unless you want to walk out of here in handcuffs, you better start talking."

I had already made up my mind that I was going to tell him the truth. That was the whole reason I made this trip. But there were many truths, and he didn't need to know all of them.

"Two more names," I said. "Ghost and The Persian. Do they mean anything to you?"

He shook his head. "No. They sound like something out of a comic book."

"Oh they're very real. And very dangerous. Ever hear of The Jackal?"

He thought for a minute. "Yeah. Professional assassin back in the '70s, right? Didn't they make a movie about him?"

"They did. And one day, they might make one about these two."

"So they're hired killers."

"They're *the best* hired killers. And one of them, I don't know which, was paid a million dollars to take out Frank and Nadia."

His eyes probed mine. The Colonial suddenly felt very much like a tight, dingy interrogation room. "Prove it," he said.

"You have their numbers? Call them."

"I don't have their numbers. Our calls are all arranged through their section chief."

Why are you having weekly debrief calls with two undercover FBI agents, Robert?

"Great, call him. See if he's heard from them since Friday."

His eyes were still probing but they lacked direction. They weren't sure exactly what they were looking for anymore. And he didn't like it.

Our waitress came around and asked if he needed anything. "I'm fine, thanks," he told her without looking up. She topped off my coffee without asking and moved along to her next table.

"How do you know all this?" he asked.

"Why did Denise tell you I left?" I countered, dodging his question yet again.

He laughed. A derisive snort full of disdain. "She doesn't know. Said you just up and left them in the middle of the night. Things had been bad at your job for a while, but they were getting better. Which is why she still can't figure why you disappeared. *I* say she shouldn't waste time worrying about the actions of a lowlife scumbag who would abandon his family for no reason."

I took the jab. I deserved it. "Without going into detail, she's right. Things did get bad at my job, and then yes, they did get better. Mostly because I started doing some side work for clients that weren't very happy when I tried to stop. So my side business kept growing, well past the point where it was just paying the bills. And the more it grew, the more danger it put Denise and the kids in. I couldn't live with that possibility, and I was in too deep to pull out, so I left."

"Jesus, Ben, what kind of side business did you get into?"

"Let's just say I don't hang around with the best people. My boring desk job that dried up taught me how to network and I've got a lot of connections back where I come from. Lots of little birdies telling me lots of little secrets all the time. And one of them tipped me off to the hits on your pals with the FBI and the others. Six agents, all doing deep cover work throughout Europe." I licked my lips. "Plus one more, here in the US."

"Who?"

I stared at him.

It didn't take him long. And when he figured it out, his first reaction was fear.

It was just a flash, quickly buried and replaced by a steely look of total control that they must teach to all rookies in the academy. But the fear was there. Out in the open like a deer before it darts into the woods once it realizes it's been seen.

He's thought about this. However he's involved, someone told him that a bullseye on his back was a real possibility, and it's kept him up at night.

"I need to know, Robert," I said, leaning across the table. "What is your connection to all of this? In a task force full of spies and federal agents, a homicide cop from Philly doesn't fit. Why would someone pay a million dollars to have you killed?"

"That was the price for me too?" He sounded both shocked and a little proud.

"You and two others. The MI5 agents. Except the hitter who picked up your contract got himself killed before he could get started, so you've got some time. Not much, because one of the other two is surely on their way to finish the job, assuming they're not here already."

"You mean one of the top two professional hitmen on the planet?"

"That's right. Do you have any idea why?"

"I need to call Jeff," he said, standing up.

"Who's Jeff? Is he the FBI section chief?"

He looked down at me. "Why did you come here to tell me this in person? Why not just tell me over the phone?"

"If you're in danger, then that means Denise is too. So's Maggie. So's Ethan." I let that sink in. "I needed you to know I wasn't just some asshole calling to fuck with you. Figured face-to-face made a stronger statement."

And I needed to make sure whatever you did after I told you didn't put my family in any more danger than they already are.

"Sitting here doesn't make you any less of an asshole," he said.

"No it doesn't. But I'm not fucking with you, Robert. And I need you to take me seriously."

"I oughta arrest you right now."

"For what?"

We stared at each other. I couldn't read him. If he made a move, I would too, and things had the potential to get real ugly, real fast. My Glock was tucked into the back of my pants. I wouldn't shoot him—the whole point was *not* to get him killed—but I damn sure wasn't leaving in handcuffs.

He blinked first. Rapped the table with his knuckles twice and shoved his finger in my face. I let him. "Stay away from my family," he said. Then he left.

I was glad I didn't order the scrapple omelet.

CHAPTER TWENTY-FOUR

"Went that well, huh?" Joey said.

"About what I expected," I said into the phone. I was sitting in The Colonial's parking lot, watching the traffic light change from green to yellow to red and back again. "He knew the names of two agents on the hit list, so he's involved in the task force. I just don't know how or why. Or what the fuck the damn task force was even investigating, for that matter, other than that it scared the shit out of Trish. And she doesn't strike me as someone who scares easily."

"So what now?" Joey asked.

"Now we wait. And we watch. I'll follow Robert to work tomorrow—"

"You mean to a police precinct crawling with cops."

"Yeah, it'll be fun," I said, wondering exactly how the hell I planned to pull that off. "You guys will need to split up. Rent another car for Erica, but use a different branch this time."

"We should have asked if Enterprise has a reward card. At this rate, we're two rentals away from getting a freebie."

"Get another boring one," I said, ignoring his joke. "Nothing flashy. A four-door sedan or an SUV. Have Erica tail Denise and Mags to the high school, and follow Ethan to the middle school. Unless you're too busy talking to your girlfriend."

"What?" The question came out too high-pitched and stretched out, like a teenager who's been caught in a lie and is stalling to think up an excuse.

"Erica said you stepped out of the car earlier to take a call from some girl. Do me a favor and manage your little black book on your own time. I didn't pay you a hundred grand to take booty calls while you're on the clock."

What started out as a ball-busting one liner had quickly escalated into genuine anger on my end. It caught me by surprise, but I was powerless to stop it. I felt my blood pressure rising with each word. To his credit, Joey didn't punch back.

"Rick, look, I'm sorry man," he said, in the most pacifistic tone I'd ever heard him use. "She's just some crazy bitch I met at a bar a few nights before we left Brussels. We hooked up, and she hasn't left me alone since. I only took the call because she was blowing up my phone and I wanted to express to her in no uncertain terms that I couldn't deal with her bullshit right now. I wasn't neglecting your family, I promise."

"I know," I said, rubbing my eyes. The pounding in my ears subsided and I could feel the color drain from my cheeks. "Erica said she gave you the okay anyway, that she had it covered. I didn't mean to snap, it's just . . ."

"Hey, we've got them," he said, filling the silence after I trailed off. I nodded, even though I knew he couldn't see me.

"Where will you be tonight?" he asked.

"There's a motel a few miles down the road," I said, composing myself. "I'll crash there. I'd invite you guys to join me, but . . ."

"No worries, man, we get it. Won't be my first overnight stakeout. Erica and I will take shifts, we'll be cool."

"Thanks."

I sat for a few more minutes after we hung up, watching the light go through its cycles. Then I started the car and was in the motel's parking lot within ten minutes. They were only at about half capacity and had plenty of rooms available. Part of that was the time of year—early March in a small South Jersey town is far from prime tourist season—but the other part, most likely the biggest part, was that the motel looked like the kind of place you stayed at if you wanted to get raped and murdered in your sleep.

There were fifteen rooms in an L-shaped row. No second floor. The sign out front alternated between spelling out MOTEL and MOT L as the pink, neon E blinked in and out of its death throes. I was in the room closest to the rental office, debating whether or not the risk of contracting an STD was higher if I slept on top of the bed sheets or beneath them, when Erica sent me a text.

It was a picture of my old house. The house where I carried Denise across the threshold, through a door that still displayed a knocker with the previous owners' name engraved on it. In all the years we'd lived there, we never took it down. My parents bought us a new one with our name on it as a housewarming gift, but it was smaller and the screw holes from the other one were visible no matter where we tried to hang it.

Rather than spackle over them and repaint the door, we just decided it was easier to be the Whiteheads. At least to anyone who actually read the engraving on door knockers.

It was the house we paid about $50,000 too much for because we bought it before the real estate bubble burst. By the time I left, it still hadn't recouped its original value.

It was the house where both of my children were born.

The house where Denise and I made love on the floor one Christmas Eve night while the kids slept upstairs.

The house where Denise and I adopted a shepherd-Lab mix named Sandy that was like a third child to us. She was twelve years old when I left, and likely long gone by now. Just like Joey's Tinkerbell.

The large evergreen against the front corner by our bedroom window was also gone, replaced by the wraparound porch Denise always wanted but I never gave her.

We didn't need it and it's too expensive, I'd said. It wouldn't have surprised me at all to learn Robert built it himself, with his rough, masculine hands, whereas I needed an hour to fix a leaky toilet tank and would still screw it up somehow.

The lawn looked good—I was always able to take care of that—but the roof was new and there was an addition over the garage that probably pushed the overall value to what we paid for it in 2002.

Parked at the curb, in front of our black, plastic mailbox that also looked the same as the one I remembered, was a police car with a Pennsylvania license plate. It was getting dark, but you could still discern the outlines of two figures through the back window.

Looks like Robert took you seriously enough to call for protection, read the accompanying message.

Good, I wrote back. Not that I thought a couple of beat cops fresh from the academy would stand a chance should Ghost or The Persian come calling, but at least it meant Robert didn't brush me off. There was always the chance Trish had in fact gotten to people in Robert's precinct, but that's why I had Joey and Erica there. *When did they arrive?*

About 5 minutes ago.

Where are you now?

Down at the end of the street. There are several parked cars and one large tree blocking their view of us but we can still see anyone who comes or goes from your front door.

Excellent. Keep me posted.

We will. It's nice here. Peaceful. Reminds me of where I grew up.

Where is that, exactly? I still can't peg your accent.

That's because I don't want you to. 😉

They say it's bad to keep secrets in a relationship.

Good thing you and I are just business partners, then. Poker rules. You want me to show my cards? Kick in an extra $10k.

Is it Poland?

No.

Hungary.

No.

Cleveland?

Goodbye, Rick.

I set the phone down on the desk across from the bed and connected it to its charger, which I plugged into a strip of electrical sockets running horizontal along the wall. I had a cheesesteak, fries, and Diet Coke delivered from the nearby pizza place and remembered that I owed Erica her first real Philly cheesesteak after all this was over. A good one from the city, not that the one from the pizza joint was bad. South Jersey is essentially East Philly, and they've managed to copy some of the best parts of the culture fairly well.

I ate, brushed my teeth and used the bathroom. By 8:00 I was lying on the bed (above the sheets) and watching a *Friends* re-run on Nickelodeon. It felt strange hearing the actors' real voices, rather than the dubbed over Dutch ones I'd become accustomed to. A new episode began as the credits for the previous one were still playing, but I was asleep before The Rembrandts finished promising they'd be there for me.

My cell phone alarm started beeping and buzzing simultaneously at six a.m. At some point overnight, I'd slid down so my neck was bent at an awkward angle on the pillows I'd propped against the headboard, but other than that I hadn't moved much. The top blanket was barely ruffled and the TV was still on, only now *Friends* had given way to *SpongeBob SquarePants.*

Both kids used to love that show, I thought. *Ethan was too young to get most of the jokes, but he liked the colors and the goofy animation. And he laughed every time his big sister laughed.*

Did they still watch *SpongeBob,* more for the nostalgia-cool of it now? Did they still do anything together, or had they grown apart as brothers and sisters sometimes do? Social media stalking let me watch them grow up, but it was all surface-level, like watching a photo montage of a celebrity you recognize but don't really know. Truth was, the two most important people in my life were strangers to me.

Based on some of Denise's Facebook posts, Maggie had gotten over her fear of sleepovers, but did she still stay up way too late, like she used to? It looked like she still played basketball, so that was good. Hopefully she was as fiery in her teens as she was at seven, hating it whenever she thought I let her win at a game of HORSE.

There were more than a few posts of drawings Ethan had done, which was entirely new. He could barely color inside the lines when I'd left, but even at two he could throw his blue, squishy baseball further than I thought was normal for a toddler. I'd had him pegged for sports, too, but apparently he got his dad's creative genes. I always loved making up bedtime stories for them, rather than reading from a book.

Christ, what I wouldn't give to hang one of those pictures on the wall of my old cubicle. Like a normal dad would.

Squidward was busy saying something snarky to Mr. Krabs and suddenly all I wanted to do was throw up. Ordinarily, I'd wash down that urge with whatever alcohol was nearby, but since there was none around, I closed my eyes, pressed my tongue against the roof of my mouth and swallowed until the bile retreated.

I sat up, swung my legs over the edge of the bed, and rolled my neck from side to side, working out the kinks. I showered, brushed my teeth again, and was out the door by 7:00, with a quick stop at the rental office to renew the room for another night.

CHAPTER TWENTY-FIVE

Across the bridge in South Philly, I spent my day moving from parking meter to parking meter within a one block radius of Robert's precinct house, like a fly buzzing between dishes at a barbecue. He made two trips outside the station. One to the Navy Yard, the other to a pizza joint for lunch with an older detective, whom I assumed was his partner.

I was invisible during lunch, but they almost made me at the Navy Yard. I'd pushed my luck and tried to follow them past the security booth, but I didn't have an appointment and the fake name I gave the guard didn't impress him. I tried to smooth-talk my way in, but the guard was an old pro and wasn't having it. Robert's unmarked car circled back around to see what was going on, but there was no one behind me so I apologized to the guard for the confusion, threw it into reverse and drove off before Robert got a good look at my face. Or so I hoped.

Once back outside the station house, I checked in with Erica at the high school where Maggie was a senior and Denise worked in the front office. Robert had a squad car stationed outside. She watched as they parked out front, only occasionally doing a circle around the school's perimeter. Lazy protection, but it allowed her to remain unnoticed from her spot in front of a house across the street. Joey gave a similar report from the middle school where Ethan attended.

After school let out, one patrol car followed Denise's old Ford Escape—which had apparently been handed down to Mags as her first car—and the other tailed Ethan's yellow school bus. Both cars remained outside the house until 6:00 p.m., when another squad car showed up to relieve them. This black-and-white with its two occupants would stand watch until 6:00 the next morning, when the first car came back to do it all over again.

That night, I ate a bland, rubber, fast-food burger with soft, lukewarm French fries and a six dollar bottle of Bud Light, while Erica and Joey had hoagies from a nearby Wawa. We talked again after dinner and I joked about how we'd spend the next week sitting in our cars, getting fat, and nothing interesting would happen. They laughed out of courtesy, but no one believed it was true. We all knew it was only a matter of time before our boring routine became far more interesting.

After dinner, I took a drive to a nearby laundromat to wash my only other clothes, the white button-down and much less expensive blue jeans I had on the night Ian was killed. A block away from the laundromat was a tiny liquor store. It was on the main drag through town, a line of small businesses that had been there long before Denise and I moved in, but which we routinely bypassed in favor of the cheaper prices and convenience of the various superstores in the area.

While I waited for my clothes to dry, I wandered down to that little liquor store and perused the shelves. It had been over a week since I'd really gotten to know the bottom of a bottle of scotch, and while I hadn't quite yet achieved the level of alcoholism where such a hiatus caused any physical withdrawal symptoms, I was definitely feeling the break.

Fortunately, they had Macallan, although it was a few bucks more expensive on this side of the Atlantic. I plunked down eighty dollars for the 12 Year Old Sherry Oak Cask single malt, and was both comforted and repulsed by the familiar feel of the bottle nestled into the crook of my arm.

There was twenty minutes left on my dryer when I returned to the laundromat and I badly wanted a taste, but again, I wasn't that kind of alcoholic. So instead I bided my time, watching my shirt and jeans tumble around, fantasizing about the first notes of peat and charred wood on my tongue.

Back in the hotel room, I tossed my Downy-fresh clothes on the bed, uncorked the bottle, and removed one of the two glasses on the desk from its protective shrink-wrap. I preferred my scotch over rocks, but there was no ice in the bucket and I didn't feel like making the trip to the vending area. Half a glass neat would do just fine.

The glass was at my lips, its rim still smudged with residue from the lips of whoever stayed in the room before me, but I didn't care. The sweet, smoky aroma was just drifting into my nose, promising me everything was about to be okay.

That's when I stopped.

We got lucky today, I thought. *We might get lucky again tomorrow, too. But one day, very soon, either Ghost or The Persian is going to make an appearance.*

Did I really want to be fighting off a hangover when that happened? Or worse, in the process of conceiving one, too incapacitated to do the one thing I risked everything to come here and do?

If I wanted to be the hero of my own story for a change, I needed to do it with a clear head. Scotch had always been a way to help me forget what I'd become since I left my family behind. I would be damned if I let it prevent me from making things right, or at least trying to.

Before I had time to second guess myself, I dumped the contents of the glass down the bathroom sink, and followed it with the rest of the bottle. I tossed the empty container into the trash, and then set the entire wastebasket on the walk outside my door so I wouldn't be able to smell it while I lay in bed.

I use the words "lay in bed" because I didn't sleep. The *SpongeBob* theme had been playing on a loop in my head all day. I couldn't shake the notion that my kids didn't watch the show anymore. It was such a little thing, though, so inconsequential. Why, then, could I not stop thinking about it? *Agonizing* over it.

I pulled out my phone and hacked into Denise's Facebook account, but this time I didn't go right to the picture of her in the black dress.

Instead, I pulled up her timeline and scrolled back ten years. The first post that came up was one cursing me—and all worthless, deadbeat men who ran out on their families. It had over two hundred comments, all either expressing disbelief in what I'd done or denouncing my worth as a human being in no uncertain terms. There was even a link to a fundraiser that, though long since closed, appeared to have netted her a few thousand dollars. (Badly as I'd wanted to dump all the money in the accounts she didn't know about into our joint checking, I was too afraid to risk it. I wanted to leave nothing behind that could tie her and the kids to me. Which was probably the right call, but doesn't make me sound or feel any less shitty.)

It was as good a starting place as any.

Hours passed, and I looked at everything. Not just on Denise's page, but my kids', too. Maggie had her own Facebook account, but was far more active on Instagram and TikTok, as was par for the course with her generation. Pictures of her and her friends, hanging out, making faces for selfies, being silly. A bunch of videos from her basketball games. More of her making passes to her teammates and playing tough defense than making shots. I smiled at that. There were pictures of boys, but none that looked as if they'd made it out of the friend zone. I smiled at that too, but in a sad way. I think all fathers of daughters are torn between wanting them to stay their little girl forever, but also to grow up and find someone who makes them happy.

By the looks of things, she'd make a good mom someday. There were dozens of pictures and videos of her with two young girls, seven to ten years old, captioned with the names Laila and Lexi. Hispanic, so probably not family. Kids she babysat, I assumed. They danced like fools in TikTok videos to Taylor Swift and Ariana Grande. In one of the videos the girls were dressed in matching pink pajamas and had used what appeared to be every item in her makeup kit to paint Maggie's face, who looked to be loving it every bit as much as they were.

Ethan had started his own YouTube channel where he played video games while others watched. He had about a dozen followers, probably all kids from school and Denise, but he carried himself like a celebrity in every video he made. And the drawings Denise had posted on her page only scratched the surface. When he wasn't playing Call of Duty for an audience, he was making time-lapse videos of him drawing comic book superheroes like Spider-Man and Wolverine, or crazy-detailed dragons that would fit right in on *Game of Thrones*. Jesus, he was talented.

I moved on from family and checked in on friends I'd left behind, gawked at newborn baby photos posted by people I never thought would get married, let alone have kids. I read inside jokes about a fantasy football league I used to be a part of. I mourned the deaths of friends' parents I'd known since I was a kid.

My own father passed away three years ago, but I'd never read his obituary. Only reason I knew about it was from seeing a post from Denise about attending his funeral. I read it that night, though. He died in his sleep, victim of a widowmaker heart attack from enjoying too many of the tastier things in life. We were close. He was the funniest person I ever knew, and was unquestionably where I got my sense of humor. They posted a picture of him with his obit, a classic shot of him in his easy chair, probably on a Sunday, watching the Eagles, one of those big smiles plastered across his chubby face. I cried for him the first time I saw Denise's post, and I cried again that night in the hotel room.

From there I turned to my brother, David, who was still teaching history at the high school we both attended, but had won Coach of the Year for the varsity boys' basketball team last season. There was an article with a picture of him, too, being lifted on the shoulders of a few boys from the team. He wore our dad's smile well, even though his face—and the rest of him—was far more fit and trim than Frank Williams ever was.

Immediately following the post about his coaching award was a heartbreaking one in which he spoke about how he'd had to put our mom in a nursing home for early stage Alzheimer's. Maybe if I'd been around to help, we could have taken care of her in her own home. Or maybe not. It's hard to say.

I pulled up the website for my old recruitment firm, the Edelman Group. Saw that they had acquired two other firms since I left and now employed nearly thirty people. One of my old coworkers was named one of the Top 40 under 40 Professionals in New Jersey according to *Jersey Man Magazine*. They seemed to be doing well without me.

That was the common thread that ran through all their stories. With the exception of my mother—whose health would have been the same whether I was still around or not—everyone I knew before I left was doing just fine without Ben Williams in their lives. It was a sobering, painful truth that had been kept submerged by untold gallons of scotch and beer. Turns out, I never drank to cope with the things I'd done or the person I'd become, even though that's what I told myself. I drank to forget about who I was.

I drank not to live with Rick Carter, but to kill Ben Williams. Because at the end of the day, Ben had the better life, and it hurt too much to acknowledge that I should have stuck with it, even through the hard times. Better to drown the bastard and move on than accept that the life I'd left behind was far superior to the one I was currently living.

But even if Ben Williams was truly dead, he still had a legacy. He had a family that was living proof he had once done something good with his life. And then Rick Carter came along and fucked the whole thing up. The least Rick could do was stay sober enough to make things right.

CHAPTER TWENTY-SIX

I spent the next two days watching Robert go to and from work, and checking in for the same reports of nothing happening from Erica and Joey. On Day Four, Thursday, Robert never left the station, which made my life a little easier. By 5:00 that evening, I was still parked across the street from the station's main entrance, but further up, so I had to use my mirrors to keep an eye on who was coming and going. It was tedious and strained my eyes, so I broke it up by playing solitaire on my phone. Robert must have come up to the car while I was trying to figure out where to put my ace, because I didn't know he was there until he tapped on my window.

It was raining—a light, steady drizzle that had been going on all day—beading on my windshield and making everyone who passed by on the sidewalk miserable. Robert didn't look any happier as he pulled his jacket collar around his neck and waited for me to start the car so I could lower my window.

"Robert, I—"

"Deptford Mall food court," he interrupted. "You like Chinese?"

"Yeah," I said, but it came out almost as a question.

"I'll meet you at the Master Wok." Then he turned and walked away. In my rearview mirror, I watched him disappear into the employee parking lot next to the station. Three minutes later, his blue pickup emerged and turned right on 24th Street, going away from me toward the Ben Franklin Bridge. I waited for a break in the traffic then did the same.

On the bridge, I called Erica and Joey for an update. All normal on their end. Denise and the kids were home, and the two squad cars were parked out front, waiting for the night shift to arrive. I told them about my dinner date with Robert and asked Erica to get there ahead of time to scope the place out. If the food court was some kind of set up, I wanted to know about it in advance. Of course, if he wanted to arrest me he could have just done so outside the precinct, but I've always been one to err on the side of caution. Once she texted me the all clear, she was to hang out of sight of our meeting. Joey I asked to stay behind and keep an eye on the house.

In an era when indoor malls were withering on the vine, the one in Deptford—a small town about twenty minutes from my old house—was thriving. It had nothing to do with the stores, which were the same as in every other mall in America, and everything to do with the dining scene. Both in the mall itself and in the area around it, upper scale restaurant chains had taken root and spread, like the purple flowers that used to blanket my lawn every April. They were nothing more than weeds, but they looked gorgeous and smelled great.

As a result, the food court in the mall itself had seen its average number of patrons dwindle, but still did enough business to keep the Auntie Anne's and Cinnabons running. Master Wok was the obligatory Chinese place, and it wasn't bad. At least, it wasn't the last time I'd eaten there. Judging by the number of full tables in its little district of Food Court Land, it still was one of the better options available. Robert was seated at one of those tables, hands folded on top, scanning the faces in the crowd. There was no food in front of him. When he saw me, he waved and headed toward the short line in front of Master Wok, leaving his leather jacket draped over the back of his chair as a placeholder.

I made my way toward him and caught Erica out of the corner of my eye, sitting alone at a table by the Salad Works, her nose buried in a book she'd likely just purchased from the Barnes & Noble downstairs.

"Can't remember the last time I ate here," I said once I reached Robert. "They still have good sesame chicken?"

"No idea, I always get the boneless BBQ spareribs," he said as he got in line. "You're buying."

I got the sesame chicken. It smelled as good as I remembered. Looked as good as I remembered. Unlike last night at The Colonial, I dug in and savored every bite of a dish I'd loved in another life.

We ate in silence as the tables emptied and refilled around us. After a while I started to wonder if Robert merely invited me here to score a free meal. Finally, as we each scooped up the last forkfuls of our fried rice, he said, "I checked you out."

I looked up from my plastic bowl and swallowed. "And?"

"Seems Ben Williams died." He moved some rice around with his fork. "Or at least, any trace of him did. Around eight years ago. Somewhere in Germany."

"Sounds about right."

"Of course, this was after he did some under-the-table, highly illegal recruitment work for not one but two organized crime families. One operating out of Philly, and one all the way across the pond in Jolly Old England. Found them some gunrunners, some IT hackers, and at least one triggerman that left two bodies in a parking lot in Kensington." He shoveled the last bit of rice into his mouth and looked up at me as he chewed, wiping his hands with a thin brown paper napkin. "Took a while for the lead detective to connect the dots, but once he did, he had you. Which meant he had the crime families, too. Major bust. The kind that can make a career. Except . . . poof." He opened both hands and waggled his fingers, like dandelion seeds blowing away in the breeze.

"Poof?"

"Just like that, before he can make the collar, you're gone. Vanished in the middle of the night. Leaving behind a wife and two young kids to wake up in the morning with no husband and no daddy." He locked eyes with me. "Just the mess he left behind."

Over my shoulder, a pack of girls giggled as they walked past. It gave me an excuse to turn around and make sure Erica was still at her post, which she was. Still engrossed in the book I knew she wasn't reading. I dropped my fork and pushed my tray away.

"Did this detective ever question Denise? Did he talk to my kids, tell them what he thought—"

"Ben fled to Europe," Robert continued, taking a sip of his large fountain Sprite. "Our hero detective—guy named Connelly—coordinated with Interpol, but despite the pile of evidence stacked against him, no one could ever seem to bring him in. Ben bounced around Europe a bit—London, Barcelona, Rome—until settling down for almost a year in a small German village just outside of Berlin. No idea what he did for a living there—maybe he bottled his own sauerkraut—but then one day . . ." He waggled his fingers again.

"Poof, right, I get it."

He smiled and pushed his own tray to the center of the table. "You know, when I first met Denise, all she told me about her ex was that he up and left one night. No note. No money. No nothing. Just left behind his ring. Which she still keeps in a box at the back of one of her dresser drawers, by the way. God knows why."

Well I'll be damned. She kept it.

"The cop part of me wanted to look you up right away, but I respected Denise and figured I'd let her tell me, whenever she was ready. *If* she was ever ready. I knew there was more. The way she got uncomfortable whenever your name came up."

So the detective did talk to her. Fuck.

"And then you called and invited me out for a cup of coffee. Told me two of my colleagues were dead, there was a target on my back and that she and the kids might be in danger, too. 'Robert,' I said to myself, 'if that isn't enough probable cause to do some digging on this guy, then I don't know what is.'"

"Not to be rude, but are we getting closer to a point?"

"When you first called," he said, ignoring me again, "I didn't know how you knew Frank and Nadia. But you did, and that was enough to perk my ears up. I called their section chief first thing Monday morning to see if he'd heard from them—"

"And?"

"No, nothing. But he did confirm those other names you gave me were a part of the same task force. I asked him to check in with his counterparts at Mossad and MI5, see if those agents had gone silent as well. Turns out the Mossad ones have been dark for about as long as Frank and Nadia—"

"Shit."

"—but MI5 abruptly pulled their men from the field. Said they got an anonymous tip from someone who knew their agents' names, along with Frank, Nadia, and the Israeli couple. The tipster claimed they were all in danger and that he was the guy who found the people paid to hunt them down."

"Do they know who it was?" I tried to make the question sound sincere, but it rang phony inside my ears.

Robert smiled again, the knowing kind that says he caught a whiff of what I was selling and it wasn't roses, no matter how much I tried to convince him otherwise. "No. Guy never gave his name and hung up before they could complete a full trace. But it got me thinking. About you and what you did for a living when you and Denise were married. What you allegedly did before you left. And what you possibly could have been up to in the decade since. 'Guy like that must be pretty well-connected,' I thought. Guy like that might have a network of little birdies, just like he said he did. And those little birdies just might not be full of shit."

"They're not." I leaned over the table toward him. "Robert, trust me—they're not."

"I believe you. That's why I put a couple of beat guys on protection duty for Denise and the kids."

I almost said, *I know*, but caught myself.

"And it's why I didn't chase you down after you high-tailed it away from the Navy Yard."

Fuck. I suck at following people.

"I appreciate what you're trying to do," he said. "But let me take it from here."

"No, Robert, listen—"

"The whole reason you came here was so that I would believe you, right?" I didn't answer, just stared. "Well I believe you. I also believe you were the one who phoned in the anonymous tip to MI5 that probably saved two lives. Which means there's at least a part of you that isn't an asshole. That's the part that I'm giving one chance to walk away. If you're mixed up in the kind of things I think you are, then your presence puts me and my family—"

My family.

"—in greater danger. It doesn't make us safer."

"I just," I started, not sure what the next word was. "I need you to understand the kind of people that are coming after you. These aren't your everyday, gangbanger hitters."

"Is there anything you can tell me about them that would be useful, other than that they're a couple of scary-ass motherfuckers?"

"No," I said with a little laugh, though nothing about this was funny. "No, that about sums it up. One's Asian, a male, and the other's Persian, a female, but by the time you're close enough to recognize them it will be too late."

"Either one got a name? A real one?"

"None that you'll find in any database."

"Then we're done here."

"But if there's something you could tell me about why you're such a threat to them," I said before he could stand up, "maybe we could figure out a way to head them off. Two of the highest-priced hitmen on the planet have been hired to take you out, and you've obviously been working with the FBI in some capacity. How are you involved in their case?"

His face slipped into the look it had two nights ago at The Colonial when I asked the same question.

"Robert, please. You said you believe me. Well then trust me when

I say if there is any chance, no matter how small, that we can get this hit called off, it's one we need to take. Why are they after you?"

He rapped his knuckles on the table then looked up. His face had softened. Not much, but enough to give me hope.

"When you called MI5," he said, "what name did you give them?"

I smiled. "What's up, Doc?"

He smiled back. Then his phone rang.

"It's Denise," he said, "hang on." He tapped the screen. "Hey honey, I'm just finishing up—"

And that's when his face turned to ash. His mouth dropped open, then pressed into a tight, thin frown covering gritted teeth. My body went weak and my bowels turned to liquid. I checked on Erica but she hadn't moved, other than closing her book and absently swiping through something on her phone. The small food court crowd looked no different than it had before. The two of us were safe. But we weren't the ones I was concerned about.

"If you touch them, I swear to Christ—" Robert said, his voice coarse and straining to maintain control over the anger that covered the fear beneath, but the person on the other end of the phone cut him off again. He listened for a minute then looked at me. It wasn't a kind look. "Yeah," he said. "He's here."

I hung my head and clenched my fists. Robert put the phone on speaker and set it on the table between us, the volume loud enough for us to hear but not so loud as to attract unwanted attention.

"Hello, Rick," the voice said. A male voice with a Chinese accent.

"Leave them alone," I said, knowing how pathetic and futile it sounded. "They've got nothing to do with this."

"You're right, they don't," Ghost said.

I'd placed him on twenty-three contracts, including this one. Over the years, I'd spoken with him directly less and less, preferring to conduct our business mostly via text. Part of the reason was for security purposes. As Ghost's reputation grew, so too did the number of people who wanted to track him down, for a variety of reasons. Secure chat rooms provided more cover than an open phone line. But that wasn't the real reason we stopped talking.

Even when he was a nobody, a young gun for hire trying to carve out some space in a highly competitive industry, his voice was as calm and emotionless as it was now. No inflection. No tone. It landed on your ears flat, almost metallic. It was an experience I loathed, so I phased it out. Quite frankly, talking to him terrified me.

And now he had Denise.

And Maggie.

And Ethan.

He didn't mention their names, but he didn't have to. They were with him. I thought of Ethan, not as the pre-teen he'd become, but as the child that I'd left behind. The sweet little boy who was scared whenever we lost power in a storm and told me all about what Donald Duck did on *Mickey Mouse Clubhouse* every night while we brushed our teeth before bed.

I thought of Maggie, my Peanut, and how I used to lay on her floor when she was getting used to sleeping in her big-girl bed. We'd listen to a CD I made of lullaby songs to help her fall asleep, often times putting me out as well. I'd wake up at midnight with a stiff back but one content little angel, her arm curled around the bedraggled teddy bear Denise and I swore would follow her to college.

I thought of Denise.

"What do you want?" I asked.

"You and Robert, back here at the house within thirty minutes. No police or they die."

"How do we know you haven't done anything to them already?" Robert asked. Ghost didn't answer. Instead, there was the sound of the phone being jostled, then Denise's scream burst from the speakers, causing them to vibrate and hum. Even with the volume lowered, people around us looked to see where it came from. That was followed by two voices, Ethan and Maggie, crying out one word in unison:

"*Mom!*"

Then Ghost was back. "Thirty minutes," he said. The line went dead. Robert picked up the phone, took it off speaker and pressed it to his ear.

"You motherfucker!" he shouted. His hand was shaking almost as much as his voice. But Ghost was gone.

He took the phone away from his ear and stared at it for a moment, then turned his gaze toward me. And I got the full force of all that rage covering all that fear. It needed to go somewhere, and I was the best target available. I also deserved it.

Before I could react, he grabbed me by the front of my shirt and lifted me out of the chair. My legs banged against the table, knocking over my half-full cup of Diet Coke. The lid popped off and it spilled over the edge into a puddle on the floor. One lonely ice cube drifted in the tiny Cola rivulet, never quite reaching the drop.

"Was he telling the truth?" he hissed into my face. "Did you hire him? Did you do this?" Our scene had attracted a small crowd, but I heard one distinct set of footsteps approaching from the Salad Works that I needed to keep away. They were more deliberate than the others, approaching not to observe but to intervene. I let go of Robert's wrist with one hand and motioned behind me for Erica to hold back, hoping she saw it. Her footsteps slowed but didn't stop.

"I recruited him," I said, knowing he wouldn't care about the semantics. "I didn't hire him."

"If they die, it's because of you."

"Then let's make sure that doesn't happen," I said.

CHAPTER TWENTY-SEVEN

If they die, it's because of you.

The words echoed in my head as I drove down Delaware Street, past the turn-of-the-century homes that Denise and I admired but could never afford. Past the courthouse and the little hole-in-the-wall delicatessen where lawyers congregated every weekday at noon.

If they die, it's because of you.

He was right, of course. I did this.

By running away ten years ago, I thought I'd been protecting them. Like a fool, I thought I could continue on with the new life I'd created for myself while shielding them from all of its inherent dangers. Turns out, all I did was destroy our marriage and rob my children of their father for ten years. In the end, they were still in danger. Because of me.

If they die, it's my fault.

I checked my rearview and saw the minivan's headlights behind me. The glare obscured Erica's face, but she was at the wheel. My ace in the hole. The only card I had to play. Robert was in front of me, and I couldn't imagine the thoughts racing around his head.

Once he'd collected himself—to say he'd calmed down would be a stretch—I told him everything, as quickly as I could. Trish, the task force, my involvement, Ian, Erica and Joey. Everything. By the end, he wanted to shove his gun down my throat and pull the trigger until it clicked dry, but the rational part of him knew that wouldn't solve anything. He needed us. That didn't mean I wouldn't wind up eating his gun at some point, just not until I'd outlived my usefulness. It wasn't an ideal way to start a rescue mission, but nothing about any of this was ideal.

Things got even less ideal when I tried calling Joey but he didn't answer. Maybe he'd turned his phone off, or was in the process of making his own move on Ghost, but that was wishful thinking. I added him to the growing list of bodies on my résumé. Joey Walls, who was a pig and a drug dealer and an attempted murderer, but who also had my back whenever I needed him. Who was excited that he got to do something good for a change.

So it was just the three of us, then. Our plan was a simple one, because simple was the only option we had. Robert and I would pull up to the house and walk inside. Erica would park at the end of the street and approach on foot, staying out of sight. She'd try to find a vantage point that offered her a clean shot. Once she had it, she'd take it. If she didn't, she'd improvise. If Ghost was alone, our chances were slim but at least had a pulse. If he had just one other person keeping a lookout, however, we were fucked.

"Guess what Donald Duck did today, Dad?" Ethan said.

The memory was crystal clear, hi-def. I could hear his little voice as if it was sitting right next to me.

"What?" I said around my toothbrush.

"He was in a car race with Mickey, and he cheated!" This was clearly a felony of the highest order.

"Oh, no! What did he do?"

"He tried to take a shortcut that wasn't part of the racetrack!"

"Did Mickey catch him?"

"Yeah. Donald got his car stuck in quicksand, and Mickey helped get him out."

"That's because Mickey's a good friend."

"Yeah, and Donald said he was sorry for cheating."

"That's good. We always do the right thing, right?"

"Yup!" Big smile, making his daddy proud.

I smiled and gave him a hug. "Go tell Mommy you're ready for bed, bud."

"Okay, Daddy."

If they die, it's because of you.

The neighborhood was as I remembered. It had always been my favorite thing about the house, the reason we never considered moving even as our tiny family began to outgrow what was supposed to be our starter home but wound up looking more and more like our forever home.

It was quiet. The homes were well-kept and filled with the kind of people that cared about maintaining that appearance. The streets were tree-lined and free of utility poles because all the electrical wiring was buried underground. It was an idyllic slice of suburbia when I left and not much had changed.

Robert pulled into the expanded driveway next to an SUV I assumed belonged to Denise. I pulled up at the curb by the mailbox. When I got out, the nostalgia swept over me despite the circumstances.

How many times had I pulled up after dark, tired from a long day at work? Listened to my shoes scrape the cracked pavement in the driveway? Seen the light on in the front window and knew the warmth of home was waiting for me?

Except there was no light in the front window. Other than the porch light, the house was dark. Robert pulled a key ring from his jeans pocket and started toward the house. I looked around but couldn't see Joey's Honda Accord anywhere. That by itself wasn't odd—he would have parked it out of sight with the police presence camped out front—but it didn't make me feel any better about him not answering the phone earlier.

I grabbed Robert's arm.

"Where's the security detail?" I whispered. The police presence that I'd assumed had chased away Joey was nowhere to be seen.

"I don't know," he whispered back. Hopefully I wasn't wrong in assuming Trish couldn't or wouldn't get to a couple of patrolmen halfway around the world, but them disappearing didn't fill me with confidence.

"Shouldn't you call it in?"

"He said no cops. If I radio the station and report that they're missing, they might send backup even if I tell them not to, assuming I'm in danger and can't talk freely. Do you want to find out what happens if they do that?"

I did not.

We climbed the steps, passing Maggie's basketball hoop. The plexiglass backboard had turned green and opaque after years outside, but it still stood in the same spot on the driveway where I'd set it up. Robert unlocked the door, and I suddenly found myself standing in a foyer I never thought I'd see again. The layout hadn't changed—it was still the open floor plan Denise and I fell in love with all those years ago, with the kitchen, dining room, front living room and rear rec room all bleeding into one another—but everything else was different. Even in the dark, I could tell. The furniture, the paint on the walls, the tile on the kitchen floor, the carpet, the curtains—it was as if Denise had spent the last decade scrubbing away as much of our life together as she could.

And who could blame her? Because of me, in addition to the new furniture and new carpet, Denise was also in the front room. On her knees, her hands tied behind her head with a scarf that probably belonged to her. It was wrapped over her mouth, so also served as a gag. On her left was Ethan, though he looked even bigger than the pictures I'd seen on Facebook. On her right was Maggie. The little girl afraid to sleep in her new toddler bed was gone. She was a young woman now, except for her eyes. They were as frightened as that little girl's had been when she swore she heard something move in her closet late at night.

There had been no monsters in her room then, but there was one here now. When she saw me, some of the fear in her eyes instinctively faded, and that broke my heart. The little girl in her thought Daddy had come to chase the monster away. Little did she know that I was the one who'd set him upon her.

"Dad?" she said through her gag, her voice breaking with an agonizing mix of confusion and hopefulness.

"Hey, Peanut," I said.

The figure standing next to her put his finger to his lips and the tip of the silencer screwed into the barrel of his gun next to her head. She bit down on her gag, holding in a scream, and squeezed her eyes shut tight. In the moonlight through the front window, I could see the tears roll down her face.

"No talking," Ghost said.

I'd forgotten how ordinary he was. He had a receding hairline and a slight build, with the beginnings of a middle-aged belly pressing against his black shirt. He wore a black suit jacket over the black shirt, to match his black gloves, black pants, and black shoes. Under different circumstances, he would be just another guy you passed on your way to work. You'd only notice him if you bumped into him, never knowing that he'd killed more people than some diseases.

Unfortunately for our plan, I also noticed that he was standing in the worst possible place for Erica to get off a clean shot. He was just out of sight of the front window, and at the wrong angle to be seen through either the kitchen window or the front door, which I had left open to help her out.

"Guns," Ghost said. Slowly, Robert removed his from its holster, checked the safety, and tossed it on the overstuffed recliner in the corner of the room closest to us.

"You too, Rick," Ghost said. I hated hearing my name in his mouth.

"Good," he said, after I tossed my gun next to Robert's. Then he took a phone from his pocket, dialed a number, and held it to his ear. In the quiet, the person on the other end could be heard loud and clear. All he said was, "Hello," but it was a gut punch for two reasons:

1. I recognized the voice.
2. It was coming from upstairs. Based on how close he sounded in relation to the steps, he was in the master bedroom, standing by the window.

"Anything?" Ghost asked into the phone.

"Just the girl," said the voice.

"Where is she?"

"Running back down the street the way she came."

"Did she see you?"

"Nah, probably couldn't get a clear shot and decided to circle around back. Want me to switch positions, see if I can locate her again?"

"No, just come down," Ghost said. "We don't need a body on the street. This won't take long."

I heard the ceiling creak above my head, then heavy footfalls on the staircase behind me. I didn't turn around. I didn't have to. When I heard him hit the landing, I hung my head and shook it slowly from side to side.

"So much for liking the way it felt to do something good for a change," I said. "You're a piece of shit."

"Don't be so dramatic, Rick," Joey said as he slipped between me and Robert into the front room, picking up my gun off the chair. "You know how the game is played. Morality don't pay the bills."

I thought of the phone call he took the other night, the one he said was just some crazy bitch from a bar. "How did she track you down? Trish call you herself, or did she have some lackey do it?"

"You're not the only one who has my number," he said with a grin that I wanted to slap off his face with a baseball bat.

"What's she paying you?"

"More than you can afford. Not just a one-time thing, either. You weren't wrong, Rick. These are some serious players. They have enough work to set me up for life."

"Think this through, Joe," I said, fighting to keep my voice calm. "You're nothing but another loose end. After you serve your purpose, you have no life. You're as dead as the rest of us."

"Wrong," Joey said. He walked over to Ghost, who pulled a second silencer from his jacket and handed it to my former friend. His gun hadn't moved from next to Maggie's head. I imagined rushing Ghost, ripping the gun from his hand and emptying it into him and Joey, laughing as their blood splattered my face.

"I'm more than just a loose end," Joey said as he screwed the silencer into the barrel of my Glock with a gloved hand. "I'm the guy that's going to testify about how you recruited me and Erica to come here and help you take out the guy who was investigating the human trafficking ring you and Leon were running."

"What?" Robert said.

"It's bullshit," I replied, my eyes fixed on Joey.

"It'll make for great headlines. The family angle will really sell it. How the same cop was engaged to your ex-wife, and in a fit of rage you took out her and both your kids before turning the gun on yourself."

I could feel Robert next to me, his body tensed and ready to spring. He'd be dead before he made it two steps and he knew it, but a big part of him still wanted to try. I know because I felt the same exact way.

"I'm going to rip your fucking throat out," Robert snarled, and Joey laughed.

"So what," I snapped, "you're going to shoot all of us, then put my prints on the gun? You're not that kind of guy, Joe. You're not a monster."

"You're right, I'm not." He finished screwing the silencer into the Glock.

And handed it to Ghost.

"But he is," he said.

Ghost stepped back from Maggie, lowered his other gun and lifted the Glock. *My* Glock. This time, it wasn't just a threat. This time, he meant to pull the trigger. My daughter would be killed with my gun.

Maggie screamed, "Daddy!"

I made a sound that was supposed to be the word "*No!*" but wound up being something much more guttural, primal.

Denise cried out for Robert, who decided it was now or never and sprang toward Ghost, but Joey was standing in the way.

All that happened at the same time. None of us noticed the room fill with bright light or the roar of the engine coming fast from outside. When Erica drove her minivan through the front door and crashed it into the banister, though, that got *everyone's* attention.

The explosion of wood and glass and other assorted debris—including a brass door knocker with the name *Whitehead* engraved on it—distracted Ghost just enough to alter his shot by an inch, give or take. Enough that the bullet grazed the top of Maggie's head, carving a little gash in her scalp but doing most of its damage to the couch behind her.

Joey caught Robert's charge and wrapped his arms around him, both of them stumbling into the antique end table against the back wall.

Ghost was a professional who never missed twice and quickly drew another bead on Maggie's forehead. But Denise was a mother, and you don't fuck with them either. I once watched her chop a five-foot long black snake in half with a shovel when it came out from under our backyard shed and went after Maggie, who was playing in her sandbox. She launched herself at Ghost's knees and sent him to the ground, his second shot punching a hole in the ceiling.

I was on him before he could reset for a third try. If I was smart I would have grabbed Robert's gun off the chair and ended it all right then, but I wasn't thinking, just reacting. I landed on Ghost and immediately began hammering his ribs and midsection with my right fist, while my left pinned his hand holding the gun to the floor. Above me, Robert and Joey continued their brawl, destroying every piece of furniture in their path. They were in the dining room now, by the sounds of it, and one of them had just broken something glass over the other one's head.

Beneath me, Ghost was finally starting to go limp. A few more blows and I'd make a move to take his gun with both hands. Before I got that far, I felt a sharp, hot pain in my right leg. I looked down and saw the handle of a knife sticking out of my rear upper thigh, just below my ass. Ghost had his hand wrapped around it and drove it in as far as it could go, the tip scraping against the edge of my femur. I screamed and dropped my elbow into his chest with all the force I could muster. I thought I heard something snap, hoping it was a rib, but I couldn't be sure. Whatever it was, it hurt enough for him to let go of the knife but not the gun. I pulled the blade out and sat back on my knees, blood quickly soaking through my pants. I looked up in time to see Ghost lying on his side, his right hand still holding his gun.

That hand never made it off the floor, though. Erica stepped on it and fired two shots into his head. Ghost's skull exploded, splattering brain and bone fragments onto the carpet Denise had installed sometime within the last ten years. I was breathing too hard to thank her, so I found her eyes and nodded instead.

As I tried to get my breath under control, I caught a strong, acrid stink of urine. Ethan, who was closest to me, stared at Ghost's body, not blinking. His mouth hung open around its gag, and there was a dark stain spreading on the front of his sweatpants. When another shot echoed from the kitchen, followed by the thud of Joey's body hitting the ground, he convulsed and began screaming. A high-pitched, frightening sound that I worried would tear his throat to shreds.

"Ethan!" I said, wrapping him in my arms. "It's okay, bud. It's okay." I started to rock him like I did when he was a baby, but when he turned and saw my face, his screams turned even higher-pitched and faster. His hands were still tied behind his head so he had to wriggle his whole body in an ugly, awkward spasm to break free from my grip.

But when Robert came over and took him from me, cradling his neck into his shoulder, the screaming stopped and the spasms subsided. He felt safe.

And I no longer felt the knife wound in my leg. Watching Robert console my son hurt worse.

CHAPTER TWENTY-EIGHT

Maggie came to me, though, and that was something. While Robert soothed Ethan, and Denise, free of her bindings, surveyed the chaos I had brought into her home, my daughter came to me. She wrapped her arms around my neck as tightly as she had when she was a little girl, only this time she didn't have to stretch. She tried to form words, asking me to make sense of everything that had happened, but her brain and her mouth weren't on the same page, so she settled for squeezing me even tighter, trying to draw strength from what little I had. I hugged her back and was relieved that it felt so wonderfully natural. There was a van where the front door used to be, bullet holes in the ceiling, blood all around and two dead bodies on the floor, but with my eyes shut and my arms wrapped around my little girl, I could pretend none of it was real.

"Rick, the police will be here soon," Erica said, obliterating the illusion.

I opened my eyes.

"We need to move," I said, letting go of Maggie, which took more willpower than most things I've done in my life. Erica nodded and handed me back the gun Joey had taken.

"You're not going anywhere," Robert said. He came around the wall between the front room and the kitchen. Ethan was still in his arms, and he looked almost like himself again, except for the stain on his pants and the lingering stink of urine. Robert set him down and he turned to Denise, who was ready and waiting to lead him away so we could talk. She caught my eye, only for a second, but long enough to let me know the words Maggie couldn't form would come much easier to her, and without anything as gentle as a hug to accompany them. For the moment, however, she was content to just be a mother, while Robert and I spoke.

Robert's lip was split open and blood trickled from his nose, but otherwise he looked none the worse for wear after his scuffle with Joey. Impressive, considering Joey probably outweighed him by about thirty pounds. I was pretty sure the blood staining the back of his jacket wasn't his, remnants of Erica's handiwork.

"Robert, listen to me," I said, lowering my voice so Maggie wouldn't hear. She sensed the tension, however, and went over to be with her mom and brother. "This isn't over. If we stick around here, none of us will make it to the end of the week."

"Enough with the drama. You'll be in a cell surrounded by cops and the four of us will be under twenty-four-hour protective surveillance."

"Oh yeah? How did that work out tonight?"

The punch came quick and landed square on my chin. I took a step back to keep from falling over and a fresh wave of pain shot out from the hole in my leg. I reached down and felt my pants squelch, like wringing out a damp paper towel.

That was going to need tending to. Soon.

"I didn't mean any disrespect," I said, sliding my jaw back and forth to make sure it still worked. "But these people won't stop until we're dead. And not just the two of us, either." I nodded toward Denise and the kids, huddled together on the couch by the window. "The entire Philly police force couldn't stop them, not when they can just keep sending one hitter after another, after another, after another. Until the job's done. And that's assuming you can trust everyone around you." I saw his arm cock back and stepped back preemptively. My leg screamed at me again, but I kept my hands held up next to my shoulders to show I didn't want to fight.

"I know for a fact Interpol is compromised," I explained, "and when I first met with the woman who hired me, she implied that she had people in other agencies as well. How big of a leap is it to assume that she has people in the Philly PD, too?"

"Rick," Erica said. She had retrieved her duffel bag from the van and was anxious to get moving. We'd need another getaway car, though. Steam poured from beneath the hood of the van, which had crumpled up like a beer can on a frat boy's forehead when it struck the banister. The windshield was spiderwebbed and useless, and judging by the way it demolished the railing and porch steps on its way to the door, the undercarriage had to be at least partially damaged.

The only remaining choice was Denise's Chevy Traverse, with its third row of seating. Perfect for taxiing gaggles of kids to practice, the movies, and back from late-night parties. Normal family stuff. It should never be used to flee a crime scene under cover of darkness, but that's where we were.

I needed to convince Robert, though. Otherwise Erica and I would be taking my car, just the two of us. Getting to it might not be easy, either, depending on how badly Robert insisted I stay.

I held my hand up to Erica and gave her a quick glance. She frowned and squeezed between the van and the jagged ruin of the wall to stand watch on the front porch, listening for the first faint wail of sirens. A crowd had already started to form across the street. Neighbors in pajamas and sweat clothes, gathering together to observe the wreckage at the Williams house.

Or maybe it was the Leap house now, if Denise had gone back to her maiden name. It wouldn't be Baglioni. Not yet, anyway.

Nobody approached yet for a closer look, but I did hear a man's voice shout out, "Is everybody okay in there?"

"Sorry," Erica yelled back, in a more than passable American accent. "I swerved to miss a cat and just lost control."

While doing 70 and forgetting how to use the brake, apparently.

"Did you call the police?" the man yelled back.

"Yeah, they're on their way now."

Maybe nobody had called the police yet, but I doubted it. A car crashes through your neighbor's house, you dial 911. The police station wasn't far away either, but it was almost 8:00 and in a small town like this, response time depended entirely on where the two or three patrol cars on duty were in relation to the scene. Still, best-case scenario we had five minutes. Probably less.

"Robert," I said, amping up the diplomacy to 10. "I'm not saying anybody in your department is dirty. But even if they *are* clean, our odds are still better on the run. You can call your captain from the road and explain everything. Call your contact at the FBI, too. But we all stand a better chance as moving targets than as stationary ones."

He bit the inside of his lower lip and turned away from me, but he didn't say no. I was close to closing the deal. Just needed to seal it.

"Blame me," I said, going for the Hail Mary. "Tell them I took you all at gunpoint, I don't care. When this is over, I'll turn myself in."

We'd cross that bridge when we came to it.

He turned back. "And when will this all be over, Ben? Or Rick, or whatever the fuck your real name is. How many more dead bodies will it take?"

"I don't know. But if we stay, there will be at least six new ones. I promise you that."

"You can't promise that. You don't know that."

"You really want to bet their lives on it?" I said, nodding toward the couch again. My leg was on fire. I was pretty sure Ghost had missed any major arteries, otherwise I'd be unconscious on the floor by now, but the bleeding hadn't stopped and the wound would definitely require stitches. The crowd outside was getting antsier and, beneath the swelling rumble of gossip and cul-de-sac chatter, the inevitable sound of approaching sirens grew louder.

But I didn't move. If I was leaving with more than just Erica, it needed to be Robert's decision. Erica poked her head back in and, for the first time since I'd known her, she looked anxious. Robert considered her, then walked over to Denise and the kids.

"We gotta go, guys," he said, ushering them up gently. I allowed myself to exhale. Denise covered the distance between us before I could take another breath.

The slap came hard. Followed by another. Then they came rapid fire, Denise's manicured nails peeling skin off my face like carrot shavings.

"You son of a bitch!" she screamed as she hit. "These people knew you! They almost killed us because of you! Your children, Ben! They tried to kill your children!"

Maggie stood watching with Ethan attached to her side. Just an hour earlier she had probably been lying on her bed, talking on the phone with her friends. Or FaceTiming. Or maybe even texting with a boy. Things any other seventeen-year-old girl would be doing on a Tuesday night. Maybe Ethan was playing video games or watching the Sixers on TV while Denise cleaned up dinner. Their life was fine and boring and happy. Then it all got thrown into a blender. Because of me. I deserved everything she gave and I took it all.

"Mom!" Maggie said, trying to pull her away. Denise resisted at first so Maggie grabbed her shoulder again and tugged harder. "MOM!"

The second time worked and the assault ended. In the dim light, I didn't even recognize the woman I'd fallen in love with back when we were two young, dumb college kids. Gone was the face I fantasized about via old pictures on my phone. In its place was the hardened look I'd seen on countless killers over the years.

"Denise," Robert said, but it was all he got out before she spun on him.

"Why did you two walk in together?" Denise said, her words short and clipped. If she had a shovel, like that day with the snake in our backyard, there might be two of Robert right now. "Did you know he was back and not tell me? Who are these people? How do they know Ben? Someone please tell me what the hell is going on!"

"I'll explain everything once we're away from here," I said tentatively, not wanting to spark a second attack. "I promise. But if we don't go—*right now*—we're going to be in a lot of trouble."

For a moment I thought the blows *would* start again. Then she looked at Robert, who simply nodded, and some of the fight left her. Reluctantly.

"We need to take your car," I said. She walked past me into the kitchen to grab her keys off a hook above the counter as if I wasn't even there.

"What will we tell the neighbors?" Robert asked, peering out the front window at the close to two dozen people congregating like groupies waiting for their favorite rock star to emerge from backstage.

"Tell them I'm your cousin and got hurt when the car crashed through the door, and you need to take me to the hospital."

"Half those people still remember what you look like," Denise said, as if explaining an exceptionally difficult math problem to an exceptionally stupid child.

"I'll keep my head down."

She made a face that expressed how little she thought of that solution but didn't argue. We went one by one through the tight space between the van and the disfigured doorframe, hopped off the porch that no longer had working stairs, and piled into the Chevy. I had my arm wrapped around Robert's shoulders and my head tucked low behind his jacket.

"Robert," the same guy called out, "everybody okay?"

"Yeah," he replied, not looking up. "Just need to get this guy to a hospital!"

"Who is he?"

"Cousin!"

There was a follow up question, but it was cut off as we slammed the Chevy's doors shut. Robert sat behind the wheel, Denise next to him. Maggie and Ethan were in the middle row, while Erica and I crammed into the two seats in the very back. The windows were tinted, so I was able to gawk at the gawkers without them knowing as we drove away.

There was Don, whose daughter used to play with Maggie when their school closed on snow days. They'd build entire Frosty families on our front lawn, then come in for hot chocolate and Denise's chocolate chip cookies, which were famous throughout the neighborhood. Vicki and Shane, whose once cute little puppy had grown into a full-sized Lab that stood obediently by their feet, despite all the commotion around it. Walt, our next-door neighbor, was nowhere to be seen, but he worked nights. Assuming he hadn't been replaced in the last ten years by a new next-door neighbor. There were other faces I didn't know, and more I thought I did but couldn't be sure. Age, poor lighting, and a few quick seconds did not make for the best conditions to identify old acquaintances.

The sirens were louder as we turned the corner. No visible lights yet, but there would be soon. Robert zigzagged through a few side streets to get to the main road, doing his best to avoid any of the more likely routes the first responders would take to get to the house. When we turned left at the traffic light onto Woodlane Road, the sirens were behind us, buried somewhere in the neighborhood's labyrinth.

The highway was ten minutes away if we made all the traffic lights. I expected his phone to ring before we reached the on-ramp, and I wasn't wrong.

"Hey Jimmy," he said into it. "Who called you?" His voice sounded strange to me, but that was likely just my nerves. And the loss of blood. Once we pulled out of the driveway, Erica had taken an extra shirt out of her duffel bag and pressed it against my leg to slow the bleeding. It worked, but I'd still lost enough to begin feeling woozy.

"Yeah, we're okay."

There was a pause while Jimmy spoke. I saw Robert's eyes flick up at the rearview mirror.

"On our way to the hospital."

Another pause.

"The two guys they found weren't the only ones who got shot. My cousin was visiting and he took a round in the leg." He thought for a second then added, "Maggie got grazed too."

Pause.

"No, I think she's okay, but my cousin's bleeding pretty bad. We wanted to get him to the hospital as soon as possible. Didn't want to risk waiting for an ambulance."

Longer pause.

"No idea, man. They came crashing through the front door then all hell broke loose."

Pause.

"No, I've still got my piece on me."

Another long pause.

"I will. As soon as we get Mags and my cousin squared away at the hospital, I'll give you a call and explain everything. I promise."

Pause.

"Virtua, the new one in Marlton."

Short pause. His eyes flicked to the rearview mirror again.

"Yeah, sure. Meet me there."

Pause.

"See you soon." He hung up and put the phone in a tray by the gear shift in the center console.

"So what happens when he gets to Virtua and we're not there?" I asked.

"He'll call me back, and I'll tell him the truth."

"Why not just tell him now?" Denise asked. "He's your partner. He deserves to know."

Those eyes back in the rearview. "I want to put a little more distance between us," he said. "Just to be safe."

"Safe from what?" Then she lowered her voice and said, "Is this what that FBI guy warned you about?"

He turned and took her hand. "I just want to be careful."

What that FBI guy warned you about.

Robert knew more about what was going on than I initially gave him credit for, no question about it. It was a conversation we needed to have. But not right now. I had more pressing matters to deal with.

"You still have that field kit?" I asked Erica, feeling the blood drip between my fingers and onto the clean, gray upholstery.

CHAPTER TWENTY-NINE

Before Erica worked on my leg, I insisted she clean the gash on Maggie's head and make sure it didn't require further attention.

"I'm fine," Mags said as Erica dabbed the last few drops of blood away from what turned out to be little more than a scratch.

God, she was lucky. Ghost didn't miss often, and certainly never twice.

When Erica went in for one last swipe with the Steripad, Maggie jerked her head away and turned to face her over the back of the seat. "Seriously, I'm good," she said. "Help my dad now, okay?"

Even though she was pissed, it still sounded lovely to hear her call me dad. Erica obliged without protest and tossed the wadded up, red-stained gauze into the pocket in the armrest of her door.

"Take your pants down," Erica said to me as she pulled out a fresh wipe. I fought the urge to make a "you need to take me to dinner first" joke. Didn't take a genius to read the room and realize it wasn't the best time for quips.

I unbuckled my jeans and pulled them down, along with my boxers, just far enough to expose the wound. Erica cleaned it off without warning, and I gritted my teeth against the sting from the alcohol.

"Hold still," she said. I don't know if Robert heard her and decided to be funny or if a pothole simply appeared at that exact moment, but the Chevy swerved hard enough to knock Erica off balance and send the suture needle right into the raw, exposed flesh she'd just cleaned. A sharp moan escaped through my clenched teeth but at least I fought back the urge to scream *MOTHERFUCKER!* at the top of my lungs.

"Sorry," Robert said, sounding anything but.

"Let's try this again," Erica said. This time Robert kept the wheel steady, but without a local anesthetic—or at least a shot of whiskey—the experience was far from pleasant. I felt every needle puncture, and the tug of thread through the freshly formed holes. My surgeon knew what she was doing, though, and in less than five minutes, eight close, tight stitches were in and tied off. Erica smeared antibiotic ointment over the whole thing, covered it with gauze and then held it in place with a large Band-Aid from the first aid kit. I pulled my pants and boxers back up, each torn and damp with blood. They would need to be replaced, as would everyone else's clothes.

"Thanks," I said as I eased gingerly onto the seat.

"Are you better?" Denise asked.

"I'll live."

"Too bad. Now tell me what the hell is going on."

"Denise, I'd rather not get into it in front of the—"

"In front of who, the kids? Your girlfriend just drove a van through the front of our house and shot two people in front of them, so I doubt anything you say could traumatize the kids any more than they already are. They deserve to know why they were almost killed tonight. We all do. So start talking."

"She's not my girlfriend," I said lamely.

"God damn it, Ben!"

I took a deep breath and started talking. No sugarcoating anything. Quick and to the point, like a doctor delivering the news to a terminal cancer patient. "The man who tied you up is a professional killer. An expensive one. He was hired to take out Robert and frame me for the murder. I found out about it and came here to try to stop him."

"A professional killer," Denise said. "And you're connected to him." It wasn't a question.

"I was the one who recruited him, yes."

"And why would you do that?"

I could have told them about my missing fingertip and the knife to my eye, but that would have been taking the easy way out. Those were the reasons I accepted the job, true, but not the reason it was mine to accept in the first place. I planted those seeds long before Ponytail flashed her shiny blade, and nobody forced me to.

"Because it's my job," I said.

"Jesus Christ, Ben." There were ten years of anger and pain and disappointment in those three words.

"Believe me, Denise," I said with my head down, "I didn't mean for any of this to happen. I didn't know Robert was involved until after the fact. As soon as I did, the very instant, I did everything I could to stop it. Including coming back here."

"Well that makes it all better, then."

"Denise—"

"What happened to you?"

"Nothing good."

"And human trafficking? You're involved in that, too?"

"No," I said, trying like hell to sound as sincere as possible. "That was a lie. Denise, come on, you know me."

"No, I know Ben Williams. Or at least I used to. And he would never be capable of anything so horrible. This person you've become, though, Rick is it?" She laughed, but it was a sad sound. Deflated. "I don't know him at all."

There was a long silence as I tried to think of something—anything—to say that would matter. Before I could, Robert's phone rang. "It's Jimmy," he said.

"What are you going to tell him?" I asked.

"The truth." Before I could protest, he answered and almost immediately started laying it all out. Bad guys. Hitmen. Denise's ex who's involved in it all and claims the police can't be trusted. It was the short version, but he omitted nothing.

"Well?" I asked, after he'd hung up.

"He'll buy us as much time as he can, but that won't be much. There are two dead bodies and a hit and run where I sleep every night, plus they found the two officers stationed outside. Harrison and Colesar. Good guys, known them for seven years. Each shot once in the head. Their car was stashed in a small patch of woods just outside the neighborhood."

"I'm sorry," I said.

"I told him it has to do with the case I'm working for the FBI, but eventually we'll all need to go in and make a statement," he replied, ignoring my worthless apology. "The longer we don't, the more questions it will raise."

"We need a place to regroup," I said. "Somewhere out of sight and low-key."

Denise thought for a moment and then said, "I still have a key to my Aunt Irene's house."

To be technical, Aunt Irene was Denise's great-aunt. Though only ten years separated them, she was her mother's aunt, and the two had been like sisters growing up until Denise's mom moved to New Jersey when she was twenty-two. Irene stayed behind in Ohio, but they kept in touch. The old-school way, too. Hand-written letters, Christmas cards printed on actual paper. They kept it up until Irene died almost two years ago.

"I thought your cousin Emily would have sold that place by now," I said. It never dawned on me that I shouldn't know anything about Irene's passing or her daughter taking ownership of her quaint, single-family home in the backwoods of Ohio. Information I would know only if I still followed Denise closely on social media, or at least closer than an estranged ex-husband probably should. If she caught my slip up, though, she never let on.

"She tried," Denise said, offering no further explanation. No doubt location had a lot to do with it. I'd only ever been there once, early in our relationship, when Denise's mother had invited me along on the annual visit. I was still accumulating brownie points with my in-laws, so I said yes to the eight-hour drive.

There was one road leading to a cluster of three or four houses at the top of a large, forested hill masquerading as a mountain. Bad weather of any kind, including a steady drizzle, made that road treacherous even for alert, experienced drivers. Cell service was spotty at best and Wi-Fi was nonexistent. I was sure technological advances had improved things over the years, but I doubted if it was by much. If indeed the place remained vacant it could be ideal. What clinched it was when Robert said, "Who's Aunt Irene again?"

If he couldn't remember who she was, then that meant he hadn't told anybody at work about the tiny little shack in eastern Ohio. Which meant that anybody close to him who happened to be on Trish's payroll—if anyone like that existed—wouldn't know about it, either. Eventually, The Persian—because it would definitely be The Persian—would discover the place in Denise's old social media archives, even after I had her delete them on the way there. But it would take her a few days. Enough time for us to figure out our next move.

I hoped.

CHAPTER THIRTY

"I need to call Jeff," Robert said, "let him know what's going on. Maybe he can help." We were on the PA Turnpike, about four hours from the Ohio border.

"Who's Jeff?"

"FBI section chief I was working with."

"Do you trust him?" In the dim blue glow of the dashboard lights, he nodded as he dialed.

"Jeff," he said after a moment, "This is Rob. Sorry to bother you so—"

As whoever was on the other end of the line spoke, his posture behind the wheel went from casual to on full alert.

"Who is this?" he said. "Where's Jeff?"

"Robert?" Denise asked, concerned.

The phone still pressed to his ear, he smacked the steering wheel, hard enough to rattle it. Then he did it again. Then a third time. I was amazed he didn't break anything in the steering column.

"Robert!" Denise shouted his name this time. In the second row, both kids sat straight and on edge as their soon-to-be-stepfather managed to get himself under control and pull the car onto the shoulder of the road. Without a word, he got out, came around to the passenger side, opened the back door and handed me the phone in between Maggie's seat and my own.

"She wants to talk to you," he said.

She.

I took the phone. Maggie slid over so Robert could release the catch that allowed the seat to tilt up so I could get out. "Hello, Trish," I said before she could speak.

"Hello, Rick," Trish replied. "You've made quite a mess of things."

"Just Ghost's head," I said, stepping out of the car. Robert shut the door behind me and Denise got out to stand with him. "Joey's too, but his was pretty much a clusterfuck even before you got to him."

"As long as we're talking about heads, don't forget your friend, Ian. I believe they're still picking up pieces of his from that dirty parking lot."

"He wasn't my friend."

"No, you don't have any friends, do you, Rick? People are just a commodity to you. A means to an end."

That's right. Because the minute you allow yourself to get close to someone, share a beer, talk sports, let them show you how to defend yourself in a fight, and shoot a gun without looking like you don't even know which way to point it, they go and betray you for a big payday and their blood winds up splattered all over the coat of the guy who's fucking your wife.

"What are you doing answering this phone, Trish? Where's the man who it belongs to? Did you buy him or kill him?"

"Well, we tried to do the former, but that didn't work, so we settled on the latter." I turned to Robert, who was hanging on every word I said and straining to hear Trish's. The rest of the car was equally rapt.

"Why are you doing this?" I asked, keeping my voice low and taking a few steps away from the Chevy. "What's so special about Robert Baglioni?"

"You mean he hasn't told you?" Trish asked, amused. "Well that doesn't seem very considerate. After all the trouble you've gone through trying to protect him, futile though it may be. You'd think the least he could do was tell you what all the fuss was about."

"Whatever it is, Trish, we can work it out."

God that sounded desperate, but my already skimpy playbook was getting thinner by the minute.

"I'll still be your fall guy," I said. "Call off the hit on Robert, and I'll be on the first flight back to London. Sign whatever confession you want. Whatever will make this all go away. Just leave my family alone."

"Oh Rick, I wish I could," she said, sounding very much the opposite of sympathetic. "But your little homecoming has forced us to activate our backup plan. And in that one, a simple confession by you just won't be enough."

"Why not?"

"Too many dead bodies, my dear. Too many loose threads we can't afford to leave dangling. If you had just gotten on your plane to Mexico like you were supposed to, none of this would be necessary. You'd be busy poisoning your liver on a beach somewhere and your family would be safe."

"Except Robert would be dead and I'd be in prison. Or worse."

"Oh yes, you both would still have needed to be eliminated. But your ex-wife and children could have been spared. Now, because of you, I'm afraid that they've simply seen too much."

My legs were weak and my hand was shaking but I fought to keep my voice steady. "Please," I said. "Tell me what I need to do to make this right."

For a moment, I allowed myself to believe that she would come back with an offer. At that point, I would have said yes to anything.

Instead what she said was, "You're going to die, Rick. And so will they. All of them."

Then the line went dead.

CHAPTER THIRTY-ONE

I stood with the phone against my ear for another minute or two, pretending to listen to the nothing coming out of it. When I turned, five sets of eyes stared back at me. The back door was still open, Robert standing sentry next to it.

"Turn this off," I said, handing the phone back to him, "and don't turn it on again. They have your number now, which means they have what they need to start tracking you."

"Okay," he said, his words flat. His gaze matched.

"No more bullshit. I need to know—"

"It's a box," he said.

"What?"

"The reason they want me dead. A tiny lead box Jimmy and I pulled from the stomach of a dead girl found inside a container on a ship at the Navy Yard. Caught the case about three weeks ago."

"What's inside the box?"

Robert sighed. Looked at Denise. Tucked his phone back in his pocket and said, "Uranium, the dangerous kind."

"Holy shit," I said.

"Twenty-two grams worth. Street value around two million. Enough to irradiate a few city blocks, or so Jeff told me in a conversation that still gives me nightmares."

"Robert," Denise said, putting her hand over her mouth.

"Omar found it while he was doing the autopsy."

"Omar?" I asked.

"Medical examiner. Captain Edwards called Homeland Security as well as the Feds right after we filed our initial report. That's when I first heard from Jeff."

"How enriched was it?" I asked. Earlier in my career, when I had just arrived in Germany, I did a little work with uranium smugglers. They weren't what you expected. Burned out, drunk Russian ex-military with mounds of debt and easy access to stockpiles of nuclear material. They were a lot of things, but professional wasn't one of them. Too many headaches. Vicious business, too. Of all the ways to earn an illicit living, dealing in uranium was one of the ones most likely to get you chopped up into tiny pieces. I was happy to leave that business behind.

So what the hell were Trish and her Board of Directors doing involved with it?

"No idea," Robert said. "I told Jeff we'd ship it to him so the Feds could test it in their lab, but he shot that down."

"Why?" Denise asked. Robert gave me a long look.

"He was worried about someone getting a hold of it, wasn't he?" I asked, trying not to be smug. "He thought someone in his office might be compromised."

"I thought he was being paranoid," Robert said. "Still did, up until you came along. Now Jeff is dead, and there are two bodies back at our house."

It wasn't an *I told you so* moment, so I resisted the urge. "Where is it now?"

"There's a dummy one filled with twenty-two grams of worthless lead pellets in the FBI lockup down in DC. Jeff had me overnight that one right after our first call."

"And the real one?"

"Somewhere only I know about. And that's not about to change, so save yourself the trouble of asking. Even Jimmy doesn't know the one I sent to the Feds was bogus. He just thinks I check in with Jeff from time to time to give him updates."

"And he trusted you with this kind of responsibility after one phone call?"

"I get the sense he didn't have much of a choice. He kept me in the dark about a lot, but it didn't take Sherlock Holmes to figure out this was a big break in whatever he was working. I'm sure he checked me out after my captain called and before he and I spoke, but it's like you said, Ben: What's a homicide cop from Philly have to do with a multinational task force? I guess he just played the odds that whoever got to his people didn't even know I existed."

"Yeah, but who's to say they wouldn't get to you eventually?"

Robert's shoulders squared and his stare hardened. "Maybe he trusted me to do the right thing. You should try it sometime."

It still seemed like a big leap of faith for someone who knew at least a little bit about Trish and what she was capable of, but now wasn't the time to argue hypotheticals. "The human trafficking ring Joey said I was involved with, the one they were going to frame me for, did Jeff think this was connected?"

"Only partially. Like I said, he didn't tell me much. From what I gather, the ring has small-fish buyers that are only interested in the girls, but there's a few whales who are interested in much bigger purchases. The girls are how they get the goods into the country."

"That's horrible," Denise murmured.

"Do you know where the box came from?"

He shook his head. "That's what we were looking into when you showed up. The girl was Polish, early twenties, but Jeff's team didn't think she was anything more than—"

He paused here, glancing at Denise.

"—packaging." Denise covered her mouth and lowered her head. "Frank and Nadia were investigating a company in Saudi Arabia for connections to the box but hadn't found anything concrete yet."

"Saudi Arabia?" I asked. Robert nodded. "No wonder someone wants you dead."

"I don't understand," Denise said.

"If highly enriched uranium is coming out of Saudi Arabia, there's a good chance it's being produced in a plant with American equipment and American technology. And for a country that signed a no-nukes treaty, a story like that would make a lot of people look very bad."

"How is the woman who killed Jeff connected to all of this?" Robert asked.

"No idea. For all I know, her organization might just be an intermediary. But now I know why it was so important that nothing be traceable back to them. No telling who would be implicated if any of this came out." I thought of Willem, the disgraced Belgian senator, and wondered how many others like him sat on Trish's Board of Directors. How many other formerly influential players clinging to whatever power they could still hold on to. "Did Jeff share any other information with you, anything at all, no matter how trivial?"

"Not really. Aside from hiding the box somewhere safe, my role was just to keep an eye on the docks and let him know if any more bodies turned up. The less I knew, the easier it was for him to trust me."

"Damn," I said. We were flying blind, and any information at all could only better help us figure out our next move. But getting our hands on encrypted FBI documents was easier said than—

"Sergei," I said.

"What?" Robert asked.

"Get in the car, I'll explain on the way."

"You still want us to go to Aunt Irene's?" Denise asked.

"It's as good a place as any."

Amazingly, nobody argued. Except Denise, who wasn't crazy about sharing the third row with Erica. But I wanted to sit next to Robert. We had a lot to discuss.

After I made a quick phone call.

His voicemail picked up after four rings, so I hung up and called again. It was 5:30 tomorrow morning in Brussels and he was no doubt sound asleep, but I couldn't wait for his alarm to go off. Every second counted.

It rang four times again, but he picked up before the voicemail kicked in a second time.

"Hello," he said groggily.

"Sergei, it's Rick."

There was the sound of rustling bed sheets and a click as he turned on a bedside lamp. "Rick? What time is it? Is something wrong with the phone?"

"No, the phone's fine. I have another job for you."

"Okay," he said. The sleep was slowly bleeding out of his voice.

"I need you to hack into the FBI's internal servers and access some files for an agent Dunbar, Jeff Dunbar." Robert shot me a look from the driver's seat but I held up my finger and he kept quiet.

"Oh, is that all?" Sergei said.

"No. While you're at it, if you could tap into Mossad and MI5, that would be really helpful. I can get you the names of the agents I'm interested in with them as well."

Sergei laughed. "And who is paying for this miracle? I hope whoever they are has deep pockets and a magic lamp with all three wishes, because that's what it will take."

"It's me," I said.

Sergei waited a beat and then said, "Do you have any real clients, or do you just recruit people to solve all of your personal problems?"

"I have several clients, in fact, and one of them is very angry with me right now."

"Would this be the same client that had someone follow you into the bathroom when you bought my phone, scaring me half to death?"

"That would be the one."

"I did not enjoy that experience, Rick."

"I'll make it worth your while."

He was quiet for several seconds, so much so that I pulled the phone away from my ear and checked the screen to make sure he hadn't hung up.

"What is in these files?" he said at last.

"I don't know, that's why I need you to open them for me, but it has to be quick because I'm pretty sure they're being deleted as we speak."

"Rick, I can't just wave my fingers over a keyboard and hack into the encrypted databases of three major intelligence organizations. A job like that takes months of planning and resources to pull off."

"I don't need everything, Sergei, just whatever you can get."

"And I'm telling you that what I can get is going to be nothing."

"Please, Sergei. I'm grasping at straws here."

He sighed. "I'll do what I can, but it won't be cheap."

"Name your price."

"Half a million, at least."

I closed my eyes. "I can get you two hundred thousand now. It's all I've got."

"And the rest?"

"Will you take an IOU?"

"Given your current situation, unless you have a three hundred thousand dollar life insurance policy that names me as the sole beneficiary, I'm going to have to say no. I'm sorry, Rick. Goodbye."

"No, Sergei, wait!" The line was silent but it didn't go dead. "Look, I know it's a big ask, but they're coming after my family, man."

Another sigh. "Two hundred thousand?"

"I'll text you my account number. There's a little over two hundred and change in there. I can't transfer it to you without drawing attention but you can hack it. Clean it out, it's all yours."

"If I do manage to access any files, what do you want me to do with them?"

"Download everything and upload it to my secure dropbox, I'll send you that info as well, along with the names of the Mossad and MI5 agents."

"Okay," he said. He didn't sound happy, but if I could have reached through the phone and kissed him I would have. "No promises, but I'll see what I can do."

"Thank you, Sergei."

He hung up. I quickly opened a new chat room, invited him and sent the relevant information.

"One of your clients?" Robert asked.

"A candidate."

"He any good?"

"I hope so," I said as I put my phone away. A tangible silence crept over me from behind, where Denise and the kids were digesting everything they had seen and heard so far that night. It couldn't have been easy, watching a man you used to love transformed into something repugnant. If there was any way to make them understand how and why that transformation happened, I would have done it. But that wasn't possible. Not tonight. Probably not ever. So instead I did my best to ignore that wave of silence, crawling over me like spiders, and said to Robert, "Tell me everything Jeff ever told you. Leave nothing out."

"It's not a lot, and none of it is terribly important."

"Let me be the judge of that."

CHAPTER THIRTY-TWO

He was right, it wasn't terribly important, and it only took him about twenty minutes to cover everything. The gist of it was no different than what I already knew:

Somebody opened a container on a ship at the Navy Yard. Inside was twenty thousand pounds of bagged rice and one dead girl, about twenty-two years old. Polish. Hanna Kaminski. Her family, from a small town outside of Warsaw, reported her missing after she ran away three years earlier. Hard to say when she got picked up by whatever trafficker found her. Probably not long afterward.

It was doubtful she was alone on the ship, but the others were likely picked up by an intermediary who then transported them to whatever sick son of a bitch still bought people like livestock in the twenty-first century. Whether the intermediary noticed the corpse and worried he'd get in trouble if he said anything or if he just fucked up the headcount no one knew for sure, but either way the dead girl got left behind for one of the dock workers to discover the next morning. She wouldn't have lived much longer anyway. Packages are meant to be ripped open when they arrive at their destination.

Robert and Jimmy saw no outward signs of foul play, but realized a twenty-two-year-old Polish girl probably didn't wind up dead in a sealed container full of rice due to natural causes, so they called in the usual teams. The crime scene guys did their *CSI* thing, Robert and Jimmy questioned the dock workers, and the dead girl was transported back to the medical examiner's office for an autopsy.

Omar Alpas, the coroner on duty, opened her up and quickly determined a cause of death: internal hemorrhaging caused by a small, lead box that had as much business being tucked in between the folds of her small intestine as the girl herself had being in the container.

Omar called Robert, who opened the box and saw it was filled with tiny gray pellets. He'd watched a *60 Minutes* special recently about the nuclear black market and recognized the pellets as possibly enriched uranium, so he called his captain, who called the commissioner, who instructed them to call Homeland Security and the FBI. Enter Jeff, who, in Robert's version of events, told Robert to hide the box about five seconds after saying, "Hello, my name is Jeff Dunbar." So that's what Robert did.

"Give it a rest, Ben," he said, after I asked him for the third time where the box was stashed.

"Fine," I said, knowing full well there would be a fourth time.

"So what's our move?"

"Get to Irene's, lay low, and wait to see what Sergei can turn up."

"Then what?"

"I haven't gotten that far yet. It'll depend on what he finds."

"For two hundred grand, he better find something."

"I can't believe you have a bank account with two hundred thousand dollars in it," Denise said from the backseat, in a voice that was more disgusted than impressed.

"I don't anymore," I said.

About an hour out from Aunt Irene's house, the roads became far more rural. The streetlights grew scarce and turns appeared out of the darkness with no warning or identifying signs. We stopped at an all-night gas station to top off the tank and allow Denise to take over in the driver's seat. The GPS still worked, but I trusted Denise more than Google Maps at that point. Robert rode shotgun, and I returned to the third row with Erica. I was relieved to see both kids asleep, leaning against each other in the middle of the second row. It was good that they were getting some rest and even better that recent events weren't plaguing it with nightmares. Especially Ethan. His fingers were gently laced with his sister's, and I suddenly wanted to cry.

It was not quite 5:00 a.m. when Denise took a hairpin right that I didn't even know was there and started our climb up the small mountain I affectionately thought of as Aunt Irene's Hill. At first glance, the road appeared to be more of an abandoned trail than anything intended for cars. Paved with potholes and crumbling hunks of asphalt, it weaved in and out of the evergreen forest that blanketed the slope. In some spots, there was a sheer granite wall on the right, and a vertical drop of up to several hundred feet on the left, with no guardrail to provide even a false sense of security. When it veered back into the pine woods, the half-moon broke the canopy just enough in places to illuminate the odd cabin or mobile home tucked among the trees. Oftentimes there wasn't even a driveway to signal the domicile's presence—just a path through the trees leading from the road to the front door, if you looked hard enough to see it.

Halfway up, at an elevation of about one thousand feet, Denise turned left through two trees that looked no different than the five hundred other trees we'd passed and onto one of those hidden driveways. Aunt Irene's place, long since abandoned, was a mere silhouette in the moonlight. A simple, rectangular rancher with the closest neighbor another half mile up the road, it was the next best thing to being invisible.

Denise pulled the Traverse to a stop just outside the front door. Robert gently roused the kids, and we all plodded up the rotting front steps with our phones on flashlight mode. The door was locked and Denise had her key, but it wouldn't have taken much to kick it in. She first undid the dead bolt, then the doorknob, but before she could open it, Robert and I both grabbed her arm and said, "Wait."

Our guns were drawn. We looked at each other and nodded to Denise, who pushed the door open so we could each step in and take a side. I went left, Robert went right. Other than something small and furry that went skittering across the floor, up the back of the couch and through a hole in the window behind it, the house was empty. No squatters, junkies, or large predators in sight.

"You guys feel tough now?" Denise said, walking between us. "You almost shot a baby possum." She flipped the switch next to the door, but nothing happened. "Emily must have stopped paying the electric bill."

"Any chance there's still a generator in the shed out back?" I asked.

"I'll go check," Robert said before Denise could answer.

"No, I'll go," I told him. "You stay with them." He didn't argue.

The generator was there, but the gas was old and wouldn't ignite. Erica held her phone light while I drained the tank, then filled it with what was left in the rusted red can next to it—which turned out to be just as old, stale, and equally useless. We found a hose sitting in a wheelbarrow with a flat tire, buried under years of cobwebs and dust. Erica brushed it off and took it with the red can to siphon some gas from the Traverse while I went back inside.

Robert and Ethan were making up a twin bed for Maggie in the spare bedroom with sheets they found in the closet. Ethan would sleep on the floor, like the gentleman Robert had taught him to be. My son's eyes still had a vacant, faraway look I didn't care for, but at least he was moving around under his own power and seemed to otherwise be okay. Maggie went in to help tidy up the room, and Robert went into the master bedroom to do the same. I planned to go talk to the kids—especially Ethan—as soon as Denise went to join Robert, but she came up to me instead.

"You stay away from us, understand?" she said, as if reading my mind. Her eyes were dancing. Or at least, that's how I always thought of it. My wife was not a crier. She fought the urge the way she refused to throw up when she was sick, preferring to choke everything back and deal with the burn rather than suffer the perceived embarrassment of letting everything go. This applied to happy tears, too. Her eyes gave her away, though. When she was feeling emotional—good or bad—they shook, side to side, ever so slightly. A lingering effect of surgery she had when she was a kid to repair her optic nerves, or so she always told me. If you weren't looking for it, you'd miss it. But I never missed it.

That little shimmer was as good as a built-in lie detector test for those inevitable occasions when she told me she was fine even though all the evidence clearly indicated she wasn't. She wasn't pretending to be fine now, though. And those beautiful, brown eyes were dancing harder than I'd ever seen them before. "Do what you have to do to fix this, but you don't talk to me or the kids any more than absolutely necessary."

"Denise, please. Let me at least tell them how sorry I am—"

"No." The word erupted from her mouth like a shell from a howitzer. That little hiccup was gone. "You gave up the right to apologize for anything when you left us."

"I only left to protect you from—"

"I don't want to hear it, Ben. I spent the first eight years after you left trying to figure out why, lying awake until four a.m., telling myself over and over that the detective who came to ask us questions was wrong, that you couldn't have done the things he said you did. But in the last two years, a wonderful thing happened: I stopped caring. You were gone and I refused to let you continue to haunt my life. And do you know what? It worked. I'm happy now, you son of a bitch, and it's all because I stopped caring about you. We never got a cent from your life insurance policy because no one could ever prove it, but as far as I was concerned, you were dead. Gone. I moved on. The kids moved on. Whatever you did, whatever you are now, we never wanted to be a part of it. You dragged us into it, though, so if we somehow make it out of this alive, do us a favor and disappear again."

I didn't say anything. I couldn't even if I'd wanted to.

"And this time," she added before walking away, "if you really want to protect us, don't come back."

Filled with fresh gas, the ancient generator roared to life, belching blue smoke and coughing several times before settling into a steady rumble that would have pissed off all the neighbors on our block back home, but out here would annoy only the few animals that hadn't hunkered down for the winter.

Robert hooked it up to the heater, the lamp in the living room, the refrigerator and the light in the bathroom. The two bedrooms we left in the dark, and it was doubtful the TV—a box-tube relic from the late '80s—would have worked even if it was hooked up. He also cut up an old tarp covering a rotting stack of firewood and used it to patch the hole in the window with a roll of duct tape he found in one of the kitchen drawers. The tape was so old, it looked like it might disintegrate in his hands, but it did the job.

Fortunately, the cell service had improved since my last time here. It still wasn't great, but I had 3 out of 5 Gs, with most of the bars full. Enough to access my chat with Sergei and my dropbox. Both were still empty, but it was early. He'd said it would take some time.

The sun was just cresting the horizon, and we were all bone-tired. For an old heater, it did its job well and the house became quite comfortable. After everyone else retired to their rooms, Erica took the couch and I took the first watch. We agreed to switch off every four hours until my family had rested enough that they no longer needed someone to stand guard while they slept. Erica protested a bit, insisting I was more tired than her, but within five minutes of her head hitting the arm of the couch, she was out. Impressive considering most of the stuffing had flattened or fallen away, so it was more like sleeping on a wooden frame than a cushion. Her mouth parted and a tiny, rhythmic snore filled the room, just audible beneath the hum of the generator from outside.

I checked the flimsy dead bolt and peered out one of the three small windows carved into the top half of the front door. Narrow rectangles lined next to each other in ascending order, a style right in line with the era from which the TV hailed.

The frost on the bed of brown, fallen detritus that made up the front lawn sparkled in the early dawn light. The wind rustled a few bare branches, but nothing else moved. From my shoulder holster, I pulled out my Glock and racked the slide, making sure there was a round in the chamber.

CHAPTER THIRTY-THREE

If I sat I knew I'd fall asleep, so I stood. Even leaning against the wall was risky. I shifted my weight back and forth from one foot to the other, absentmindedly, the way I've always done since Maggie was born and that gentle rocking motion was the only thing that could soothe her infant cries. Back and forth I swayed, staring through the little window in the front door all the way to the left, then the one all the way to the right, watching the frost melt and the wind whip dried leaves and pine needles around the wheels of Denise's SUV.

After exactly four hours, Erica's cell phone alarm beeped three times before she turned it off. She woke as if she'd never slept. Simply sat up, pocketed her phone and took my place at the door. Like a robot that just finished charging. I set my own alarm for exactly four hours later—2:03 p.m.—checking the chat room before lying down.

Nothing from Sergei.

When my head settled against the hard, stiff arm of the couch, I knew why Erica had found sleep so quickly. It felt wonderful.

The sun had nearly set when Erica shook me awake, the sky outside a dull, faded blue. It was almost 4:30 in the afternoon.

"Why did you let me sleep so long?" I grumbled, rubbing my eyes.

"You needed it," she said.

"I'm starving."

"We all are. Your wi—"

She caught herself. The corner of my mouth twitched in the slightest hint of a smile.

"Denise," she continued, "said there's a little corner store a few miles in town. You okay if I make a run?"

"Sure," I said, pulling out my phone. When I opened it and saw my new notifications, I forgot about the hunger pangs in my stomach.

There was a message in the chat room.

Files in dropbox, it said. *Not much, best I could do.*

Thank you, I wrote back, fingers shaking. Then I killed the chat and opened the dropbox. It showed that just under 1 MB of data had been deposited within the last hour. If that was all text, it was a lot. If there were videos and images mixed in, not so much. I called Robert over to take a look. Someone must have found a deck of cards somewhere, because he was in the middle of a game of rummy with Denise and the kids at the kitchen table.

"Whaddya got?" he asked, sliding a chair over to the couch. The metal legs screeched against the yellowed, curling linoleum floor.

"Don't know," I said absently as I punched in my pass code. When it opened, I saw it was mostly emails and word documents, with some PDFs and a few scanned photos mixed in as well. No video.

"Is that all from Jeff's computer?"

"Hard to say." Sergei had taken the time to create separate folders based on the file type, but there didn't appear to be any indicators about where they came from. I couldn't complain. He did this job on short notice and at a discount. Like I always tell my clients: you get what you pay for.

I skipped over the heaviest folder marked "Emails" and opened the one marked "Documents." This was a mix of scanned images, Excel spreadsheets, and traditional Word docs. After scrolling through the first dozen pages, it became apparent that Sergei's haul was haphazard.

Either many of the files to which Trish had access had already been deleted, or these were simply the ones he could access with no help and limited resources. Whatever the reason, it was a data dump in the most literal sense. Like trying to solve ten different puzzles with only a handful of pieces from each one, all mixed together in the same box. Still, the methodology didn't change. How did you solve a puzzle? By putting matching pieces together. Find the corners, look for patterns.

For the next two hours, that's what we did. Robert and I, side by side, while Erica went grocery shopping and Denise and the kids went about making Aunt Irene's old homestead as livable as possible. Ethan sulked the entire time, which was actually kind of reassuring—it's what a twelve-year-old boy should look like when dusting old furniture. Hopefully that meant he had come fully around from his shock last night.

"That goes there," Robert said, pointing to the folder we'd created marked "Suspects." Sorting through the jumble of evidence, the only pattern that emerged was that most of it revolved around either individuals or companies, so we created a new folder for each and were in the process of grouping them together. It helped that I was familiar with a lot of the names in both folders. Some were from my days doing executive search—those were mostly the American corporations—but the rest were from the network I'd built in the decade since. I was not at all surprised to see that the two often overlapped. Multi-billion dollar companies don't get to that level by only doing business with Boy Scouts.

"This guy's an arms dealer," I said, pointing at a surveillance shot of a middle-aged Arab man getting into a car outside a nondescript office building. "Connected to at least a dozen militant extremist groups around the world."

"Any in the US?"

I nodded. "A few."

"There has to be a connection to the uranium there, right?"

"Maybe. Hard to say for sure. That's not our concern right now anyway."

"Not our concern? Preventing a terrorist from killing thousands of innocent people is not our concern?"

"No, it's the task force's concern."

"The task force is gone, remember? You made sure of that."

"Not all of them," I said, ignoring the shot. "MI5's agents are hopefully still alive. Besides, the uranium's hidden away someplace safe, right? *You* made sure of that. Right now, my focus is on protecting the people in this house. That's it."

He clearly wasn't happy with that answer, but he didn't press the issue.

When we were done, there were 113 files in the Company folder, and 57 in the Suspect folder. Many of those files contained information about the same suspect or the same company. In all, there were maybe a dozen companies of interest, and ten suspects. I knew all of the companies and had dealt directly with four of them. All legitimate businesses with global footprints. The four that I'd worked with before were headquartered in America.

The word "legitimate" did not apply to the suspect list, which was full of career criminals. I knew them all. Their specialties were all over the map, ranging from robbery to murder. There was no common denominator. Two of them, though, stood out more than the others:

General Li Xin, former head of the Chinese Ministry of State Security.

And Arthur Lynch, a serial entrepreneur who founded dozens of Silicon Valley startups before he renounced his citizenship and emigrated to Russia right before his businesses were all investigated for tax evasion.

Neither of them had been seen for years. They weren't presumed dead, like Willem Van de Berg, they just sort of fizzled out, the way well-known people sometimes do when they step out of the public eye.

"So what's the connection?" Robert asked, more to himself than to me. Knowing he wasn't looking for an answer, I simply shook my head. If he wasn't going to give up the location of his secret box, then I wasn't inclined to share what I knew about Trish's organization. Not yet, anyway. Besides, it was just a hunch that Xin and Lynch were part of her Board of Directors. I could be totally wrong.

We sat staring at the tiny five-inch screen on my phone, our chins resting in our hands, the universal image of the adult male stumped. It's the same look I wore at some point during every Christmas Eve that

I spent assembling an overpriced toy with eight hundred thousand tiny plastic pieces. Every now and then one of us would reach down and open a specific file, read it—or at least pretend to—then close it and resume the position.

"What's the endgame here, Ben?" Robert said as he stood up, arching his back to stretch the muscles. Denise was at the stove, boiling water for a quick spaghetti dinner. The supplies in the country store had proven to be somewhat limited, but they were enough to provide a real meal. "Let's say we figure out what all this means. How do we use that information to call off this Persian person you say is coming for us?"

"If we can figure out what the task force knew, maybe we can use it to leverage Trish to call off the hit. Clearly, whatever evidence they'd already compiled was enough to spook her pretty bad. And from what I know about Trish, she doesn't spook easily."

"That's your plan? Try to 'spook' her?"

"I'm open to better suggestions."

"My suggestion is dinner," Denise said as she set paper plates around the table. "You both need to eat."

As suggestions go, it wasn't a bad one. Especially since Denise said it without sounding like she hoped I choked on the noodles. I'd take every small win that I could get.

After dinner, we stared at the files some more. Tossed out multiple theories as to how everything was connected. Argued about them. Argued about if this was all just a waste of time. Argued about what we should do instead. Then Robert got tired of arguing and suggested we call it a night, following Denise into the bedroom before I had a chance to argue with him about that, too.

It was just after midnight when Maggie came out of her room and joined me by the front door. I wasn't nearly as tired as the night before, so I felt safe pulling a kitchen chair over to the front window where I could look out and prop my foot up on the sill during my watch. My phone was charging on the counter. It needed a break, and so did I. Erica was asleep on the couch. Fitting, since she'd practically become a piece of furniture since we'd gotten here, melting into the background while Robert and I argued, and eating her dinner by the front door instead of at the table with us.

Maggie pulled a matching chair over, an ugly, garish thing that looked like it belonged in the break room of a post office from the 1970s. Irene's decorating tastes had been . . . *unique.*

"Hey, Peanut," I said. "What are you doing up?"

"Can't sleep," she said, spinning the chair around backward and straddling it. She was wearing blue fleece pajama pants with little sheep printed on them, and a plain white sweatshirt. Same outfit she had worn the night before. The little country store didn't have a women's clothing section, apparently.

"You could try counting your pants," I said.

"What?" she said, giving me a quizzical look. I pointed at the cartoon sheep on her legs, and she groaned. I laughed quietly. She rolled her eyes. "You always had the worst dad jokes."

"The worst dad jokes are the *best* dad jokes," I corrected.

She smiled and it lit up her whole face, just like when she was little. "I miss them."

My own smile faded and I turned back to the window. "Me too."

"Why did you leave?"

The smile was gone and her face was older, nearly adult, reminding me just how much of her life I had missed. "Maggie, I don't know that now is the best time to have this conversation."

"Well, now isn't the best time to do anything, is it? Given that we're hiding in an abandoned house waiting for someone to come kill us. But we have to pass the time somehow, so it might as well be doing this."

"I can't imagine what this must be like for you," I said, dodging the subject at hand.

"Yes you can. It sucks. But I try my best not to think about it so I don't lose my mind and I go on. I'll be fine."

I smiled. "You always were my tough one. How's Ethan doing? I feel like he's been a ghost."

"He's better. Just scared. We all are."

"I bet. You're such a good big sis—"

"Why did you leave?"

"Maggie—"

"Why?"

I sighed. "Your mother doesn't want me talking to you. I don't want to make things worse than—"

"Dad, stop. I'm not five anymore. No bullshit. Why did you leave us?"

She wasn't going to let this go. I glanced over her shoulder to make sure Denise and Robert's door was still shut, then I said, "We needed money."

"What does that mean?"

"It means the economy crashed and nobody was hiring anybody, let alone paying someone like me to find people for them to hire. Your mom had just started working at the school and wasn't making much. When my income dried up, we burned through what little savings we had. I tried finding part-time work, even applied to be a greeter at Walmart, but there just weren't any jobs. Your grandparents gave us what they could but it wasn't a lot. Then we stopped paying bills. Then people started calling who didn't like that we stopped paying bills and threatened to take away things like our cars and our house."

"But Dad, they didn't take anything away. We kept our house, we kept our cars. I even remember taking a vacation to Niagara Falls the year you left."

I nodded. "That's because I did what I had to do."

"What did you do?"

I looked away, out the window, trying to figure out how much to tell her.

"Dad," she pressed, "what did you do?"

I turned and saw her mother staring back at me. It was still just the two of us in the room, but Denise was all over her face. She really had turned into a mini version of her, minus the freckles. "I did my job, but not for my company."

"For who, then?"

"Bad people, Maggie."

"What kind of bad people?"

"The kind that paid me a lot of money to find other bad people to help them do bad things. And when those bad things started piling up, I realized that you and Mom and Ethan weren't safe anymore. So I left. To protect you."

I saw her face start to crumple, saw her try to swallow back the lump in her throat. When she was a toddler she cried openly and freely, but the older she got the more she fought it. Like her mother. When she realized she would lose this battle she turned her head and wiped her eyes angrily with the palm of her hand.

"We would have been fine," she said, sniffing. "Even if we had to move and never go on a vacation again." Fresh tears replaced the ones she wiped away, and when her face broke this time, she didn't try to stop it. "I missed you, Daddy," she said. And then she wept. I got off my seat and knelt in front of her, wrapping her in my arms. She hugged me back and squeezed, sobbing into my ear.

"I'm sorry," I whispered into hers. "I'm so sorry, Peanut. And not just for leaving. For everything."

We held each other for a long time. On the couch, Erica slept, or at least pretended to. If we woke her, she gave us the courtesy of not letting on. When at last we let go, both of our faces were wet. I dried mine with the sleeve of my shirt, then smiled and laid my hand against Maggie's cheek.

We stared at each other for a moment, neither one saying anything. A car drove past on the road, its headlights briefly illuminating the otherwise dark living room. I curled my hand around the Glock resting on the windowsill, but the car moved on without slowing down. I let it go and Maggie asked, "Are there really more people coming? Bad people?" She may be my tough one, but it was obvious she was terrified. She was only seventeen, after all. Facing the prospect of her own murder—after barely surviving an attempt already—was not something she could simply ignore, no matter how much she tried to convince herself.

I hesitated just a second before nodding. No point in lying to her now.

"Can't you do anything to call them off? Aren't you their agent or something?"

"It doesn't work like that," I said. "I find them, yes, but they don't work for me. They work for the people who pay me to find them."

"What about the stuff you and Robert were looking at all night?" she asked, her voice hitching a bit. A stray sob that betrayed her fear. "Anything useful in there?"

"Not yet. It's just a bunch of companies and random people. Nothing connecting them, at least not that we can see."

"Do you recognize any of them?"

"Some. The people are not the kind you want to make friends with, but the companies are all legitimate ones. I even had a few as clients back when I was in my old job."

"Do you know anyone who still works at any of them, someone you could call and get more information?"

I shook my head. "No, we never did a lot of business with them. They're all big, global companies who use vendor management—"

Systems. They all used vendor management systems.

"They all used vendor what?" Maggie asked, confused.

"Hang on," I said, standing up. My phone was at 90 percent now, so I pulled the connector from the jack and opened up my dropbox. I was flipping through documents, scanning the emails between the task force agents when Maggie came up behind me.

"What is it, Dad?"

"We didn't work with those companies because they were all part of a VMS," I said, my eyes never leaving the screen and its bright, bluish-white glow. "VMS stands for vendor management system, which basically means they paid one agency to do all of their staffing and recruiting for them, instead of farming out the work to multiple firms. The VMS company didn't actually find the candidates, though. They just turned around and used smaller firms like ours anyway and funneled all the candidates we found through them, charging both sides a fee for being the go-between. It's cheaper and easier for the big hiring company but smaller recruitment firms like mine hated it because it meant we had to go through whatever VMS company they hired, which paid us less for our candidates than we would charge on our own."

My fingers moved quicker as I started to find what I was looking for. I created a new folder and began sliding documents into it, both from the Suspects and Companies folders.

"I don't understand," Maggie said, looking over my shoulder. "What does that have to do with the people who are after us?"

"Maybe nothing," I said, glancing at the time in the top-right corner of my screen. It was 12:17 a.m., which meant it was 5:17 in London, and 7:17 in Saudi Arabia. Too early for normal working stiffs to be in the office, but the exact window when most high-level executives liked to clock in so they could have the place to themselves for a bit before the worker bees arrived. I thumbed through the Companies folder until I found the one in Saudi Arabia where Robert and the FBI suspected the smuggled uranium came from.

Coperion Industries. Ahmir Uddin, CEO.

"Only one way to find out," I said.

CHAPTER THIRTY-FOUR

By the time everyone else woke up, I was in the zone at the kitchen table. I'd made my way through all the Middle Eastern companies in Sergei's files and was halfway through the ones in Eastern Europe, starting with the C-Suite and working my way down until I found the person I was looking for, the connection between that company and Trish. Almost all the employee profiles were on LinkedIn, and getting their extension was as easy as dialing in and entering their name into the company directory.

Just like the old days when I lived on the phone, prospecting to either poach a candidate away from a client's competition or pitch my services to a brand-new company. I was damn good at it, and even though I hadn't flexed those particular muscles in a while, I was happy to see they hadn't atrophied at all.

It was Headhunting 101, and never while I was sitting in any of those boring, all-day training seminars my old boss loved so much did I ever think those particular skills would one day save my life. Yet here we were, because apparently the universe has a nasty little taste for irony.

Erica was standing guard by the door and Maggie, who had vowed to stay up and help in any way she could, was asleep on the couch beneath the hand-knit afghan that Irene had given me when I slept on that same couch all those years ago. Robert was the first one into the kitchen, bleary eyed and slovenly with a thick morning stubble. Not that I looked any better.

I had just punched in the last name of the CFO for a Hamburg company called Innovative Technologies and was listening to it ring while it connected to her extension, wondering if it would be a live voice or a recorded message that answered. When she picked up and said her name, I got the same little thrill I used to get sitting in my old office, when every answered call held the possibility of a future commission check.

"Marianne Muller," she said, her German accent thick. I decided to reply in English and see how it went.

"Good morning, Miss Muller," I said. It had been easier to slip into my polished, professional recruiter voice than I'd anticipated. Like putting on an old jacket from high school that still fit.

"Good morning," came the reply, in better-than-expected English. Her LinkedIn profile did say she studied at Cambridge before moving back to Hamburg. So did one of the seven emails between the FBI and MI5 in which her name was mentioned.

"My name is Rick Carter, I'm a recruiter. I came across your profile on LinkedIn and have a proposition I'd like to discuss with you. Do you have time to talk, or did I catch you at a bad time?"

"I'm sorry, Mister . . ."

"Carter."

"Yes, Mr. Carter. I'm quite happy in my current role and am not looking to make a move at this time."

"Of course, I'm sorry for not being clear. I'm not calling you today about a job, Miss Muller, but more of a business opportunity."

"Whatever it is, Mr. Carter, I'm not interested. Now if you'll excuse me, I'm very busy—"

"I know about the processing chips you're buying from Patricia Baum. The ones your competitor came up with a year before you did but they haven't been able to patent yet."

Dead silence, other than a small click that might have been her pen falling from her fingers onto a desk that probably cost more than Aunt

Irene made in her best year at the textile mill. Robert replaced the tea kettle on the stove and leaned against the counter with his freshly topped off mug of instant coffee, watching intently. When Denise plodded into the kitchen with a loud yawn, he politely shushed her and pointed at me.

"How did you say you got my name?" Marianne asked after she picked up her pen. I could hear her clicking it furiously in the background.

"LinkedIn. Wonderful platform. Connecting people from all over the world."

"Well, while I appreciate your phone call, I have no idea what you're—"

"Sorry," I said, snapping my fingers close enough to my phone's mouthpiece that she could hear. "Forgot to mention that I also saw your name pop up on some files over at MI5."

More silence, but it was weighted, tugging on my phone's earpiece like a bent fishing pole.

"That's impossible," she said, but even she didn't believe it.

"Don't worry; I'll email you the files after we hang up. Along with a few more that show a direct link between you and a man named Junan Collins who specializes in industrial espionage, among other types of theft."

"What do you want?" The German accent was back and thicker than ever. Fear tends to do that, revert people back to their most base level in all facets.

"Call Trish and tell her your partnership is over effectively immediately," I said. "Tell her Rick Carter threatened to go public with your dealings unless you did as you were told."

"That won't end well for you, Mr. Carter."

"Your concern is admirable, Marianne, but at the moment I'd be more worried about what will happen to you and your company should the information in my possession ever get to the press. Or maybe I'll just send it directly to the company you're stealing from, see how they'd like to handle it."

"Okay, okay," she said. Anything else she had planned that day had taken a backseat in terms of importance to ending this call as quickly as possible.

"Good. I'll send the files once we hang up. Email me back as soon as you tell Trish. If you lie to me, I'll know. And Marianne?"

"Yes?"

"Don't forget to tell her my name. Rick. Carter."

I hung up, feeling better than I had in a long time.

"What was that all about?" Robert asked as I sent the files linking Innovative Technologies to Junan Collins and a stolen set of prototype microchips that powered the next evolution of smartphones, one with full AI capabilities. An evolution that Innovative Technologies paid good money to cash in on in a less than honorable way.

"That," I said, "was my third victory of the day."

"I'm gonna need a little more than that."

"I figured out what Jeff was investigating." Robert and Denise both stood up straighter, the leftover sleep suddenly gone from their eyes. "I'm pretty sure the woman who hired me, the one who answered Jeff's phone the other night, is part of an organization that profits off being the middlemen between criminal organizations and legitimate businesses. That's why the suspects in those files were all over the place in terms of their rap sheets. We were trying to solve a puzzle last night, Robert, when what we should have been doing was playing connect-the-dots."

"And you connected them?"

I nodded. "Those two guys I told you were the big fish, the Chinese general and the Lynch guy?"

"Yeah."

"They match the profile of someone who I know for a fact is on what my client calls their Board of Directors. Except they're not some group of criminal masterminds bent on world domination—they're a bunch of washed-up has-beens who spent their lives abusing their power, skimming off the people who did the real work, and are desperate to continue doing so. They connect criminals of all kinds to large, wealthy organizations that want what those criminals have to offer but don't want to risk being connected to them directly. So Trish's group acts as the go-between. They make introductions, they set up meetings, they broker deals—all of it kept completely in the dark and safely away from their clients. And all for a sizable fee."

"Isn't that essentially what you do?" Denise said, not without judgment.

"Yeah, but this is on a much bigger scale. And they are way more organized and have their hands in way more illegal shit than I ever have."

"So this is all about money?" Robert asked.

"It's always all about money. Human trafficking is just a part of what they're into. It also appears to be their acceptable loss, a line of business they're willing to sacrifice, with me and Leon set to take the fall. While the media and authorities are focused on the horrors of their disabled sex slavery ring, they can continue profiting from everything else on their list of services."

"Including smuggled uranium," Robert said.

I nodded again. Coperion's CEO, Ahmir, had cracked just as quickly as Marianne. Anything to keep my information from going public. In less than ten minutes, he'd confessed to knowing about his company's illegal enrichment activities. Hardly made them unique. Most people in the US intelligence community suspected that the majority of Saudi companies had some type of enrichment activity going on, but it would never advance to nuclear capabilities as long as our two countries remained on good terms. It was a contingency plan the Saudis hoped to never use.

What Ahmir hadn't planned on was one of his scientists smuggling a box's worth of pellets out one night, and handing it off to an arms dealer working with Trish. Ahmir claimed to not know anything about Trish or who her client was that would be interested in purchasing the uranium, but he and I both agreed that whoever it was probably wasn't interested in using it as a paperweight. The box being in my possession compromised not only Trish and her client, but Coperion as well.

"So how does knowing that help us?"

"Trish is part of a big business, Robert, and like all businesses—legitimate or otherwise—she cares about two things: Her money and her reputation. I say we fuck with both."

"And how do you plan on doing that?"

"By calling the companies on that list and threatening to go public with what we've got unless they sever all ties with her and her Board. The woman I just hung up with was the third one so far to agree."

"But your candidate only got a small portion of the evidence the task force had."

"Right, but we're not trying to mount a criminal case against them. The most valuable service Trish provides to her clients is anonymity, the security of knowing that they will never be connected to the criminals they're doing business with because Trish and her Board are the only ones dealing directly with the bad guys. If we take that anonymity away, Trish's reputation is shot and all of a sudden all the money and influence her Board of Directors crave dries up like a housewife with a headache."

"Eww," Maggie said from the couch. She had woken up at some point during my call and listened with the afghan wrapped around her shoulders.

"Sorry, Peanut, thought you were asleep." I felt my face flush. Turning back to Denise and Robert, I said, "We don't have enough evidence to take them to court, but we've got more than enough to burn down every business implicated if that information ever goes public. I'll give it a day, then call Trish and tell her I'll back off if she calls off the hit on you."

"But I'll still be a threat to her because of the uranium."

"You won't be," I said, pausing because I knew what came next would not go over well, "after I let her know that you told me where it's hidden, and I moved it to a location only I know about. Puts the target on me and me alone."

"No way," Robert said angrily.

"Trust me, I can handle my—"

"I don't give a damn about you, Rick." I caught Maggie flinch out of the corner of my eye. Even Denise seemed a bit taken aback by the remark. "These people are kidnapping girls and selling them into slavery. They're smuggling nuclear material into my country and doing God knows what else. Not to mention they tried to have us all killed. They deserve to be put in jail, not just blackmailed."

"And eventually they will. MI5 and the other agencies will reassemble their task force and they *will* catch these people, I believe that."

I didn't. Not really. It's generally accepted that money may not buy you happiness, but it can buy pretty much any other fucking thing you want. Including immunity from the consequences of breaking laws the rest of us must abide by. If my new career had taught me nothing else, it was that people with money always come out on top, even when it looks like they won't.

"When they haul Trish and her people into court," I said, "I will gladly turn over the uranium. But at least until that happens, I'll know that they're only trying to kill me and no one else. The whole reason I came back was to protect all of you. This is the only way."

"Dad," Maggie said, "there has to be another—"

"Do it."

Ethan stood in the doorway to his bedroom. Before he said those two words, the last time I'd heard him speak was when he still called memories "rememberies." His voice had deepened since then, but not all the way. It still had some cracking and creaking to go before puberty was done with it. More importantly, the sweet, exuberant innocence that I remembered was gone. It might be there under normal circumstances, but not now. Not while I was within earshot.

"Tell him what he wants to know, Robert," my son said, "so he'll go away and leave us alone."

"Ethan," I said. My own voice cracking, but for entirely different reasons. I never got to finish the sentence, though. The instant my eyes met his, he turned and went back into his room, slamming the door shut behind him.

If Robert took any joy in Ethan's simple, brutal dismissal of me, I didn't know it. I never looked his way. I couldn't take my eyes off Ethan's door.

"Finish your calls," Robert said, mercifully ignoring Ethan's comments. "See if you can get the rest of the companies to go along. If that part of the plan works, we'll revisit the uranium discussion."

I nodded, still focused on the simple brown door and the boy behind it I barely knew, who wanted nothing more than to forget about me.

"You really think you can pull all that off from here?" Denise asked.

I turned, wiping my eyes with the heel of my hand, and held up my cell. "All any good recruiter needs is a phone."

CHAPTER THIRTY-FIVE

I dialed and texted and emailed the rest of the day and into the night. By the time I took a break for dinner—chicken and carrots, the latter drizzled with melted butter and dusted with brown sugar, another Denise staple—my phone once more radiated heat, and I worried all the charging would burn out the battery.

The rest of the calls went about the same as the one with Marianne. Some, like the CEO of a Silicon Valley startup that was desperate for a good hacker to wage cyberwar on a competitor, were more hesitant. Fear of Trish and her Board of Directors was strong, but when I gave them a little taste of the information I'd gleaned from the hacked files, most were willing to take the risk in exchange for my silence.

Erica took my shift standing watch that night so I could get some sleep. It had been quiet anyway. The Persian hadn't yet sniffed us out, but I knew that was just a matter of time. The following day was long and anxiety-ridden as I gave the companies time to get in touch with Trish and give her the news. After a dinner of instant rice and beans, I stepped onto the porch and called her.

"You must be getting desperate," Trish said in lieu of a traditional hello. At least a few of the people I'd contacted must have called her.

"I am," I said, "but that doesn't make what I'm doing any less effective."

"Effective?" she scoffed. "You blackmail a handful of our clients into backing out of their deals with us and you think that moves the needle? Oh darling, it's cute when you try hard."

"I didn't try hard though, Trish, that's the thing. Took me less than twenty-four hours to get those ten to back out of their deals with you. How many more do you think I can get in a week? Or a month?"

"A month?" This time she actually laughed. "Every sunrise you see at this point is a miracle. No, you won't be around long enough to become more than a nuisance."

"Yeah, but that uranium will be."

"Once Detective Baglioni is gone, that won't be a problem anymore either. Its whereabouts—and the problems it may cause us—will die with him."

"That would be true, if he was the only one who knew where it was."

There was a pause. "What do you mean?"

"Robert told me where the uranium's hidden. It's yours if you want it."

Another pause, but more hopeful than the last. "Name your price."

"Call off the hits on me and Robert. Leave my family alone. And forget any notion of framing me for your human trafficking operation. Let Leon take the fall for that one by himself."

"Is that all?"

"I'm a fair negotiator. Do this and we both walk away happy. I'll even stop pissing in your pool as far as blackmailing your clients goes."

"How very generous of you. I'll need proof you actually have the box, of course."

"Naturally."

A final pause, one spent making sure she hadn't missed anything, some con I was trying to pull. "Okay. Send me visual proof you have the box then name your place to do the exchange."

"I'll be in touch," I said, then I hung up. Nothing had changed. Trish was not going to call off anything just because I claimed to know where the uranium was. We were all still in as much danger as we had been a few minutes ago.

But now she was intrigued. If there was even a chance she could get her hands on that damned box she owed it to her Board of Directors to at least explore the opportunity. Because the guy who supplied her arms dealer wasn't the typical drunk Russian ex-general, but an employee of a US-backed Saudi energy company. If the uranium was tied to them—and it would be—then there would be more attention on her and the Board than there had been at any point yet in their existence. More attention than even she would be able to deflect.

I hadn't landed her yet, though. Trouble was there was no bait on the hook right now, and she wouldn't stay interested if it remained that way for very long. I didn't have a lot of time.

"You look like shit," Robert said. He had joined me on the front porch.

"Title of my autobiography," I said. "I need to know where the uranium is."

Robert grunted and flexed his arms against the railing, assuming the same defensive posture I'd come to recognize whenever I asked him to do something he didn't want to do. This time, I cut it short.

"No," I said, "no more of that. The first part of the plan worked. Every single company I called told Trish they were ending their partnership."

"She pissed?"

"Less than I thought she'd be but more than she let on. But she was *very* interested to know that I had moved your uranium to a new location that only I knew about and no one else."

"Why the fuck did you tell her that?"

"Because I knew you'd try to wriggle out of telling me where it is, so I needed to put some pressure on you."

"Jesus Christ, Ben, this isn't a game."

"No it's not, so stop playing around. I need to know where it is to draw her away from you and onto me. Otherwise, you're about to spend the rest of your lives running. Trust me: it's no way to live."

His jaw clenched, but he knew I was right about this too. In the end, he settled for a weak threat. "If I find out you sold it back to her or anyone else, I swear to God . . ."

"That's never been the plan, Robert." I'd like to say I felt bad for lying to him, but I didn't. I had no idea what would happen to that box of uranium once I handed it back to Trish, who she would turn around and sell it to, or what they would do with it once they had it. Chances are, it would wind up being used to make a dirty bomb, yes. But dirty bombs were made all the time. It's what keeps the uranium black market afloat. Fortunately, the authorities apprehend the assholes who make the bombs before they ever get a chance to use them. I was betting what little morality I had left on them doing so again. It was the only option I had to keep my family safe, which made it a risk I was willing to take. Does that make me a cold-blooded asshole? Yes. But we've already established that to be true.

Robert shook his head and bit his tongue, but he was out of moves and he knew it. "It's in a lockbox," he said. "Stashed underneath the floor panel in my uncle's boat, out near Warminster."

"Jesus Christ, you told your uncle about it?"

"Even if I did, he wouldn't remember. My uncle's been in a nursing home for the past two years with late-stage dementia. I go by once or twice a month to check on the house, clear out the junk from his mailbox, mow the lawn in the summer. Nobody gets suspicious when I drive up there to make sure the box is where I left it last time. The boat hasn't been in the water for at least a decade. Just sits in his driveway, rotting in the sun."

"Still seems risky to me."

"I don't give a shit what you think. Do you want the address or not?"

CHAPTER THIRTY-SIX

The next morning, Robert and I went car shopping. He, Denise, and the kids were to stay at the house with Erica while I made the drive to Warminster, but I wanted them to have the Chevy in case they needed to get out of Dodge quick. As far as Trish knew, until I sent her proof that I had the uranium, this could all be one huge bluff. She wasn't going to call off The Persian until that box was in her hands.

We passed by a small dealership and went browsing on the side of the road instead, where owners sold for cash and didn't ask any questions or require any paperwork. . Robert spotted a 1994 Buick Regal parked on the front lawn of a small ranch house about five miles outside of town. The handmade sign in the windshield said $950. It had 149,000 miles on the odometer. The metal had rusted away from the bottom of the passenger door so it rattled like a gong when you closed it. The owner was a widower and the car belonged to his son, who had upgraded to a model made in this century. We talked him down to $900 and paid in cash. Robert checked the engine before handing over the money and felt confident that it wouldn't crap out on me halfway to his uncle's house.

The fan behind the center dashboard vent squeaked, but the heater worked fine otherwise. I had it on full blast as I sat behind the wheel, parked outside Aunt Irene's house, after saying my goodbyes. They weren't anything special. Ethan never came out of his room. Of all the failures I'd accumulated in my life, my son's persistent condemnation of me was the one I knew would stick around the longest, and hurt the worst. Denise wished me luck and told me to be careful, but only because their survival depended on my success. Robert spent another ten minutes trying to talk me out of it, being more obstinate than usual. Maggie gave me a hug, squeezed me tight, and started to say something but then turned away, her eyes glassy. She came out to finish her thought as I was getting ready to leave.

"Hey, Peanut," I said, as she opened the door and sat in the passenger seat. "Everything okay?"

"No," she said, shaking her head back and forth, as if the motion would jar loose the rest of the words she wanted to say. "It's not your fault, Dad," she managed at last.

"Yes," I said, staring at her. "It is."

"You couldn't have known any of this would happen when you took that job. You had no choice, you said so yourself. Look what they did to your finger! You're not a bad—"

"Maggie," I said softly. "Stop. Honey, I love you, but we both know what I am."

"Don't say that," she said, and now the tears were building. "You're a good person. You wouldn't have come here to help us if that wasn't true. You're making them go after you now, not us. You could die." That line came out as a croak. "You saved our lives."

I smiled, but only because that's what she needed to see right then. "Too little, too late, sweetheart," I whispered.

"It's not fair."

It wasn't. And that was my fault, too. I leaned over and hugged her, and she hugged me back.

I heard the cars before I saw them. My eyes were shut, the lower half of my face pressed into the soft spot between Maggie's shoulder and her neck, not wanting to let the world back in, not wanting the moment to end. Even over the roar of the heater, though, I heard the crunch of the tires on loose stone. When I looked up there were three of them, older model Ford Tauruses, two with the classic red and blue lights flashing on top and one, unmarked, with a single red globe spinning on the front dash. The other two had the words "Wright Township Police Department" stenciled in black letters on the sides.

"Dad," Maggie said, pulling away. Her eyes were wide.

"Just relax, Peanut," I said, although my voice betrayed the confidence of my words.

The three cars pinned us in against the cabin. One behind, one in front, and one next to my driver's side. Two uniformed officers each spilled from the cars behind and to my left, their guns drawn and pointed at me and Maggie. From the unmarked car, parked in front, came a big guy, thick in the arms and the chest. He was wearing a plain gray sweatshirt but no jacket against the cold. Black jeans and boots, with a gun holstered on his belt. There was a badge clipped next to it. He stood six-three, six-four maybe. Smooth, bald head and a no-nonsense face.

"Come on out of the car now," he said, his voice booming through my window.

Maggie said, "Uncle Jimmy?"

Fucking. Robert.

"Hey Mags," Robert's partner said, catching her look.

She got out of the car and stared at him over the roof, disbelieving. "What are you doing here?"

"I called him," Robert said, walking down the steps. "Get out of the car, Ben. Don't be stupid."

You're the only stupid one here, pal.

Still, it wasn't like I had any other options. I got out and one of the officers with Jimmy immediately spun me around against the car and cuffed my hands behind my back.

"Hey!" Maggie shouted.

"Take it easy," Robert said, "he's not a threat."

Uncuff me and come down here, we'll test that theory.

The officer eased up on the rough stuff and pulled me away from the car.

"Thanks for coming, partner," Robert said, walking up to Jimmy and doing one of those hand-shake-into-one-armed bro hugs. "What's with the vest?" he asked, tapping Jimmy's chest.

"Figured better safe than sorry," Jimmy said. "Meet Officers Napoli, Tocco, Whelan, and Hinchey of the Wright Township PD. They're going to take care of you while we get all this straightened out."

"Straightened out?" I asked.

"Yes," Robert said, "as in letting the authorities handle this, which is what we should have done in the first place."

"You mean the same authorities that tried to have me killed back in Belgium? The same authorities that your buddy Jeff didn't trust, before he was killed?"

"No, I'm talking about my partner and the police force where I've dedicated nearly half my life. And as far as trust goes, Ben, I trust this man right here to protect me and my family far more than any half-assed blackmail scheme you could ever dream up."

I shook my head and kicked the old Buick three times. "You can't be this naïve."

"Put him in the back of your car," Jimmy said to one of the four officers who collectively sounded like a law firm that ran infomercials on daytime TV.

Have you been assassinated by a hit man due to police corruption? Call Napoli, Tocco, Whelan, and Hinchey to talk about what kind of settlement we can get for you!

I caught a glimpse of Maggie and what I saw in her expression toward Robert gave me a small moment of fatherly pride. It was full of betrayal and anger.

That's my girl.

"Where's the other one," Jimmy asked, "what was her name? Erica?"

"I didn't see her when we came out," Denise said as she and Ethan came down the steps. "She must be in one of the rooms."

"Did you know about this?" I asked her as Officer Whoever sat me in the back of his squad car. Denise didn't answer. Didn't even look at me.

"Napoli, Tocco, go inside and find her," Jimmy said. After they entered the cabin, he turned to Denise and laid his hand gently on her back. "Why don't you and the kids wait in my car. We'll all get out of here in a minute, back to the station where it's safe."

Safe. Sure. Even if Robert's right to trust you, Jimmy, he'd be an idiot to trust everyone else. Corruption and the law of averages go hand in hand. Eventually, somebody always takes the bribe.

Denise and the kids settled into the back of Jimmy's unmarked car while he and Robert remained outside.

"Once we're at the station we'll arrange something more secure back home, but it will take a few days to set up," Jimmy said to Robert. "You're gonna have to testify. Him too," he said, jerking his thumb over his shoulder to me.

"That won't be a problem," Robert said.

"We won't be alive long enough to even testify at the deposition," I yelled through the window. Robert glanced up, as if surprised that I'd been able to hear their conversation, then came over and opened my door.

"I'm getting a little sick of this 'can't trust anyone' bullshit," he said, fuming. "This man's had my back for over ten years."

"That's touching," I said. "It also means he'll likely catch the first bullet from whoever Trish gets her claws into at your precinct once she finds out that's where we are."

Before Robert could reply, Jimmy said, "Where the hell is your girlfriend?" Then, to the young officer standing by the steps, he said, "Find out what's taking so long."

The cop, who looked barely a year out of the academy, said into his walkie, "Aaron, did you find her or what?" He released the button and waited. When no response came from his colleague, he clicked it again and said, "Napoli, Tocco, what's your status?"

Release.

Silence.

Before he clicked the button a third time, he drew his pistol and held it at his side. "Napoli?"

Pause.

"Tocco?"

No answer.

My eyes were glued to the front door of Aunt Irene's cabin, right along with Robert's.

"Sam," Jimmy said, "go see what's going on."

Sam seemed less than enthusiastic to lend his fellow officers a hand. He climbed the stairs like a kid on a dare approaching the neighborhood haunted house, holding his gun like he'd just found it lying on the ground a minute before. The front door hung partially open, but he kicked it as if it were secured by a top-of-the-line dead bolt. It swung in violently and then drifted slowly back on its rusted hinges. He stepped inside, gun sweeping first right, then left.

Well, *almost* left. If he'd been able to fully check out that side of the living room, he might have seen the person who swung a cast-iron skillet at his face before it connected with his nose, spraying the front porch and doorframe with a geyser of blood. His body hit the wooden planks as total dead weight, his gun skittering unfired from his hand.

"Son of bitch!" Jimmy shouted. The last officer remaining outside, a blonde with former high-school quarterback good looks, panic-fired two shots at the door before Jimmy told him to stand down. Then he and Robert both trained their guns on the door.

"Call her off, Ben," Robert demanded.

"Sure," I said. "Just uncuff me and send your partner back to Philly."

"Ben, god damn it, this is serious!"

"I've been trying to tell you that since we first met, Robert."

He glared at me, then went back to watching the door with Jimmy and the All-American. I could only see their backs, but their heads were in constant motion, trying to spot Erica before she could launch a fresh attack.

It didn't work.

Three shots rang out from around the corner of the cabin and the QB, about ten feet to Jimmy's left, flopped backward on the ground.

"Shit!" Robert called out, but it quickly became apparent that Erica was no cop killer. The QB writhed in obvious pain, but there was no blood despite the three puncture holes in his neatly pressed shirt. The body armor he wore beneath it had stopped each slug before they pierced his skin, but at such close range, and in a tight, triangular cluster around his heart, at least one or two of his ribs were likely bruised, if not cracked outright.

None of us saw Erica, but that didn't stop Jimmy from squeezing off another four rounds in the general direction of where the shots came from. The bullets pinged off trees and the side of the cabin, no more effective in taking her out than if he had grabbed a handful of stones and tossed them toward the same area. He stood for a moment, icy puffs of breath pulsating from his mouth as he considered his options while Robert holstered his gun and came back to where I sat in the back of the squad car.

"Get out here, and call her off," he growled, yanking me out of the seat. He never heard Jimmy come up behind him, so he never even tried to defend himself as his partner of ten years, the one who always had his back, smashed the butt of his gun into the base of his neck. Robert collapsed in a heap at my feet. Denise got out of Jimmy's car and screamed but Jimmy ignored her, grabbing my cuffed wrists and shoving me toward the center of the yard, picking up Robert's gun and tossing it into the woods as we went.

I was getting tired of being right.

Denise and Maggie both cried out, but I couldn't make out what they said. Jimmy told them to be quiet and stay in the car, which they did. On the ground by Jimmy's car, the QB was undoing the Velcro on his body armor, reaching a tentative hand underneath to make sure his torso really was still intact. Lying on his back, his breathing labored, he wasn't going anywhere anytime soon.

"Drop the gun and come out or he dies," Jimmy said, his gun pressed hard against the side of my head. His voice was loud, but it wasn't a yell. He knew she was close by. Some of the fear in his body language had subsided as well. A human shield tends to have that effect on armed assholes.

We stood there for a moment, waiting for Erica to comply or make her move.

"When did Trish get to you?" I asked.

"Shut up," he said.

"Was it after Robert called you or before?"

"I said shut your fucking mouth." He was pissed, but also a little scared. He couldn't hide it all the way. It was good to hear. I kept pressing.

"If we hadn't fled Denise's house that night, would you have killed us all then?"

That earned me a smack on the back of the neck with the butt of his pistol, but not as hard as the one he gave Robert. He needed me awake. Gray spots exploded in my vision but I shook my head until they cleared.

"How much they paying you?" I asked, pushing my luck. I needed to keep him distracted enough for Erica to make her move, whatever that move might be.

As if reading my thoughts, she stepped into view from the corner of the cabin where she'd taken out the QB. She had her HK P30 leveled at Jimmy's head, or at least the half of it that was visible from where he hid behind me. The bullet would go right through my brain if she was off by even half an inch, but I wasn't worried. Her hands were steady, and her eyes were laser-focused.

"Drop it," Jimmy repeated, although it came closer to sounding like a plea than a demand. "Now," he added, trying to sound tougher.

Erica held her pose for another few seconds, then noticed the QB at her feet, struggling to get to his knees. She lifted her foot and brought it down hard on the side of his face. His head whipped into the loose dirt and he lay still.

Jimmy pressed the gun harder into the side of my head. I squeezed my eyes shut but refused to give him the pleasure of a grunt or cry. "I'll blow his fucking brains out," he said. "Swear to God. Drop the gun."

I kept my eyes shut, waiting to feel the zip of the bullet as it passed by my ear into his head. What I heard instead was the sound of Erica's pistol hitting the ground by her right foot, next to the unconscious QB. I opened my eyes and stared at her in disbelief.

"Kick it behind you," Jimmy said.

She did. I tried to ask her what the hell she was doing with no more than a look, but she never took her eyes off Jimmy. I was starting to feel less confident about her plan. When Jimmy spoke, I felt even worse. It was little more than an exhalation of breath tinged with the hint of words. If his mouth wasn't pressed against the back of my ear, I never would have known what he said. But I did hear, and knew it wasn't good.

"Forgive me," he whispered.

"Erica!" I shouted. Not soon enough.

With quicker speed than I expected for a man his size, Jimmy took his gun from the side of my head, pointed it at Erica, and pulled the trigger.

He got only two shots off before I reacted, but they both found their target. Erica's shirt puffed out tiny bursts of thread where the bullets punched through. I saw her legs buckle but never watched her hit the ground. The adrenaline had kicked in, and all my attention was on Jimmy.

My head jerked back like a hydraulic hammer. I was hoping to find the weak, rubbery cartilage of his nose, but whatever I hit was as solid as the back of my skull. It wobbled me for a second, but I still gave better than I got. The hollow clunk I heard in my own head must have been echoing through his because he let go of my arm and took a step back. Before he could recover, I turned and swept his feet out from under him with one swift leg hook. All 220ish pounds of him dropped without any attempt to break his fall. When his head bounced off the gravel, his hand opened and the gun popped out. I kicked it as far as I could, not caring where it landed, then pulled back with every intention of punting his chin through his brain.

Maybe if I'd broken his nose earlier instead of just conking him on the forehead, I'd have had better luck. As it happened, he wasn't quite dazed enough and caught my foot before it could connect. With a renewed sense of purpose, he twisted my leg and pulled me off balance. I landed hard on my shoulder, biting my tongue. I spat out a mouthful of blood just as he climbed on top of me, lifted my upper half off the ground by the collar, and began pounding the side of my face like a man working out his anger issues on a heavy bag.

Three punches in I must have become too heavy to hold up, because he let go of my collar and my already throbbing head hit the ground. I couldn't see out of my left eye, partially from the shock of the blows and partially from the steady stream of blood flowing into it from a gash in my eyebrow that felt big enough to dock a canoe in. Sharp, stinging pain spiked out from my orbital bone. If it wasn't broken already, one or two more good shots would do it. Jimmy's arm was cocked back to finish the job when his body jerked, and a strange look came over his face. With my one good eye, I saw his expression go from rage, to surprise, to fear.

And the fear was pure white. It spread across his face like water soaking through a paper towel. He reached over his shoulder and touched a spot just below the base of his neck. His fingers came back bloody and he staggered to his feet, but that didn't last long. His legs gave out and he sat hard on the ground, holding a spot just above the top of his bullet proof vest that was leaking blood at an alarming rate.

Erica stood over him, the barrel of her HK P30 still smoking from the two shots she put into the back of his body armor, and the third that clipped the top of the vest and got lodged in the base of his neck. The vest slowed it down, but it was still dangerously close to his spinal column. He needed to get to a hospital, but that wasn't high on her priority list at the moment.

"Are you okay?" she asked me.

"Yeah," I said, blinking the blood out of my eyes.

Erica produced a set of handcuff keys she'd taken from the unconscious QB. As she freed my wrists I said, "Are you okay?"

"Fine," she said. "A little sore."

I stood and faced her. The two holes in her shirt, like those in the QB's, were blood free. She tapped her knuckles against the bulletproof vest beneath it. "Good thing one of the guys they sent inside was about my size."

I smiled, then shook my head. "Wait, was that your plan all along, to let him shoot you?"

"It was the only way I could think of to get him to take his gun off of you."

"Why didn't you just shoot him first?"

She looked at me like I'd just asked why she didn't fry him with her heat vision. "He was standing behind you."

"Yeah, but you're a professional assassin. Aren't you supposed to be able to do some Angelina Jolie, bending bullets around corners shit?"

"You watch too many movies."

Denise and Ethan ran to Robert, who was starting to come around, while Maggie came to me.

"I'm okay, Peanut," I said as she reached for the cut on my eyebrow, hesitant to touch it. Instead, she wrapped me in her arms and I hugged her back, turning my face away so I wouldn't stain her shirt.

"She's got my kids," Jimmy said. We all turned to look at him, still sitting on the ground, color draining from his face.

"Who does?" Robert asked, on his feet and rubbing the back of his neck. I didn't need Jimmy to answer to know who he meant.

"Some woman. Middle Eastern. She called me the day after everything went down at your house. Told me I needed to find out where you were. She," his voice caught in his throat, but he cleared it and went on, "she sent me pictures of the girls at recess, playing on the swings. Said if I didn't tell her where you were, she'd kill them."

"Laila and Lexi?" Maggie said, her hand over her mouth.

The girls in her TikTok videos. The ones painting her face in their pajamas and hopping around to "Shake it Off." Now I knew who they belonged to.

Jimmy continued, "And if I pulled them out of school or sent them to stay somewhere else, she swore she'd kill the rest of the kids in their class."

"Did you tell her where we were?" I asked.

Jimmy nodded. "I had to. I'm so sorry, Robert. She has my babies."

"What do you mean she has them?" Robert asked. The concern in his voice was natural, but there was far less anger than I expected considering the man he was talking to had just cold-cocked him and admitted to working with the people who were trying to kill us.

"After you called," Jimmy went on, "I told her where you were. She showed up at my house. Told me to come up and make sure you weren't lying, then call her when I got here and keep you all occupied until she arrived with the girls. If I did that, she said she'd let us go."

"If you sold us out, you mean," I said, with enough anger to compensate for Robert's lack of it.

"She said it was the only way."

"And you believed her?" Erica said, dumbfounded.

"No, of course not! That's why I looped in these local guys. I figured we could make a stand if we had some help."

"Why didn't you just tell me?" Robert said, and there was some of that anger, if only a little. "All the shit we've been through, did you honestly think I wouldn't have your back?

"I'm sorry," Jimmy said, twin tears sliding down his cheeks. "I'm sorry, brother, but I didn't know if she had tapped my phone, hacked my computer. I couldn't risk it. I just want my babies back, Robert. I just . . ." And then the tears took over, and the rest of what he said didn't make any sense.

"Hey," Robert said, grabbing his partner's arm. "We'll get them back. You hear me? We'll get them back."

Jimmy nodded and the sobbing eased, replaced by a groan as he leaned on his elbow, blinking his eyes against the nausea that was hitting him.

"Robert, he needs to get to a hospital," Denise said. She was right.

"You need to go, too," Jimmy said. His voice sounded weak. "She knows where you are. She'll be coming."

"Not without your girls."

"Get him up and into the Chevy," I said. Denise, Ethan and Maggie all helped Jimmy to his feet. I pulled Robert aside and said, "Drop him at the nearest hospital and then take off."

"In case you missed it, I just made a promise to get his kids back. Running away's your move, Ben, not mine. Where's my gun?" He turned and started looking on the ground, scanning for wherever his beloved partner had kicked it after knocking him out cold.

"Listen to me," I said, grabbing his arm, but he spun out of it and bunched up the front of my shirt with his fist.

"No, you listen, you son of a bitch. It's not bad enough you drug your own family into this shit, now you've put Laila and Lexi in danger, too? You want to go hide somewhere, fine, that's what you do best, but I'm done playing it safe."

"Then how about playing it smart?" I shouted. "If you stay here and try to take on The Persian by yourself, or even with Mayberry's finest," I motioned to the cops Erica had dispatched with ease, "then you're dead."

Robert started to protest but I ripped his hand from my shirt and said even louder, "You're dead, Robert. She is a trained, expert killer, and there is no way she just has the girls waiting in her car to be dropped off like she's taking them to a playdate. She will have anticipated every possible move you can make and come up with ways to beat them. You think you'll take her by surprise? People like her don't *get* surprised. You cannot win this fight, I don't care how pissed off you are."

Again he tried to speak and again I cut him off. "I can still get Trish to call her off, but I need to know where the uranium is."

He shook his head. "This again? I already told you."

"Your uncle's boat?" I scoffed. "You're not that stupid, and neither am I. If you called Jimmy because you didn't trust me, then you sure as shit didn't tell me its actual location the first time. Where is it?"

He took a breath and looked over my shoulder. I didn't follow his gaze, but I could hear Maggie and Ethan both crying as they helped Jimmy into their car.

I lowered my voice. "I'm the best chance those girls have got. And you're the best chance my family—" I swallowed, "—*your* family has of making it through this alive. You and Erica. Please don't put all of them at risk out of some admirable but misguided sense of honor."

He turned his pained expression toward me, desperate for there to be any other way, knowing there wasn't.

I said, "Let me end this."

"I'll call you as soon as I have the box," I said to Erica. She was standing next to my open car window, having cuffed the deputies to the steering wheels of their squad cars. After they dropped Jimmy at the hospital and were a safe distance away, she would make an anonymous 911 call telling the rest of their squad where to find them. Other than some bumps and bruises, they would all live.

Everyone else was in the Chevy, its engine idling. Denise sat behind the wheel, the kids were in the back, and Jimmy was leaning against Robert in the middle row, a balled-up rag from beneath Aunt Irene's sink pressed against the bullet hole in his back. "Drop him at the hospital and then make sure you get everyone else away. Just keep driving. If you don't hear from me once every hour . . ."

I didn't need to finish the sentence. We'd already been over it.

"I still agree with Robert," Erica said. We'd been over that, too. She was firmly in the stay-and-fight camp. "We know she's coming. We can prepare."

I started shaking my head before she finished speaking. "We can't risk it if Jimmy's telling the truth about his kids. Besides, even if we manage to take her out, which is far from a sure thing no matter how much we prepare, it still won't be over. Trish can just send someone else. And they will keep coming. Unless I shift the focus onto me."

She disagreed, but held her tongue.

"Please keep them safe."

"You know I will," she said, then turned back to the Chevy.

I grabbed the gearshift to drop the car into reverse when Denise appeared at the window. "Hey," I said.

Her eyes were dancing again. She started to speak and then stopped, as if unsure what she wanted to say now that she was standing there. She settled on leaning over and gently brushing the butterfly bandage covering the cut Jimmy's fist had opened in my eyebrow. "How's your head?" she asked.

"Hurts."

She pulled her hand away and grabbed the open window frame of the door. "You really fucked things up, you know?"

I nodded. "I know. But I'm going to fix it. I promise."

She shook her head and wiped at her eyes with the hand that wasn't holding the door. "I don't mean just that." When she stopped, those brown eyes had stopped dancing and stared straight back at me. "We had something good, me and you. I just wish you would have talked to me before you did what you did. We could have worked things out, could have—"

Her voice broke, and she dropped her forehead against the edge of the door. I rested my hand on the back of her neck. For a minute, she let it sit there, let me feel the subtle shakes as she fought back the emotion she hated anyone to see. When I let my hand drift into her hair, though, that was a step too far. With her head still down, she reached back and grabbed my hand, squeezing it once before removing it and placing it on the door. Then she picked her head up and sniffed.

"Be careful," she said. It was the same two words she'd said to me earlier, before I'd been cuffed and beaten, before her fiancé's partner had been shot, before her already fucked-up world took another dramatic turn into Shitville. But these two words were different. This time, it sounded like she actually meant them.

"I will," I said, but she was already walking away.

I watched her go, watched her get behind the wheel without another glance back, then pulled the old Buick out of the driveway and watched the Chevy follow behind me, down the windy mountain road. At the base of Aunt Irene's Hill, they turned right, to the west.

I headed east.

CHAPTER THIRTY-SEVEN

"It's a little nothing stream about a half mile off one of the main hiking trails by the resort," Robert had told me, finally resolved to letting me do what needed to be done. "My dad used to take me fishing there every summer. Got a few salmon in it, some trout. Never caught much of anything big enough to keep, but that wasn't the point."

"Father-son fishing trips are rarely just about the fish," I'd said, thinking of the first and only time I'd taken Ethan fishing with Maggie and me, off a small dock on a man-made lake in a park near our house. He'd had a Spider-Man fishing rod that was about two feet long, but still awkward for his three-year-old hands to hold. I'd had to help him not only bait the hook but cast and reel in the line, too. Still, when he made his only catch of the day—a sunny no bigger than six inches—he grinned like he'd just hooked a great white.

"No they're not, are they?" Robert said. He didn't pursue that particular line of philosophical thought, and for that I was appreciative. "Anyway, no one else knew about the spot but us. The stream ran too shallow a lot of the time to make it worth the trip for serious fishermen, and getting to it was a pain when the brush got thick in the spring and summer. I don't recall ever seeing anyone else there in all the times he and I went. It's easy enough to find, though."

"And you're sure the box is still there?" I'd asked.

"I take a drive up every week to check."

"Nobody ever questions you? That's like a six-hour round trip."

"Jeff told my captain he needed me to do periodic check-ins on an informant they had stashed in the area, which was good enough for him. No one else needed to know. When you're an unofficial part of an FBI joint task force, you get to throw the word *classified* around a lot."

The stream was nestled on the grounds of a ski resort in the heart of the Pocono Mountains. I made it there a little after 2:30 in the afternoon, the rusty old Buick doing better than I expected once she got humming with no traffic in front of her. The resort was a fancy one called Woodlake, just outside Big Bear at Masthope Mountain. Truly gorgeous. On-site spa, golf course, four-star restaurants. Everything all-inclusive. The kind of place I fantasized about taking Denise back when we had no kids but no money either. Treating ourselves to a weekend away in those days meant renting a hotel room down the Jersey Shore in the offseason. Dropping $1,000 for one night in the Poconos would have been the equivalent of financial suicide. Assuming we could have made a reservation anyway. According to their website, they were booked solid nearly a year out.

I pulled into a small lot behind the main building, popped the trunk and removed the shovel I'd borrowed from Irene's shed.

Robert's directions were deceptively simple:

Start at the mouth of the blue hiking trail and follow it about a mile until you reach a large granite boulder covered in moss by the side of the path. Easy to spot and the first such boulder you'll encounter.

Cut through the woods directly across from the boulder and head due west for another half mile or so until you reach the stream.

Follow the stream north a few hundred paces until you come upon a tree with the words "Jay and Abby 4Ever" inside a heart carved into its bark.

A few feet from the trunk sits a flat hunk of stone that looks vaguely like the shape of Texas, about a yard across. Easy enough to lift but too heavy to tempt any kid passing by to toss it into the stream just to watch it splash.

About two feet directly underneath of that stone is the box, sealed inside a plastic evidence bag.

Easy, right?

Except now that I was standing next to the boulder, there was no clear path cutting through the woods, at least none that I could see. Instead, there was a thick menagerie of sharp, dry branches, thorny brush, and patches of soggy ground just starting to thaw, camouflaged by a blanket of fallen leaves and pine needles. I had passed only three other hikers on the trail before I reached the boulder, an old couple out for a stroll and a jogger lost in his playlist. Everyone else was either on the slopes or warming themselves with a glass of whiskey by the big stone fireplace in the lodge.

Anybody wanna trade places? I thought before breaking off the trail into the true wilderness.

By the third stretch of mud, my shoes were soaked through and I regretted not stopping to pick up a pair of rubber muck boots on the drive in. I'd tried poking around with the shovel, looking for drier land, but the mud extended so far in both directions I was afraid of straying off course just to avoid a case of frozen feet.

When at last I reached the stream, I could see why Robert chose it as a hiding place. Between the hike through hell and the shallow water, there had to be a dozen better spots for anyone looking to drop a line in the water. The current was moving quickly, forming little whitecaps in places where a branch or the tip of a submerged stone broke the surface.

I made my way along the bank until I came to Jay and Abby's tree, about twenty yards from where I'd run into the stream. I scanned around the trunk, certain the Rock of Texas would be gone, washed away by the rain or tossed in the stream by the only other person stupid enough to make it this far, but it was right where Robert said it would be. I flipped it over and watched an earthworm dig itself deeper into the wet earth while a family of little gray pill bugs scattered.

I took off my suit jacket, hung it on a nearby tree branch, rolled up my sleeves, drove the tip of my shovel into the dirt and started digging.

CHAPTER THIRTY-EIGHT

At the risk of sounding like Denise at the end of our fifth date, it was tinier than I expected. I had pictured something the size of a cigar box, when in actuality I could hold the container easily in the palm of my hand. Robert assured me it was safe to open, that in pellet form the radiation was lower than a standard X-ray, but I still turned my head as I lifted the lid, as if that alone would shield me from whatever deadly rays were emanating from within. There were maybe two dozen of the little gray pellets, filling up half the box. I tilted it from side to side, watching them roll back and forth like a contained wave.

There are a couple thousand lives in this box. Give this to the wrong person with the right set of skills, and you've got the terrorist attack on domestic soil that keeps Homeland Security chiefs up at night. One of many possible attacks, anyway. Not the one with the mushroom cloud in Midtown Manhattan, but the one that fills up the hospitals with radiation poisoning for months to come, leaves the water undrinkable and the air toxic to breathe. All that in the palm of my hand.

Holding it steady, I snapped a picture and sent it to the chat room I had just opened.

"Happy?" I said, returning the phone to my ear.

There was a pause as she examined the photo I'd just sent, then Trish came back on the line and said, "Very much."

"Good, because the price just went up. One million dollars, cash, in addition to calling off the hits. Call it punitive damages for pulling that shit with Robert's partner."

"Don't push your luck, Mr. Carter. You should be grateful I took this call at all, after keeping me waiting for so long."

"And you should be grateful I haven't gone public with this already."

"Don't be silly, Rick. Going public does nothing good for anyone, and you know it."

"Send the money with The Persian," I said, refusing to get sucked into a back and forth with her. "Alone. I find out she hurt Jimmy's kids and all bets are off."

"What's the location?"

"I'll text it when we hang up. And if anything happens to Robert or my family in the meantime—"

"Yes, yes, I know, you'll disappear with the box and leak your own story to the press."

"And continue my quest to cut you out of every deal you've ever brokered."

"I wouldn't puff my chest out over that too much, Rick. We have ways of dealing with clients and suppliers who deviate from our arrangement. Don't think we'll hesitate to dole out consequences for their disloyalty. Forcefully, if necessary."

"And the pile of bodies will stack up, like one big arrow pointing back to you, Van De Berg, General Xin, Lynch, and the rest of your publicity-shy Board of Directors." I paused to let those three names sink in. Her silence felt wonderful. I pictured her on the other end of the line, wondering what else I knew about her organization.

"Your family will not be harmed, Mr. Carter," was all she said.

"Glad we understand each other."

"I've always understood you, Rick."

"I think you mean 'underestimated.'"

I hung up, my heart racing. After a quick look around to make sure I was still alone, I texted the following:

Blue hiking trail on the ground of Woodlake Resort and Spa. Poconos. Midnight tonight. The Persian comes alone with the cash in a black duffel bag. Unarmed.

I watched the little bubbles dance in the chat room as Trish typed her reply. It didn't take long.

She'll be there.

Then I resealed the box in the evidence bag, dropped it in the hole I'd just dug and started to refill it.

CHAPTER THIRTY-NINE

"Everything good?" I asked.

"No different than the last time we spoke," Erica replied. They were currently westbound on the Ohio Turnpike, stopping only for gas, food, and bathroom breaks, as per my instructions. They'd dropped Jimmy off at the nearest ER and took off, not even giving their names. Been driving ever since. Robert still wasn't happy about it.

"Tell him Laila and Lexi are still alive," I said. "Hopefully that will make him feel a little better."

"Turning this car around and heading back home to face things head on is the only thing that will make him feel better. Can't say I blame him."

"Tonight," I said. "If all goes well, you can be Jersey-bound tonight."

"Any sign of her yet?"

"No."

I'd been standing by the little wooden sign that had *Blue Trail, 4.7 Miles* carved into it since 11:00 p.m. From this vantage, I could just make out the main resort parking lot in the orange glow of the sodium lights. The last car pulled in at 11:17. None had come or gone since. A soft quiet had settled over the place, the kind that usually only comes on the heels of a snowfall. It was 11:45. The Persian was due in fifteen minutes.

"Are you ready?" Erica asked.

I took a deep breath and let it out. "As I'll ever be."

After re-burying the box, I'd driven to a Bass Pro Shops and picked up a pair of brown leather boots and a wool-lined denim jacket. In the pocket of that jacket was a new chrome flashlight, powerful enough to light up the woods like Yankee Stadium. I opened and closed my hand around its shaft, my palm slick with sweat despite the cold night air.

"Good luck."

"Call you in an hour."

I hope.

I'd been leaning against the sign during my check-in with Erica and started to stand up straight as I pocketed the phone when something hard and cold pressed into the tender space between my jawbone and skull behind my right ear. The silence around me would have given a librarian wet dreams, but I never heard even a single footfall.

"You were supposed to be unarmed," I said, hands at my side, palms out. Slowly, she reached around my chest and pulled my Glock out of its holster. She popped out the magazine, thumbed the slide release, and the pistol landed next to my feet in three separate pieces.

"Any others?" she asked. Her voice tickled the hair on the side of my neck. Under different circumstances, it would have been incredibly sexy. Now, I was just hoping they weren't the last words I'd ever hear.

"No ma'am," I said, but she patted me down anyway. "Trish told you what would happen if I die, right?" I took a tentative step away from her, waiting for the muzzle to jam back into the bundle of nerves behind my ear, or for her to force me down onto my knees and press it into the back of my skull, but none of that happened. I took two more steps and turned.

It had been a long time since we last met face-to-face. Several years, in fact. Nima Heydari, The Persian, was not beautiful, at least not in the traditional sense. She also wouldn't give a shit whether you thought she was or not. She had an athletic build that filled out her clothes in all the ways some men liked, but her face had a hardened quality that dulled her eyes, which were a deep, haunting shade of green.

She was dressed in black from head to toe, like Ghost had been, but it wasn't some kind of tactical outfit. Just a pair of black leggings with matching boots, sweater and leather jacket. Combined with her jet black hair and olive skin, she was damn near invisible in the dark. Taller than I remembered, too. Almost my height. In one hand she held a Desert Eagle L5, which normally looks huge in a woman's grip but seemed custom made for hers. The nail of the finger stretched out along the trigger guard was also painted black. In her other hand was a black duffel bag, its sides bulging with what I hoped was neatly wrapped stacks of hundred-dollar bills and not something more nefarious, like plastique.

"You kill me," I continued, "and in twenty-four hours, every news station in America gets a detailed report on what's in that box. Not to mention a healthy list of all the CEOs that Trish has been working with, and the details on what she's done for them."

That stoic face betrayed nothing as she continued to point the Desert Eagle at my chest.

I wasn't bluffing. Erica had strict instructions to dump everything we got from Sergei onto all the major news sites if I missed a check-in by more than ten minutes. Standing there in the dark, though, with even the breeze through the naked trees no more than a whisper, staring into the face of a woman who had made a career out of killing, the threat of destroying Trish's cash flow felt like a flimsy suit of armor indeed.

Slowly, never taking her eyes off mine, she dropped the bag and pulled her phone from her jacket pocket. She thumbed in a code, scrolled a few times, then punched in something else. The Desert Eagle never wavered. Never even quivered. My phone buzzed against my hip just as she put hers away. I reached for it, asking permission with my eyes. She twitched hers down, like a snake flicking its tongue. I pulled the phone out and saw there was a new message in the chat room I'd established with Trish. But this message was from The Persian.

It was a link.

"This better not be some kind of malware," I said, "because I already gave the last of my money to a Nigerian prince who really needed my help."

No response. The statue with the gun just kept staring at me, her blackened fingernail resting on the trigger guard. I clicked the link.

It was a live feed from a webcam. On the floor of a modest living room sat two girls, between seven and ten years of age. They wore matching pink pajamas that I'd seen before. Except this time they were alone, Taylor Swift wasn't playing, and they weren't giggling. They couldn't even if they'd wanted to, since their mouths were sealed with a thick strip of black duct tape. The same tape secured their hands behind their backs, and also bound the two girls together where they sat, back-to-back, tears streaming down their delicate chestnut-brown skin. The video feed had no sound, but I didn't need it to know what their cries sounded like. Every father would.

They were bound together another way as well. Each wore a vest, far too big for them, laden with bricks of plastic explosive. A red light blinked on the chest of each vest, and a tangle of wires connected the two.

"Goddamn you," I said, but it was little more than a whisper. I don't know if she heard me. It wouldn't have mattered if she did. The words would have no effect on her. "I told Trish the kids weren't to be harmed."

"And they won't be," she said, "unless you're lying about the box. In that case," she held up her phone, which displayed a keypad. A four digit code was pre-entered. Detonator by way of Samsung. What a world we live in. "All I have to do is hit Send. You're not the only one with an insurance policy, here."

"I'm not lying about the box."

"Take me to it, then."

The faces of the girls were all I could see, dancing in my mind's eye, but I couldn't let her know that she'd rattled me. If my head wasn't in the game, then this wasn't going to work.

"Let me see the money first," I said.

Her hardened features cracked the briefest of smiles, the sardonic kind, and she unzipped the duffel, revealing neatly wrapped stacks of hundred-dollar bills.

"Would you be insulted if I count it?"

She closed the bag, kicked the pieces of my disassembled Glock into the underbrush, and gestured toward the trail with her Desert Eagle.

"It's a good thing you have a trustworthy face," I said as I stepped past her.

Good, keep joking. Let the quips and one-liners smother the sound of those silent cries in the video feed. And keep breathing. Just keep breathing. Mr. Cool, you do this kind of thing all the time.

God, I hoped my legs didn't give out as we walked. Or my bladder.

CHAPTER FORTY

The Persian wouldn't let me use my new flashlight. I pulled it out of my coat pocket when we started, but she snatched it out of my hand and tossed it into the woods.

"No weapons," she said.

"It's a flashlight," I replied, but the conversation was over. If she thought I would pull some Jason Bourne shit and blind her with it, then she had clearly overestimated my combat abilities.

The moon was nearly full, but it didn't make the going any easier. Twice I nearly slipped on fresh mud patches, and my face had to have almost half a dozen tiny scratches from branches I didn't see until I was right on top of them. The nub at the tip of my pinkie finger throbbed from the cold, almost in time with the hole Ghost had gored into my leg. I pressed my hand against it, counting all eight stitches beneath my jeans, making sure none had popped out.

The Persian followed, nonplussed by any of it. It was as if she was taking a leisurely stroll down a well-lit park path.

"We made a lot of money together," I said as a fresh tangle of branches brushed against my face, tearing off one of the scabs Denise's fingernails had left behind during our less-than-Rockwellian reunion. "It's a shame you're throwing it all away to turn corporate shill for that bitch, Trish, and her Board of Directors. I never pegged you for the sellout type."

"How much further?" she asked.

"Not much, I can hear the stream."

It was actually closer than I thought, waiting for us on the other side of a dense clump of thicket. We reached it and took a moment to pick bits of twigs and leaves out of our hair.

"So, they give you dental?" I asked as I patted my coat to knock loose any lingering bits of debris. "Vacation, holiday pay. What's their 401(k) match look like?"

"Where do we go from here?" she said.

"Like, in our relationship? I was thinking couple's counseling but wasn't sure if you'd be into it."

The gun barrel was back at my chest.

"That way," I pointed upstream, "about twenty feet. You never did have a sense of humor."

She gestured the Desert Eagle in the direction I'd indicated.

"Okay, we need to work on using our words," I said.

She raised the gun and drew a bead on a spot just above the bridge of my nose. "Move."

"See, that wasn't so hard," I said, hands up. "Baby steps."

We baby-stepped our way along the bank until she suddenly said, "Stop."

"What?" I asked, turning around. The gun was still on me, but her eyes were everywhere else. Scanning the trees, the ground, upstream and down.

"Where are you taking us?"

"To the box. That's what the money in the bag's for, right?"

Her eyes, still dancing, finally settled on mine. It had taken longer than I anticipated for her to get anxious about our walk in the woods. Then again, maybe I should have been flattered that she was worried at all. When you're not known for being a hero, no one ever expects you to do anything heroic. "You go get it, then bring it back to me," she commanded.

"A little paranoid, aren't we? Besides," I said, pointing to the tree just ahead, "it's right there." She scanned our surroundings once more, with the trained precision of someone who can spot a sniper by a single glint of light off a filling in his tooth. Seeing nothing but still not happy, she got me going again with a shove.

We made it to the tree, and to the rock at its base, the one shaped roughly like Montana. "There you go," I said, tapping it with my foot. The Persian looked at the rock, then back up at me.

"There what?" she asked.

"There's what you're looking for, the box. Well, underneath the rock, anyway."

"And how do we get it out?"

I stared at her blankly, then blinked. "You didn't bring a shovel?"

"No." Her anxiety had been replaced by frustration.

"I can't believe Trish didn't tell you to bring a shovel. I specifically told her to remind you to bring a shovel. I remember saying, 'Trish, tell Nima to use the bathroom before she leaves and have her bring—"

The gun was back on the spot above my nose, but this time she cocked the hammer. What little patience she had was wearing thin. "Dig it up."

"With what?"

"Your hands."

"Fine," I sighed.

I bent down, lifted the rock, and hurled it at her gun. She saw it coming, but not quite fast enough. A second sooner and the bullet she fired would have blown out the back of my head, just like Ian, instead of ricocheting off the tree behind me. In that regard, the move worked.

Except in the sequence of events I ran through my mind a hundred times throughout the course of the day, the rock hit its target and knocked the gun out of her hand. Turns out highly paid assassins hold on to their weapons the same way highly paid running backs hold on to the football, which meant I had to resort to Plan B:

Run. Or more specifically, run like hell.

Her second shot hit the tree again, but by then I'd ducked behind it. The trunk was wide enough to cover me as I sprinted to the next tree further upstream. She put a bullet into that one too, right after I spun behind it.

That was three shots. She had six left.

There were more trees in front of me, but their trunks were thinner and made for inadequate cover. I darted right, into the tangle of brush, and felt her fourth shot whiz past my ear, snapping branches and shredding leaves. Shot five actually tore a hole in my jacket as it flapped next to me while I ran. I dove face first into the loose, wet dirt, and heard shot number six sail high where my back would have been.

Down to three. Holy shit, how did I not have any holes in me yet?

There was another large tree off to my right, about twenty yards away. I crawled on my hands and knees, hoping the combination of thick brush and poor lighting would provide cover long enough for me to make it to the oak undetected.

That's when the flashlight beam hit me.

"Fuck," I said. "Why did you get to keep yours?!"

Shots seven and eight kicked up bits of mud on my right and left, and that's when it dawned on me. She wasn't missing because she suddenly forgot how to aim, she was missing because she needed me alive in case I was lying about the location of the box.

Her goal wasn't to kill me, just to slow me down. Turns out my bullet-dodging *Matrix* skills were not as advanced as I initially thought. Armed with a bit of extra confidence from this epiphany, I got to my feet and sprinted for the tree.

Almost made it, too.

Shot nine ripped another hole in my jacket, but this one took a chunk of my shoulder with it. I screamed and slid behind the massive trunk. About fifty feet away was a hunter's perch, ten feet off the ground. I eyeballed it, gauging the distance. It lit up, or at least half of it did, as her flashlight beam fell on the tree at my back. I heard her release the spent Desert Eagle magazine and slam in a new one.

"I'd turn that light off if I were you!" I shouted.

"And why is that?" she asked.

The shots came almost simultaneously. There would be much debate afterward, but based on the brief muzzle flash I saw, the first originated from the hunter's perch. It hit her in the chest, and would have been enough to finish the job on its own. I didn't see shots two and three, but I saw their results. It wasn't pretty. One punched straight through her neck, and the other entered her back and got lodged in her lung, causing blood to bubble out through both her mouth and the newly formed tunnel in her throat.

Nima's eyes were open as she fell to the ground. The flashlight was still on, illuminating the ground in a widening cone from where it landed next to her. My shadow fell long behind me as I walked up to her and picked it up. I flicked it off, then shook it in her face.

"Makes you an easy target," I said. I'll never know for sure if she heard me before everything in her world went permanently dark, but I like to pretend she did. It's a nice thought to hold on to.

That nice thought dissolved like powder in my stomach when I saw the phone in her hand. The four digit code that had been there back at the start of the trail, the one that would detonate the suicide vests strapped to Jimmy Ramirez's little girls, was gone.

And her dead thumb was covering the Send button.

CHAPTER FORTY-ONE

John Stanton, who had been in the hunter's perch, was the first to reach me. He was a rail of a man, his elongated face hidden beneath a layer of black face paint.

"Made that a little harder than it had to be, didn't you?" he said as he slapped me on my wounded shoulder.

I winced and held up my finger as I dialed my phone, fingers trembling. The video stream still showed the two girls sitting on the floor, the vest very much unexploded, but that didn't mean anything. The video had been playing on a loop for the last two hours.

"Pick up, pick up, pick up, you old son of a bitch."

When he did, I let out a long exhale and wiped my hand across my forehead.

"Jesus Christ, Frank, you scared the shit out of me," I said. "What took you so long to answer?"

"Sorry," came Frank Cochran's grandfatherly voice, "me and the girls were just finishing up a game of Candy Land."

"Oh yeah, who won?"

"Laila won this round, and Lexi won the first two, but they cheat."

I heard giggling in the background. Not the same giggles that came after they gave Maggie the world's worst makeover, but good to hear nonetheless, especially given their current circumstances. "Too bad they don't play poker, you could cheat them right back."

"I might just have to teach them," he said, his smile coming through loud and clear over the phone. "What were you so worried about anyway? You know I disarmed the vests hours ago."

On my way to the Poconos, I'd made a few calls. Some were to arrange the group of hitters that had just taken out The Persian, Mr. Stanton here and two others I'd worked with during my early days. The other was to Frank, the only person I knew within a hundred miles of Jimmy Ramirez's place that could observe his house without The Persian getting suspicious. After all, who would look twice at a cable repair guy nearing retirement age? The Comcast jumpsuit had been in the back of the old van when the cable company sold it to Enzo's for scrap. Frank had hung on to both, liking the easy cover they provided if he ever needed it. After Nima left, I told him to enter the house. I thought it unlikely she'd be working with anyone who'd be standing sentry—Nima always operated alone—but told him to be wary of booby traps. There weren't any, but he quickly spotted both the webcam and the two frightened young girls on the floor that it was pointed at.

"Can you disarm the vests?" I'd asked when he called to give me the lowdown.

"She's using an older model TR-580 remote detonator. I've sold more of these in the last five years than I can count. Lots of wires strung between them meant to spook any amateur heroes, but anyone who knows what they're doing can disable it in less than five minutes."

It had taken Frank three. After he was done, I told him to stay with the girls until I called with the all clear.

"I know you *claimed* you disarmed them Frank," I said now, "but until I knew for sure—"

"Until you knew for sure there was some doubt that old Frank had lost his touch, huh?" He sounded mad, but I knew he was just busting my stones.

"I don't know what I was thinking," I said. "You sure you won't let me pay you?"

"For helping out these two little angels and getting me out of the house during the wife's Scrabble party with that group of cackling old biddies? Not a chance. Happy to do it. Still need me to stick around?"

"Nope, Frank the Comcast Cable Repairman can call the police and let them contact Jimmy's ex-wife so she can come be with her daughters until their daddy gets home."

"I can do that."

"Stick around in that old van until they get there, though, if you don't mind." I doubted the cops in the sleepy little Philly suburb of Ardmore were on Trish's payroll, but the whole experience had my nerves on high alert. "There'll be a six pack of beer in it for you, and I won't hear any arguments about it."

"Now that's a fee I won't say no to."

"Don't forget to take the looping equipment off the webcam before you go."

"I may be old, Ricky, but I ain't *that* old."

Now it was my turn to smile, "See you around, Frank." I hung up and turned to Stanton.

"What was that all about?" he asked.

"Just thanking a friend for a favor. Speaking of which," I punched him in the arm, "who hits someone right on a fresh bullet wound as a way of saying hello?"

"Well maybe next time don't run around like a rooster in a shooting gallery," he teased back.

"She didn't drop the gun, I had to improvise. Still got her to chase me, though, and that's all that matters. No way she walks into that turkey shoot unless she was distracted."

It's still amazing she did. Sometimes it pays to be the last person anyone expects to be a hero.

"Been a while since I went night hunting," he said, slinging his long rifle over his shoulder. "It was fun."

"Don't count if you use a laser sight." This came from Richie Marchese, who had fired shot #2. He had a ridiculous ghillie suit made of straw and fake earth draped over him like some kind of mutant Chia-Pet bathrobe.

"My ass it doesn't count," John fired back.

"I made a tougher shot from further away with just a scope," Richie argued.

"Tougher shot? Look at my entry wound: bullseye on the heart from thirty yards out, in the dark."

Richie rolled his eyes and poked The Persian's corpse in the neck with the barrel of his rifle. "*Neck shot*, forty yards, no laser sight."

The third shooter, Craig Serano, called out as he splashed over from across the stream. "You guys see that? I dropped her!"

"*You* dropped her?" Richie hollered back.

"Dude, you shot her in the back on the way down!" John added. "Get the fuck outta here."

And thus the debate started. I stepped aside and let them go a few rounds. When you call three local hitters to work the same job, there's bound to be a pissing contest. While they traded insults, I retrieved the duffel bag from where she'd dropped it by the tree and counted the stacks of hundreds inside.

One million dollars, even.

I took out ten stacks of bills and shoved them in my various pockets. Then I lifted the bag and went over to settle the battle of egos before more shots were fired, but it was like breaking up a shouting match between my kids. They only shut up when I whistled loudly through my fingers, an ear-piercing sound that used to stop Maggie and Ethan mid-sentence. "You wanna keep bickering like you're on *The View*, or you wanna get paid?"

I held the bag open, putting the cash on full display. The bickering ceased at once.

After distributing their share to each, I thanked them all for showing up on such short notice.

"Hey," John said, "Rick Carter calls, we know the job's gonna be good."

"Thanks," I replied.

"Was not expecting to hear from you today, that's for sure. What's it been, almost ten years? We all thought you were dead, pal."

"The world's just not that lucky, I guess."

"Got anything else lined up?" Richie asked.

I shook my head. "Sorry fellas, I'm not hanging around long. This is a one-and-done."

"Well," Craig said, "it was good working with you one last time, at least."

"*Very* good," Richie said with a smile as he shouldered his backpack full of cash.

We shook hands and they made their way back to the trail, the arguing starting up again almost right away. Half of me expected to hear a shot ring out before they parted ways, but none did. Maybe it was because their hands were busy carrying The Persian's corpse, mummified in a plastic drop cloth and a whole roll of duct tape.

Once their voices were too faint to hear, I went over to the stream, dropped the duffel bag (now refilled with the $100,000 I had kept hidden from the guys; it's never wise to tempt three armed killers with extra cash), took off my jacket, and splashed cold water on my tattered shoulder. With the blood washed off, it didn't look too bad. No worse than any of the other injuries I was currently nursing. It would need stitches, but I could hold it together with some butterfly bandages until I found a guy to sew it up. I could always find a guy.

I sat by the stream bed for another half hour, just to be safe, listening to the water lap over the rocks, and the occasional rustle of leaves as some small, nocturnal mammal scampered past, unseen. The Persian's Desert Eagle was in my lap, in case something more sinister made itself known, but nothing did. Still, it felt good to take someone else's gun for a change.

When I was positive none of my three old candidates stuck around to see what I was up to, I started walking downstream, past where I had originally emerged with The Persian, past the rock shaped like Montana that was lying half in the water, and kept walking until I reached the back of Jay and Abby's tree. The rock shaped like Texas was right where I had left it that afternoon, as was the shovel I had stashed in the branches above it.

My shoulder wasn't happy about it, but I moved the rock and dug up Robert's box for the second time. I held it out and snapped a picture of it, then sent it to the chat room along with one I'd taken of The Persian's body before the boys dragged it away. I waited five minutes before I called, letting her digest the significance of the images. She answered on the first ring.

"What do you think of my photography skills?" I asked before she could speak. "The lighting's not great, but I think the overall quality doesn't suffer too badly."

"We had a deal," Trish said. Her voice was flat. Emotionless. It was disappointing. I'd hoped to coax some more of the cockney out of her.

"Yes, we did. None of which involved strapping ten pounds of explosives to a couple of elementary schoolers."

"Then next time you should be more specific with your instructions."

"Was I not clear enough about The Persian coming unarmed? Not that it matters now, anyway."

"I can send others. You haven't won anything, just delayed your inevitable loss."

"Now Trish," I said, as patronizingly as possible, "we've been over this. Do you really want your clients' dirty little secrets smeared over every corner of the internet?"

"Go ahead, I can clean it up."

"If that were true, then this little box wouldn't be worth half the trouble you've gone through to keep it hidden."

"What will you do with the box now?" she asked, not even bothering to back up her own weak bluff. "Sell it yourself? I'm sure you have plenty of potential buyers already lined up."

"I think I'll hang on to it for a little while. I don't like the idea of a dirty bomb going off just so I can turn a profit."

Robert would be so proud of me.

She snorted derisively. “You think there won’t be other boxes, other bombs? The world is a cruel place, Mr. Carter, filled with very dangerous people who are very passionate about reshaping that world to match their own twisted ideals. And as long as they’re willing to pay, there will always be someone else willing to sell them the means by which to make those ideals a reality.”

“I’m well aware,” I said. “But I’m not interested in saving the world, Trish, just protecting my little corner of it.”

“And what of the other half of our deal, are you reneging on that as well?”

“Not at all. As long as my family and I remain safe, I see no reason to continue interfering in your business relationships. But I can start back up whenever I want. If I even think they’re in danger because of you, I will use every connection I have to gut your operation. I might not be able to bring you down, but I can damn sure set your house on fire trying.”

She laughed, a soft, breathy taunt filled with malice. “Okay, celebrate your little win. We’ll pick up the pieces from this minor setback and move on. Our operation will continue to expand until you, your family and that damned little box are nothing but a distant memory. Remember that, Rick, in case you or Detective Baglioni ever get a sudden attack of morality and decide to go to the authorities with the information in your possession. I can be everywhere and see everything, whenever I want.”

“No cops, Trish, remember?” I said. “That’s my guarantee.”

EPILOGUE

Erica took the phone from Robert and put it to her ear as she stepped outside the car, onto the shoulder of the Ohio Turnpike. She walked with the traffic, what little there was at this late hour.

"Do you really think Robert will let it go?" she asked as she paced.

"I think so," Rick said on the other end of the line. "I *hope* so."

All Robert had to do was stick to the story: Two hitmen he didn't know broke into his house and threatened to kill everyone. Then Denise's ex and some crazy blonde woman crashed through the front door, killed the bad guys, and forced Robert and his family into Denise's car at gunpoint. They fled to Denise's family cabin where Robert was able to sneak away and contact Jimmy for help, who looped in the local police to assist. Things went bad, Jimmy wound up in the hospital, but Denise's ex and his partner panicked and let them go. No idea what they were after, but Robert suspected it had something to do with the dead body he and Jimmy found in the container ship and its connection to an ongoing FBI investigation. Too bad the guy running that investigation got himself killed, or he might have been able to shed some light on things.

"Robert's got a strong moral code," Rick went on, "and he wants to be a part of bringing Trish down, but I told him MI5 is likely already assembling a new task force and to let them handle it. There are already news stories coming out of Belgium about Leon being the mastermind behind the human trafficking operation, so hopefully that means Trish sacrificed that business to protect the rest. If there's one good thing to come out of this, it's the end to that."

"You think Leon will ever make it to trial?"

"I don't think Leon will make it to next weekend. Bad things happen to people in prison all the time. How's Jimmy doing?"

"He'll be okay. They did surgery to repair some nerve damage, but nothing that won't heal. I think Robert's as happy about that and his girls being okay as he is about finally being able to go home."

"Jimmy was fully prepared to turn all of us over to The Persian, and his partner doesn't even hold a grudge."

"Jimmy wanted to make a stand, remember? Not turn us in."

"So he says. Something tells me if things went south, he'd have a mighty quick change of plans."

"He was just trying to protect his family, Rick. Surely you can understand that."

His silence served just as well as an actual answer.

"Robert wants to go back to the hospital and check on him. Do you want me to keep an eye on them while he does?" she asked.

"If you don't mind," he said, "just until you all get back to New Jersey. I can't ask any more of you than that. You've done so much for me already."

"Where are you headed?"

"I haven't figured that part out yet," he said with a soft chuckle. "Back to Europe, eventually, but not right now. Trish says we're square, but I don't expect her to keep that promise for very long. At least I've got some fresh walking around money, courtesy of the corpse formerly known as The Persian."

"Well, once you find a place to spend it, call me. I'm planning to lie low for a while, same as you. Might as well buy you a beer."

"Only after I buy you one. Or two. Or ten. I've lost count of how many times you've saved my ass in the last few days."

"It's a date," she said with a smile as she pivoted and headed back toward the SUV. A semi rig towing a gasoline tanker blew past her, easily topping 90 mph.

She would have to buy another car after she left Rick's family behind, but that wouldn't be a problem. There was an exit a mile up ahead, spilling into another small, podunk town like the one Aunt Irene called home. Used cars sprouted like weeds in such places. At least, that had been her experience as she traversed America over the years, from backwaters to big cities. Sometimes she felt she knew this country better than her own.

"Erica," Rick said, "thank you. All kidding aside, you came through for me when I had nobody else. My family is alive today because of you. I can never fully repay you for that."

"Well, let's start with the beer," she replied. "Take it from there."

"Sounds like a plan."

Denise and Robert were talking, their hands linked together as Erica approached. They didn't acknowledge her, but she didn't take that as a slight. These poor people had been through hell. Denise had stopped crying but the tears remained on her face. Erica watched through the windshield as Robert brushed them away. Maggie and Ethan were passed out in the second row, sharing a large blanket they took from the cabin. Shocked as she was to admit it, she would miss them. She had barely shared more than a few words with them over the last several days, but she'd grown attached to the family, in her own cold, distant way. She wished them a speedy return to their happy, boring suburban lives. Where games of cards were played around the kitchen table after a family meal, not to pass the time in an abandoned cabin, waiting for a killer to knock on the door.

"Actually, I do need you to do one more thing for me," Rick said. "This one will get you a shot of premium whiskey to go along with that beer."

"I'm more of a tequila girl," she said, smiling.

"Anything. Name your bottle."

"What's the favor?"

"I need you to tell Denise something for me. Not that I'm sorry for what I did to her, even though I am. She's already heard me say that and she doesn't care. Nor should she." He took a breath. "I want you to tell her I blew it. I was happy, with her and the kids and my normal, boring job, and I blew it. Whether it was for what I thought were the right reasons or not doesn't matter. I destroyed not only my life but theirs as well, when all I ever wanted to do was protect it. I own that. And I won't do any more damage. I'll stay away, just like she told me to, and I hope that makes her happy. Because she deserves to be happy. They all do." He coughed, just once. It was as if he was trying to dislodge the last remnants of what he'd said. "Will you tell her that for me, please?"

She nodded. "I will."

"Thank you."

Nobody in the car looked up at her as she walked past them and continued down the highway in the opposite direction while she listened to Rick's speech. To his confession. Nobody saw her dial another number on her phone after her and Rick said their goodbyes.

A recording answered, asking for a code. She spoke four numbers and a letter, taking care to enunciate each one. The wind had picked up and if it distorted anything she said, she wouldn't get a chance to repeat them. After a few clicks and beeps as her code was verified, a male voice came on the line.

"The job's done," she said. "The Persian's dead. She was the last of the three."

"Excellent news," the male voice said. It was hoarse, like he'd just gotten over a bad cold. "Our client will be pleased. What about Carter? Is he what we thought he was?"

"Oh yes," she replied. "He might be even better."

"How does he handle himself?"

"You need him to be a recruiter, not a fighter. That's why you have me."

The voice paused to consider this, then cleared his throat. It was an awful, juicy sound. "You haven't checked in since you took out Ian Matthews. I was starting to get worried."

"Circumstances wouldn't allow it. Besides, you should know better than to worry about me by now."

"Does he know you were the one who popped the kid? He was standing right next to him."

"No."

"I'm told he and Matthews were close. If he suspects you at all then we have to be careful how we—"

"He doesn't suspect anything. He trusts me."

More nauseating throat clearing, but he didn't press the issue. "Do you know where he is now?"

"Not yet, but I will. He's going to call me to get a drink after he settles in somewhere."

"What if he doesn't?"

"He will."

"But if he doesn't? This next job is everything, Erica, and it doesn't stand a chance of succeeding without Rick Carter."

She had reached a bend in the road. The SUV was just out of sight. Since the tractor trailer rocketed by, not a single other vehicle had appeared. Not even the faint twinkle of headlights in the distance. It was so quiet that the thin dusting of snow on the asphalt lay undisturbed. After a quick check to make sure Robert hadn't followed her, she pulled the blonde wig off and ran her hand over her short, military-cut hair, scratching her scalp where the adhesive strips left it red and irritated.

"If he doesn't call, I can track him down."

"Good," the voice said. "Go get him."

ACKNOWLEDGMENTS

You made it! Either my debut novel didn't suck as much as I feared or you're one of those people who refuses to put a book down until you've finished it, even if you think it's hot garbage. Regardless, I appreciate you spending not only your money but your time on the previous ninety thousand words.

Now that the credits have rolled, so to speak—and I hopefully didn't piss you off too much with that cliffhanger—I'd like to ask for just a few more minutes of your time so I can shout out some very important people.

Mom and Dad come first, because of course they do. Ever since they submitted the short story I wrote in elementary school to *Highlights Magazine*, they have supported me in my writing journey. (That story, "The Horse Raised by Wolves," can be read in its four-paragraph entirety on my website, by the way. While you're there, check out the article my local paper wrote about it in which my father, whose name is NOT Larry, is nonetheless referred to as Larry several times throughout the piece. Classic.) Seriously, though, you both set the bar for what I hope to be as a parent, and I strive to reach it every day.

Next up are the three people to whom this book is dedicated. My wife, Kristina, has been putting up with my shit for longer than anyone who knows me would have thought possible. It takes a special woman to not only stay with the douchebag who fake-proposes to her as a joke, in a gazebo under the moonlight, but then to also say yes when he proposes for real a few months later. Our marriage is proof that Paula Abdul and that cartoon cat were right all along: Opposites really do attract. She was the first person to read this book, and has been one of my biggest cheerleaders. Love you, babe. You're amazing. And I'm sorry in advance for the next stupid thing I do.

My kids, Kayla and Evan, remind me every day what's really important in life. Their enthusiasm and excitement on my behalf has been one of the most rewarding experiences of writing this book. I can only hope they are half as proud of me as I am of them.

My brother, Jeff, didn't really have anything to do with this book, mainly because I never told him about it until after it was sold. But if nothing else, his constant drive and desire to be the best at whatever he does likely served as subconscious motivation during those times when the writing wouldn't come, or the rejection letters from agents started to pile up. Thanks, little bro.

My in-laws are some of my favorite people, and have been ever since they laughed when Kristina told them about that gazebo prank, instead of throwing stones at me like they probably should have. Too numerous to list by name, if you're a Mazza, Krick, Leslie, Wright, or Vasapollo, I love you. A special chest-pat and point to the sky for my mother-in-law, Mooneen, who passed away before I told anyone I had written this book. As the biggest reader of the bunch, I bet she would have loved it. Miss ya, Ma.

As incredible as my real family has been throughout this process, my work family has been equally amazing. Emerson Group is a second-generation, family-owned, boutique staffing and recruitment firm operating in the South Jersey/Philly area. Submitting my résumé to them thirteen years ago was the best decision I ever made in my non-writing career, and would eventually lead to the inspiration to write a book about a recruiter. (For the record, NONE of what Rick does in this book would be sanctioned by Emerson Group. Cool? Cool. Nobody call the cops on them, please.) In an industry that gets a bad rep, they are a shining example of how to do things the right way. It starts at the top with Bill Emerson, who has built a culture of respect and professionalism that is truly special. Your constant support, both for my work as a recruiter and an author, has been invaluable.

My literary agent, Dan Milaschewski, is a rising star in this business. When he agreed to represent me, I felt like I'd just bought stock in Amazon during the early days. He gets my humor, digs my writing, and works his ass off to make sure my career stays on the proper trajectory. Dan's the man.

Addison Duffy and Orly Greenberg, my film/TV agents, are lending that same work ethic to putting this book in a position to be on a screen one day. My friends who don't read are eternally grateful to you both, as am I.

Blackstone Publishing is cool. There's nothing else to say. As soon as Dan told me we had an offer from them, I started researching the company online, and everything I read made my decision to accept a no-brainer. They run a big business like it's a family, are on the forefront of marketing, and their covers rock. (Thank you, Alenka Linaschke, for mine.) Daniel Ehrenhaft believed in this book from the moment it hit his inbox and has been in my corner every step of the way. Josie Woodbridge earns her living by keeping a thousand plates spinning at once, and I count myself lucky to be merely one of them. Celia Johnson got her hands on the original manuscript and, through her editorial genius, made me appear to be better at this than I actually am. Cannot wait to work with her again. Cole Barnes caught all the typos I missed, so thank you for making me not look like an idiot. My marketing team of Tatiana Radujkovic, Rachel Sanders, Brianna Jones, and Francie Crawford are likely the reason you even knew this book existed. And to anyone else behind the scenes at Blackstone who had a hand in this process, thank you.

If you want more in-depth knowledge of the people who have helped bring this book into existence—because I know this acknowledgments section is dragging on, but it's my first one, so bear with me—please check out the Beyond Words section of my website, GreggPodolski.com, where I interview those individuals and give them the due credit they deserve. Including Sierra Godfrey, a talented author in her own right, who also designed that very website for me.

There are plenty more people to thank, including my friends, all of whom are like an extended family, but the orchestra is starting to play me off, so I'll just offer a blanket thank you to anyone I've left out. Particular nod to my beta readers, Junan Collins, Avanti Centrae, and Sam Richey, all of whom read the manuscript after my wife and provided valuable feedback before I began querying agents. To anyone else who read an advance copy and offered advice, praise, or criticism, every bit of it is appreciated.

Finally, I want to thank you. A book can exist without a reader, but it's a sad, lonely existence. My words live on with every fresh set of eyes (or ears) that takes them in, and that's a gift I could never repay. Whether you liked what I wrote or not, thank you just for reading it.